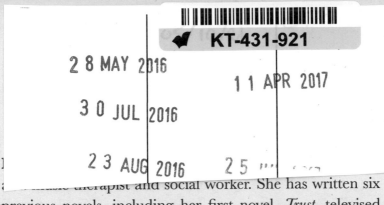

KT-431-921

... therapist and social worker. She has written six previous novels, including her first novel, *Trust*, televised by Granada; *The Perfect Mother* was also a NYT Notable Book of the Year, *The Drowning Girl* was chosen for the Oprah Summer Reading List, and *The Soldier's Wife* was a Goodreads Historical Fiction finalist. Her books have been published in twelve languages. She is married with two children, and lives in London.

A Brief Affair

Margaret Leroy

sphere

SPHERE

First published in Great Britain in 2015 by Sphere
This paperback edition published in 2016 by Sphere

1 3 5 7 9 10 8 6 4 2

A CIP catalogue record for this book is available
from the British Library.

ISBN 978-0-7515-5179-2

Typeset in Baskerville MT by Palimpsest Book Production Limited,
Falkirk, Stirlingshire

Printed and bound in Great Britain by Clays Ltd, St Ives plc

Papers used by Sphere are from well-managed forests
and other responsible sources.

MIX
Paper from
responsible sources
FSC® C104740

Sphere
An imprint of
Little, Brown Book Group
Carmelite House
50 Victoria Embankment
London EC4Y 0DZ

An Hachette UK Company
www.hachette.co.uk

www.littlebrown.co.uk

I am deeply grateful to Cath Burke and Lucy Malagoni at Little, Brown for their inspired editorial suggestions, and to my brilliant agents, Kathy Anderson and Laura Longrigg. Thanks as well to Thalia Proctor at Little, Brown, and to Madeleine Fullerton for showing me the tomb in Ashbourne Church.

Of the many fascinating books I read to research the novel, two were particularly memorable: Juliet Gardiner's *The Blitz*, which is at once a masterly account and an enthralling read, and Henry Green's novel, *Caught*, which draws on Henry Green's own experience as a fire-fighter in the London Blitz.

My love and gratitude, as always, to Mick, Becky and Steve; and special thanks to Izzie, who has been a constant source of emotional support and literary wisdom during the writing of *A Brief Affair*.

Prologue

At one of the houses in Selborne Street, the front door is half open. You push it wider, step cautiously into the black of the hall.

'Hello? Anyone home here?'

There's no answer, which doesn't surprise you. Your voice is thin with exhaustion. And how could anyone possibly hear you above the noise of the raid?

You glance in the rooms that lead off the hall, but they all seem dark and empty. At the top of the stairs, a little red light is leaking under a door; it looks like friendly fire-light from a hearth fire. If there's anyone still in this house, you know that's where they'll be, up there in the fire-lit bedroom.

You climb the stairs. The last bomb fell very close, but

this building isn't much damaged. If there's someone here, there's quite a good chance that you're going to find them alive.

You come to the door, open it.

There's a woman in a rocking-chair, on the hearthrug. Her back is to the doorway, her face towards the fire. She has a baby in the crook of her arm, swaddled in a blanket; you can see the top of the baby's head, a tuft of pale hair poking up. The fire is dying in the grate, but it still gives out a little heat: she must have brought the baby in here to be warm by the fire. You wonder why she didn't go to the shelter. Perhaps she simply couldn't face it any more – the overcrowding, the stench of sweat and urine and fear. A lot of people are starting to feel like that.

The way she's sitting, cradling her baby, you half expect to hear her crooning a tender lullaby, like the ones you once sang to your children. As you stand there, the sweet old words slide randomly into your mind.

> *Golden slumbers kiss your eyes*
> *Smiles awake you when you rise . . .*

But she sits so still: no singing. Perhaps she's fallen asleep – though how could anyone sleep here, with all the sound from outside, the bark of the guns, the whistle and thud of bombs falling? The windows of the bedroom have been broken by the blast, and rags of blackout curtain are flapping. Through the jagged shards of shattered glass, you can see the night sky – the flames from the

2

burning city reflecting in the clouds: scarlet, rose pink, vermilion.

You move your torch over the room. The beam of light catches on anything shiny – a mirror on the dressing table, a grip in the woman's dark hair. In spite of the tumult in the streets around, the room seems somehow peaceful. As though all the chaos of the night were far removed from this place.

You step forward softly.

'Excuse me, ma'am.'

The woman doesn't respond.

You notice how silently you are treading. Almost as though you're spellbound. As though you might waken something that is better left undisturbed.

'You shouldn't stay here. It's really not safe,' you tell her.

Still she doesn't reply.

You walk round her chair, turn to face her.

'It's a really bad one tonight.' And your voice falters.

The woman and child are both dead. They seem whole and uninjured, undamaged; yet their stillness, that seemed like tranquillity, is the stillness of death. You've heard of this, but never seen it – how you can be killed by the blast. How the high-pressure suction can impact on your body's internal cavities: ears, lungs, stomach, intestines. So inwardly you'll be ravaged, yet outwardly you can look entirely untouched.

Bile fills your mouth: you swallow hard.

And then all the regret comes flooding in.

If I'd only come half an hour earlier. If I'd only turned along here, instead of going down Hamilton Street.

3

You imagine it. How you'd have rushed up the stairs and found them, the baby wailing, the mother smiling politely but privately thinking you rather officious, saying yes, they'd go to the shelter, she just had to fetch a few things, you saying there's no time for that, and ushering them downstairs, hurrying them along the street, hurrying them to safety. You can see – hear – all this so vividly. As though it had actually happened.

Your thinking is frayed with exhaustion, and it doesn't seem so much to ask, to have made a different choice then. As though the impossible wish could be granted. As though you could turn back the skies and begin again, and this time not get it wrong.

Part 1

1

Saturday 7th September 1940

I dress with care – my cornflower-blue woollen suit, my black suede high-heeled shoes. I study myself in the mirror. I look pale, and reach for my lipstick. The pretty silver casing has a soft grey shroud of dust: it comes to me that I haven't worn lipstick for over a year – not since I heard about Ronnie. I press my lips together and smooth colour over my mouth.

My Sunday-best handbag is buried at the bottom of the wardrobe. This, too, is dusty. I always used to take this handbag to matins at St Michael's – but I haven't been to a single service since the telegram came. Except for the funeral. I dust the handbag with a clean hand-kerchief. I find my bottle of Après l'Ondée and spray a little behind my ears; the wistful heliotrope scent wraps round me.

I'm almost ready to go now. I pick up the case that holds my gas mask, then put it down again.

We were all very conscientious when war was first declared, keeping our gas masks with us always. But it's been a year now, and the war feels unreal here in London. The sirens sound from time to time, but they're always false alarms: we used to rush to the shelter in our garden, but now we mostly don't bother. People who sent their children off to the country have gone to fetch them back home – like my friend Phoebe, who brought her two boys back from Somerset. And everybody dislikes the Air Raid Precautions wardens, who don't have enough to do and poke their noses in everyone's business. We're not really much concerned with precautions any more – in spite of Mr Churchill's warning: *The whole fury and might of the enemy must very soon be turned on us* . . . It's started to look a bit feeble – to go everywhere with your gas mask under your arm.

I desperately want to impress this man, to seem sophisticated and smooth. I decide to leave it.

The front door clicks as Aggie lets herself in. I give a small sigh of relief. Polly is ten now, and old enough to look after Eliza herself – but I prefer to leave them with Aggie. If something happened, I'd never forgive myself.

Out on the landing, honeyed September sunlight falls through the tall arched windows. I've criss-crossed the glass with sticky tape, and the mellow light throws a pattern of golden lozenges everywhere: over the floor and up the wall and across the door of the girls' room, leaving the door at the further end of the landing in shadow. The door I rarely open, which leads to the room I don't use.

The girls are in the dining room. Eliza is on the floor with her little painted animals, with Hector the cat curled up beside her. She's tunelessly singing a rhyme.

> *Oranges and lemons*
> *Say the bells of St Clements . . .*

Her hair, silky-thin, pale as barley sugar, is falling over her face. She has Rabbit tucked under her arm, his knitted legs dangling. He was her present from Ronnie and me two Christmases ago, and she won't be parted from him. She's engrossed in her play with the animals: she doesn't stir as I go in.

But Polly looks up at once from her drawing at the table, pushing her cloud of dark wavy hair out of her eyes.

'You look really nice, Mum. Like one of the photos in *Woman's Journal*,' she says.

'Thank you, sweetheart.'

I admire her picture. It's a perfect storybook room – intricate and detailed, with a chandelier, a vase of tulips, a budgerigar in a cage. No people. All drawn in very sharp pencil, filled in with pastel colours.

'That's beautiful,' I tell her. I kiss the top of her head. She smells of the rose geranium bath salts I gave her for her birthday.

With a quick, fastidious movement, she reaches up and picks a loose hair from my sleeve. Polly always likes everything to be neat and perfect and clean. In the bedroom she shares with Eliza, she has stretched a dressing-gown cord across the middle of the floor, in an attempt to confine Eliza's mess to just one side of the room. On Polly's side, all is immaculate: her clothes exactly folded, her lace-up shoes polished and parallel, her hair ribbons smoothed out and straightened, and arranged according to shade.

Aggie comes in from the kitchen where she's put the kettle on to boil. She looks me up and down appraisingly; her smile is wide and approving, and deepens the kindly wrinkles at the corners of her eyes.

'Goodness, you look lovely, Livia. It's such a treat to see you all dressed up,' she says.

I know Aggie thinks I've let myself go over the past few months. But what's the point in getting dressed up, if there's no one to dress up for?

'There's some stew in the food-safe,' I tell her. 'And you really mustn't bother with the washing-up I've left . . .'

'Don't you worry, Livia. You just take yourself off and have a great time,' she tells me.

I feel a rush of gratitude: I don't know where I'd be without Aggie.

'Bless you,' I say.

Eliza looks up suddenly. Her eyes are an elusive colour, grey-green, the colour of rain. And in this moment, unblinking and sternly fixed on my face.

'Mummy, you've forgotten your gas mask.'

'I thought I might leave it behind, just this once . . .'

'But that's not *fair*. You make us take ours everywhere.'

I feel ashamed. I was only thinking about myself, and now I've set them a bad example.*

'Yes, you're right, of course, sweetheart. I'll get it.'

I straighten my velvet pill-box hat in the mirror in the hall. A rich blue light falls on me from the picture glass over the door, which has a stained-glass bluebird, webbed in a gilded skein of convolvulus. I've put sticky tape across it, but the colour still shines through.

I step out of the house, the gas mask under my arm. As I wait at the bus stop, then take the bus through the city, I find myself thinking again about that speech that Mr Churchill made: *Hitler knows that he will have to break us in this island or lose the war . . .*

I stare through the mesh on the bus windows at the streets of London spooling past, just the same as they always were – filthy, teeming, vivid – and it all seems so implausible. I shut the words away at the back of my mind.

I realise that I feel, for the first time since Ronnie died, a little thrill, a surge of something like happiness.

2

The office of Ballantyne & Drummond is in Paternoster Row – one of a labyrinth of lanes around St Paul's Cathedral, where medieval clerics used to walk, reciting *Pater Noster*: Our Father. I find that I also am praying, though in a rather more self-centred way.

I find the place, in an elegant terrace, where even the sandbags look stylish – they're duck-egg blue, to match the paintwork. There's a brass plaque next to the doorbell.

I ring, and a woman comes to the door. She has a severe expression, her hair austerely scraped back, discreet pearl earrings. She ushers me into the office, gestures towards an armchair.

'Mr Ballantyne will see you shortly,' she says.

I sit, feeling nervous: my pulse is cantering off. The woman goes back to her typing.

The room has a wonderfully intellectual air. There are shelves full of books, all arranged to display their front covers: they're mostly about journeys in exotic, distant lands – Samarkand, Ceylon, Patagonia – places whose very names sound like poems; and there are books of maps and photographs, and biographies of explorers. This all seems so glamorous to me – a place of such order and artistry, which celebrates wonderful images and the clear, pure life of the mind. I think of the messy, disorderly household I left behind in Conduit Street – all the washing-up in the sink, and Eliza's toy animals scattered. I feel like Alice in the storybook: I have passed through the portal in the Looking Glass, and entered a separate, magical world.

The door to the inner office opens. The man standing there has the glow of someone who eats a lot of very good lunches. He's dressed immaculately – Savile Row suit, crisp shirt, gold cufflinks. His greying hair is still thick and falls forward over his face.

'Mrs Ripley? I'm Hugo Ballantyne.'

He has a lingering handshake, an accomplished charming smile; the most upper-class voice I've ever heard, except on the wireless. He makes me think of Alvar Lidell reading the BBC news.

I follow him into his office. I'm glad I put on some lipstick. I think: *Every woman who walks through this door will be wearing her very best clothes. Every woman who comes here will want to seduce him in some way – because of what Mr Ballantyne can do for her, if he chooses.* The thought unnerves me.

He gestures me to a chair. I sit, and put down my gas mask. I rather wish I hadn't brought it now. He offers me a cigarette from a silver box on his desk. I take one; he leans in to light it for me. He has a scent of cloves and vetiver – a luxurious, spicy male smell. I hope he won't notice that my hand is shaking with nerves.

'You'd like tea?' he asks me.

'That would be lovely. Thank you.'

He calls through the door.

'Miss Cartwright, could we have tea?'

He seats himself behind his big mahogany desk. He has my portfolio open, my pictures spread out in front of him. I can see some of them from here. The rose garden at Polesden Lacey after a brief summer storm, the flowers dishevelled, a drift of translucent petals over the paths. Shadow and light on the lake at Stourhead. Lavish hollyhocks in an Oxford college garden; above, a lowering sky, a promise of rain.

He looks up at me; he has a slight smile, as though he's a little amused.

'You really like dim light, Mrs Ripley.'

'Yes. It's softer – no strong shadows.' My throat feels like blotting paper. 'The thing is – you see the world differently, when you start to take photographs. You learn to love clouds, and low light. You can sometimes get the loveliest pictures on the darkest days.'

His gaze is rather intense.

'You have a wonderful eye,' he tells me. He gestures towards a photo I took in the gardens at Stowe: a dreaming pool in hazy sunlight, fringed with ravelled bulrushes, the skin of the water crinkling under a soft summer breeze. 'The angle you've taken this from. The way the light falls. So beautiful.' There's a hint of something extra, in his words, in his look.

'Thank you.' I feel my face go hot. I'm so flattered.

'Tell me the story,' he says. 'How you became a photographer. How you came to take these photographs.'

'Well, I've always taken pictures . . .' I sound hesitant: I realise I should have a ready answer. But this has all happened so rapidly – since Phoebe showed my photographs to her friend who works in publishing, and he told me where to send them. I don't feel properly prepared. 'I was given a camera of my own when I was just sixteen. Ever since then, I've taken pictures. Though not so much since I got married and my children came . . .'

I leave it at that. I don't want to say anything negative about Ronnie.

Hugo Ballantyne has a rueful, understanding smile. 'Children do tend to push out other things.'

He makes a slight gesture towards a silver-framed picture on his desk: a woman, a child, a backdrop of velvet, a palm. The woman remote and willowy, her long dark hair swept up, the child very fair and slender. I feel a brief spasm of curiosity about the woman.

'I know just what you mean,' he says.

I swallow hard. I'm not sure how much to tell him.

'The thing is . . .' My voice thins. 'My husband died last October . . . He'd joined up just a few months before war was declared.'

I feel awkward. I prefer not to talk about it really. This grief makes a little rip in the fabric of things. People never quite know what response to make.

He composes his face into an expression of condolence. 'Oh, I'm so sorry,' he says. 'On service?'

'Yes.' There's a break in my voice.

It's not exactly true – or it implies something that isn't true – but it's easiest. I don't want to dwell on the awful randomness of Ronnie's death; I don't want to share all that misery with this polished, self-assured man.

'I'm so very sorry,' he says again. And gives me a slightly anxious glance, as though worried I might start crying.

'I didn't know how to keep going . . .' I remember all those sleepless nights, all the self-blame and grief and regret. I clear my throat. 'But in the end, I realised what I had to do to get through it. That I had to become the person I'd been before I met him. To start doing again the things I used to love to do . . .' I lose my nerve. 'Does that sound stupid?'

He gives an encouraging smile.

'Not at all. I'd say it made perfect sense. Sometimes we have to look back before we can start to move forward,' he says. The aphorism has a formal, literary sound.

'So I started taking pictures again,' I tell him. 'To begin with, just shots of my daughters or of things I saw in the street. But it's always been landscape photography that I especially loved. So I took the girls on a trip to the country, photographing gardens . . . It was their summer holiday; I'd saved up my petrol ration . . .'

'And was the process consoling?' he asks me. 'Restorative in some way?'

'Yes. Yes, it was, actually.'

'I think that's very admirable.'

He sips his coffee, thoughtful. I find I can't quite meet his gaze.

'One or two technical points. I was wondering – do you do your own developing?' he asks me.

'Yes. I have a darkroom. It's nothing grand – just the cupboard under the stairs. But I love the whole process. Especially that moment when the image begins to emerge . . . It's just a hint, at first. A promise of something . . .'

I feel so shy, but I find I have a lot to say about photography.

'And how did you get permission to take the pictures?' he says. 'Some of these are private gardens.'

'I just asked people – I can be quite pig-headed, actually. Quite determined . . .'

His face is wreathed in some private amusement.

'You know, I can imagine that. That you could be very determined. The iron hand in the velvet glove,' he says.

'People are usually perfectly happy – if you promise to send them a print . . .'

Miss Cartwright brings in the tea. She pours it, hands me a cup, and then discreetly withdraws – though not before glancing adoringly at Hugo Ballantyne.

He turns the photographs over, pauses at one of my favourite shots, a single calla lily, silkily unfurling: you can see its poised, perfect shape, its stamens, its wide-open throat. I watch his hands moving over my picture. He has graceful hands, long-fingered, at once masculine and elegant, and I find myself feeling something I haven't felt since Ronnie died: a little stirring of attraction. As though something that was dormant in me is waking up again.

He comes to a picture I took at Montacute House – a sweep of lawn, tall cedars and sweet chestnuts; a garden of slanting shadows.

'I had to wait for that shot,' I tell him. 'I wanted the long light at the end of the day.'

'Your patience was certainly rewarded,' he says. 'There's such grace in these pictures. What I love: it's the way you take something so familiar – the quintessential English garden – and see it in a new way. That's what it's all about, I suppose. To see what other people pass by. The unexpected conjunction.'

I don't know how to respond to this praise.

'I'm so glad you like them,' I say, rather primly.

'And do you take portraits?' he asks me. 'Do you photograph people at all?'

'No, not really. Only my daughters. I don't think I quite have the confidence for portraits,' I say.

He considers this.

'I look forward to seeing what you can do – once you find that confidence,' he says. Warmly, his eyes on my face.

I'm embarrassed to feel myself blushing.

He closes my portfolio, takes a long drag on his cigarette. Leans away a little.

'Of course, we're not publishing very much at the moment. With all the uncertainty.' His voice is more brisk now, more matter-of-fact.

'No, of course you wouldn't be.' Trying to keep my voice level. Composing my face, so I won't look too disappointed. I want to seem a sophisticated woman who can take all this in her stride. As though I expected nothing of this meeting.

'Everyone's very cautious. Even some of our best authors aren't getting new contracts,' he says. 'And, of course, the paper shortage doesn't help . . .'

'Yes, I can see it must be difficult.'

'To be frank, some people view this kind of activity as rather frivolous, with a war on.'

'Yes, of course. Well, it is, really, I suppose . . .' My voice fading.

He runs one finger slowly across the cedars at Montacute House.

'But, let's face it, people could do with a bit of uplift. We need some beauty in our lives. We need reminding what it is we're fighting for.' He leans towards me again, across the mahogany desk. He has the satisfied smile of a man about to proffer something valuable. 'So I'm going to take a punt on you, Mrs Ripley,' he says.

I'm speechless, breathless.

'We'll need a bit of text,' he tells me. 'Just a few sentences for each picture.'

'Oh. I'm not sure if I—'

I bite my tongue. I wish I didn't sound so hesitant. I should be saying *yes of course* to everything he says.

'If you could just get something down on paper about each photograph – where you took it, any thoughts about it – we could work from there.'

'Oh. All right. Yes, I could do that.'

He closes my portfolio. I know our meeting is over.

'Thank you, Mr Ballantyne.'

'Please call me Hugo,' he says.

'I'm Livia,' I tell him.

There's a slight hesitation – as though he's trying to work something out, or wondering about something.

'Well, Livia. I'd like to meet up again before too long. Would that be possible, do you think?'

'Yes. Yes, absolutely.'

'What days are good for you?' he asks.

'Any day, really, as long as I have plenty of notice. I have someone who helps with my daughters.'

'That's excellent. I'll be in touch.'

'Right.'

He comes round to the front of his desk. I stand; he shakes my hand.

'Livia. It's been a real pleasure.'

His eyes on me, his skin warm against me. Again, I feel that shimmer of desire, which at once delights and troubles me. He holds onto my hand for just a little too long.

3

I take the bus home through London, and feel an unfamiliar happiness, and a sense of possibility that I haven't felt for an age now. Not since that morning last October when the telegram came.

Phoebe was with me, drinking coffee in the kitchen, when it happened.

The doorbell rang; I went to answer the door. The telegraph boy was standing there, and I remember noticing his expression, how he looked so very solemn. He handed me a telegram.

I had the strangest feeling then – as though I was high up, out of my body, looking down on this scene. The idea forming in my mind, with an odd kind of detachment, that this meant bad news for somebody.

I didn't open the telegram in the hallway. I took it through to the kitchen and dropped it on the table. Stood looking at it. Out of the corner of my eye, I was aware that Phoebe's face was entirely drained of colour, her skin so weirdly white against the red of her hair.

'I can't open it,' I told her. Puzzled. Watching myself – and the way I was somehow unable to move: how I couldn't reach out my hand to the thing. 'Could you do it? Would you mind terribly?'

She picked it up. Her hand was shaking. She opened it, read it; sat there, looking up at me. Warily. As though I'd become an entirely different being – some unpredictable wild creature.

'Liv, dearest, I'm so sorry. It's Ronnie,' she said.

'Ronnie?'

She got up, put her arms around me, steered me to a chair. She tried to hand me the telegram.

'No – just tell me,' I said.

'Something's happened. He's been killed, Liv. I'm so so sorry . . .'

I heard the choke in her voice.

'No, he can't have been,' I said at once. Very brisk and confident, though my body felt weak as water. 'I got a letter from him yesterday. He said he was right as rain, never better. Anyway, he's only been on exercises, he's only on Salisbury Plain . . . You know that . . . I told you . . .'

Phoebe knelt in front of me, wrapped her arms around me.

'There was an accident, Liv.'

I still couldn't touch the telegram.

'It must be a mistake,' I said, my voice rather odd and high-pitched. 'We need to tell them. Is there someone we can get in touch with? Does it say? So they can find the right family. The people who need to be told.'

'Liv – you have to read it.'

She put the thing into my hand. I read it, let the knowledge in.

I heard a sound of keening, a strange high animal wail. I wished the wailing would stop; then realised it was coming from me, from somewhere deep inside me, that it was beyond me to stop making it. I hadn't known my body could produce such feral sounds.

Later, someone from the army visited. With his face set in a practised expression of sympathy, he told me what had happened. Ronnie had been driving a tank on an exercise; the tank had overturned.

I felt so furious with God – that He could let this happen. Such a stupid, pointless way to die – a random death on an *exercise*. And only a few short months after Ronnie had enlisted, when he hadn't even been really fighting the war. If only he'd been fighting, perhaps it wouldn't have seemed so meaningless. If he'd been fighting, perhaps it wouldn't have hurt quite so much.

Then, for weeks, months, afterwards, I was tormented by guilt. We'd had a stupid row when last he'd been at home – about my housekeeping, as usual. Ronnie's mother had been a ferocious housewife who always kept her home pristine: he had very high expectations. He'd complained that I'd let my standards drop in his absence; that the whole house looked like a pigsty. I'd been upset, furious. I'd shouted at him – that he didn't know how hard it was, bringing the children up on my own; that perhaps he'd like to try helping out sometime, he'd find it wasn't exactly a walk in the park . . . I'd added, unforgivably, that his mother might have kept that damn house of hers very tidy, but she sure as hell had been a terrible mother to her son. That she could have brought him up to show an ounce of *consideration* occasionally . . .

. We hadn't reconciled properly, when the time came for him to leave. Then, a few days later, the telegram. Perhaps he'd been distracted; perhaps he'd had a lapse of attention because he still felt angry with me. I'd lie awake for hours, staring into the darkness, wishing I could return to that moment and not get angry at all, but be understanding and patient. Wishing I could go back in time and do it all again. And this time, do the right thing.

A feeling, a torment, that I recognised so well: that was already horribly familiar to me.

I hadn't known how the loss of him would take me. I'd pictured it, of course – as every soldier's wife must do. But it wasn't how I'd expected. Ronnie had been such a *big* man – voluble, talkative. *Larger than life*, people said: *the life and soul of the party*. Blond and forthright; always standing people drinks and telling stories that made people laugh. That was what had drawn me to him, when I first met him, at a church social: he'd seemed so jovial, convivial. I've always been rather retiring and shy: he'd had enough presence for both of us. I felt I was nothing without him – that I needed him to complete me. With him gone, I felt so *small*. As though I wasn't quite solid. As though I was thin, just two-dimensional, like one of Eliza's cut-out paper dolls, and the very least breath of wind might blow me away.

It wasn't as though our marriage had been perfect. We seemed to argue so often. And I found our love-making such an effort. This perplexed me – when I'd enjoyed all the kissing and courtship, all the thrilling early touching. But when it came to sex itself, the excitement all dulled down. I never really felt anything – just somehow untouched and separate: distracted, running through household tasks and laundry lists in my mind. Except when I was pregnant, when I was full of desire, but Ronnie didn't want to know. He thought it was unnatural – for me to want sex when I was expecting a child. And it was even worse once Polly arrived, and I was too tired to pretend.

Sometimes I wonder if I really loved him. But if I didn't love him, why do I miss him so much?

I had to be strong for my children. Polly was heart-broken. I'd hear her sobbing in the night, and I'd go to her, hold her, feeling so helpless. After a time, she stopped crying so much, but she still seemed very distressed: she'd pull strands of hair from her head, and rip the skin at the sides of her nails. It was around this time that she started drawing her detailed, immaculate rooms, with their vases of bluebells, flowered teapots, canaries in cages of gilt. Always flawless, but uninhabited, the table set for tea; just waiting for the perfect family to enter them.

25

Her little sister has seemed to cope much better. Perhaps for Eliza, the loss still isn't quite real. She's only five: too young to fully comprehend the way the world works, the immutable laws of existence. Sometimes I wonder if she doesn't really believe that her father has gone. I talked this over with Phoebe; and she told me that Freddie, her youngest, reacted just the same when his beloved grandmother died – refusing to believe it. She'd try to explain that his grandma was dead, and he'd ask when she'd next be visiting. Perhaps that's how it is for five-year-olds. They don't realise death is final, that it's something that can't be undone. It's as though the dead still exist for them: as if those who've passed on are just hanging around in some great ante-room in the sky.

As though one day they'll come back to us.

The girls rush up to me the minute I'm through the front door.

'What happened? Did the man like your pictures?' Eliza asks me.

I kneel down to hug her.

'He's going to publish them,' I say. 'They're going to be in a book.'

'Ooh, Mum. That's wonderful,' says Polly.

'Will you be famous?' Eliza asks.

'No, I don't suppose so.' Then, seeing how her face falls, 'Well, maybe just a little bit.'

Aggie is in the parlour, crocheting a tea cosy: she's always making useful things to sell in the Red Cross shop. She looks up and smiles, and her brown eyes gleam, bright as ginger wine in the sunlight.

'You look like the cat that got the cream,' she tells me.

'Yes, it all went really well . . . And everything was all right here?'

'Don't you worry, Livia. The girls were good as gold.'

She's washed up all my dishes, even though I told her not to.

Aggie started out as my babysitter – but now she's so much more, an honorary great-aunt. Her life hasn't been easy: her husband had emphysema, and she had to nurse him for years. If I remark how hard it must have been, Aggie is cheerfully philosophical. 'The way I see it, Livia, everyone has their bag of stones – something they have to drag behind them. And that was mine,' she'll say.

'Thank you so much,' I tell her now.

'A pleasure, my dear. It's lovely to see you looking so happy,' she says. Then she hesitates, lowers her voice, as though unsure whether to say this. 'I've been so worried about you, Livia, since – you know – since it happened. Maybe this is the moment when things will start to look up.'

'Yes. I think it could be.'

And as I say it, I believe it. I have a sense of this whole past year as a darkness that's starting to lift.

Aggie gathers up her things, and we go to wave goodbye to her, beneath the fragile bluebird in the glass above our front door.

4

We'll have sardines and lettuce and toast for tea, and then some flapjacks I've made. I slice the bread and grill it.

Eliza wanders through the kitchen. She has her skipping rope, and Rabbit under her arm.

'You were singing, Mummy.'

'Was I?'

'Is it because you're happy?'

'Yes, it must be . . .'

'Is it because of your book?'

'Yes, I think so, sweetheart.'

Yes, it's because of my book. *And Hugo Ballantyne.*

She goes out to the garden, where she'll skip or play hopscotch on the terrace, or push herself on the mossy swing that hangs from the old apple tree.

My kitchen is full of lavish late-afternoon sunlight. I've always loved this room at the back of the house. It's very quiet. This is one of those tall, thin London houses that seem to reach back a long way, and you can feel quite secluded here, only a little noise from the street filtering down the side alley, looking out on the sweetly disordered garden with its hollyhocks, lupins, rambling roses, its cherry and apple trees, its high laurel hedges. And of course the Anderson shelter in the middle of the lawn, with its corrugated iron walls, and its roof covered over with turf.

Through the open window, I can hear Eliza on the terrace – the patter of her sandalled feet and the rhythmic swish of the rope. Polly is playing 'Für Elise' on the piano in the parlour.

When we inherited and came here, Ronnie and I, after my mother died, we changed as much as we could afford to. All the heavy dark furniture oppressed me: it reminded me of my childhood, of all the guilt and the sadness: of Sarah, my sister, of things I was trying to push from my mind. I did keep a few of my mother's possessions. The dresser with the crockery patterned with meadow saffron flowers. The Holman Hunt picture, *The Light of the World*, which hangs above the dining-room fireplace, showing a rather mournful Jesus holding an old-fashioned lamp. The sampler that says, *There's no place like home,* in faded magenta cross-stitch. But it all looks much more cheerful than in my mother's last days, with family photos in ormolu frames on the dresser and potted geraniums flaring redly on the window sills.

I spread the butter – thinly, because butter is on ration now. Mostly, I use margarine. The kitchen fills with the friendly, welcoming smell of hot buttered toast.

And then it comes: the familiar mournful wail of the siren, rising and falling, rising and falling. The sound always makes you feel nervous – even when you're sure it means nothing. I swallow down my anxiety. I tell myself it's certainly another false alarm.

The cups and saucers on the dresser begin to rattle faintly, as though a tremulous hand is holding them. The water in the washing-up bowl shivers all over its surface. There's a distant droning, something at first more felt than heard, like the far-off thunder of some massive waterfall. Rapidly coming closer.

I rush to the window, look up.

Oh God oh God oh God.

The sky is full of planes, shining in the sunlight like a swarm of glittery insects, the ones in the middle in forma- tion, the ones on the edges, the fighters, weaving and darting around. Their noise swells to a roar, slams into me.

For a moment, I'm paralysed.

It's over. We've lost the war. This is Hitler's invasion. When these planes begin to bomb us, there'll be nothing of London left. It's all over.

At once, the guilt rushing in.

I should have sent the girls out of danger. I didn't, and now it's too late. Everything I do is wrong.

And then, a brief sense of very personal outrage.

This can't be happening now. *Just when the darkness is lifting. Just when my life is starting to make a kind of sense again.*

I'm transfixed, staring up at the planes, all these thoughts racing through me. Polly has seen: she runs through from the parlour. Eliza notices us at the window: she comes in, grabs my hand.

Polly tugs at me.

'Mum – shouldn't we go?' Her voice shrill, urgent.

'Yes. Yes, of course.'

I have a basket kept ready, with biscuits and crayons and books. Polly fetches the basket. Eliza drops Rabbit and makes a dive for Hector, who is skulking under the table. He skitters away from her. She pursues him into the hall.

'Eliza, what on earth are you doing?'

'We have to catch Hector,' she tells me. 'He doesn't want to be bombed.'

'No, we can't take him. For God's sake, Eliza. I thought we'd been into all that.'

My voice is stern. She comes back reluctantly into the kitchen.

I grab our gas masks.

'*Now*,' I tell them.

I take them out to the garden, lock up the house behind us, run over the lawn to the shelter, open the door.

Eliza hangs back, a slight frown etched in her face.

'But Rabbit isn't here,' she tells me. 'Rabbit got left behind.'

'*No*, Eliza. I don't *believe* this . . .'

'It was an accident, Mummy,' she tells me limpidly.

The world is pulsating with sound – the wail of the siren; above us, the drone of the planes. It makes it hard to think clearly. What if I went back for Rabbit and they started to bomb and I died? But then I imagine Eliza fretting for hours in the shelter.

I give Polly the torch.

'You two go on. I'll get him.'

I race back into the house, find Rabbit on the dining-room table. I snatch him, run back to the shelter, slam the door shut.

We used to take shelter here frequently just after war was declared – there were a lot of false alarms then – but we've never had to stay in here for more than half an hour. There are deckchairs, blankets, a mattress, a supply of candles and matches, but it's cramped and claustrophobic and has a smell of sour earth. I find the matches and light a candle, to save the batteries in our torch. The candle flickers weirdly. It's strange to leave the bright day behind and suddenly find ourselves here, huddling together fearfully in this shadowy, flickery cave.

I wrap the girls up in the blankets: they've already started shivering. The shelter needs some form of heating, with the wet clammy earth all around. I should have done more to make it comfortable. It comes to me that I'm all wrong for these times. If only I was more practical; if only I'd been a Girl Guide as a child, and learned to do helpful, sensible things: knots, and cooking on campfires, and sing-songs to make people smile. What use are pictures of roses in wartime?

There's a shrieking whistle, an ominous thud. Polly screams.

'What was that? Was it a bomb?' Her face pale as wax in the candlelight, her voice serrated with fear.

'Yes, I think so, sweetheart.'

I'm shaking, my teeth are chattering; but I have to be brave for my girls.

Eliza climbs on my lap and wraps around me like a vine. I feel the tremor that passes through her with every whine and whistle and crash, as though we are one body. I feel her heart beating against me, as though it is beating inside me.

'Poor Hector. What will happen to him?' she asks me.

'Hector will be fine,' I tell her. 'He'll find a corner to hide in. Cats are really good at looking after themselves. Don't worry too much, Eliza . . .'

We can hear the shriek and crash of the bombs, but there's no sound of our guns. Why aren't we shooting back at our enemy? Have we just given up?

'They won't kill us, Mum, will they?' says Polly.

'We'll be safe in here, sweetheart. It's all designed to protect us.'

'But people will get hurt, won't they?'

There's a great rumbling eruption, much closer to us this time.

'Yes, some people, probably. If they don't manage to get to their shelters. But the doctors are ready for them.'

'But what if they bomb the doctors?'

'Polly . . .'

'And what if they bomb our house,' she says, 'and all my drawings are spoilt?'

33

'*And* my animals,' says Eliza.

They start to list all the things that could get destroyed in the house – Eliza's painted elephant, Polly's beloved coral necklace, the sampler and the piano and the apostle spoons – chanting the names of all these things over and over. This lugubrious litany seems to soothe them.

'What if the bluebird gets bombed?' says Eliza.

I think of the flower-wreathed bluebird in the glass above our front door. I don't say anything.

At last, the noise of the planes and the bombing recedes; and then the glorious All Clear sounds.

'It's over. We can go back to the house,' I tell them.

I'm almost sobbing with relief. *It was terrible, but it's over now.* I glance at my watch: it's half past six. The raid seemed to last for an age, but we've been sheltering less than two hours.

I push open the door of the shelter. It's surprising to find that out here it's only twilight, the greens of the garden fading to lavender, long sepia shadows slanting, the sky deepening into evening in a void of cobalt blue. In the east, there's a lot of smoke billowing – off towards Stepney, towards the docks: many fires must have been started there. But the burning all looks quite distant, and our street still seems to be here.

In the dining room, our tea is waiting on the table. The toast, of course, is soggy now, and I have to make some more. I'm cross that the butter was wasted.

The girls are very hungry, but I can scarcely eat at all.

*

34

Polly and Eliza go upstairs to clean their teeth and get ready for bed. I'm exhausted: I long for sleep myself. I wash the dishes and tidy the kitchen, taking a kind of comfort in these simple, everyday tasks: trying to reimpose some order on our life and our home.

And then the sirens start to howl.

No.

The girls lurch down the stairs two at a time, Polly still clutching her toothbrush.

'Please say it's a false alarm. *Please*, Mum. Say it. You *have* to . . .'

I run to the window, fling it open. You can already hear another wave of planes.

'But they'd *gone*,' says Polly, in a little rag of a voice.

We run back to the shelter through the gathering gloom of the garden. Many of the fires from the earlier raid are still burning; they're more obvious in the thickening dark, as the colours of the flames reflect in the billows of smoke and the clouds – copper, bronze, rose, crimson. London will be all lit up by these fires. Perhaps that's why the Germans did this – dropping thousands of fire bombs to guide the second wave of bombers. The blackout is point-less tonight: the night will be bright with the flames, the entire city illuminated.

This time, the bombs fall much closer. We listen, shud-dering, to all the noise out there – the droning of the bombers, the scream of the bombs as they fall, the thun-dering crash as they land and explode. This is so much worse than before. Fear consumes me. I don't have any

35

strength left – I used up every last shred of courage in the first round of bombing. I can't fight the fear any more, can't push it away.

Eliza is on my lap again: I clasp her to me. Polly is sobbing. I find that I'm praying fervently – even though I don't really believe.

I try to imagine what is happening out there on the streets of London. Will anything be left after this night of devastation? And I have an insidious, traitorous thought. *If Hitler has invaded, why don't we surrender at once? If we surrendered, at least there wouldn't be any more bombs. If we surrendered, we could at least come out of this horrible place . . .*

There's a thud, very close, so the earth beneath us trembles. We hear glass splintering somewhere: the shards ricochet off our metal door with a fearsome clattering sound. Polly screams and clings to me. Are we going to die and be buried here? Is this the way everything ends?

We huddle close together, clutching one another, shrouded in damp blankets and the smell of sour cold earth.

5

The raid lasts the entire night.

I feel we have been in the shelter for a lifetime, when it comes to me that I haven't heard any bombing for a while. I have a sense of confusion: I must have fallen asleep. The candle that I lit last night has burned right down to a stub.

The All Clear sounds, the long level note – the most welcome sound in the world. I disentangle myself from Eliza and put her down in the empty deckchair. She stirs a little, her pale eyes open and close.

'Is it over, Mum?' says Polly.

'Yes, I think so.'

My body is stiff and achy from sitting so tensely all night. Fear, it seems, can wear out your body.

I go to the door of the shelter. My heart is pounding. I

wonder what I will see out there: perhaps the end of the world. I push the door open, step out.

It's morning. But the daylight looks all wrong, unreal: in the east, towards the docks, there's a glow as red as sunset. There must be vast fires burning there. There are great banks of cloud that hold the violent colours of the fires – sulphur, scarlet, ochre. I stare for a moment at the unreal flamboyance of the sky. The air smells strange; it's sooty, acrid, heavy with brick dust and smoke. No gas, I think – though I'm not entirely sure what gas would smell like. But if there were gas, they certainly wouldn't have sounded the All Clear.

When you breathe, the brick dust scratches your throat, like you've swallowed a handful of briars.

'The raid's all over,' I tell them cheerfully. 'There. It wasn't too bad, was it?'

Eliza is awake now. She stretches, yawns widely. Her eyes are sticky with sleep.

'It was horrible,' she says.

'Well, we seem to have got through it,' I say. 'We still seem to be in one piece.'

'You were really frightened, Mummy. You were shaking. I could feel you.'

Polly frowns at her sister. 'How do you know that anyway? You were fast asleep,' she says.

'I heard it. Every single bomb,' says Eliza.

She looks too sleepy to walk, and I pick her up in my arms, and take them both out into the garden.

Our house is still standing. *Thank you, God*. But when I

look to either side, across the other back gardens, I can see that a house in the street behind ours has been quite badly damaged – the roof and chimney torn away. I don't know who lives there: poor people. But St Michael and All Angels, the church round the corner in Stapleforth Street, looks to have survived intact: I can see its familiar steeple, still pointing up to the sky, and the sight is oddly comforting.

A window at the back of our house has been broken. The lawn is strewn with shards of glass, which have a rosy sparkle in the light of this strange dawn. The glass must have been what so frightened us, when it bounced off the door of the shelter. Fragments crackle and shatter under our feet as we walk.

'Be careful where you step, Polly.'

'That's *our* window that's broken, Mum. Mine and Eliza's. Our bedroom window,' she says.

'Yes, I'm afraid so. But it's just the glass: I don't think your things will be damaged.' I pick my way cautiously between the glittery shards. 'You two will have to sleep in my bed, for what's left of the night,' I tell them.

'What about you, though, Mum?' says Polly. 'You need to sleep as well.'

I'm touched by how considerate she is – thinking of me, after everything we've been through.

'Don't worry about me, sweetheart. I can sleep on the sofa,' I say.

I suddenly feel an exhaustion so complete that I can scarcely move, can scarcely carry Eliza, who is almost asleep again, and heavy in my arms, like something soaked through with water.

Polly opens the back door, and I take Eliza up to my bedroom and lay her down on the bed – just as she is, in her day clothes, only pausing to pull off her shoes.

'You can sleep in your clothes as well,' I tell Polly.

'I'd rather change, Mum. I feel so dirty,' she says.

But I won't let her fetch her pyjamas. I want to be the first to look in their room, in case the damage is upsetting. For the moment, I can't face it.

'You can change later, sweetheart. Just try to get some sleep,' I say.

She acquiesces.

Eliza is asleep already, her lashes making a fringe of gentian shadow under her eyes, Rabbit clutched against her. Polly climbs in beside her. I pull the blankets over them, as though they were going to bed at the end of an ordinary day. Seeing their heads together on the pillows, I feel the tears well up, all the emotion of the night that I've tried to keep tamped down surging through me. I leave the bedroom hastily, so Polly won't see my tears.

I go to the parlour. My legs give way; I feel utterly unravelled. I find myself huddled up on the floor, weeping inconsolably, oppressed by a sense of utter hopelessness. How can we endure this? What will become of us?

And I think of the people I love – Aggie; Phoebe and her family. What has happened to all of them? I think of Hugo Ballantyne. Is Hugo still alive?

I weep for a long time.

At last, the tears slow. I fetch my winter coat from the hall, lie down on the sofa, cover myself with the coat. The silence is astonishing. Outside, the streets and gardens shiver and shake with birdsong: pigeons, softly turning the same phrase over and over; the liquid fluting of a thrush; the wet yellow whistle of a blackbird in one of the poplars in the street. All the usual sweet, peaceful sounds of a Sunday. If you didn't look out of the window, at the fires and the smoke in the sky, you could imagine it was a perfect Sunday morning.

Now, there are no more tears left in me. Sleep comes swiftly.

6

The girls are still fast asleep in my bed when I get up.

I cautiously open the door of their old bedroom. It's unnerving, to see their things all blown about by the blast: Polly's coral necklace, her *Chalet School* stories, her manuals of First Aid; Eliza's dolls and picture books, all scattered. A movement of air through the broken window rifles through the room, ruffling my hair and turning the pages of Eliza's *Rupert Annual*. Splinters of glass are everywhere, glinting malignly. But nothing else seems broken – though there's a new jagged crack in the outer wall, which has an ominous look.

I'll have to deal with the window myself – I won't be able to get a workman. Our house can still be lived in – we won't be a priority, unlike those poor unfortunate souls whose houses were badly damaged; we won't be at the top of anyone's list. I can probably find a linoleum off-cut in the shed in the garden, that I can tack over the window. But the room will get very cold at night, and it won't get any daylight, and the crack in the wall is worrying. The girls won't be able to sleep in here anytime soon.

I could put one of them in the little spare room, but there wouldn't be room for them both. The solution to this is obvious. Yet I feel a profound reluctance.

I shut the door of their old bedroom, step on along the landing. I feel so tired suddenly, my body heavy and slowed, as though I were wading through deep water. I stand for a moment at the door of the room I rarely go in. My hand against the door knob, just waiting; taking a breath. Then turn the knob, push the door open.

It's entirely dark; in here, I keep the blackout curtains permanently drawn. I go to the window, pull back the curtains. Moving slowly, cautiously, as though I might disturb something. There's a soft pall of dust on the sills, and a spider has set its embroidery all across the pane, the sun shining silver through the filaments, so they seem pellucid, luminous. I put my finger to the cobweb: it's sticky and clings to my hand. There's a dingy smell of neglect, a backwash of old clothes and dust, and the touch of the air is cold here – this room hasn't been heated in years. It has the chill of air not stirred, not breathed; a chill that can get inside you, and bring goosebumps up on your arms. Even on a bright September morning.

Outside, my whispery garden, looking different from this

43

angle, is suddenly unfamiliar, all littered with bits of roof tile and shards of glass from last night. A blown leaf is splayed against the glass, so you can see its intricate veins. Branches of the cherry tree that grows too close to the house are almost touching the window. In windy weather, the tips of the branches could knock against the panes, perhaps disturbing whichever girl is sleeping here. I think routinely that I'll have to get the cherry tree pruned – then reflect that I would never be able to find a gardener to do this.

I stand there for a moment, resting my hands on the sill.

This was Sarah's room when we were children. My mother kept it just the same, for years and years, like a shrine. Sarah's ecru lace bedspread smoothed down; her collection of dolls in national costume lined up on the bookshelf; her clothes still hanging from the rail, still smelling faintly of her, of the sarsaparilla drops she loved, and of flowery talcum powder. After my mother's death, when Ronnie and I inherited and moved here, I cleared out most of Sarah's belongings, all except one or two things – her prayer book, her Bible, the jewel box our grandmother gave her; but I couldn't quite persuade myself to bring this room back into use, except as a kind of lumber room. I only come in here when I absolutely have to. Once or twice a year, perhaps, to look for something we've lost.

Standing here, I think about Sarah: I can't stop myself. Aware of the pit that opens up at my feet even now, whenever I let myself think of her, the dark and shaming knowledge that laps at me like black water. All through my life since it happened, when I was ten and she was twelve, I've never quite known what to say, if people ask if I have a sister. Do you say, *Yes*, or *No*, or *Once I did, but now I don't any more*? It's the same disturbing uncertainty I have today, with Ronnie. What should you do with the dead? What part should they play in the lives of the living? How should you think about them, talk about them? Where do the dead belong?

There are no answers to these questions.

I drag my mind back to the present, to immediate, practical things. There will be a lot of clearing to do, to make enough space for a bed. There are so many boxes, packed with the stuff that builds up over the years that you don't really need but can never quite get rid of. Old curtains and bedspreads, neatly folded; a trunk with Polly's discarded dresses, which Eliza will one day grow into; toys they played with when they were younger. Things from the past that one day might possibly come in useful again.

I make my decision. Polly can sleep in the spare room and Eliza in here. Polly likes everything to be orderly, and she'd undoubtedly hate all the clutter, but it shouldn't bother Eliza. And it will look so much more cheerful once it's cleaned and Eliza's moved in – the boxes stacked, her friendly toys and books all strewn around. I remind myself it will only be for a little while. Just until I can get the window glazed.

I close the door behind me with a slight sense of relief. And the thought flickers in me that Eliza might feel exactly the same about the room as me – that she won't like sleeping here. But I'm probably being fanciful. She's only a little girl; I've never told her about Sarah. She won't feel the weight of it – all that history, all that sorrow and grief. Of course the room won't bother her.

7

Eventually, Polly and Eliza come downstairs, in their crumpled clothes from yesterday, blearily rubbing the sleep from their eyes.

Eliza finds Hector huddled behind the piano in the parlour. She tries to haul him through into the kitchen, but he scratches her and wriggles out of her arms.

'Poor thing, he's really upset.' She studies the delicate red thread that he's incised on her wrist with interest. '*Somebody* was mean to him. *Somebody* wouldn't let him into the shelter,' she says, with a meaningful glance in my direction.

When war was declared, a lot of people had their pets put down. Myself, I couldn't face it – though I often regret my decision: our bad-tempered, raggedy cat is just another mouth to feed. But whenever this thought occurs to me,

Hector will seem to fix me with those knowing eyes of his, which are the exact feral yellow of dandelions, and I'll feel guilty that I thought it.

'Mum, I really want to change,' Polly tells me. 'I feel disgusting.'

'You can change after breakfast. I'll try to find you some clean clothes.'

They spread margarine on their toast. I pour tea for Polly and milk for Eliza.

The air that drifts in through the window has a smoky, sulphurous smell. People are up and about now, and starting to mend the wreckage of the night: you can hear hammering and sawing, and the brittle percussion of glass shards being swept up.

'I've had a look at the damage,' I tell them. 'And I'm afraid you won't be able to sleep in your bedroom for now. Sorry, girls.'

'So where shall we sleep, Mum?'

'Polly, you can go in the little spare room at the front. And I'm going to sort out the lumber room for Eliza.'

'*Yes*. My own bedroom. At *last*,' says Polly.

I can imagine just how ordered and pristine Polly's new bedroom will be.

I expect Eliza to protest, but she seems rather pleased by this news. There's a glint of interest in her eye.

'There are lots of things in the lumber room,' she says, her voice dreamy with nostalgia. 'The pull-along chicken I had when I was small. The picture made from butterfly wings . . .'

She has her most demure goody-two-shoes expression. This usually spells trouble.

'Yes, but it's all in boxes. Now, I don't want you poking around in there and getting things out, Eliza. I shall be really cross if you do that.'

'Perhaps I could look at just *some* of the things? If I was very very tidy?'

'*No*, Eliza. Anyway, it's all just boring old stuff.'

'But I like old things, Mummy.'

She puts down her mug with a neat little click, to underline her words.

'Eliza. I mean it.'

Eliza doesn't respond to this. She bites crisply into her toast.

'Mum, we want to have a look in our bedroom,' Polly tells me.

Eliza nods. For once, they're united.

'We do. We want to see what Hitler has done to our room.'

'You can look at it from the doorway,' I say, 'but you absolutely mustn't go in. Not till I've dealt with the broken glass.'

After breakfast, I show them, and gather up toys and clothes from their shelves. I expect them to be upset by the damage, but for the moment they seem remarkably calm, as though this is all an adventure to them.

8

The front door clicks open.

'Livia!'

It's Aggie, her voice frayed with fear. I run down from the lumber room, where I've nearly finished cleaning.

'Oh, my dear,' she says. 'What an absolute joy to see you all in one piece.' She wraps me in her arms, and I breathe in her comforting smell, of Wright's Coal Tar soap and freshly laundered linen. 'I just wanted to check that you and my favourite girls were all right.'

'Their bedroom window got broken. But otherwise everything's fine . . . And what about you? And your house?'

'Both still standing, thank the Lord.'

I take her through to the kitchen. Eliza comes to join

us, with a book of colouring-in: she's always happy to see Aggie. I put the kettle on the hob.

'Aggie, you're all dressed up,' I say. She's wearing her Sunday-best hat – petunia felt, with a jaunty feather. 'Don't tell me you made it to church . . .'

Aggie is very devout – though she rarely talks about her faith, and never remarks on my lack of one.

'I did, actually, Livia. I went to St Michael's for matins.'

'Goodness. They still had a service – even after last night?'

'There were only a few of us there,' she tells me. 'We prayed for all the poor souls who've been killed or lost people they loved.' Her eyes are suddenly full of sorrow. 'There must be an awful lot of them, Livia.'

'Yes. Yes, there must be.'

But it's strange to think of this – here in the peace of my kitchen, the kettle whistling cheerfully, birdsong trickling in from the garden. The stench of smoke is fading, and you can smell the Duchesse d'Angoulême roses that grow very close to the house, their scent languorous and heady, so sweet that you feel you could never smell it enough. The night seems utterly unreal now, like something imagined or dreamed.

'So you stayed here, in your Andy?' she asks me.

I nod. 'It wasn't much fun, but it did the job. And you?'

'I went to the crypt at St Michael's. It was quite a night, I can tell you. Poor old Mrs Cavendish fainted clean away. It was lucky I had my eau de cologne, to rouse her. And some of the others spent all night sobbing, poor things.'

'Well, I don't blame them,' I tell her. 'I had a weep myself, this morning.'

But I think to myself that I'm glad we've got a shelter of our own – even though it's cramped and chilly. I wouldn't want to spend the night in the crypt, with a whole crowd of other terrified people.

'It's funny how folk react,' says Aggie thoughtfully. 'As I say, some of them couldn't stop crying. And there were some who just played dominoes and didn't seem to care.'

'Well, it takes all sorts . . .'

Aggie turns to Eliza.

'And what about you and Polly? I bet you were ever so brave.'

Eliza considers this.

'*I* wasn't frightened, Auntie Aggie,' she says.

'They both coped very well,' I say.

Eliza frowns. 'Mummy, that's wrong, you know it is. Polly got really upset.'

Aggie smiles.

'Sometimes I think the little people can take these things in their stride. The trouble with us older ones is we always think far too much. We dwell on things; we imagine the worst that can happen.'

'You're too right, Aggie. I know I do,' I tell her.

I hand her the teacup; she sips gratefully. Eliza colours her picture, working with great concentration. A thrush is singing rapturously in my cherry tree.

'Some of those poor refugees came to the crypt to shelter,' says Aggie then. 'You know, the strangers you sometimes see at the shops. There's a man and his wife from Frankfurt – Dr and Mrs Rosen. They're staying at Orchid Villa, Mrs Parkinson's place. He was a doctor, in Frankfurt, he told me.'

'That must be terribly hard . . .'

There are lots of strangers in London now, fleeing from Hitler. I can't begin to imagine it – to leave behind the land of your birth and everything you have known; to come to a foreign country and lodge in a dreary boarding house that smells of cabbage and Dettol; to lose everything you have built up over the years. To be an *exile*.

We are quiet for a moment. You can hear the little homely sounds – the scratch of Eliza's crayon, the stir of the coals in the boiler, Polly in the parlour playing a Haydn Sarabande. I feel such a profound gratitude, that I still have my house. For now, at least.

Aggie puts her cup down in the saucer and flicks some lint from her sleeve, her gestures neat and careful. Sometimes she makes me think of a little brown bird – so busy, cheerful, humble.

'It's quite well organised, at St Michael's,' she tells me. 'We've got a new vicar – the Reverend Connelly. I wondered if you'd come across him at all?'

I shake my head. 'No, not really.'

How could I have come across him, when I never venture inside the church any more?

Though I still sometimes think about services, and remember some of the words. *We have done those things which we ought not to have done . . .*

'He was mostly out on the streets, in the raid. He runs the wardens' post here,' she tells me.

'Does he? That's quite impressive . . .'

I think how the wardens put everyone's backs up at the start of the war – how they'd knock on your door and tell you off if your blackout was inadequate. Nobody liked them. But after last night, they seem like heroes, putting their lives on the line.

'He dropped in to see us in the shelter,' says Aggie, 'to check that things were all right. Well, as all right as they could be, with poor old Mrs Cavendish lying flat out on the floor . . .'

There's a gleam of amusement in Aggie's eyes.

'Oh. I haven't heard of him.'

'He's only been here a few weeks,' she says, and a shadow crosses her face. 'A lot of people don't like him. Well, you can see where they're coming from. He's a bit of a fire-brand, Livia. His sermons are far too socialist, and he can be rather abrupt.' She illustrates her point with small upheavals of her hands.

'Really?'

In spite of myself, I feel a slight stirring of interest in this controversial clergyman.

'I can understand people objecting: church isn't the place for politics. And he's very keen on silent prayer,' she tells me. She's thoughtful, frown lines bunching in a knot between her brows. 'It can make you feel rather awkward. Myself, I like a good rousing hymn. *Eternal Father, strong to save* – that kind of thing,' she says.

'I know what you mean,' I tell her. Though I don't have opinions on hymns.

She leans towards me across the table. Uncertain, not sure how I'll respond to what she's about to tell me.

'The thing is, Livia, he told me he used to be a conchie. He was in Dick Sheppard's Peace Pledge Union.'

'Oh.'

I remember reading about the Peace Pledge in my *Daily Herald*. The Reverend Dick Sheppard was a canon at St Paul's. He urged men to send him postcards with a pledge that they'd never enlist, that they'd never support another war. Over a hundred thousand responded. It was seven years ago now, and at the time it had seemed so admirable, after the carnage of the Great War – people solemnly vowing, *Never again*.

But since Hitler became so powerful, things don't seem quite the same.

'I don't suppose that goes down very well with people,' I say.

Eliza looks up from her colouring-in.

'Why not, Mummy?'

I hadn't realised she was following our conversation. My heart sinks a little: this is so hard to explain to a child.

'Those men all promised they'd never fight for their country,' I tell her. 'But now, people think that's cowardly – when there are so many brave soldiers who are risking their lives.'

'Like Daddy did,' says Eliza.

It's as though a dark lacquer of sadness is spreading over

the room. There's a sensation of falling inside me. I haven't told the girls exactly how their father died. I don't know what to say to her.

Aggie can see how upset I am, and briskly intervenes.

'Anyway, Livia, he says he's changed his mind, this war. He's got a bad leg and he couldn't sign up, but he'd fight if they'd let him, he said. I think that's right, to be honest, Livia. He's not a conchie, in his heart. Or, if he is – well, he's the most ferocious conchie I ever clapped eyes on,' she says.

She straightens her hat, picks up her handbag.

'So I imagine you'll be looking for a new church to go to,' I say.

Aggie's smile is warm and wide and softens the lines in her face.

'Oh, bless you, Livia, no, not at all. I didn't say *I* didn't like him. You feel he wouldn't take no for an answer . . . I respect that, to be honest. A bit of determination – that's what you need in a man. Especially in times like these,' she tells me.

We say goodbye on my doorstep.

The street has been changed by the bombing, even though we escaped the worst of the damage. There are slices of sky where there shouldn't be, where roofs and chimneys have vanished. It's unnerving to find yourself seeing so much further than ever before.

9

On Sunday evening, there's another raid.

We huddle in our shelter and hear the bombers circling above us. Polly shivers.

'It sounds like they're hunting for us, Mum. It's like they're saying: *Where are you? Where are you?*' she says.

We hear a long shrieking whistle, and then a vast dull thud. The ground in the shelter shudders beneath us; the flame of the candle goes out.

Polly screams. I have Eliza on my lap; with one hand I reach for Polly in the darkness, pull her against me. She's shaking.

'Where did that land?' she says then, her mouth muffled against my shoulder.

'I don't know, sweetheart. Not too close, I hope.'

'Will our house still be there?' she asks me.

'Yes. I'm sure it will.'

'Are you just saying that, Mum? How can you be so certain?' she says.

If the bomb had hit our house, our shelter wouldn't survive. We wouldn't still be sitting here.

'I just am,' I tell her.

I turn on my torch, find the matches, light the candle again.

Later, the planes move away, and we manage to grab a little sleep; though I keep jolting into wakefulness, my heart racing, and Polly too keeps shifting, murmuring words I can't make out. Only Eliza sleeps soundly.

And then, at last, the All Clear, and we head gratefully back to the house. Polly and Eliza go to bed in their new bedrooms. I tuck Eliza's blankets in around her and pull her eiderdown up; the lumber room always feels so chilly. Then I take to my own bed. I sleep restlessly, in a feverish kaleidoscope of dreams.

I wake suddenly, heart pounding, as though something has disturbed me. I listen before I look, before I open my eyes, but all is blessedly quiet. I look around uncertainly. When you wake in the blackout, you can't tell what time of day it must be. I never get used to this.

I reach to turn on my bedside lamp. My clock says five to nine. *Bother*. I've overslept – but maybe it doesn't matter: the girls will be late for their lessons, but so will most of their classmates. I could keep them at home, I suppose; but I'm determined to send them to school, to keep their lives as normal as possible.

I push aside the curtains and look out across Conduit Street. It's another gorgeous morning, no cloud, the light all golden and syrupy. But across to the east, above the docks, smoke smears the blue of the sky: fires must still be burning there. A blackbird is singing his heart out in one of the pollarded poplar trees.

I pull my dressing gown around me, and go to wake Polly and Eliza.

Out on the landing, I push the blackout curtains aside, then open the door of the room that is now Eliza's. A little light from the landing leaks in over the bed.

Oh God.

Panic surges through me. My heart thuds, hurting my chest. The bed is empty.

I rush to the window, push back the curtains. Sunlight spills into every corner, illuminating everything. And then, in the clear gilded light, I see her, lying curled up on the floor – just in her pyjamas, with no bedclothes. Rabbit is clutched against her, and she's absolutely still.

I kneel, put a hand on her arm. Her skin feels cold; she must have got chilled after the night in the Anderson shelter, and then lying here for hours in the draught on the floor. Her chest scarcely moves, her breath is silent. For a brief bitter moment, I think she is dead; I'm still flooded with fear from the night.

'Eliza!'

Her eyelashes flicker, she opens her eyes. All the breath I didn't know I was holding rushes out of my mouth.

'Sweetheart, are you all right?'

Her eyes seem entirely without colour in the brightness, and are rather wide and unfocused; she blinks at the daylight, looking vaguely around. She's confused perhaps by finding herself in this unfamiliar room.

'Yes, of course I am,' she says.

She stretches languidly. Her face is smudged with violet shadow.

'What on earth were you doing?' I gather her up in my arms. Her body is soft with sleep. She's shivering; her skin has goosebumps. 'You must have been frozen, Eliza. Why didn't you sleep in your bed?'

Eliza yawns noisily on my shoulder. She smells of soap and biscuits and bedclothes; and something else, something musty, worn, neglected, that must have come from sleeping in this unused room, as though some essence that lingers in here has clung to her.

Then I see that one of the cartons has been pulled out from under the bed. I'm surprised she could do this – it's heavy. A bit of the Sellotape that fixed down the flaps has been ripped.

'Were you trying to open that box?' I ask.

Eliza hesitates, frowns.

'Maybe, Mummy.'

'Eliza, *no*. You know you mustn't. It's just old things in there. Boring baby toys, and so on.'

And some of Sarah's things as well. But I try not to think about this.

It's very quiet in here, and I can hear the smallest sounds – her breath, and the rasp of her eyelashes when she rubs at her eyes. Her skin is so pale it seems translucent; there are blue nets of veins in her wrists.

'Eliza, why were you lying down on the floor?'

'I was frightened, Mummy.'

'You didn't need to be, sweetheart. When the All Clear goes, it means the bombers have all gone away.'

'It wasn't the bombs. I'm not scared of the bombs. I'm not like Polly,' she says.

'Well – what was it then, sweetheart?'

'I didn't like the fingers. They stopped me from sleeping,' she says.

For a moment, I'm bemused.

'What fingers, Eliza?'

She frowns.

'You can't sleep if people keep knocking. They went *tap tap tap* on the pane.'

And then I think of the cherry tree.

'Oh, Eliza, it's just the cherry tree branches. When the wind blows, they rub on the glass. It's nothing to be scared of.'

'Someone was trying to get in, Mummy.'

'No, sweetheart.'

But a little shudder goes through me, and Eliza sees.

'What is it, Mummy? Are you frightened as well?'

Pull yourself together, woman.

'No, of course not, sweetheart.' I tell myself it must have been something that Polly said to her – that Polly was trying to scare her. I make my voice cheerful and brisk.

'Eliza, I know it's rather confusing to wake in a different bedroom. But you'll get used to it soon enough. And now, you need to get dressed and have breakfast . . .'

But I feel it again – how I really don't like this room.

After breakfast, when Eliza is upstairs cleaning her teeth, I speak to Polly.

'You shouldn't have teased Eliza like that,' I tell her.

Polly is brushing her hair in front of the dining-room mirror. You can see all the rippling auburn highlights in the wavy dark hair, where the sunshine falls across her. She turns to face me, puzzled.

'What? I haven't been teasing her. Well, not today, anyway . . .'

'I thought you teased her this morning, when we got back to the house.'

'No, I didn't. Why would I? You know I didn't. I went straight to my new room. It's lovely having my own room, Mum . . .'

'Eliza had this idea that the cherry tree branches were fingers . . .'

My voice sounds sterner than I'd intended.

'Well, you know what she's like. She's always making things up.' Polly's voice is shrill with protest. '*And* she's always getting me into trouble,' she says.

Her eyes, which are soft and brown as gillyflowers,

suddenly glitter with tears. At once, I wish I hadn't said anything. I think how strained we are, how the least little thing can upset us.

Polly swallows down her tears, and reaches for her satchel.

'Anyway, Mum, can't we get a move on? We're horribly late as it is.'

10

Today, I take the girls to school myself, though they usually go without me. I feel they need an adult with them: there could be dangerous craters or unexploded bombs. I bring my bicycle. Nowadays, I cycle everywhere: my car is in a garage, and I don't use it any more. After I've left the girls at school, I cycle on to the shops.

I cut across Fountain Place and turn into Carpenter Street, on the way to Mr Bradley's butcher's shop. *Oh.* Abruptly, I get off my bicycle. *Oh my goodness.*

Carpenter Street has been hit. I remember the bomb that we heard at the start of the raid, that blew out the flame of our candle. There's a desolation that chokes the breath. Two houses have completely collapsed: where they stood, there's a great heap of rubble. There must have been a fierce fire here: the broken masonry is blackened, and there are filthy pools of water lying in the road, from when the firemen fought the blaze. There's a rank smell of sewage. Charred timbers stick up out of the rubble, like bones – the burned, blackened skeletons of these buildings. The Tarmac is littered with rubble, but I can just about thread my way through. The air is dusty and scratches my throat: I wrap my scarf over my mouth.

Men from the heavy rescue squad are digging in the rubble, their faces dark with soot and grime, their movements weighted and slowed; they must have been working here for hours. There's a dogged determination about them – no urgency: I feel they've almost given up hope of finding anyone alive. But then one of them calls for silence, and they all stop working at once. They listen, all alertness; then someone shakes his head wearily, and they dig their shovels and pickaxes into the rubble again.

A few people are standing watching. A couple of women; a burly man and a little boy, holding hands. The little boy is impassive, but the man is crying silently, making no attempt to wipe the tears from his face. I glance rapidly away from him. It's disturbing, to see a grown man weeping openly, out in the street. Above us, storybook clouds are sailing through a sky of ravishing blue. It's a perfect autumn morning.

One man in the rescue gang draws my eye. There's nothing exceptional about his appearance – he's rather tall, thin, angular – but you can't help noticing him: there's a kind of intensity to him. He's dressed like the other men – a boiler suit, a tin hat – and his face like theirs is black with grime and streaked with runnels of sweat, but above the neck of his boiler suit you can see his clerical collar. He's not somebody I recognise. I realise that this must be the man who Aggie described – the controversial vicar who has recently come to St Michael's, who runs the local wardens' post.

As I watch, the man lowers his shovel. He takes off his helmet and rubs his hand over his head, and I see that his hair is grey as iron. This surprises me. When Aggie talked about him, I'd pictured someone young and fiery, with all the passion of youth, but this man must be at least in his forties.

He lights a cigarette, takes a grateful drag. Then he puts his helmet back on, and takes up his shovel again.

There's a van parked a few yards away: it says *Williams & Wylde: Fine Bakers since 1890*. It's filthy, and someone has written *Please Clean Me* in the film of dirt on the door. I wonder why the van is waiting here.

One of the men in the rescue squad suddenly drops his shovel. He's leaning in to the mound of rubble, moving bricks fastidiously, easing them out with his hands, tugging at something. I hear him cursing quietly.

There's a suspenseful, electric feeling; the air seems thin and glimmery. The other men all stop their work and stand there, watching him.

A voice starts to whisper inside me: *Go. Go at once. Don't look back.*

I don't move.

You don't need to see, you don't need to know, says the

whispery voice in my mind. Small, but imperative. *You can't do anything to change it. You should turn around now, while you can.*

But I feel a sick, chill fascination.

The man pulls out a few more bits of masonry. Everyone is staring.

'Jesus wept,' says somebody.

And then I see the thing that he has exposed there under the rubble – a blackened, twisted, burned thing that used to be a man. Someone who only yesterday was breathing, talking, loving, as full of hopes and desires as I am. Just a few hours ago. The hands of the thing are stretched out, as stiff and crooked as claws, as though in the moment of death he was trying to grasp at something. On the top of the head, you can see a clump of burned and crinkled hair.

Another man goes to help, and they lift the body together, one at the head, one at the feet, but the thing is brittle, it falls apart, like a plank of wood rotted through. They're each holding a piece of charred human flesh. Nausea rises in me.

The door of the baker's van opens: for today, it seems, this vehicle doubles as a mortuary van. Two women pull out a stretcher, bring it over. The men lay the remains on the stretcher, but there's nothing to cover them with. Someone grabs a scrap of filthy fabric from the mound of rubble, and lays it over the body.

The vicar goes to stand by the stretcher, makes the sign of the Cross, murmurs something.

'*He that believeth in me, though he were dead, yet shall he live . . .*'

I recognise the words from the last time I was at church. They're from the Burial Service.

The burly man who was waiting with the boy has sunk to his knees. He's sobbing, his whole body shaking. The vicar turns to him, kneels beside him – just kneeling there with him, his hand on the other man's shoulder. I wonder what he is thinking, this cleric – feeling a sudden strange stab of empathy with him. Curious about him – what he has faith in: what he believes can be saved. How he can endure this.

He looks up: his eyes fall briefly on me. Will he be appalled that I'm standing here – useless, just feeling a kind of morbid fascination? But I have the sense that he doesn't see me at all – that he's almost past noticing anything.

I know I shouldn't stay here, a bystander, just watching. It feels so wrong, so intrusive, to stand here and witness such grief.

I wheel my bicycle through the rubble and cycle on to the shops.

I wait in the queue in the butcher's, just behind Mrs Dixon and Mrs Yates. I feel utterly unreal, cut-off, as though by walls of glass. I can't reconcile these things – the everyday-ness of the butcher's queue, the bright sky, sun-drenched pavements, people talking, laughing, going about their business – and the horror of the thing that I saw in Carpenter Street.

There's a murmur of talk around me.

'I heard that the docks really caught it again . . .'

'My Eddie was down there. He said it looked like the whole bloody world was on fire . . .'

'We went to the shelter in Howlett Street. We didn't get a wink of sleep. All these people jabbering on and on – no consideration at all. I'm telling you – tonight, we're going to take our chances at home . . .'

'How I see it, there's not a lot you can do, is there? If it's got your name on . . .'

Mrs Dixon turns to me. She's wearing a glossy sable coat, rather too hot for the day and smelling of mothballs: she must have just taken it out of storage. I don't like Theodora Dixon. She sees herself as a fount of knowledge on child-rearing: she raised seven children herself, as she often likes to remind you, and nothing makes her happier than dispensing gratuitous advice.

'So how are your daughters doing, Mrs Ripley?'

Her face is doughy and soft, like white bread, and she has a disapproving expression.

'They're doing fine, thank you, Mrs Dixon.'

'Coping all right with the bombing?'

'Well, obviously it's frightening for them . . .'

Theodora Dixon frowns.

'You should keep very calm at all times, Mrs Ripley. Children are very sensitive. They can tell at once if you're nervous. It's up to the mother to set the tone,' she tells me, rather severely.

I murmur some sort of agreement – just for the sake of politeness. But it's hard to talk: when I try to speak, I start coughing. My throat is clogged with the dust of Carpenter Street.

11

Phoebe is at the school gate before me. I see her at once, standing there in the mellow afternoon sunlight: you can't miss her vivid gestures and the dazzling red of her hair.

I rush up to her.

'Oh, Phoebe. It's so good to see you. How are you?'

'All still here, for the moment at least . . . And you, Liv?'

'Just a window broken . . .'

Her smile is as warm as ever, and she's wearing a pretty sprigged frock, and yet she looks somehow older – the lines in her face etched more deeply; inky hollows under her eyes. I probably look much the same – greyer, ravelled, haggard. There are stories of people whose hair went white in a single night, from fear. Now, I can imagine that.

'And how about Bill and Freddie?' I ask her.

'The boys are doing fine. Rather better than me, to be honest. I think they're finding it all a bit of a thrill.'

'Yes, I imagine boys could do.'

'We went to the Milton Street shelter.' Phoebe doesn't have a garden, so she can't have an Anderson shelter. 'Freddie thought it was wonderful that I let him sleep in his shoes.'

'Bless him . . .'

'I don't know, Liv . . . Are we right, do you think, to keep our children here in London?' Her summer-blue eyes are clouded.

I think of what I saw in Carpenter Street, and a shudder goes through me.

'The thing is – you can't know, can you?' I say. 'Maybe nowhere's safe from the bombs.'

A lot of people sent their children away at the start of the war. You were encouraged to. I didn't. I had some notion, perhaps, that they'd be safer here with me – because nobody else could love them as I love them. But now I wonder if that was just misguided and selfish: if it was just because I couldn't bear to let them go.

Phoebe did send her boys to the country, with labels pinned to their coats. Howard, her husband, had been very keen to send the boys out of harm's way: it would be a load off their minds, he felt. Though Phoebe wept a little, telling me about it – how she'd taken them to Waterloo and waved them off on the train, running along beside the carriage until she couldn't keep up.

They'd stayed on a farm in Somerset, with a Mrs Vera

Blythe. Phoebe had thought it would be lovely there – all apple trees and clotted cream, and good fresh country air, to put the roses in their cheeks . . . But it hadn't turned out as she'd imagined: Mrs Vera Blythe was foul. She made the boys work from dawn to dusk on the farm, and often beat them. Bill wrote a heartbreaking letter; he'd only just learned to write – it was all misspelled and tear-blotched. *Deer Mum and Dad, its horible here pleas come and take us away.* So Phoebe headed off to Somerset. She gave Mrs Blythe a piece of her mind and brought her boys back home.

At the time, Phoebe's experience had reassured me, confirming that I'd made the right decision for my girls. But now neither of us is so certain.

'I used to say, when I brought them back – "Well, if we go, at least we'll all go together,"' she tells me. 'But it was a kind of joke, when I said it: I was rather blasé, really, once I'd brought them home. I didn't think it would come to that. Now, I wonder if I should have left them there, with the ghastly Mrs Blythe.' Her face eases into a grin. 'Though to be frank, that bloody woman was an absolute bitch,' she says.

The shocking language delights us both.

The bell rings for the end of lessons, and we watch as the children come flooding out of the school.

'I've been longing to tell you, Phoebe,' I say. 'I've got a bit of nice news. I had my appointment at Ballantyne and Drummond. On Saturday. Though with everything that's happened since, it seems like weeks ago . . .'

'Oh, Liv. How exciting. Tell me everything.'

'Mr Ballantyne was very charming . . .'

And, speaking his name, I feel a thrill, something deliciously shivery and illicit.

'Yes, people do say that,' she says.

'And he wants to publish my photographs.'

'Oh, Liv, that's such wonderful news.'

'I'm so grateful to you for urging me to send them to him,' I tell her. 'It all only happened because of you.'

Phoebe comes from a very different background to me. She went to a convent boarding school, her father worked in the theatre: she *knows* people. I'd never have sold my pictures without her.

'They're such beautiful photographs, Liv,' she says. 'I'm not in the least surprised that he was crazy about them. You deserve this . . .'

Her words are warm, but there's something reserved in her face, and I know just what she's thinking. What chance is there that my book will be published, with London under attack? It seems such an insignificant thing to want, amid all the horrors of wartime. But I can't help wanting it.

'I'll keep my fingers crossed for you, that it all works out,' Phoebe tells me.

Eliza rushes up, and I kneel and hold her tight against me. She smells of school, and I find myself thinking of all the classroom things – inky fingers, chalk dust, chanted times tables, murmured secrets. She presses against me; her silk hair brushes my face. Then Polly saunters along, chatting with two of her friends, Christina Paige and Nancy Baxter. I'd like to hug Polly as well, but I know she'd be appalled.

Freddie comes running up to Phoebe. He has red hair, like his mother, and a cocoa-powder spill of freckles on his nose.

'Chin up, Liv,' says Phoebe, waving goodbye.

We'll have tea earlier than usual, in case the bombers come again.

The dining room seems so peaceful and homely in the lavish afternoon sunlight, the grandfather clock ticking blandly, geraniums glowing red on the sill. Polly is at the table, sketching a diagram of a rift valley: it's meticulous and perfect, like everything she draws. Eliza is in the parlour, playing with her animals. Today she's unusually quiet – I can't hear a sound from the room. There's a good smell from the macaroni cheese that is cooking in the oven. Afterwards, we'll have some little fairy cakes that I've made.

I'm going to the bathroom, when I glance into the parlour.

'Eliza – what on earth are you doing?'

She's kneeling on the hearthrug, hunched down over her play. The parlour floor is a shambles. Toys the girls played with as babies are strewn everywhere around her – the pull-along duck, a teething ring, lots of fat wooden bricks. She must have opened up one of the boxes in her new room, even though I expressly forbade her to touch them. And there are things that she sometimes uses for cutting and sticking or making models – figures she's cut from the *Daily Herald*, silver paper, cotton reels. There are scraps of fabric, and clothes pegs. There's a swan from the bathroom, made of shell, that once had bath-salts in, scented with lemon verbena. Rabbit is propped up against the sofa, as though surveying the scene.

More work, I think – tidying it all up or trying to get her to do it – when life's already so difficult. I feel a quick flare of rage.

'Goodness, Eliza. Just look at all this clutter.'

'I'm building a special place, Mummy. It's my London Town,' she says.

I look more attentively at what she's done. And I start to see the pattern, and the way it's all designed. A blue hair ribbon of Polly's for a river, the swan swimming serenely along it. The wooden bricks making bridges; a tower built from cotton reels. The teething ring is a little round pond, with silver paper inside, crumpled to look like lapping water. Her painted animals have been incorporated into the plan. The lion stands majestically on top of the cotton-reel tower; the leopard, sleek and predatory, peers out through an archway; the giraffe admires her reflection in the silver-paper pond. One of Eliza's newspaper figures, a tiny Veronica Lake, is sprawling rather languidly across the elephant's back. It's ramshackle, but enchanting.

'Eliza, you shouldn't have got those toys out. You know perfectly well that you're not allowed to open those boxes,' I say.

'I closed them up again,' she tells me limpidly. 'I was very, very tidy.'

My anger leaks away. Does it really matter? At least while she's playing here, she's busy, quiet, content.

76

'Well, you can go on playing till teatime. But you must promise that you'll never ever open those boxes again . . .'

I leave her to it.

When the macaroni cheese is ready, I call her, but she doesn't come. I go back to the parlour.

Her construction is rippling outwards across the parlour floor, and she's bending down over it, talking in a little whispery voice. I can't hear what she's saying. She speaks, then is silent for a moment, almost as though she's listening.

'Eliza.'

She startles, hearing my voice, as though she's somewhere else entirely. She glances up. She has a dazed look.

'Who were you talking to, sweetheart?'

'All the people, Mummy. The people who live in my town.'

'Well, it's teatime now,' I tell her. 'You'll have to tidy up really quickly, in case the sirens go off.'

'What do I have to tidy up?' she asks me.

'All this.' I wave my hand towards her arrangement.

'*No.*' She's outraged.

'Yes, you have to, Eliza.'

'But I want to play with it again. And it's taken me hours and hours . . .'

Her face begins to crumple; her eyes are desolate as rain.

I ought to insist, but there isn't time for the scolding, the upset, the tears. We need to eat our tea at once, in case the bombers come back.

'All right. Just this once, you can leave it. But you absolutely must put Polly's ribbon back in her room.'

In the dining room, I spread the cloth on the table. Polly closes her geography book and packs it away in her satchel. She studies herself rather doubtfully in the over-mantel mirror, putting her hands to her wayward hair, trying to flatten it down. Then she takes her satchel out to the hall, all ready for school in the morning.

She comes back, looking alarmed.

'Mum, have you seen what Eliza's done in the parlour? It looks like a jumble sale in there. She's made the most horrible mess.'

'I know. It's a bit of a nuisance. But I'm letting her leave it for now.'

'You *can't*.'

'Polly, there isn't time to tidy it up. We need to eat our tea so we're all prepared – in case anything happens tonight.'

There's a stitch of a frown in her forehead.

'I bet you wouldn't say that if it was *me* who'd done it,' she says. '*And* she stole my ribbon. I saw her sneaking it back to my room.'

Eliza comes into the dining room with Rabbit under her arm. I serve the macaroni cheese. Polly still seems aggrieved; Eliza has an absent look, a dreamy otherness in her grey eyes, as though she's somewhere else entirely. The fairy cakes were made with dried egg and don't taste quite as they should, but we're hungry and eat them anyway, and we manage to finish our tea before the sirens start to wail.

12

Tonight, the bombing is distant, thank goodness. We all sleep a little.

When the All Clear has sounded, we head back indoors, and I take Eliza to her new bedroom. I'm quite stern with her.

'Now, you're to stay right here in your bed,' I tell her briskly. 'There's nothing to be frightened of. I'll be very cross if I find you sleeping down on the floor.'

She studies me, grave as an owl.

'Yes, Mummy. Should I say my prayers?'

'Not now. It's too late for prayers.'

Her eyes roll upwards; she gives a small sigh. She's asleep in an instant.

I'm exhausted. But for a while I don't sleep. I think

about Eliza – worrying about her. I remember her expression when she was playing in the parlour – that absent look in her face then. The way she said she was talking to the people in her town. It's as though only her fantasy world is real, and everything else is just a distraction. Isn't she too old for this? She's nearly six – she should be living in the real world now.

I think of Polly at six. She was sensible already, like a miniature adult. She didn't like books with magic in – dragons, witches, talking animals. She always wanted stories that were set in a world that she knew, where children might have adventures but would still be home by dinner time. And she loved to knit or embroider, and to help me bake sponge cakes for tea.

Though, now I come to think about it – myself, I was more similar to Eliza. Like her, I had a very vivid inner life as a child.

I remember it: how, just as she's done, I'd conjure up a whole imaginary kingdom. I would breathe on the window in my bedroom, and make a little opening in the oval of mist on the pane, tracing a circle with my fingertip, like a small round secret doorway; and I would slip through this door in my mind, and enter a magical landscape, a place of many gardens, all elaborately planted with flowers, so beautiful, bright, intricate. The flowerbeds very formal, a chequerboard of pattern, the gardens opening one out of another through little doors in low walls, the colours vibrant, singing out – scarlet, orange, saffron – a carnival blaze of colour; or palest pink and amber, delicious as

Turkish delight: everything enchanting. It was all rather like the grounds of the Red Queen's palace in *Alice in Wonderland* – one thing becoming another, and full of metamorphoses and mysteries: hedges cut in the shapes of animals, and flowers cunningly planted, so the patterns of the planting spelled the letters of my name. And sometimes the flowers would talk, or sing, or whisper secrets to me. I can still remember the various voices the flowers had in my mind: the shrill excitement of day-lilies, the rich bell-tones of hollyhocks, the high-pitched chattering of gerberas, the soft lisp of the sweet pea. It was a place I didn't want to come back from. I can see now that this was where my love of gardens began – in these gardens of my mind, these enchanted places I imagined.

I first summoned up these images when I was very small – about the same age as Eliza. But it all became much more intense in the months after Sarah was lost. My dream world became, I suppose, an escape – a place of safety for me. And it comes to me that this could be what's happening with Eliza: she's using her fantasy to escape from her grief – from all the misery of her father's death.

Yet I still feel uneasy.

13

Thursday 12th September

After I've washed up the tea things, I read my *Daily Herald* at the dining-room table.

The newspaper says that the invasion may be this weekend. It says that Hitler 'has been accumulating shipping in the Channel ports, Hamburg and the Baltic, and obviously does not intend to let them rot. As the prime minister said last night, this invasion may never materialise: equally from present indications, it would seem that its attempt will not be long delayed. It may come anywhere in several heads from the coastline which is now in German hands. It is certain that everywhere it will meet with terrific opposition . . .'

I put the newspaper down on the table, light a cigarette. My hand is shaking.

Polly is sitting beside me, writing an essay on Henry VIII. She pulls the newspaper towards her. Her eyes widen.

'What will happen when they get here? What will happen to us?' Her voice is ragged.

'I don't know exactly, sweetheart. Let's hope it doesn't come to that . . .' I ought to be able to comfort her, but I don't know what to say.

'Do I still have to do this stupid composition?' she asks me. 'I mean, what if Hitler invades now, and all my work goes to waste?'

Her eyes are shining too brightly: I see the tears that glimmer there. I wrap my arms around her, breathe in her rose geranium scent.

'You should still do your homework,' I say, my mouth in her hair. 'It's important. If you want to get a good job when you grow up and leave school.'

It's the sort of thing that mothers routinely say to their children. But I don't know if it's true now – don't know what shape our future will take.

'Will I still be able to be a nurse when I grow up?' she asks me.

'Of course you will, Polly.'

'You don't sound very certain, Mum.'

She moves away from me, brushes a tear from her face. The weekend passes. Hitler doesn't invade.

During the next week and the one that follows, we start to get used to our strange new life – the ordinariness of daytime, the frenetic bad dream of our nights.

Our daylight hours aren't so different from the way they always were. Every day during the working week, I send the girls to school. I'm grateful their school is still open: so many in London have closed. Usually I accompany them, bringing my bicycle with me. Afterwards, I cycle on to the shops.

You have to spend a lot of time queuing, but sometimes you learn useful things. I see Mrs Yates in the queue in Mr O'Callaghan's greengrocer's shop. Mrs Yates is always full of useful information and tips. She says there's a butcher's in Soho where they are selling horsemeat – and horsemeat is off ration, so you can buy as much as you want.

'They say it tastes quite good,' she tells me. 'A bit like beef, but gamier. It would fill up your daughters nicely.'

I resolve to go there one day soon, though Soho's a bit of a trek – especially with all the road closures.

It's a struggle to keep us well-fed. I make hotpots and stews, with potatoes and carrots to make the meat go further, and fish-and-potato pancakes, and Woolton Pie, from cauliflower and turnip, with a lid of shortcrust pastry – it's rather like steak-and-kidney pie, but without the steak and kidney. The food is bland and not quite satisfying. The girls miss all the little treats they used to take for granted. Sugar's been rationed since the summer, and there aren't many sweets in the shops.

'I wish you could still get sherbet lemons. And candyfloss. I love candyfloss.' Polly's voice is plangent, mournful. 'D'you remember when we went to Brighton? It was so hot, the Tarmac was melting. And Dad bought us candyfloss, and Eliza managed to get some stuck in her hair.'

'I did *not*,' says Eliza.

I think of that day at Brighton beach: it was two years ago now – the summer before Ronnie died. I picture the sea so gentle and shimmery, like some great lithe glittery creature shifting slightly in its sleep; the seabirds lifting into light; the women all in cotton dresses, rose pink or yellow as sherbet; Polly and Eliza laughing, their sunburnt skin smelling of salt. I feel a pang. If I could only have that summer back – all the freedom, my husband, no war, all those things I took for granted – I'd live each moment so differently; be so grateful.

'Yes, I remember,' I tell her.

'I like butterscotch best.' Eliza has a pensive look. 'Peter Grayson brought some to school today, and Jenny wanted a bit.'

'Did she? And what did Peter say?' I ask her.

'He said if she took her knickers down for him, he'd give her some,' she says.

I'm appalled.

'I hope Peter isn't a friend of yours. That's no way to behave.'

Polly sighs. 'Boys are like that, Mum,' she says, rather world-weary.

'She did it though,' Eliza tells us. 'Behind the caretaker's hut. And the butterscotch was really lovely, she said.'

Every day is washday now: our clothes are permanently grubby. Because the air is so dirty, I usually dry the clothes inside, on lines hung round the kitchen, in the warmth from our Ideal boiler, or sometimes on the fireguard in front of the parlour fire. In the afternoons, I sew: I get out my Singer sewing machine and turn sheets sides-to-middle, or I take up sagging hems, or darn the girls' jumpers and socks. There's always so much darning.

When the girls come home, Polly starts on her homework, and Eliza plays in the parlour. And we have our tea together, and then the girls get ready for bed. Our evening routine is shortened now: I don't read Eliza a story, I don't listen to her prayers. I try to keep it simple. If it's bath night, we start especially early: Eliza hates having her hair washed and needs a lot of persuasion. And they clean their teeth, and put on pyjamas, with winter coats on top.

And then, the sirens, tearing apart the quiet of evening; and so our other life begins – the life we live underground.

The fear starts to take a different form, after all these nights of bombing. It's not that you stop being frightened: your heart still leaps up into your throat at the scream and thud of a bomb. But the fear changes – the quality of it. You're so used to being afraid, you become rather jaded and dulled – as though your body still reacts, but your mind is somehow switched off. It's a kind of fatalism, perhaps – something that settles all over you like a fine dust sifting down, the edges of everything blunted.

Phoebe, too, has noticed this. She remarks on it at the school gate.

'It's like everything feels a bit unreal. It's all kind of muffled and blurred.' She holds Freddie tight against her, pushing the bright hair out of her eyes. 'Or I suppose it could be just that we're so very very tired. Honestly, Liv, half the time I feel I'm sleepwalking. Sometimes it gets to the point where I start to see things that aren't there. A bit like when the boys were babies – only an awful lot worse . . .'

Sometimes the bombing is near, too near, and we shudder and cling together. Sometimes it's further away, and we manage to snatch a few moments of sleep.

And then, at five or so in the morning, the glorious All Clear. Coming out into the open air, and feeling a rush of triumph, that another night is over and we're still alive. Glancing around at what's been destroyed, at the lights of fires in the sky – bronze, pink, red as arterial blood – strangely beautiful; unnatural. Going back into the house, which feels chilly, uninhabited. Trying to get some proper sleep before the day begins.

In the dawn hours after the raids, I dream. These dreams are heightened, and very precise and vivid – more intense and vibrantly coloured than the waking world; rather like the imagined worlds of my childhood.

Sometimes I dream about Ronnie – that he's still alive, and sitting on the sofa in the parlour. Smoking his pipe, perusing his Reader's Digest; drumming his fingers impatiently if he doesn't like something he's read. This all feels unsurprising and very matter-of-fact. As though things are as they always were; as though the telegram with the news of his death was just a stupid mistake.

Sometimes I have a recurring dream, one I've had since

87

I was ten. I'll be doing something ordinary – walking in the street or shopping, everything cheerful, sun-drenched – and I'll suddenly remember that I've done something I shouldn't have done, the knowledge heavy in me. In the dream, the sin – the thing I've done – is vague as night or shadow. Though when I wake, I know at once the meaning of the dream. It's about my childhood, about Sarah.

Once, I have a very different dream – a dream I don't want to wake up from. Hugo is there in the dream with me, and we're out in some vast open landscape – wide fields, wide sky above us, the land all around us bathed in a strange unnatural light, suffused in the unreal colours of sunrise after a raid – the cornfields yellow as sulphur, the sky a livid purple. I can't see Hugo in the dream, I just sense him, standing behind me: I can smell his spicy scent of vetiver and cloves. He comes close, lifts up my hair; I feel his mouth on the nape of my neck. Then he wraps his arms around me, moves his hands over my body. I can feel his erection pressing against me, and all the warmth of his skin.

I wake from the dream with a sharp sense of longing, like a hunger. The intensity of the feeling shocks and startles me. Especially when he's someone I've only met so briefly. Is this an effect of the raids – of being constantly in peril? An unspoken secret about the weirdness of desire? I think of the strange sexual cravings of pregnancy, when I'd be throwing up all day long, then crawl into bed so hungry for sex. Ronnie didn't like this at all: he'd usually turn away from me, and if we did make love, it was just as unsatisfying as ever. Can the nearness of death also do this to you – make you ache with desire?

The feeling stays with me all day – so I can picture my dream, re-enter it. It's as though I can still feel the sweet sensation of Hugo's mouth on my skin.

I find myself briefly wondering, *Does he think of me at all?* Then I tell myself this is stupid, I'm getting carried away. There must be so many beguiling women in the glamorous circles he moves in. I'm just a photographer who's taken some photographs that he likes: I can't possibly mean anything to him.

The girls seem pale and brittle, with lilac crescents underneath their eyes. The lack of sleep makes them bad-tempered: they're constantly quarrelling. The pattern is always the same. Eliza provokes Polly; Polly ignores her for a while, then loses her temper, and slaps or pinches Eliza, who then starts sobbing noisily. At this point I'll intervene – making Polly still more annoyed.

'Eliza gets all the sympathy. But *she's* the one who starts it,' she'll say.

I can't dispute this.

Eliza still worries me – the way she lives in a fantasy world, utterly impervious, so nothing I say seems to reach her. Her London Town has expanded across the parlour floor. There are trees made from twigs from the garden wrapped around with green wool, bushes of crumpled brown paper, little matchbox houses. Sometimes she works assiduously, reorganising her things. But some of the time when she plays she doesn't seem to be doing anything much – just talking to herself in a breathy, whispery voice.

Polly comes to find me. There's a flicker of rage in her eyes.

'Mum, other people have *tidy* houses. I don't understand why you let her leave her junk all over the floor. It's stupid, it's embarrassing.'

I feel a pang of guilt. As though I am complicit in something.

'Sweetheart – it keeps her happy—'

'And she was talking to herself, like she'd got a screw loose,' she says. 'You shouldn't let her do it. *And* she stole my ribbon again.'

I take Eliza a ribbon from my sewing basket.

'Look, you can have this for your river. But you are *never* to take Polly's things. Do you understand, Eliza?'

'Yes,' she says, all innocence, her eyes as cool as rain. 'And now I want to get on, Mummy . . .'

I wish that the girls had a better relationship.

'Why don't you two play together any more?' I ask one day, after yet another squabble. 'Couldn't you play princesses or something, with the dressing-up clothes?'

There's a trunk of old clothes in my bedroom. My mother's hats and dresses that I wore when I was younger. A frock of eau-de-Nil crêpe de Chine, embroidered with glimmery beads. A kimono, spangled with dragons. A nurse uniform – a navy cloak, starched hat, white apron – that Polly adores. A fox stole, which frightens Eliza with its bright, carnivorous eyes. They used to love dressing up in these things – though Polly could be a bit patronising and always took the best roles. But now they never show any interest in them.

Polly shrugs. 'She only ever wants to play with that wretched London of hers.'

Eliza protests. 'I didn't like playing with Polly anyway. We always had to play nurses. I got really fed up with being *bandaged*,' she says.

Perhaps the problem is simply that they're so far apart in age. Polly is quite grown up now, and has other interests. It's so different from my own childhood, when Sarah and I would play together happily for hours.

Sometimes Polly invites her friend Christina round to the house. They try out different hairstyles, and listen to Cole Porter records on the gramophone. Christina is very maternal and likes to hug Eliza and ruffle her hair, which Eliza tolerates with gritted teeth.

'Christina thinks Eliza's really sweet,' says Polly drily. 'Little does she know . . .'

But if I suggest to Eliza that we have one of her own school friends round, she always shakes her head emphatically.

'No, thank you, Mummy. I don't want to. Today I'm busy,' she'll say.

One morning, on my way back from the shops, I come to a street that was very badly bombed in last night's raid. The Tarmac is strewn with broken bricks: I have to get off my bicycle. Where a couple of terraced houses and a grocer's shop once stood, there's now a mound of rubble. Men with shovels and pickaxes are digging into the mound. A few people are watching, very still, not speaking. I look around for the clergyman, but he doesn't seem to be here.

A woman comes up to me as I stand there. Her clothes are torn and grey with dust; her eyes are bloodshot and wild.

'I've lost my boy. Have you seen my boy?'

She stands too close, she plucks at my sleeve. She smells sour, like the ruins behind her.

'No, I'm sorry, I haven't seen him.'

'Look. Here he is. This is my boy,' she tells me.

She has a crumpled photograph in her hand. She thrusts it at me. I try not to look, but I can't help myself. A little boy of six or seven, wearing his Cubs uniform. Freckled, bright-eyed, mischievous, like the boys at my daughters' school.

'That's my Tommy. Have you seen him? He had a blue pullover on.'

'I don't know where he is. I'm terribly sorry,' I say.

'I can't find him. He ought to be here. That was our arrangement,' she tells me. 'If ever we lost one another, this was where we were going to meet. In front of Treadgold's grocery shop.' She makes a vague gesture behind her: her pale hands flutter like birds. 'Only, Treadgold's grocery shop isn't there any more.'

I glance behind her, at the heap of rubble.

'No, I'm afraid it isn't.'

She looks around, her eyes not quite focusing.

'We were bombed,' she tells me. 'That's the thing. We were bombed and all the lights went out and I reached for him in the dark, but I couldn't find him.'

'I'm so sorry,' I say again.

'I put out my hand . . .' She shows me, stretching out her hand, which is trembling violently. 'But Tommy wasn't there.' She presses my wrist with shaking fingers. 'He must have got out before me. D'you think that's what happened?' she says.

'It could be,' I tell her.

'Perhaps he couldn't find the meeting place. The street looks all different,' she says.

There's a strange singsong note to her voice. She seems half-crazed with anguish. I know she'd have been a respectable, sensible woman – just a few hours ago: her filthy coat is made of good cloth, and has a fox fur collar. But she's become someone else now: she's no longer the person she was. It can happen in just a single night, when your entire world falls in on you. Because if you lose the people you love, you also lose the person you were.

'Yes, it does look different,' I tell her.

She could be me. She could so easily be me. I don't want to think about this. Her fingers are still on my wrist: she clings like somebody drowning.

'I'm so sorry,' I say. 'But I can't help you.'

Her fingers are like sticking plasters: I peel them from my arm. I turn, and start to walk away, pushing my bicycle. I can feel her eyes on me, watching me for a moment. I'm afraid that she will follow me.

93

But then I hear her move on to the next person who passes.

'Have you seen my boy? I can't find my boy . . .'

There's a chill rain falling. The drops slide down my face, like tears.

14

I'm seized by a sudden resolution. Today I shall do the writing for Hugo Ballantyne.

It's over two weeks since I met him. And I've been postponing this work, because it seemed so pointless. I think of the doubt in Phoebe's eyes when I talked about my book. What possible chance can there be now that my photographs will be published? I don't even know if the publisher's office has survived so far. But I decide I will do this, nonetheless. This can be my own personal piece of defiance, a small act of faith in the future: to behave as though all is normal, as though life will carry on. The days have been pulled out of shape, and they won't go back: the bombers keep on coming. But I can at least behave as though there could be a future for us: as though good things could still happen.

I gather my photographs, a notebook, my silver Parker fountain pen. I shall write with pen to start with, and type it up when it's done. I make coffee, sit at the table.

Just for a moment, I rest my head in my hands. I feel a great helplessness suddenly. It's been fifteen nights now. How much longer can we bear this?

And a familiar, treacherous thought slithers into my mind. *Wouldn't it be better if we just surrendered? At least if we surrendered we wouldn't be bombed any more. At least there'd be something of London left then . . .*

Then I'm ashamed of myself that I thought that.

I open my folder of photographs. A conservatory with orange trees in terracotta pots, the fruit glowing against the dark of the leaves like little planets and moons. Cypress trees, their black flickery branches held up against a bright sky. A single camellia, perfect as a phrase of music.

I look at the pictures for a moment, wondering what I should write. I could perhaps tell the story of how each photograph came to be taken. At Montacute House, how I waited for ages for the long light of evening, wanting to capture the shadows of cedars stretching out over the lawn. How we came to Polesden Lacey in high summer after wind, the roses falling voluptuously open and spreading out their perfume, pale petals scattered everywhere: how I'm drawn to gardens that are a little disordered – ragged at the edges, the flowers overblown. How I love a random, only just cared-for loveliness.

The pen feels like velvet, the writing flows. As I write, I see these places so exactly, feel them, smell them. It's easy to enter the memory of them – as easy as entering my imaginary world as a child, when I made the doorway with my finger in the moisture on my window. And it's soothing, to think of these gardens – to know that there are still such tranquil places in the world, where things have their old meanings: where a spiral of smoke just means that someone has made a bonfire of leaves, where the red in the sky is the gorgeous fieriness of the sun as it sets. Losing myself in this knowledge.

And as I write, I think of Hugo Ballantyne reading my words. *If he's still alive; if the office of Ballantyne & Drummond is still there,* I add superstitiously. I think of the dream I had of him, and heat rushes through me. I like to think of him rifling through my photographs and reading what I've written: this feels somehow intimate. I remember his lingering handshake and the warmth in his eyes.

15

Polly has a subdued air as we're walking home from school.

'Did you have a good day?' I ask her.

She shrugs and doesn't reply.

I know that Polly doesn't like to confide in me in the street. And Eliz, as usual, is bursting with all the events of her day: it was chocolate sponge for pudding, and they had such horrible spellings, and Peter Grayson got given the cane for saying a very rude word. I decide to ask Polly nothing more for the moment.

We turn into Conduit Street. In one of the houses we pass, there's an old woman in the window, looking out, framed in shadow. I think how I'd love to photograph her. I'm drawn by the symmetry of the image, her stillness, the absent look in her face.

Later, when I'm cooking, Polly comes to the kitchen to find me. I see that she's been ripping the skin at the sides of her nails: her fingers are bleeding.

'Mum. Nancy Baxter wasn't there. Nancy wasn't in school.'

My stomach feels cold and heavy as lead. But I try to keep my voice cheerful.

'Well, her family might have left London. Lots of people are going, if they've got relatives in the country . . . There could be all sorts of reasons why Nancy wasn't there . . .'

But I know I'm just postponing something. There's such sorrow etched in her face.

'No, Mum. Colin Parker said—' She makes a small choking sound. She clears her throat, begins again. 'Colin Parker told me that Nancy died in the night. They don't have an Andy in their garden, and they didn't go to the shelter. He told me there was a direct hit on their house.'

'Oh, sweetheart. I'm so sorry . . .'

I try to put my arm around her; she moves a little away.

'We said a prayer for Nancy. Colin Parker told Miss Taylor, and she made us all say a prayer. But it's a bit late for that, isn't it? To say a prayer for somebody, after they're already dead?'

'It's so terribly sad,' I say again.

I think of Nancy Baxter. I used to chat to her mother sometimes. Nancy was just the same height as Polly, and lithe and rather sporty; she loved to turn cartwheels in the playground, her slender white legs flying, her candy-stripe skirt fanning out like a flower. She seemed so vivid, robust, full of life. There's a hard knot of tears in my throat.

'She had the desk just in front of me,' says Polly. 'I kept looking at her empty chair.' Her voice is so full it spills over. 'Her things are still there in her desk. Her exercise books. Her atlas. The pictures she draws. She's really good at drawing horses. I mean, she *was* really good . . . She wanted to be a nurse, like me. She'll never do that now, Mum.'

I put my arms around her.

'Oh, sweetheart,' I say helplessly.

'I couldn't believe it. I kept staring at her desk and I just couldn't take it in. It's so hard to believe it, when somebody dies,' she tells me. 'Like when Dad . . . you know . . .'

And then the tears come. She cries softly, despairingly; and I know that she's weeping for her father as well. I hold her, and this time she clings to me. My own eyes are filling up too. She cries for a long time.

Eventually she quietens. Her face is flushed and blotched, her eyelashes clotted with wet. She takes out her handkerchief, scrubs at her eyes.

'Why do these things keep happening, Mum?'

I push the hair from her face; a strand that fell over her eyes is drenched with her tears, like drowned hair.

'It's the war, this terrible war. And one day it will be over, sweetheart,' I tell her.

Though this is so hard to imagine.

'But why did it have to happen now – to me and Eliza and Nancy? Why to *us*, Mum? Why to *Nancy*? Why did it have to happen when she hadn't even *lived*?'

I don't know how to answer her.

16

'You never read to me, Mummy.' Eliza grabs at my arm; she sounds a little aggrieved. 'We never have a bedtime story any more.'

'The thing is, everything's such a rush now, sweetheart,' I tell her. 'There isn't much time in the evenings, before the sirens go off. And it would be hard to read in our Andy.'

In the early days of the war, I'd imagined that if there was bombing, I'd read to the girls in the shelter, to comfort and distract them. I always kept some books in the basket, ready to take. But I've found it isn't possible. There's all the cacophony of the bombing, and the candlelight makes my head hurt; and I'm usually far too frightened to concentrate on a book.

But Eliza is insistent.

'I want a story. *Really*, Mummy. I want to have one here in the house, before we hide from the bombs.'

This pleases me – that she's interested in something apart from her play.

'All right. If we can finish tea nice and early, we'll try to squeeze in a story,' I say.

After we've eaten, I go to the girls' old bedroom. Most of their books are still here. Enid Blyton. Beatrix Potter – *The Tailor of Gloucester*. Polly's *Chalet School* stories, and the old St John Ambulance manuals that she loves to pore over. And some books from my own childhood. Hans Andersen. King Arthur. Perrault's fairy tales.

I pull out the book of King Arthur stories. These were stories I especially loved when I was a little girl, when our father used to read to us, and our mother too, when she was well. I loved to hear about the knights, the wizards, the sorcery. About the great king who will come again in the hour when Britain needs him; and Morgan le Fay and Nimue, the glamorous, wicked enchantresses; and Avalon of the apples, that elusive, magical land.

I sit with Eliza in the parlour. Polly comes to join us: she's brought her history homework, but I know she's here for the story. I open the book. It has beautiful colour-plates in a lush Pre-Raphaelite style, and Eliza wants to see all of them: the pale hand clad in white samite reaching up through the glistening water; Lancelot clad in shimmering armour; Morgan le Fay in a robe green as forests, her hair very long and straight as water and black as a night-winged bird.

Polly watches us, frowns.

'Mum, you need to get on with the story. Or Jerry will beat us to it,' she says.

So I turn to my favourite story – the one that tells of the quest for the Grail. And I read how the knights rode out from Camelot and searched all over the land, beset by many dangers, bravely confronting every peril, going wherever their quest took them. Not knowing if they'd ever find what they were looking for.

'And now each one went the way upon which he had decided, and they set out into the forest at one point and another, there where they saw it to be thickest . . .'

There are spellbound castles, monsters, maidens weeping under willow trees. Eliza is rapt, lost in the story. I feel her warm breath on my skin.

I turn the page and her concentration is broken; she stirs.

'I don't know what the Grail is, Mummy.'

'Well, nobody knew exactly.'

'There ought to be a picture,' she tells me, rather severely.

'The thing is – the Holy Grail was said to be the most precious thing in the world. But people weren't sure what it looked like . . .'

There's a small frown etched in her forehead. This doesn't satisfy her.

'But how can you tell if you've found it, if you don't know what it looks like?' she asks me.

And then, the sirens, ripping apart the stillness of the evening, and we rush out to the shelter to hide from the bombs.

17

I open the window. It's the most beautiful late-September morning. The grass is pearly with dew, everything still, wet, shiny; a whisper of mist in the shadows under the hedge. We have a leisurely breakfast, as it's Saturday.

Once I've washed up the breakfast things, I fetch my camera. It's the first time I've felt like doing this since the bombing began. But the light is so lovely today, at once bright, and softened by haze. It lures me, I can't resist it.

My garden is tidy again. I've cleared away all the glass and the broken tile from the lawn, and it all looks much as it always looked – as though nothing unusual had happened here, as though we hadn't been bombed. There's a spray of birds in the sky, and the bushes are caught in nets of gossamer. I take several wide shots of the garden, seeking to capture the soft autumn light; then I experiment with some close-ups. A ladybird poised to fly, its translucent wings half-open. A bee hovering over a ripened apple that's fallen on the lawn. A clutter of flowerpots making sharp-edged shadows. A speckled spider on a rose bush, ringed by its glittery web. I'm hoping the shots will come out clearly because the light is so bright.

I'm happy, doing this. There's a particular kind of peace that comes to me when I take photographs. Just for the moment, everything in you is focused on the image, and all the things that normally trouble you seem to fall away, like a tattered coat that you can simply shrug from your shoulders.

But back in the house, the sense of contentment leaves me. The girls are both in the dining room: Polly struggling with her long division homework; Eliza at the table beside her, doing some colouring-in. But Eliza won't be quiet, she keeps on singing.

> *Polly put the kettle on*
> *Polly put the kettle on*
> *Polly put the kettle on*
> *We'll all have tea . . .*

'Mum, tell her to stop,' says Polly. 'She's just singing that song because it's got my name in. She's just doing it to annoy me.' Polly throws down her pen, frustrated. 'I can't think with all her racket. These are really horrible sums.'

I'll take Eliza to the shops, to try to give Polly some peace.

We walk down the street together, Eliza's hand in mine. There's a spring in our step: it's the kind of day that makes your heart lift, in spite of everything. Eliza is still humming the nursery rhyme under her breath, and the crispness in the air brings a healthy flush to her face.

She goes to talk to a cat that's curled up in a circle of sun on a doorstep. His fur is dirty and matted: I wonder if he's feral. A lot of pets have been abandoned because the people who owned them couldn't feed them any more.

'Be careful, Eliza. He might be hungry, he might scratch you.'

'No, he won't, Mummy . . .'

She strokes the cat assiduously. He arches his back and purrs with pleasure, and weaves his body between her legs, in a complex figure of eight.

'Look, he really likes me,' she says.

We walk on, and the cat walks with us for a while, then sits in the road and abandons himself to a little frenzy of washing. Eliza smiles up at me. For the moment, we are happy.

We turn down Cressington Street. I hear my quick in-breath.

'Oh my goodness.'

A bomb must have fallen here in the night. There's a great heap of rubble, a gang of weary, dogged men with pickaxes and spades, an ambulance waiting.

I look around for the Reverend Connelly, but at first I can't see him. I'm aware of feeling a surprising little sag of disappointment. And then my eye falls on him: he's working up at the top of the mound. He has his back to the street, but I can recognise him immediately – it's his height, his hunched-over body; something quietly determined about him. I remember Aggie: *You feel he wouldn't take no for an answer. That's what you need in a man. Especially in times like these . . .* I find myself wondering when he reads the Bible, or writes his sermons, or prays. He always seems to be right in the thick of things, wherever the damage is worst, digging down into the rubble, his face and hands blackened with brick dust and grime.

As I watch, he accepts a cigarette from a man who is working beside him. He turns, and I see his face in profile, and glimpse his rueful half-smile at some quip the other man has made. I haven't seen him smile before. Then he wipes the sweat from his forehead and raises his pickaxe again.

Perhaps we should retrace our steps and take a longer way round. But there's a narrow path through the debris, and you can just about make your way past. We walk on carefully. There's a stench of sour earth, sewage, domestic gas, decay. The smell of the aftermath.

'I don't like the smell,' says Eliza.

'No. It's horrible, isn't it? We'll walk past as quickly as we can.'

Two houses are utterly destroyed, but the front wall of a third is still standing. The roof has been torn away, it's just a broken façade: it looks as flimsy as a children's play-house cut from a cardboard box. It would make such a striking picture if you could get the angle just right. There's a sad little pile of possessions heaped on the pavement in front of the house – a copper pan, a ration book, a battered trilby hat. One of those clocks in a domed glass case where you can see the parts inside: it looks miraculously undamaged.

'What happened to the people who live in that house?' says Eliza.

'I expect they were fine. They were probably safe in the shelter,' I say.

Eliza seems to accept this.

My eye is caught by something up on a first-floor window sill. It's a woman's shoe, rather stylish – a T-bar, a neat curvy heel. I once had some shoes that looked remarkably similar: mine were made of burgundy suede, and I used to wear them for dancing, when Ronnie and I were courting. I thought they looked quite the thing with my dove-grey crêpe de Chine dress . . .

There's something stuffed inside the shoe. I tell myself it's a rather oddly designed shoe tree. Or a wad of news-paper pushed inside, to keep the shoe in shape and stop the suede from creasing. That's a good thing to do with your favourite shoes, to keep them looking their best. The paper has turned a filthy browny-black colour.

I'm about to point out the shoe to Eliza – because it looks almost comical, perched randomly there on the window sill – when I see that the thing stuffed inside the shoe is a *foot*. The flesh is torn off at the ankle, clotted with black blood, ragged.

Bile rushes into my mouth. I swallow hard, to stop myself retching. Strange convoluted thoughts are skidding into my mind. *Maybe the person survived. A foot isn't really essential. You don't absolutely have to die if you've gone and lost one of your feet . . .* Trying to make it all right, as a child might do – to push the horror away.

I glance down at Eliza, but she's turned to look for the cat, to see if the cat is following: I don't think that she saw it. I walk briskly on to the corner of Cressington Street.

'Mummy, you're pinching.' She snatches her hand away from me. Her small face darkens. 'I really hate it when you hold my hand too tight,' she says.

We wait in the queue at the butcher's. There's the usual chatter around us, but it seems to come from far away. The smell of raw meat turns my stomach.

Mrs McKenzie joins the queue just behind me.

'Morning, Mrs Ripley . . .'

I turn to her gratefully, wanting distraction. Wanting to push the thing I saw out of my mind.

Mrs McKenzie is a talker: she always knows all the latest news, about everyone's children and husbands. Someone's daughter has joined the WAAF, and looks very trim in her uniform; someone else's son is on one of the ships, and it all sounds very hush-hush . . . For once, I'm glad of all her chatter.

She has some information that she thinks might interest

Eliza, something someone told her about the Regent's Park Zoo – a friend of her husband's is working there. The pandas and elephants, she says, have been evacuated to Whipsnade, and they've chloroformed the black widow spiders and the poisonous snakes. But the lions and tigers are still at the zoo; they wouldn't be easy to move. There are men with rifles whose job it is to patrol there during the raids, in case a cage should get damaged by a bomb and a lion or tiger escape.

She smiles at Eliza, who is hanging on every word, wide-eyed.

'I thought young Eliza might like to hear about it, Mrs Ripley. I remember how your girls always used to enjoy a trip to the zoo.'

'Yes, that's right, we used to love it . . .'

I think of a family outing, way back before war was declared. The girls in pink gingham frocks, Ronnie smart in his summer blazer. Eliza was enthralled by the tigers; Polly preferred the flamingos, who looked like ballet dancers to her. Afterwards, we sat in the Regent's Park rose garden, and ate vanilla ice creams.

As I remember it, the colours all seem too bright and brilliant, like in the imagined landscapes of my childhood, shining out, lavish, luminous. It's one of those pictures that come to me sometimes, from the world of Before. A world that now seems so remote, so impossibly far, so desirable: a world in which you would never see what I saw in Cressington Street.

Eliza listens intently to our conversation.

As we make our way back home with a packet of oxtail and kidneys, carefully avoiding Cressington Street, she looks up at me quizzically.

'You're frowning, Mummy. Are you worried about the lions and tigers?' she says.

'No, it isn't that . . .'

I take light, shallow breaths to keep the sickness at bay.

'But what if a tiger escaped? What if it was dark, and there was a bomb, and a very fierce tiger got out?'

'That wouldn't happen, Eliza. That's what the men with rifles are for.'

'But what if it *did*? What if the tiger escaped, and nobody saw? What if it got into our garden?'

I think how there's something primeval about the things that children fear. They're always so scared of carnivorous animals – being swallowed whole by a snake; finding a crocodile under the bed or a big cat in the garden. The far more terrible things that men have made don't frighten them nearly as much.

'Eliza, it won't happen. Really.'

'But it *could*. And it could hide in our shed until it was dark, and jump out on people,' she says.

Back at home, she peers through the window of the shed in the garden. She's so much more frightened of the tigers escaping than of the bombs.

18

One afternoon, I pick the apples from my apple tree. They're Worcester Pearmains, the loveliest eating apples, with their pinkish flesh, their strawberry fragrance: good keepers, which if anything taste sweeter as they age. I'll lay them out on cardboard trays, and they'll last the whole winter long. I wonder if we'll be around to enjoy them.

It seems so peaceful out here, in the quiet of the daytime, after the fury of the bombing. The afternoon is overcast, with a mournful sepia light, and in the astonishing stillness I can hear the tiniest things, all the little sounds of the garden. The incessant seethe of grasses. A bird alighting on the bench beneath the cherry tree. The creak of the swing in a breath of air, as though an unseen hand is pushing it, or as though a child has just jumped off, and left it swinging there. A rustle of leaves, like a footfall.

As I stand here in the afternoon hush, memories wash through me – memories of Sarah. I'm not sure what has triggered these thoughts. It's opening up Sarah's old room, perhaps. And Nancy Baxter dying, and the reminders of death all around – even on a walk to the butcher's. And the exhaustion as well, which leaves you undefended somehow, unable to protect yourself against your old regrets and your fears. It's as though all these things have opened up the floodgates in my mind, released a wash of memories.

Sarah and I used to play out here in the garden a lot. Sometimes she'd get exasperated with me, sometimes she found me too childish. But mostly she was patient, and we played together well – much better than Polly and Eliza play together. Sarah looked after me – *mothered* me, really – did so much more than any child should ever have to do. During our mother's black moods and absences, when she'd take to her bed and turn her face to the wall, Sarah had to do everything.

I think of the games we used to play here. Two-ball, against the wall of the house. Hopscotch. Skipping on the terrace – our skipping ropes swishing, our clever sandalled feet *tap tap tapping* on the paving stones, chanting our favourite skipping songs – the questions that would be answered when you tripped over the rope.

Who shall I marry? Tinker, tailor, soldier, sailor?
What shall I be married in? Silk, satin, muslin, rags?

Sarah would always be really cross if she tripped on *rags* or *muslin* – she longed to be married in satin. She wanted a white satin dress, she'd say, a coronet of white roses, a lace train to whisper behind her: not knowing she'd never get married, that she'd never even have a chance to be a woman at all.

These memories have such clarity; except that I can't see her face. Something surprising happened soon after she died – I found I couldn't picture her. I'd have to glance at a photograph to remind myself how she'd looked. Which was strange – when her face had been more familiar to me than my own. I could still remember the scent of her: Devon Violets talcum powder; sarsaparilla drops, her favourite sweets; and the musky perfume of her hair, when it hadn't been washed for a while. Hair the exact same colour as Polly's, always escaping from her braids. At night, undone, spreading out on the pillow, a soft dark cloud round her face. But the precise disposition of her features – that eluded me.

They're so odd, the tricks the mind plays. It's as though my mind was protecting me, by making her somehow unreal, by blurring or seeking to erase my knowledge of her. Because if I hadn't had a sister, if she'd never existed at all, then none of it could have happened. I couldn't have killed her.

Our favourite game was hide-and-seek. There were nooks where we used to hide, the secret corners of the garden, places that my daughters have discovered in their turn. Behind the trellis of summer jasmine that shields the

116

compost heap from view. In the wet-smelling hollow between the laurel hedge and the raspberry canes.

One time, I found a new hiding place, up in the cherry tree. Our mother had warned us not to climb it – the tree was young and slender, she worried the boughs would break under our weight – but I so wanted to impress Sarah. It was summer, the tree was in leaf – I was certain I'd be completely hidden. I climbed, the branches held me. Sitting up there in my murmuring bower of summer leaves, in my mantle of light and dappled shadow, I felt triumphant, invincible.

I could hear Sarah counting. Counting down from twenty, her voice growing louder as she got nearer to one. *I'm coming to find you* . . . I peered out through the leaves. I could see her hunting round the garden, coming closer and closer. I made myself so tiny, trying not to breathe. Her footsteps stopped at the foot of the trunk. She stood there, looking up at me. Her eyes were bright with laughter.

'You found me. I thought you wouldn't,' I said, my voice a little snappish. I had such a sense of let-down – bitterly disappointed that my new hiding place hadn't worked, that the cherry tree hadn't concealed me.

'No such luck, Livie.' Sarah smiled. 'I'll always find you,' she said.

19

I hear the click of my letterbox. There's a letter addressed to me. I rip it open, stare at it.

The letter is from Hugo. This is a miracle – or several miracles in one. That the post is still working and he received the writing I sent. That he was able to reply. That he's still alive, still here in this world. Or was at least when he sent this.

The letter is handwritten – not typed out by his formidable secretary. This surprises and pleases me: it makes it seem more intimate. Though of course it may mean nothing, I assure myself hastily. Miss Cartwright might have been bombed out; she might just have caught a bad cold. The letter might be handwritten for any number of reasons . . .

Dear Livia,

I do hope you've not been too inconvenienced by the unfortunate events in our city. I wanted to thank you so much for the writing you sent, which is extremely promising and will form a perfect complement to your enchanting photographs. There are one or two issues which I thought it might be helpful to discuss – a couple of places where the writing needs a little more development. I wondered if you'd be able to come to my office at four o'clock on Friday, and perhaps we could go for a drink and talk it all through . . .

He's just signed the letter *Hugo*. It's one of those male upper-class signatures that take up half the page: a signature full of self-assurance, that asserts its right to be there, to take up lots of space in the world. But *elegant*. I run my finger over it.

I write back, to say I'm delighted he's pleased with what I've written; to thank him for the invitation; to tell him I will be there, on Friday, at four.

20

'Don't forget to come back, Mummy,' says Eliza.

I hug her.

'Oh, sweetheart. Of course I'll come back.'

I'm checking my appearance in the hall mirror when Aggie lets herself in.

'Goodness gracious, Livia. You're a sight for sore eyes in that frock.'

I smooth down the skirt of the dress. It's a smoky-blue shantung silk, with a pattern of swallows in flight: my best dress.

'So, Aggie – if I get held up, you'll take the girls to the crypt? Though I really don't think that will happen . . .'

'Don't you worry, Livia. You just go off and have a good time.'

Travelling there, I feel a mixture of things. Thrilled and nervous at once, and more nervous the nearer I get. With a trickle of the anxiety that I always seem to feel when I'm parted from my children. I remember a recurrent nightmare, from when the girls were small: that I'd had a baby and carelessly left it somewhere – in my bedroom drawer, on a shelf in a grocery shop – and I'd search for the baby everywhere and wouldn't be able to find it. Or I'd find it – but it would be shrunken, deformed, a blood-red, jelly-like thing; a thing of horror. When I was still breastfeeding, I dreamed this dream every night.

I ring the bell at Ballantyne & Drummond. The door is opened by Miss Cartwright, who's wearing a suit so severe it could probably do her job on its own. Hugo comes out of his office, with his briefcase and hat in his hand.

'Livia – how lovely to see you. Now, I think a drink is in order?'

Miss Cartwright is watching me with cool, knowing, fastidious eyes: watching both of us. As though something familiar is happening – something of which she doesn't approve.

Do I mind? Not in the slightest.

'I thought we could go to the Balfour Hotel. It's just round the corner,' he says.

The street has a smell of coal, petrol fumes, Virginia

tobacco, and a wisp of autumn fog follows us into the foyer of the hotel. Hugo ushers me through to the Sandringham Bar, where there are deep leather armchairs, a fire in a wide marble hearth, a dinner-jacketed pianist languidly playing Gershwin. There's a restrained opulence to the place, and a scent of port and cigars. A handful of people in uniform are drinking up at the bar: a woman and several young men – the woman a Wren, in lipstick of a startling carmine shade. They seem rather febrile, knocking back brandies – *as though there were no tomorrow,* I think, and shiver a little – sometimes laughing too loudly at off-colour jokes.

We sit by the fire. Discreet waiters hover. Hugo orders gin martinis.

He opens his briefcase, takes out the writing I sent him.

'This was very good, Livia. I especially liked the more personal passages. Where you talk about the process – how you came to take the shot.'

'Oh, good. I'm glad you thought it was all right . . .'

He's marked the pages for me. He shows me the changes he wants me to make – a little more here, a little less there; a more elegant shape to this phrase.

'It's all a question of confidence, as I said before,' he tells me. 'I'd love to see what you could express, if you really believed in yourself. If you became truly confident, if you really trusted your feelings . . . There's so much that's unexpressed in you . . .'

He looks at me intently when he says this. His face is

so close I can see the amber flecks in his eyes. I remember the dream I had of him, his hands on my body, his mouth on the back of my neck. I turn away to hide my blush.

He takes out his cigarettes, offers me one. I have a sense that this is a piece of punctuation: the business part of our meeting is over; now we can move on to more personal things. As he leans in to light my cigarette, his hand brushes mine, and I feel a vivid red thread of sensation running through me.

'So – was it all right for you, coming here to see me today?' he asks me.

'It was absolutely fine. I have someone who helps with my girls.'

'They're still with you, then? You didn't send them to the country?'

I feel guilty. Will he think me an irresponsible mother?

'The thing is, I don't have any relatives that I could send them to. They'd have had to live with strangers. And there are people I know who did that, and it didn't really work out . . .' I think of Phoebe.

He smiles ruefully.

'I guess it's a bit like going to boarding school. And God knows, that can be grim.'

'Maybe.' I smile sympathetically – though I know nothing about boarding school. 'I've started to wonder, of course. For the first few months of the war I was certain I'd made the right decision. And then the bombing started, and now I'm not so sure.'

'You have to do what feels right,' he tells me. 'What

seems to work for your family. To be blunt, you can't be certain that anywhere's safe any more.'

'London's the big target, though . . .'

I think of what Mr Churchill once said: *With our enormous metropolis here, the greatest target in the world, a kind of tremendous fat cow tied up to attract the beasts of prey . . .*

'But if your daughters are happy here,' he says, 'well, that's surely the best you can do.'

'I don't know. I hope so.'

I wonder whether to tell him my worries – about Polly's sadness, about how Eliza gets lost in a fantasy world: all the anxious thoughts that assail me. I could ask for his advice, perhaps. But I sense that this isn't the kind of conversation he wants.

'So, tell me more,' he says lightly. 'What are they like, these daughters of yours?' He smiles engagingly at me. 'Do they take after their mother? Are they pretty?' he says.

I feel my face colour again, at the implicit flattery. I look down, into my drink, moving the olive around in the slithery oily liquid. I tell him a little about them. About the pictures Polly draws. About Eliza and the tigers – and I add vaguely that it worries me that she has such a vivid imagination. But I say nothing about Polly's grief, or the way Eliza will sometimes talk to people who aren't really there.

'Do you have any pictures of them that you carry around?' he asks me.

'I don't, I'm afraid . . .'

I resolve to take some appealing shots, so I can show off my daughters to him.

There's a little lull in the conversation. We listen to the music: Cole Porter, *Anything goes*. One of the soldiers up at the bar is tapping along in time. In the heat and opulence of this room, it's hard to believe in the raids – that in two or three hours' time we'll all be taking shelter.

'And what about you?' I ask boldly. I remember the photograph on his desk: the willowy woman, her hair swept up; the ethereal-looking blond child. 'You have a family yourself?'

'My wife's in the country, with Giles, our son,' he tells me. 'In Wiltshire, in our house there. I go down whenever I can, but it's hard – the trains are so bloody slow. You can spend the entire day travelling.'

'That must be frustrating . . .'

'It's more than that. You start to feel disconnected, after a while . . .' He blows out smoke, thoughtful. 'You know, Livia – I never really *knew* my father: he was rather cold and aloof. And I vowed it would all be different when I had children of my own. And then, of course, all this happens . . . I can feel we're drifting apart . . .'

I'm surprised to sense a sadness in him that I didn't know was there: he's always so confident, charming, easy. Instinctively, I reach out to put my hand on his sleeve, in a small gesture of comfort; but his sleeve is pulled back, and I touch the warm skin of his arm. I take my hand away quickly – but I can sense he's aware of my touch.

'I don't quite know how to talk to my son now,' Hugo goes on. 'Something that used to be there between us isn't there any more . . . And to be frank, I think it's happening

125

with my wife as well . . . We have such separate lives now – me and Daphne. We live in different worlds, since she went off to the country,' he says.

Daphne. I store the name away in my mind. I'm so curious about her.

'It's all very complicated, in wartime,' I tell him blandly.

'I can feel us moving away from one another.' His eyes are on me, and the look in them brings a wave of heat to my face.

'Well, so many people are in that position, of course,' I say. Trying to sound casual. 'So many people are being driven apart . . .'

The room is all shimmer and glitter around me: the lustres of the chandeliers, the mirrors, his cufflinks as he flicks the stub of his cigarette into the fire. I'm dazzled.

'I couldn't sign up,' Hugo tells me. 'Unfortunately, I'm too much of a wreck for the Forces.' He pulls a deprecating face. 'A touch of heart trouble, very annoying. I decided to stay in London and keep the office open. And I do a couple of nights a week with the fire service,' he says.

'That's impressive.'

'Not at all. I felt I had to. Some of my authors were putting me to shame – all mucking in really wonderfully. Doing their bit on the Home Front.' He has a slight crooked smile. 'I happened to be in Tavistock Square when some incendiaries had just come down, and there was quite a blaze there, and I counted four progressive novelists manning the pumps . . .'

I smile, and sip my cocktail. The gin is sliding into me,

smoothing away the rough edges of things: my body feels fluid, easy.

'But it's been all change on the domestic front,' he goes on. 'We've let out our house in Kensington.'

'So – where do you . . .?'

'I'm staying here, for the moment. They have a shelter in the basement. It's all a bit impersonal, but it's fine for now,' he says.

I'm staying here. So he has a room in this hotel. Somewhere just above us, he has a room, with a *bed*. This frightens me, and thrills me.

I've finished my drink, I ought to go. He sees that my glass is empty.

'Livia, let me get you another.'

I hesitate. I shouldn't, I know I shouldn't. I have to get back to my girls.

But something overwhelms me, in this moment. Such a yearning to escape for just a little while. To escape from all of it. From my worries about Eliza, and the pain of Polly's grief, and the fear I feel for them always. From powdered egg and ration books and the taste of dust in my mouth. From my sadness about Ronnie, and the rage that he died as he did. From all the day-to-day grief and horror – Polly's school friend dying, and the things that I've seen in the street, the broken bits of bodies. Above all, from the nights in the shelter, thinking, *Is this when we die?*

Wanting to forget all this – just for these few short moments. To think about something utterly different. Or not to think at all.

I feel his eyes on me – how intently he's waiting for my answer.

'You know, I'd really love another,' I say.

He beckons the waiter over, orders more martinis.

'You look a bit preoccupied, Livia,' he says then. 'Tell me what you're thinking.'

I can't, of course. I try to think of something bland to say.

'Just that – well, it's so good to be out, and having a drink,' I tell him vaguely.

'You deserve a treat. We all do. Enduring all this, as we are.'

I glance around the room. 'I mean . . . To be honest, I haven't been anywhere nice like this since Ronnie died,' I tell him.

'It must take such a long time.' His voice delicate, careful. 'To recover from something like that.' There's a question in him, and I know with a sudden, absolute certainty that he's asking this for a reason. 'Well, I don't suppose you ever do recover entirely,' he says.

I let myself meet his eyes.

'I think I'm maybe starting to come through it. Sometimes I feel that, anyway. That I'm beginning to feel that life is possible again. That life could open up for me . . . I feel like that tonight,' I tell him.

'That's good. That's very good,' he says, his warm eyes holding mine.

We are quiet for a moment, looking at one another. I could fill up the silence with bright chatter, but then the moment would pass.

The waiter brings our martinis. There's a raucous shout from the group of people up at the bar. The Wren is laughing, a little hysterical, out of control – her head thrown back, her lipsticked mouth wide open.

Hugo puts his hand on mine, and I feel a surge of desire.

'We could go to my room. It's quieter there. Would you like that?'

'Yes. Yes, I'd like that.'

He ushers me up the stairs. Thoughts flit through my mind, all the reasons this shouldn't be happening. These thoughts seem strangely removed from me, as though someone else is thinking them. Because he has a wife in the country. Because I have my children to care for. Because I'm not really in love with Hugo: in fact, I scarcely know him. Because I'm still grieving for Ronnie. Because any night, any moment, we could be blown to smithereens.

But in some crazy way, in this upside-down world we find ourselves in, I know that these are also the reasons *why* this is happening.

He unlocks the door to his bedroom and ushers me inside. A sombre oil painting of a stag – *The Monarch of the Glen*. A trouser-press. A Gideon Bible. And a bed with a walnut headboard, and a blue satin quilt, folded back.

We should stop. We should stop now.

But I can't. Nothing could stop me.

He closes the door, stands there looking at me. He comes over to me, takes my glass from my hand, puts it down, his eyes never leaving my face. He cups my face in his hands, as though just for this moment I am something infinitely precious. He pulls me to him, kisses me. He tastes of gin and tobacco: his mouth is sweet on mine. When at last he pulls back, I'm breathless.

'I'm a bit out of practice,' I tell him.

He stops my mouth with a kiss.

And then I find I don't care any more – whether I should be doing this, whether I'm any good at it; I don't think about my troubled daughters, or Ronnie, or the bombs. The war, the city, my everyday life – all these things seem worlds away from me. There's nothing but this moment – his mouth, his skin, his scent of cloves wrapped round me; the movement of his clever hands; the cries that break from me. I have a sensation of floating, as though I have no substance, as though I am all sensation. As though this room were glimmering water, stretching out all around us; this bed the boat on which we're drifting, weightless, far from land.

Afterwards, I lie with my head on his shoulder. I can feel his heart slowing.

He stirs, and lights our cigarettes. I glance at my watch, which I've put on the bedside table. *Oh.* It's later than I'd thought. I feel a shiver of alarm.

'I need to get home,' I tell him. 'Before the sirens.'

'Of course. I'll call you a taxi.'

We dress and go downstairs.

As the taxi glides to a stop at the pavement, he kisses me lightly on the lips. My body still feels sweet – fluid, carefree, amazed. But at the edges of my mind, I can already sense guilt lurking: my familiar assailant, hiding round a corner with a stocking over his head, waiting to leap out and floor me.

'Livia.'

He pushes a strand of hair from my face, and I feel a rush of desire.

'When can I see you again?' he asks.

'Oh. I'd love that . . . Anytime, as long as Aggie can look after my daughters . . . If we're both still here,' I add superstitiously.

'I'll write to you. Soon,' he tells me.

Back at Conduit Street, all seems peaceful. Aggie is by the fire in the parlour, with her crochet.

'Goodness. *You* look pleased with yourself,' she tells me.

'Do I? Well, we had a good conversation . . .'

I'm slightly alarmed to hear myself lying so effortlessly. Unblushing.

'We've just finished tea,' she tells me. 'The girls are up in their rooms. The power was off for a while, though.'

'Oh. How awful for you.'

'Don't you worry, Livia, it was fine. We all sang hymns in the dark.'

'Bless you, Aggie.'

I feel such relief – that everything is fine here. That I've not been punished for my transgression.

'By the way, Livia – when are you going to get Eliza to tidy her things in the parlour? She refused outright when I asked her. She said, *But, Auntie Aggie, my mummy never makes me clear up my town.* I thought she was having me on, to be honest.'

'Actually, she's right – I don't bother with it,' I say. I'm only half paying attention: part of me is still back at the Balfour Hotel, my body wrapped around Hugo's, under the blue satin quilt. 'Eliza loves playing there. It keeps her happy.'

Aggie frowns.

'Livia – I hope you don't mind me saying – but I don't think you should stand for it. If you're always giving in to her, she'll run rings around you,' she says.

I know she means well, but I always bridle when people give me advice. Even when it's Aggie.

I try to justify myself.

'I know that it's horribly untidy, but I think her play helps her to cope – after losing her father and everything . . .'

Aggie looks doubtful.

'Well, it's up to you,' she says, a little briskly. She packs her crochet away in her sewing basket. 'I'll be off then, shall I? The sirens could go any time.'

'Yes, of course, Aggie. Thank you so much . . .'

I'm back in my day-to-day world, and the familiar worries crowd in – the war, the bombing, my children. I feel fraught, oppressed, exhausted.

But I can still smell his faint scent of vetiver, on my hair and my skin.

Part 2

21

Saturday morning. I sing to myself as I tidy the kitchen after breakfast. My secret colours everything, like the afterglow of a dream.

The day seems to fit with my mood – it's a lovely October morning. There's a slice of light through the window, furred with dust motes, so you feel if you touched it a soft yellow powder might brush off onto your hand. It's quiet – no sounds of glass being swept: no bombs fell here in the night. You can hear the velvety rufflings of pigeons in the cherry tree.

I remember how Hugo wanted to see a picture of my daughters. I decide that today I will photograph them, so I have a picture to show.

There's a single shot left on the film in my camera.

'You two, come here. I want to take your photograph,' I tell them.

Eliza is willing, but Polly protests.

'Not today, Mum. *Please*. My hair's like a rats' nest,' she says.

She's reaching the age when girls become self-conscious. Sometimes I'll come on her standing in front of the mirror with a concerned, disapproving expression, and I know she's fretting about her appearance, as women always will, and this saddens me a little.

'Your hair looks perfect, sweetheart. You're lovely, just as you are,' I tell her.

'You're only saying that because you're my mother,' she says. But she joins us anyway.

The two of them stand as instructed, with their backs to the wall, just to the side of the Holman Hunt picture. They look so neat and trim, in their matching Fair Isle cardigans, their Start-rite lace-up shoes; I'm so proud of them. Sunlight dappled by the cherry tree is falling through the windows; it lays yellow lozenges over the floor and glints in Eliza's fair hair.

I study the composition through the lens.

'You need to move closer together. And, Polly, you could put your arm around Eliza . . .'

I want to have them looking affectionate – to demonstrate to Hugo just how sweet my daughters are. I want him to be charmed by them.

Polly inches towards Eliza. Eliza puts out a hand and pushes her sister away.

'Stop shoving, Eliza,' says Polly.

I feel a surge of irritation, my happy mood seeping away from me. Why won't they just do what I tell them? I have such an urge to snap at them. I get cross so readily nowadays, with the exhaustion and the bombs. I'm like the Tailor of Gloucester in one of Eliza's picture books – worn to a ravelling.

'Eliza – don't push her,' I say.

'But there isn't any room. Polly's crowding me, Mummy,' she says.

'Nonsense. There's masses of space for both of you.'

It's such a simple thing to ask, for them to stand still for a photograph. I remember Theodora Dixon: *It's up to the mother to set the tone.* Perhaps I'm too lenient with them.

I put on my sternest voice.

'Look, girls, just do as you're told. Just *try*. It will only take a moment . . .'

And to my surprise, they do as I say. Eliza nudges up, and Polly puts her arm around her. Eliza rests her head on Polly's shoulder; they both smile careful smiles. Maybe there's something a little satirical about them – their expressions are rather contrived and deliberate. But the composition works beautifully, Polly's arm solicitously wrapped around Eliza, their two heads close together, against the sun-dappled wall.

I can't wait to develop the photograph. I'm lost in a little reverie: I'm showing Hugo the picture, he's saying how pretty they look, so like their mother . . .

*

'Now, you mustn't come in, remember? Not for any reason. If you need me really badly, you'll have to shout through the door.'

'Yes, Mum, we *know*,' says Polly.

I switch on the light, which is red, so as not to damage the film, and close the door behind me. I'm happy. I love to spend time here in my darkroom.

I always used to look forward to science lessons at school. I relished everything about science – about chemistry, especially. The distinctive sour smell of the science labs; the array of glass bottles of chemicals, with their gorgeous colours and their mysterious names – the amethyst richness of permanganate, the lavish jade colour of copper sulphate; the fierce blue of the Bunsen flame. The shivery sense of danger, when you handled caustic things. The exquisite formation of crystals, and the miracle of what you might see in the test tube – one thing becoming another, in the heat of the crucible; or the marriage of the chemicals – the two becoming one.

I'd have loved to have been a scientist. But that's something that women don't do – or only exceptional women, those with money and opportunity, the privileged women *allowed* such ambitions. Never women like me. Who mostly study typing, as I did, and work in tedious offices; then marry, bring up children, run the house and make the meals.

But maybe that passion for science explains the pleasure I feel in my darkroom: to watch the chemicals at their subtle work, to see something new and intriguing emerge.

I take the strip of film out of the camera; uncoil it,

holding it carefully by the perforated edge of the film so my fingertips won't smudge it; slide it into the developer, in an old washing-up bowl.

I hear footsteps approaching the door. *Oh no. Not now, at the very worst moment.*

'Don't come in,' I shout through the door.

'I wasn't going to.' Eliza sounds affronted. Her voice fades as she heads towards the back garden to play.

I wait several moments. Then I rinse the film with water from a jug into a bucket, and peg the strip up on the line; it hangs there dripping, full of promise.

The pictures are tiny as postage stamps. Negatives are so strange – this weird reversal, everything its opposite: the white things looking dark, the black things pale. I have a magnifying glass to examine the images with: I'm always so fascinated, so curious, to see the picture begin to appear. You can't make out exactly how it will look, but you start to get a sense of it.

I move along the strip of film, study each picture through the magnifying glass.

They were mostly taken a while ago, before the bombing began: they're shots of London in summer. The pelicans in St James's Park, the white birds deeply dark in the negative: I hope they'll look luminous, magical, when I've developed the shot. The Embankment on a summer day, and a nanny pushing a pram, the nanny with a dreamy, inward look in her eyes, and, beyond, the great slow shimmering river. The wedding-cake steeple of St Bride's against a threatening sky, just before a summer thunderstorm.

I have a melancholy thought. When I took these pictures, I thought these things would all be there for ever. I wonder how many of these scenes still look the same; how many are now ruined.

I come to the pictures I took in my garden, just a few days ago. It's hard to tell from the negatives, but they don't look as good as I'd hoped. The close-ups aren't quite in focus, even though the light was so bright. I feel cross with myself.

I move on to the last shot, the shot of my daughters; I peer at it through the lens. Studying it, trying to work out how it will look when it's developed. This one, at least, I'm pleased with. The composition is perfect, and the girls look so different somehow – affectionate, Eliza leaning on her sister's shoulder, as though Polly is just her adored and trusted older sister, their two heads close together, one softly dark, one pale. As though they aren't always squabbling. As though there's real tenderness there.

The world tilts. I can feel my heart pounding, shaking me. In the stillness and smallness of the image, these children look just like Sarah and me. So like us, that in a moment of chill confusion – for the space of a breath, a heartbeat – I feel this is truly what I'm looking at: an image of the two of us. As though I can peer down the tunnel of the past to the way things used to be – before catastrophe struck us.

The air feels tight as a violin string; the hairs lift up on my arms. There's a vibrancy to the atmosphere – it's the way it feels during a bombing raid, that weird electrical feeling; but there hasn't been a raid for hours. It's suddenly hard to breathe. The dense smells of my darkroom are suffocating me: the sour smell of the chemicals, and something else as well, a mingled sweetness: a flowery scent of violets; a piquant smell, like the sweet winey breath of someone sucking sarsaparilla drops. Scents that come from nowhere, that don't belong in this room, that make memory wash through me.

In that moment, as I stand there, unmoving, the strangest notion comes to me: that this world of ours, the world of our senses – that seems so solid, so grounded, so real – is illusory, flimsy, fragile. That what we call reality is thin as cellophane, or the membranous layer around an egg, or the delicate coating round a soap bubble – just a frail skin on the surface of all that is. And that something is pressing at this surface, distorting it and seeking to break through it, like something born from an egg, or like a hand that pushes at a sheet of cellophane.

I stand there for a long moment. Transfixed. Paralysed. I feel a creeping cold, a sense of being chilled right through. And a vast resistance.

I find I am speaking to her. As though she is there with me. As though she has some kind of reality – like a ghost, a haunting, a shade.

No. Don't do this. Please go, please leave me alone. I can't handle this, it's all beyond me, life's hard enough without this. Please go now . . .

All these protestations inside me.

Please go now. Leave me. Please please please.

At last, the smell seems to fade. Whatever it is – a strange hallucination, or a memory – it eludes me. I can only smell the chemicals and the smell of my own body. Even though I'm cold, I'm sweating: I can feel the wetness under my armpits, and at the back of my neck.

I stare again at the photograph. It's just my children, holding a rather uncharacteristic pose.

I feel my pulse steady and slow. It's because of the raids, I tell myself. When you're tired, your senses get muddled. As Phoebe said, you imagine things – you see and hear things that aren't there. *Smell* them, even. It's as though the boundaries of things are breached. As though it's harder now to keep the past back where it belongs.

When the pictures are developed – when I've submerged them in the bath of hypo, rinsed them, hung them up again – the image looks quite normal. It's Polly and Eliza, looking unusually loving; it's exactly the photo I'd hoped for.

And yet I still feel unnerved. I know I won't show this picture to Hugo.

22

Monday – a gloomy, heavy morning: the clouds soak up the light like a stain. Once I've left the girls at school, I cycle on to the shops.

I'm just going down Kimberley Road – past the library and the scout hut, past Mrs Bence's hair salon, where you can see all her customers in the window, huddled under hairdryers with magazines on their knees – when I notice a man on the pavement, talking intently to someone. He has a clerical collar, and I recognise him at once: the Reverend Connelly. You couldn't mistake him, though he looks very different today – no grime and no tin helmet, and he's lost the great weariness that I've seen in him. There's something fierce in his face, and I remember how Aggie described him as a firebrand. I find myself recalling a line from a history book – the thing that King Henry I said about Thomas à Becket. *Who will rid me of this turbulent priest?*

Mr O'Callaghan has some cooking apples for sale – Bramley's Seedlings, so richly green and fat and glossy; they'll have a lovely tart taste, refreshing, perfect for puddings: the eating apples from my garden just fall into mush if they're cooked. I start to picture some of the lovely puddings that I could make. Perhaps Apple Charlotte, with a bit of bread-and-butter left over from tea – sweet and appley underneath, crunchy and golden on top. Or I could bake the apples with a few sultanas and cloves, and some of the Tate & Lyle Golden Syrup that I've kept stashed at the back of my larder. My mouth waters.

Everyone in the queue ahead of me is buying a few. I watch anxiously – willing for there to be some left when it's my turn.

Theodora Dixon is just in front of me. She's wearing her sable coat, and a rather fancy headscarf that has pictures of horses on, and she has a crocodile handbag. She turns to me, and I groan inwardly.

'Morning, Mrs Ripley.'

'Morning, Mrs Dixon.'

She leans in. I can see the powder that flours her white face, and smell the astringent scent that always hangs about her, of mothballs and carbolic soap.

'I feel I should mention something, Mrs Ripley.' Her voice at once conspiratorial and surprisingly loud. 'You need to take rather more care with your blackout. When

I walked down Conduit Street yesterday evening, I saw a distinct chink of light.' She leaves a slight pause, for dramatic effect. 'I'm afraid it was coming from your front window, Mrs Ripley,' she says.

'Oh. Oh dear.'

I feel my face blazing red. Everyone in the shop is staring. Why on earth couldn't she just knock on my door and tell me? Why does she have to do it in front of a shopful of people like this?

'You'd be amazed how bright the smallest beam can look from up there . . .' She points to the sky, and I find myself stupidly glancing upwards. 'We don't want to give Jerry too much help, now, do we?' she says.

'No, of course not. Well, thank you for letting me know.' But I'm not in the least grateful. I feel like a naughty child who's been hauled in front of the class. 'I'll look into it, of course,' I tell her. Gritting my teeth.

'I should hope so, Mrs Ripley . . . And how are those girls of yours doing? I trust that you're keeping them to a stringent routine?'

'Oh yes, absolutely . . .'

'The little ones need a good firm hand, especially in troubled times. It's important not to be too *indulgent*, Mrs Ripley,' she says.

She's at the head of the queue now, and turns away to be served. At least she doesn't buy any of the Bramley's Seedlings I want. Something to be grateful for.

She pays for her turnips and swedes, and closes her bag with a snap.

'Now, remember what I told you, Mrs Ripley,' she says as she goes.

The woman behind me catches my eye and gives a slight, empathic smile. Theodora Dixon is always making comments like these – the blackout gives plenty of scope to people who want to seem morally superior. Though sometimes I feel she delights most of all in saying these things to *me*. Perhaps it's because I don't stand up to her: I'm always very placating with women. Phoebe remarks on this sometimes – she says that women pick on me because I don't defend myself: that people can scent weakness.

I tell her she'd be just like me, if she'd had a mother like mine.

It happens just outside Mrs Bence's salon, as I'm heading back home, with the apples in my bicycle basket.

I'm already in a low mood – and Mrs Dixon's made everything worse, with all her criticisms and her doubts about my child-rearing. Maybe she's right and I'm too indulgent. Maybe I shouldn't let Eliza live in that secret world of her own . . .

But that's the way I am. I always handle everything wrong . . .

I'm preoccupied. Not looking where I'm going.

My front wheel hits a broken brick. My bicycle swerves wildly, out of control. I grab for the brakes, but my hands don't seem to be working properly. The bicycle thuds into something solid, slams to a halt. *Damn.* I feel myself falling, arms and legs flailing, helpless. I crumple up in the road, with my bicycle on top of me, the wheels still spinning. I push down my skirt, which is all rucked up. I'm intensely embarrassed: I curse my clumsiness. My heart is slapping around like a bee in a jar.

Someone is sprawled in the road in front of me. I see to my horror that it's the clergyman. I've knocked him over: he's lying there in the road. He's muttering obscenities softly under his breath. Apples that spilled from my bicycle basket are scattered around, some of them still rolling.

'Oh God,' I say, getting up.

Then I think I shouldn't have said that: he's bound to be offended, because I've taken God's name in vain. Another reason for him to dislike me, on top of my knocking him down.

Though to be honest, his own language is quite off-colour as well.

'Oh my goodness – I'm so sorry. Are you all right?' I ask him.

A stupid thing to say, when patently he isn't.

He stands and begins to brush himself down.

'Absolutely. Just a bit shaken.'

He has a chain-smoker's voice – gravelly, nicotine-stained – and he sounds more working class than you'd expect. Standing here, quite close to him, I can see all the detail of his face: the deep lines coming, in his brow, round his mouth. Something restless in him, his eyes the colour of stormy seas. He gives me a thoughtful look. I decide at once that he doesn't like me. I can imagine just how he sees me – as a sheltered, standoffish woman. Someone who isn't pulling her weight, who can't even get her blackout right. Not at all the kind of person of whom a turbulent priest would approve.

'I'm Justin Connelly,' he says.

He doesn't smile. He's not, I think, a very smiley person.

I tell him who I am.

'I've seen you around, Mrs Ripley,' he says.

'Oh. Have you?'

I think of Carpenter Street, when he spoke the words over the terrible burned body. Did he see me standing there – watching, curious – when I should have walked on?

'I'd shake your hand,' he tells me, 'only . . .'

He shows me the palm of his hand. The skin is raw and bloody, where he tried to break his fall.

I feel dreadful – first my inadequate blackout, now this.

'Oh no, you're bleeding. I'm so sorry. I wasn't looking where I was going. I was a bit preoccupied. I was thinking of something I keep doing wrong . . .'

'Were you?'

There's something about the way he stands there, his head on one side. Waiting. You can tell he's used to listening – that he listens to people a lot, their stories, their confessions. I'm disinhibited, after the shock of the fall. I have a sudden stupid impulse to pour everything out. *My husband died, and I'm so worried about my daughters. One of them is still grieving, the other seems lost in a fantasy world . . .*

I swallow down the words.

'I got distracted. It was all my fault,' I tell him.

148

'Do you always do that?' he asks me.

'Do what?'

'Think that things are your fault?' As though he's genuinely interested in my answer; but why would he be?

His eyes are on me – that subtle, complex colour, dark grey with a sea-green flicker. He's being far too intense, when he's only just met me. He feels this too, perhaps; he takes a step away.

'Probably,' I say, shrugging, smiling; trying to sound nonchalant.

'You've hurt your leg,' he tells me.

I look down. My stocking is laddered beyond repair, and there's a gash in my knee, which is dripping blood. For some reason, this just makes me more embarrassed.

'It's only a graze,' I tell him. Though in fact I'm starting to feel a shrill ring of pain.

The door of the hair salon opens and Mrs Bence comes out, bringing with her a whiff of setting lotion and an air of drama. Behind her, all her customers are staring out of the window. I hate to be the centre of attention like this.

'Poor Mrs Ripley, you took quite a tumble. I saw it all,' she tells me. 'And you, too, Reverend. Can I fetch you each a glass of water?' she says.

We assure her we're all right. She goes reluctantly back to her work, with a yearning glance over her shoulder.

I pick up my bicycle. It seems undamaged. Though I'll have to wheel it home; my knee is hurting far too much to ride it. I lean it against a bollard, and start to pick up the scattered apples and put them back in the bicycle basket.

Justin Connelly helps me. I notice he's limping. Does he always walk like that or have I inflicted some horrible injury on him?

'Look – the vicarage is just round the corner,' he says. 'Would you like to come in and try to patch up that knee?'

But I don't want to prolong the embarrassment.

'I'll be fine,' I tell him. 'I've got a First Aid box at home.'

He picks up the last apple, holds it out in his hand. Studies it, with a rather forensic look.

'They're bruised,' he says. 'A bit like you and me. What a shame.'

He places the apple carefully with the others in my basket.

'It really doesn't matter. Damaged fruit can still be useful. They'll be absolutely fine for purée,' I tell him.

His smile is startling, lighting up the stark angles and lines of his face.

'That's the spirit,' he tells me.

I think of something we were once taught in a chemistry lesson at school, about the literal meaning of spirit: it's what you see dripping down from the retort when you do a distillation. The very essence of a thing, distilled out by the heat of the flame.

'I am *so* sorry,' I say again.

And walk painfully home, pushing my bicycle, cross with myself for being so clumsy and making a scene.

23

At home, I bathe my knee in salt water to try to get out the grit. The graze is still quite painful. Then I peel the apples, cut out the bruises, and put them on to simmer: I'll make a whip with honey and egg whites that we can have for our tea.

When all this is done, I sit at my kitchen table, sipping coffee. I feel shaken.

I think back over that brief, strange conversation.

Do you always do that?

Do what?

Think that things are your fault?

I think how I should have answered.

Yes, because they are. Because I make bad things happen.

I sit there, my head in my hands. Remembering. As

though the things that have happened over the past few days – that strange, haunted moment in my darkroom; the conversation with Justin Connelly – have opened up something in me, a door I strive to keep bolted. I feel so ragged, tired, defenceless: I can't fight the memory any more, can't keep it shut it away.

I watch the scene that spools out in my mind: watch with horror. The day it happened. Sun, snow, blue hard sky; the sun shining on the fields and the river near our grandmother's house, the snow all frosted over, the river frozen and white. Everything immaculate, glittery, crystalline, cold. Walking on the river path with Sarah and Rufus, my dog, our feet crunching in the frosted snow. I remember feeling vaguely cross and uncomfortable because there were holes in my gloves and the cold was stinging my hands.

They come out of nowhere, those moments that change everything. Like a bolt, a lightning strike. They happen so fast. While you watch, paralysed, smitten, unable to move.

I remember the sound, the splintering. How she was there, then she wasn't. How her body seemed to fold up, how smoothly, rapidly, fluently, she slid down under the ice. How as soon as I could move, I tried to get to her, creeping across the splintering ice towards her, reaching into the crack of bitter black water opening up. How I grabbed for her. Felt her fingers. I have the sensation again, remembering – the exact moment of nightmare, the precision of it. Trying to grasp cold fingers: the fingers slipping away. Then, only water against my hand. How I saw just her red woollen hat, floating there in the vein of dark water. How I looked around for help, tried to shout out, tried to breathe, but there was nobody – just the great white emptiness of snowbound pastures and woods.

Then, running and running back to my grandmother's house. My father coming to the door. I could only say, *Sarah, Sarah*. But he must have known at once – seeing me there with Sarah's dripping red woollen hat in my hand. Rufus running with me. No Sarah.

My father shouted for my mother, went lurching down to the river, dragging me with him. I pointed to where it had happened. There was nothing there. Just the line of chill black water where the ice had pulled apart.

Later, they found her body in the river under the ice. My grandmother kept me up at the house – they didn't want me to see. But I watched the search from an upstairs window. There were policemen, huddled together, and a frogman in a rubber suit, and I could see that the snow on the river bank was all trampled and muddy and soiled, not shiny and white as it had been. I remember how, as I watched, I tugged at a loose woollen thread on my jumper, tugging and tugging till it began to unravel, all the rows of careful knitting coming undone, and I knew I would get in trouble for this, that people would be angry with me, but I couldn't stop doing it. I stared at the tiny figures, so black against the white river. So far away, like a picture in a storybook, as though those little dark figures had nothing to do with me. So far away, I couldn't see what they pulled from the water.

They asked me what had happened – my parents, the

policemen. Everyone staring and staring at me, their faces ashen and tight.

Why did she go on the ice, your sister? The policeman, his eyes on my eyes, his forehead trenched in a frown. *Why? She was twelve, she should have known better.*

I don't know.

She's a sensible girl, our Sarah. Was *a sensible girl.* My father, his voice fracturing. *Such a good, responsible daughter. She knew not to go on the ice. Why? Why did she do it?*

I don't know.

Why, Livia? Why?

I don't know, I don't know.

Pressing my hands to my ears.

I didn't tell them what had happened – I've never told anyone. Not even Ronnie, nobody. Though it's all imprinted on my mind for ever. How I was the one who had killed her. How I killed the person I loved the best in the world.

They never scolded me because I unravelled the jumper. In fact, they never scolded me about any events of that day. I knew this wasn't right: that if there was justice in this world, I should get in terrible trouble. But nobody said anything. I waited for the punishment that I knew I deserved, but it never came.

I waited. Through those grim days after her death. Through the funeral service, everyone singing *Abide with me*, their faces hollow, their voices serrated with grief. Through all the long years, all the sand in the hourglass, running out since that time.

I'm still waiting.

24

'Goodness! Do I smell flapjacks?'

Phoebe breezes into my hall, with Freddie trotting ahead of her. She looks lovely. She's wearing her pleated Gor-Ray skirt and a blouse she's sewn herself from some flowery printed Viyella, the lime and tangerine colours as delicious as New Berry Fruits. Phoebe was a needlework teacher before she married Howard, and her sewing is impeccable.

It's Saturday. Music floats down from the gramophone in Polly's bedroom: *Stormy weather*. Freddie darts into the parlour, where Eliza is kneeling on the hearthrug, surrounded by her London Town. Freddie is clutching a tiny balsa-wood boat he's brought to show her. She grins at him, and it warms my heart that she's being friendly again. But I can see Phoebe swallow: I can tell she doesn't entirely approve of Eliza's extravagant untidiness.

'Well, *someone's* been busy,' she says, a little thin-lipped.

We go to the kitchen, drink coffee and eat the flapjacks – which taste surprisingly good although they're made with margarine.

'So how are you, Phoebe?'

'Still in the land of the living. A bit sick of the Milton Street shelter, though. We try not to go to the toilet, and of course it's frightfully noisy. You'll be lucky if you manage to get a wink of sleep,' she says.

'Yes, I can imagine that.'

I don't like the sound of it. I'd hate to go to a public shelter.

'You're still using your Andy?' she asks me.

I nod.

'It's rather claustrophobic. But it's held up. So far . . . And Freddie and Bill are coping?'

'More or less,' she says. 'Well, children don't think about things, do they? Though they do seem to draw an awful lot of tanks and planes and guns.' She smiles briefly; then her face clouds over with thought. She runs one finger pensively round the rim of her cup. Her head is bowed: I can see that her vivid hair is dusted with grey. 'I don't know, Livia . . .' She's suddenly so serious. She looks up at me and her expression is troubled, the frown lines tracing out a fleur-de-lys between her eyes. 'It's not dying I'm afraid of, exactly – it's more *how* it might happen. You know, being buried alive, under a great heap of bricks. Being drowned or gassed or something. And leaving the boys without a mother if I died . . . Goodness, sorry to be so maudlin.'

I put my hand on hers.

'We all think these things. You're bound to. It's how our minds work,' I tell her.

We sit quietly for a moment. The window is open, and the scent of my Duchesse d'Angoulême roses drifts in from outside – drowsy, delectable.

'Any more news from Howard?' I ask her.

She nods.

'We've had another letter. Though the censor had got to it as usual, and half the words were cut out. He's worried about us, bless his cotton socks.' She gives a crooked smile. 'He seems to think that we're in rather more danger than him . . .'

Howard is serving abroad now, though Phoebe doesn't know where. They'd agreed on a code for his letters. Normally he'd write, *Dearest* – but if he was posted overseas, he'd start with, *My dear Phoebe*. The letter had come in August, just before the bombing began: *My dear Phoebe*. Three such innocent words, she'd said, to make your heart sink like a stone.

You can hear the little sounds of the house, sweetly familiar and comforting: the languid tick of the grandfather clock, the fizz of a fly at the window, the children playing in the parlour. I hear Freddie saying something, though I can't make out the words, and then the xylophone ripple of Eliza's laughter.

Phoebe shifts in her chair.

'Anyway, let's talk about cheerier things. It's so lovely about your photographs.'

'I have you to thank,' I tell her.

'They're such beautiful pictures,' she says. 'And Mr Ballantyne – what did you make of him?'

'He's very nice,' I say cautiously.

'He has a reputation as a bit of a charmer,' she says.

'Yes, I can imagine that . . .'

I think of his arms around me, his mouth on me, in the bed with the blue satin quilt. Heat rushes through me.

'You must be absolutely thrilled, Liv. And goodness knows, you deserve it, with all your talent,' she says.

'It's very exciting,' I tell her carefully.

But my voice is too brittle and bright. I need to change the subject rapidly. I'm worried that I'm blushing – that she'll be able to look in my face, and read what's happened, read what I've done.

'Phoebe, I wanted to consult you – to pick your brains a little.'

Phoebe is at once intrigued. She loves to be asked for advice.

'It's about Eliza. She worries me,' I tell her. 'You saw what she's built in the parlour. And she's adamant she won't clear it up, and it seems easiest just to leave it.' I feel embarrassed, telling her this. 'And she has these imaginary people who she talks to all the time . . .'

'Well, she's certainly gone a bit overboard on your parlour floor,' says Phoebe, smiling a little wryly. 'But then, young Eliza has always been one to live in a world of her own.'

'I suppose so . . .'

Phoebe is thoughtful.

'And, let's face it, we all need something to help us through,' she tells me. 'With everything that's happening. We all need some kind of escape . . .'

'But it just all seems so intense. Almost as though her imagined world is somehow more real than this one . . .'

A shadow crosses Phoebe's face.

'She did lose her father, Liv,' she says. 'That's bound to take its toll.' Her voice is very gentle.

'Yes, of course . . .'

'I'm sure that's the explanation. She finds her game a comfort. A bit of a prop, in these terrible times.' She hesitates, and her eyes narrow, as though to glimpse something that's just out of sight. 'That must be the answer, Liv,' she says then. 'I mean – what else could it be?'

The question hangs in the air for a moment. I find myself thinking of my mother.

In the silence between us, we hear the creak of the stair: Freddie and Eliza going to play in Eliza's bedroom. I hope they won't rummage around in the boxes and get out all the old things.

Phoebe stirs.

'Don't let it get to you, Liv. Don't take it all so seriously. It can make us feel so weird, all this.' She makes an expansive gesture, taking everything in: London, the bombing – all of it. 'You can feel so *raw*. We're like snails who've had their shells ripped off. It's like we have no protection, like all our nerves are exposed. Or that's how it feels to me, anyway.'

'I know what you mean.'

She reaches out and puts her hand on my arm.

'She'll grow out of it, mark my words,' she tells me. 'Don't worry too much about her. Children have phases, don't they? I bet it's all just a phase.'

There isn't a single sound from upstairs. Eliza's new room is just above us, and you'd expect to hear the pair of them moving around: their play can be very boisterous.

'Those two are rather quiet. I hope they're not up to something,' I say.

I ought to go and check on them – but I'm reluctant to move: it's so pleasant, sitting here in the sunlight, mulling things over with Phoebe. When you let yourself relax, you can feel how exhausted you are.

'I wouldn't worry,' says Phoebe. 'I'm sure they'll be perfectly fine. By the way, these flapjacks are *scrumptious*.'

We sip our coffee and chat about what we've seen and heard. Talking lightly now, amusing one another. I tell her how I bumped into Justin Connelly. How I knocked him over and took the name of the Lord in vain and almost certainly appalled him. She tells me how her local police station was hit the night before last.

'There's a whopping great hole in the roof, and the front wall's half demolished. They've stuck a notice up on the door: *We are still open. Be good.*'

And then, for a while, as people always do, we talk about food. Phoebe tells me about some nice Cheese Frizzles she made, from cheese and flour and oatmeal, fried to a golden brown in some dripping: the boys absolutely adored them. And she had a go at cooking tripe, though that wasn't such a success.

'Well, not unless you really fancy a bit of boiled knitting,' she says.

I write out the flapjack recipe for her.

She licks the last crumbs from her fingers.

'I guess we'd better be going,' she tells me. 'We're having tea rather earlier. I like to get the kitchen tidied before the siren goes off.'

We go through the dining room into the hall. I'm about to call up the stairs, when I hear a small rustling sound from the parlour.

Eliza is there. She has her back to us; she's rearranging her animals.

'Where's Freddie?' I ask her.

She doesn't turn.

'In my bedroom, Mummy.'

Phoebe rushes upstairs. I follow.

There's a little sob from Eliza's room.

Freddie is sitting on one of the boxes. He's clasping the balsa-wood boat to his chest, and his face is shiny with wet. He's crying silently.

'Freddie! Whatever's the matter? Did you get hurt?' asks Phoebe.

'She wouldn't play with me,' he says.

'Eliza wouldn't? Why ever not?' says Phoebe.

I can hear all the rage in her voice.

'She just wouldn't,' he tells his mother. 'She had something more important to do.'

'Freddie – have you been sitting here all alone all this time?' says Phoebe.

He nods mournfully. He's still weeping, his eyelashes clumped together, clotted with tears.

'Oh, my poor poppet,' says Phoebe.

My heart plummets. I go downstairs, storm into the parlour.

'Eliza, whatever happened? Why didn't you play with Freddie? I thought you two were very best friends,' I say to her, in my sternest voice.

She turns to me. But my crossness doesn't touch her. She has a look of absolute innocence.

'Mummy, I have something else to do now,' she says, in a tone of sweet reasonableness.

I'm intensely embarrassed.

'But, Eliza – you shouldn't have just gone off and left poor Freddie like that. You shouldn't have *ignored* him. Freddie's really upset.'

'He has to learn,' she says primly. Talking just as an adult would talk. She can sound exactly like Mrs Dixon sometimes.

I glance at Phoebe. Her eyes flare like blue gas-flames. I feel the anger blazing off her.

'We'd better be off,' she says briskly. 'Come on, Freddie.'

She puts an arm around him, steers him into the hall.

'Phoebe – I'm so sorry . . .'

She turns to me as I open the door.

'I *do* see what you mean, after all.' She's speaking half under her breath, but her words sear into me. 'I take back everything I said. You can't let Eliza get away with that kind of behaviour,' she says.

She leaves, pulling Freddie behind her, her red hair streaming out like a flag.

Eliza just stands there, with that look of limpid innocence. A hot rage seizes me.

'Why were you so horrid to Freddie? He was really hurt,' I tell her, furious.

Eliza flinches slightly.

'I didn't *hurt* him,' she says. 'I didn't even *touch* him.'

'Maybe not. But he was hurt *inside* – because you wouldn't play. You shouldn't hurt people like that. It's very selfish,' I tell her.

Her grey-green eyes are untroubled.

I don't know what else to say, or how to make her understand. I feel helpless and incompetent. I think how angry Phoebe was, and the thought comes into my mind – *What if one of us dies tonight, and we've parted like this, on bad terms?*

I feel an ache rising like dough beneath my breast bone.

25

Saturday 19th October

There are a couple of things on my doormat when I get back from the shops. The parish magazine with all the news from St Michael's, which is still delivered, though I scarcely ever glance at it. And something else – something more welcome: a letter from Hugo, inviting me to meet him the week after next, on Thursday, at four. I run my finger over his signature, feeling desire wash through me.

For lunch, we'll have a casserole, made with scrag end of mutton, bulked out with swedes and carrots. As I cook, I'm lost in a daydream: imagining his mouth on me, yearning to be back in the bed at the Balfour Hotel.

Eliza comes in from the garden to join me. She sits at

the table in the warmth from the boiler, drawing princesses with beribboned shoes and complicated hair.

'You were singing again, Mummy.'

'Oh. Was I really, sweetheart?'

And then the doorbell rings.

My first thought is that it's Hugo. I feel a hot, thrilled certainty – that he's come here to see me; he wasn't able to wait. I'm so sure it's him that I glance in the mirror on the way to the door. My face is flushed from the heat of the kitchen, my hair is messy and frizzing. I pat down my hair, rip off my apron. My heart slams like a tennis ball against the walls of my chest.

I pull the door open.

'Oh.'

It's Justin Connelly, in his severe black clothes, standing there on my doorstep beneath the stained-glass bluebird. His expression thoughtful. No smile.

I wonder if my disappointment shows in my face. And at once I'm so cross with myself for my fevered imagining. As though Hugo Ballantyne would ever visit me *here*. I doubt he's been anywhere as humble as Conduit Street in his life.

'Mrs Ripley. I hope you don't mind me coming round uninvited,' he says.

'No, of course not. And do call me Livia . . .'

Then I wonder why I said that. He'll think me far too informal.

'I wanted to have a word,' he says. His eyes are on me, and I notice again what a subtle colour they are.

165

'Of course. Do come in.' I compose my face into a welcoming smile. 'I'm afraid we'll have to go through to the kitchen. I haven't lit the fire yet – it's the only room that's warm . . .'

I think how standards drop in wartime. My mother would turn in her grave if she knew I was entertaining a clergyman in the *kitchen*.

I usher him past the parlour and through the dining room. I hope he hasn't noticed Eliza's clutter in the parlour. I'm worried he'd think me a terrible mother, indulgent with my children – and I realise I'd hate him to think that. I find I don't want him to have too bad an opinion of me.

In the kitchen, I gesture to a chair at the table; he sits. He has an air that tall men sometimes have, of not being quite sure how to arrange his body.

Eliza looks up from her drawing, shaking her pale hair back from her face.

'This is Eliza,' I tell him.

'Delighted to meet you, Eliza,' he says. He sounds as though he means it. He's pleasant with children – not patronising. I like him for this, at least.

'Do you come from the church?' she asks him.

'I do.'

'Do you live at the church, with all the dead people?' she says.

He answers her very seriously.

'No, not exactly, Eliza. I live next door to the church, in the vicarage.'

'Mummy doesn't go to church. She used to take us, but now she doesn't.' Her voice as clear as a bell.

He absorbs this information silently. I'm embarrassed.

'Can I make you a cup of something?' I ask him. 'The kettle's just boiled.'

'Well, then. Some tea would be lovely . . .'

'How are you?' I ask him, pouring water into the teapot. 'After – you know – being knocked over?'

He looks so different when he smiles. Younger. Warmer.

'I'm happy to report a complete recovery,' he tells me.

I take two cups from the dresser – the cups that were my mother's, patterned with meadow saffron flowers. I pour the tea, pass him his cup. He has the hands of a labourer, rather callused and worn, and the bone-china cup looks too delicate as he cradles it in his palms. As though he could break it just by holding it. It's strange to see him in my kitchen, surrounded by all my possessions. My house has become too feminine, somehow, in Ronnie's absence: all patterned chintz and potted plants and flowery bone china, with the masculine things – Ronnie's pipe, his fishing rods, his Reader's Digests – cleared away.

I wonder why this man has come to see me: whether he wants to save my soul from damnation – or, less ambitiously, to try to persuade me to go to matins again.

He leans towards me across the table.

'I wanted to ask you something, Mrs Ripley. Livia. Whether you'd consider becoming a warden,' he says.

'*Me*?' My voice too shrill.

He's amused by my reaction. Little lights glint in his eyes.

'Yes, you, Livia.'

Horror floods me, appalling images rushing into my mind. The burned remains on the stretcher, the torn-off foot on the window sill. The woman who'd lost her son, and the way she clung to my arm, how I couldn't bear her anguish.

'I couldn't do that,' I say swiftly.

'Couldn't? Or *wouldn't?*' he asks me.

This isn't entirely polite. You can see how he might upset people, just as Aggie once said.

His eyes are on me, awaiting my answer; his gaze is intense, as though he can see right inside. I can feel myself colouring.

What would he think if he knew about me? If he knew I had a married lover? Still worse – if he knew about my childhood and the thing that happened then?

We have done those things which we ought not to have done, and there is no health in us . . .

I rally my arguments.

'I wouldn't be any use to you. I'm not remotely practical. Besides, I'm only a woman – and isn't that kind of thing all man's work, really?' I say.

He puts his cup down in the saucer, with a small, significant click.

'But women make the best wardens,' he tells me. 'A woman can go in a house and make sense of it all in a moment. She can read a room, in a way that a man couldn't do.'

I'm intrigued, in spite of myself.

'A woman can see the playpen that means there's a baby,' he goes on. 'Or the chair pulled up to the fire for the elderly person who lives there. If the kettle's on the stove, she knows the people are still in the house.' As though to illustrate the point, he's glancing round my room. 'Details mean a lot to a woman. But a man will almost certainly miss those things,' he says.

But not all men, not *this* man. I feel he wouldn't miss anything.

He's silent for a moment, looking past me, and I know he's caught sight of the family photographs on the dresser. Our wedding photographs. School photos of the girls. Ronnie in his sergeant's uniform.

I open my mouth to explain that, anyway, I have my daughters to care for . . . But he isn't paying attention. His eyes move back to my face; I can see the question in them. He's wondering about Ronnie.

'I'm a widow,' I tell him.

'I'm so sorry to hear that,' he says.

There's a sudden quietness about him. He waits, to see if I will say more.

'Ronnie died last year, in an exercise on Salisbury Plain.' I don't usually tell people how it happened. 'He hadn't even seen action. It's stupid – but I think that makes it harder to bear . . .'

'That isn't stupid at all,' he says.

Eliza is watching us, with her eyes the colour of rain. Missing nothing. And I know I shouldn't talk about this with Eliza here. But I have such an urge to tell him.

'I felt – if he had to die, why couldn't he have been fighting? So there would be some purpose to it?'

I'm surprised by the anger that flares in me. My voice sounds too loud for the room.

'I can see that that would make it harder,' he says.

'Mummy was cross with God when Daddy died,' says Eliza. 'That's why she doesn't like going to church any more.'

To my intense embarrassment, I feel the tears welling up. I take out my handkerchief, blow my nose.

'I'm sorry.'

'Don't be,' he tells me.

He pulls out his Woodbines, offers me one. I'm trembling, and the cigarette is shaking in my hand; and as he leans forward with his lighter, he puts one hand on mine, to steady it. There's a surprising tenderness in the gesture.

We sit quietly for a moment, smoking.

I remember when I saw him in Carpenter Street, saying some words over the burned broken body. Kneeling by the weeping man. I think how hard it must be for him – to always have to be strong for others. To know what to say, what to do, when people are blasted by grief.

The tears are still very close, and I desperately don't want to cry. I change the subject rapidly.

'About being a warden . . . I mean, I want to help the war effort, of course. I ought to be doing more really. But I just don't think it's the kind of work I'm suited for,' I say.

He considers this.

So what are *you suited for?* says a sceptical voice in my head. I tell myself that I have my photography, my talent. I remember Hugo: *People could do with a bit of uplift. We need some beauty in our lives* . . . That's what I do – I provide a *bit of uplift*, with my camellias and lily ponds. Yet, with this man with the fervent eyes sitting here at my table, the sentiment has a flimsy sound: my arty photographs suddenly seem so frivolous to me. I'm briefly angry with Justin Connelly – for making my gift, my only talent, seem like a thing of little worth. Just by the way he sits there, looking at me.

As though he expects so much more of me.

'I'd be useless. Really,' I tell him. 'I scarcely know any First Aid.'

'You could learn,' he says. 'I'm organising training. But the main thing is that you know how to stop bleeding. Just to keep people going, until the stretchers arrive.'

I imagine it. Entering a bombed building. Finding somebody horribly injured, their life's blood streaming from them; trying to keep them from dying until the stretchers arrive . . .

'The thing is, Livia,' he goes on, 'you'll have lived in this area for a while, I imagine?'

I nod.

'This was my home, as a child. And then Ronnie and I inherited and moved back here when my mother died.'

'That kind of local knowledge would be like gold dust to us,' he says. 'As you may know, I'm new here. Well, not *entirely* new – I grew up not so far from here. But I still don't know my parish well.'

It's as Aggie said – you feel he wouldn't take no for an answer. Perhaps he'll just sit at my table until at last I relent. I play my trump card.

'I've got my girls to look after. I need to be with them during the raids. Eliza's too little to be left . . .'

Eliza's eyes spark.

'I'm nearly *six*,' she says, outraged. 'And anyway, Auntie Aggie could do it. We could go to the crypt with Auntie Aggie.'

I ignore this.

I push my teacup aside. Briskly. Trying to signal that I want this conversation to end.

'I'm sure you can find someone better. I'm really not the kind of person you need. I'd be absolutely no use to you.' Making my voice sound emphatic and final.

He smiles a small, crooked smile.

'I think you'd be exactly the kind of person we need.'

In that moment, I understand why he makes me so uneasy. It's as though he sees something in me that I didn't know was there. Something I couldn't possibly live up to.

I take him out through the dining room, past Holman Hunt's mournful Jesus. He glances at the picture.

'Do you like that painting?' he asks me.

'I'm not sure. It was my mother's.'

'You don't think it makes Jesus look a bit too *meek*?' he says.

'Well, maybe . . .'

'Sometimes I think the Jesus of the Gospels is so strange,' he tells me. 'The way he cursed fig trees and

172

lost his temper with people. There's that whole ferocious side of him that we tend to forget.'

'Yes. I suppose so.'

But I'm startled by his lack of manners. This is rather tactless, isn't it? To criticise a painting I have hanging on my wall? He isn't gracious, like Hugo.

Though I do know what he means about the picture – the way Jesus looks rather feeble. I've sometimes thought this myself.

On the doorstep, he turns to face me.

'Look, if you change your mind, just come round to the vicarage. Any time. We'd be delighted to have you.'

'I'll think about it,' I say politely.

Though my decision is made. I don't intend to think about it at all.

26

Sunday night. A bad raid on our borough.

I don't sleep at all until we get to bed in the morning.
And I dream that my hand has been partly sawn off and
hangs from my wrist on a vein, like a child's glove on a
woollen string, the vein purple, glimmering, pulsing with
blood. Even though I'm exhausted, it's such a relief to
wake up.

Eliza is unusually quiet at breakfast. She raises her slice
of toast to her mouth, then puts it back down on her plate
without eating anything.

'Eliza – are you all right?'

She shakes her head emphatically. There's an unhealthy
red flush in her face.

'What's the matter, sweetheart?'

She pushes away her plate and puts her hand to her neck.

'It really hurts. It hurts me *here*,' she says.

'It's probably just a sore throat,' says Polly. 'Everybody gets them.'

Eliza gives a melodramatic shake of the head.

'No, it isn't. It's worse than that. It feels like I've swallowed a fishbone. A *great big* fishbone,' she says.

'Eliza, you make such an awful fuss,' says Polly.

'That's enough, both of you. Polly – leave her alone.'

'I'd leave her alone,' Polly tells me, 'if only she'd grow up a bit.'

The air is always full of brick dust and fragments, from the bombing, and perhaps this is all that's wrong with Eliza: the dust is hurting her throat. But when I put my hand on her forehead, I find that her skin is hot to the touch.

I decide to keep her at home, to be on the safe side.

I walk to school with Polly. It's cold, the weather rushing towards winter. A bitter wind swirls the litter, and the leaves on the poplars rattle, and the sun is pale in the sooty sky, like a lamp covered over with gauze. Above us, jackdaws flap emptily.

Polly is anxious.

'Will she be all right, Mum?'

'Yes, I'm sure she will.'

'I shouldn't have got cross with her. But she can be really annoying.'

'I know, sweetheart.'

Sometimes I wonder why Polly is always so riled at Eliza: whether she misses playing with her sister, even though they always argued. Whether she feels rejected, now that Eliza seems to live half the time in a world of her own.

'I should have been nicer,' she says. 'When she was feeling so poorly.'

'Polly, really, don't worry,' I say. 'It's just a nasty cold. She'll be right as rain in a day or two.'

'D'you *promise*, Mum?' she asks, as we turn the corner into Laurel Road.

But I don't reply: I don't say anything.

Laurel Road was hit in the night. There's rubble, the heavy rescue squad digging, a few people watching, not speaking: a man in an ill-fitting suit, a hollow-faced woman fumbling distractedly in her handbag. In front of the broken buildings, there are things laid out in the street – the scatter of belongings found as the workmen dug down, the flotsam of the storm of destruction that has swept through here. Saucepans. A biscuit barrel. Half a wooden rocking-horse. And several cylindrical packages, loosely wrapped in scraps of cloth that someone has pulled from the ruin – torn curtains, grubby carpet. The wind finds its way inside the fabric and makes it ripple and flap.

I quicken my step. But Polly has seen, and grabs me; her fingers bite into my arm.

'Mum. Are those the bodies of people?'

'I'm afraid so, Polly. That's terribly sad, isn't it? I expect they stayed in their house and didn't use their shelter,' I say.

But perhaps they *did* use their shelter; perhaps they did

everything right, and it's just a random act of horror. Why do we pretend to our children that the world works according to rules? That there's any kind of justice, that life isn't as cruel as it is?

There are seven of them. A whole family. It strikes me how precisely they have been laid there, the bodies neatly parallel. As though this was the best that the men who dug them out of the ruin could do for them. As though laying them out like this was the only kind of respect they could give.

'Some of the bodies are very *short*.' Polly's voice is a little thin shred.

'Try not to think about it, sweetheart.'

But you can't stop Polly from thinking.

'Did Nancy Baxter look like that, when they dug her out of her house?'

Her voice sounds so old and weary and bitter – far too old for her years.

'Sweetheart . . .'

'Did Nancy get dumped on the pavement in a bit of carpet?' she says.

'Oh, Polly. Hush. Don't say that.'

'Why do they even kill the children?' she says. 'Children haven't done anything.' She's angry. Angry with me as well – as though I am complicit, because I can't stop this happening. Because I'm part of the generation who have let the world come to this.

When I leave her at school, I try to put my arm around her, to comfort her. She moves away from me, embarrassed.

'*Don't*, Mum,' she hisses at me.

I try to take my own advice – I try not to think about what we saw. But when I blink, I can still see the line of bodies there, in the darkness behind my closed eyelids.

By now, the mortuary van should have come for them. But I still take a different route home.

Eliza is listless and hot to the touch, with a cough that's deep in her chest, that hurts her. I know this is more than irritation from the dust in the air. I tuck her up in bed, and give her some thick brown cough mixture, but she spits it out into the spoon.

'It tastes of *spiders*. It tastes of *turnips*,' she tells me. Conjuring up the most disgusting things she knows.

I rub Vicks Embrocation on her chest. I bring her Lucozade to drink, and some colouring-in on a tray.

For lunch, I make her some nourishing soup from chicken bones and vegetables, and she swallows a few spoonfuls. I sponge her face to cool her down, then leave her to sleep for a while. Perhaps I should send for the doctor, but I very much doubt that he'd come: he'll be busy patching up people who were injured during the raid.

After an hour, I check on her. To my surprise, she's wide awake. She's sitting up, looking alert – *too* alert: her eyes glittery with fever, her back straight as the stalk of a flower. Hector has found his way in and is on the bed beside her, sleeping, a ramshackle, torpid heap of raggedy fur.

I sit on the chair by her bed.

'How are you, sweetheart?'

'Shh, Mummy.'

'What is it, Eliza?'

'You have to be quiet, or you won't hear them,' she says.

Her voice is high-pitched, with an unnerving, bell-like clarity: her fever voice. Making everything sound as though it's of huge significance. Both girls are like this with a temperature: they'll suddenly sit straight up in bed and speak in a shrill, certain tone, making some bizarre pronouncement. Usually about things they think they can see that aren't there – spiders, creepy-crawlies. It can be a little uncanny.

'Who won't I hear, sweetheart?'

'The people talking,' she says.

Hector, hearing the thrill in her voice, opens one witchy yellow eye.

'What people are these, Eliza?'

'All the dead people, Mummy. The people killed by the bombs.'

I shiver, the goose bumps prickling all along my arms. *Pull yourself together, woman.*

'Sweetheart, it's just you and me here. And Hector.'

'No, Mummy. Can't you hear them?'

'No, I can't . . .' I put my hand on her forehead. She's still very hot. 'Sweetheart, sometimes we can think we hear things that aren't real. Especially if we're poorly. It's nothing to be frightened of.'

'I'm *not* frightened.'

I pull up her blankets, start to tuck them in.

'You should lie down, sweetheart, and get some rest.'

'No, Mummy, I don't want to. It's too hot under the covers.'

'All right, I'll fold the covers back. But I still want you to lie down.'

In spite of her protestation, she slithers down in her bed. Her eyes roll up, her eyelids flicker. You can see the delicate tracery of lilac veins in her lids. She falls asleep instantly, like a door closing.

All afternoon, the thing she said haunts me. Maybe the bombing is affecting her more than I thought.

In the end, I go to check on her. She's utterly still and the blankets are twisted tightly round her body, as though she was tossing and turning, then suddenly fell fast asleep. I think of the bodies we saw in Laurel Road, and I feel a chill go through me.

But when I put my hand in front of her mouth, I feel her warm breath on my skin, and this comforts me.

27

Aggie pulls some things from her shopping basket: a Flower Fairy picture book, and then, with a conjurer's flourish, a bulging brown paper bag.

'Oranges! Oh, Aggie!'

'I had a word with Mr O'Callaghan. He had them under the counter. They'll be just the ticket for little Eliza,' she says.

'That's so wonderful. Thank you, Aggie.'

I stare at the glorious fruit: it's an age since I saw an orange. In the afternoon sun, they glow golden, like the fruit of fairy-tale trees.

'I'll just go and see her, then, shall I? And she can have a look at her book.'

'Yes, she'd love that,' I say.

I make a pot of tea for us.

When, ten minutes later, Aggie comes back to the kitchen, I can see the anxiety in her, the splinter of doubt that floats in her eye.

'Poor little mite. She's not right yet, is she? She still doesn't seem quite herself.'

I wonder what she's said to Aggie.

'She's still coughing a lot. It's worst at night in the shelter. But at least her temperature's gone back to normal,' I say.

'You're still using your Andy?' says Aggie.

I nod.

'Livia, I think that may be part of the problem. I hope you don't mind me saying this, but I think you should come to the crypt at the church.'

'I don't know . . .'

'It's dry there. All that damp in your shelter will be bad for her chest. She'll never get over that cough of hers if Jerry keeps on coming. Especially now the days are drawing in . . .'

I'm hesitant. I remember what Phoebe said about the shelter she goes to. I hate the idea of spending the night with strangers, who could be drunk, or ill, or rowdy; trying to sleep in their company; all the embarrassment of using a bucket behind a screen.

I hand Aggie her teacup. I'm intensely aware of the smell of the oranges. Their scent delights me, transports me, conjures up Sicily, Italy, Spain – places I've never been, but love to read about. I dream of groves of citrus trees, the fruit all shining like treasure, a warm wind heady with herbs and salt, a glimpse of dazzling blue sea.

'There are just two rules,' Aggie tells me, bringing me down to earth with a bump. 'No animals, no alcohol. I'm not saying it's perfect. There are folks who come who you'd maybe rather not spend the night with, of course – but it takes all sorts to make the world. And he's got it kitted out a bit. He's got some acetylene lights. It's better for morale, Livia, not to have to sit in the dark.'

'The Reverend Connelly, you mean?'

She nods. 'He's busy during the raids. But he pops in and keeps an eye on us.'

Justin Connelly. I think how I knocked him over. How he asked me to be a warden, how I absolutely refused. I wonder whether to tell her all this – but something stops me. A furtive sense of embarrassment – because my encounters with the man always seem to go horribly wrong.

'You'll need to bring blankets – it's chilly, of course,' she goes on. 'But, like I say, there's no damp there. And he's trying to get some heating, for when the cold really kicks in.'

'It doesn't sound too bad,' I say.

She pushes her hand through her hair in a random, abstracted gesture.

'The thing is, Livia, you can feel that little bit safer in the House of God,' she says.

'I can imagine that,' I say vaguely.

But I've noticed how people always have faith in their chosen place of shelter, always believing it to be safer than anywhere else. You have to, really. Or how could you bear it?

'And it's easier to pray there . . .' Aggie is thoughtful for a moment, moving her finger over the table, as though she is tracing out a mysterious word. 'Though to be honest, I never quite know what to pray for during the raids. You know – what to ask for. You can pray for the planes to pass over – but they have to drop their bombs somewhere. So really you're just praying for some other poor blighter to cop it,' she says.

'I know what you mean.'

But I think, rather guiltily, of how I pray in the raids. I *do* pray for the planes to pass over: I pray for the people I love the most – for my children and Hugo and Phoebe and Aggie to be kept safe from harm. So many urgent prayers, to a God I'm not sure I believe in.

She looks up. Her face opens out in a sudden grin: perhaps she's worried she's been too solemn.

'And we always say, if the worst did happen – well, it's handy for the graveyard. At least they wouldn't have to move us very far.'

I give a rueful smile – as people always do when somebody jokes about dying.

We sit quietly for a moment. The scent of autumn comes in through my open kitchen window – wet, rotting leaves, late roses; smoke, that you could almost pretend was the smoke of garden bonfires. I can see a starling pecking around on my lawn. I love starlings: they seem so brown and nondescript, but if you really look at them, you can see the iridescence under the drabness, and all the gorgeous colours hidden in their wings – jade green, cobalt, shimmery purple.

I sip my tea and think it over. I still feel reluctant to go to St Michael's. But I wonder if my reluctance is in part because I don't want to see Justin Connelly – and that's such a trivial reason, when Eliza's health is at risk.

'You're probably right. We'll try it.'

Aggie lets out a small sigh of relief.

'Thank goodness for that, Livia. Trust me, you won't regret it,' she says.

28

'Right, you two. There's a change of plan. We're not going to use the shelter in our garden any more. Instead, we'll go to the crypt, like Auntie Aggie.'

'*No*, Mum. Why?' says Polly.

'Because our shelter is damp, and Eliza's chest will only get worse.'

'But I don't want to. The crypt is weird. There are all those dead people,' she says.

She's suddenly pale, her eyes dilated and wide. She's more frightened of the tombs in the crypt than the bombs. I remember Eliza's fears about the tigers escaping. Are we all like that? Not most dreading the things we *ought* to be afraid of, the things that truly threaten us, but instead, the unreal things that chime with the fears in the depths of our souls: our most profound horrors and nightmares.

'*I'm* not scared of dead people. They're only people like us,' says Eliza, boastful.

'No, they're not. Worms eat them,' says Polly. Perhaps ashamed about being afraid, and wanting to make her little sister alarmed in her turn.

'No, they don't,' says Eliza. 'Not *all* dead people.'

'Polly – that isn't helpful. There's no need to be so *graphic*. Anyway, the crypt is just a room underground. With a few stone tombs and so on. There's nothing to be afraid of. It's meant to be quite comfortable . . .'

I gather our things together on the dining-room table: blankets and pillows; the basket of reading books, drawing books, crayons; cheese sandwiches and flapjacks and a Thermos of sugary tea. Everything is ready when the sirens start to sound.

'It's time we were off. It's further to go,' I tell them. 'You'll have to get your skates on.'

They fetch their coats obediently, but Polly still looks upset.

'Auntie Aggie's been on at you, hasn't she, Mum?' She's frowning. 'Auntie Aggie may like the crypt, but that doesn't mean that *we* will. Anyway, she's got a bit of a crush on the vicar,' she says.

This startles me.

'Auntie Aggie? Has she?'

'Yes, of course. On the Reverend Connelly. She's always talking about him. She seems to think he's rather exciting and wild.'

'Really, Polly, I don't think—'

'She has this look when she talks about him, Mum. I bet that's why she shelters there. She told us he's always popping in to make sure that everyone's happy. I bet Auntie Aggie would really like that,' she says.

They've already started bombing when we get there.

The church is strangely illumined by the lights of the raid, which are flashing through the stained-glass windows, the jewel colours dancing and spinning across the dark of the floor: ruby, emerald, sapphire. It looks like some infernal fairground – though you'd never think of Hell as having all these colours and lights. We walk cautiously down the stone steps and arrive at the cavernous under-ground room.

There are acetylene lamps set here and there. Some of the tombs round the wall are brightly lit by the lamps, and where there are stone figures, they cast precise black shadows – a stern, sad face in profile; beseeching hands steepled in prayer. But the corners of the room and most of the tombs are shrouded in darkness. There's a smell of the years, of dust and mould, like when you lift an old stone.

Polly's hand is tight in mine. I can sense how this place alarms her.

'You'll get used to it, sweetheart,' I tell her.

'*I'm* not scared,' says Eliza.

About forty people have gathered here. They're settling down for the night, with their blankets, their flasks of tea or soup, their newspapers, card games, sewing. Some have brought with them precious things that they want to keep safe from the bombs. A thin, stooped man I don't recognise has an oboe or flute in its case. I wonder if he's one of the refugees that Aggie once described, who were staying at Orchid Villa.

Aggie waves to us. There's a stack of chairs in the corner, but Aggie, like most people here, is on a blanket on the floor. Later, she'll stretch out her limbs and perhaps be able to sleep for a while. She's resting her back against one of the tombs. We join her.

She smiles broadly.

'Oh, I'm so glad, Livia. I'm sure you've done the right thing . . . And how's my little Eliza?'

'I'm all right, thank you, Auntie Aggie.'

'She loved the orange juice,' I say.

I notice Theodora Dixon on the opposite side of the crypt: at least she's too far off to talk to me. She's knitting a jumper that seems to be the colour of porridge; sometimes she glances up, and her eyes sweep rapidly round the room. Looking, I imagine, for someone to disapprove of. She nods curtly in my direction.

I arrange the pillows at our backs. They're thick, but you can still feel the cold of the stone.

I look at the carving on the tomb behind us. A little girl, lying asleep; a flounced, old-fashioned dress, elaborate, ringletted hair. She's called Jemima Codrington; from the dates engraved on the stone, she'd have been just seven when she died. There's an inscription running along the side of the tomb, and I peer at it, expecting some

189

consolatory quote from Scripture, but the words are bleak and melancholy. *I was not in safety neither had I rest, and the trouble came . . .*

I glance to either side, to see who will be our neighbours for the night. There's a man in a shabby sports jacket, sitting on one of the chairs and reading a copy of *Picturegoer*. He has a high colour and prominent veins in his nose, and I wonder if he's a drinker. His eyes flick over us, taking us in, seeming to linger on Polly – so I too turn to her, wondering if there's something awry in her appearance. He says hello in a friendly enough fashion, but doesn't introduce himself, then goes back to his magazine.

There's a rattle of guns, and the sound of bombs falling, not very close. I feel less exposed than in our garden shelter. Perhaps we were right to come here.

Polly is looking round warily, at the tombs and the sinister shadows. I push the basket towards her.

'Why not do some drawing, sweetheart – to take your mind off things?'

Obediently, she pulls out her drawing pad and crayons, and sets to work on one of her perfect, immaculate rooms. A vase of lilies with speckled throats, a grandfather clock: no people. She's breathing more easily now, the tension seeping away as she draws.

I turn to Eliza.

'Would you like a story?' I ask her.

It's less noisy, less claustrophobic, than in our Anderson shelter. I should be able to read here.

Eliza takes out the book about King Arthur.

The book falls open at the tale of Lancelot and Guinevere. I start to read: I'm self-conscious at first, but soon I'm lost in the story. It tells how Lancelot was reared in the fairy kingdom of Avalon; how he came to Camelot to be knighted, and when Guinevere saw him, she blanched, for he was so fair to look upon, the very flower of manhood. How they yearned for one another. How he performed the most valiant deeds, inspired by his love for his beautiful queen.

The story is told very simply, to make it suitable for a child, and I know it well, yet tonight, as I read, it seems fresh and vivid to me. I think of Guinevere, torn between the two good men she loved – the one, the just King in Camelot; the other, the perfect, chivalrous knight, unconquerable on the battlefield. I think of the choice she had to make, how hard that would have been for her. Because to choose between these two men was also to choose who she herself was.

Eliza traces her finger across the colour-plate – Guinevere in a dress of gorgeous cornelian brocade, though the harsh white lamplight leaches all the colour from the picture.

'I'm going to be a queen as well, when I grow up,' she says.

She yawns, her eyelids flicker, she falls asleep in my arms. I lay her down on the blanket and cover her.

It's quiet, except for the distant gun barrage. Just the clacking of knitting needles, the whisper of pages turning, and people snoring or sleep-talking, speaking blurred words you can't quite make out.

Then – the whine and thud of a bomb, very close. The stone of the crypt seems to tremble, the lights stutter. Fear surges through me. I hear the man next to us jerking awake, calling out.

'*Jesus Mary Mother of God.*'

Praying or swearing or both at once.

My heart is galloping off, and I find myself praying as well, for all the people I love. For my children and Aggie; for Phoebe and Bill and Freddie; for Hugo, in the basement of the Balfour Hotel.

The next bomb that falls is much further off. And a little sigh moves round the crypt, like a parcel passed round in a game, as though everyone is breathing out. And then, the small, companionable sounds of the shelter resume.

I doze, and dream of Hugo.

I wake as the door at the top of the steps swings open. Justin Connelly comes down the stair, pulling off his helmet. He looks weary, and his face and hands and hair are blackened with dirt. He glances around the crypt, checking that everyone's here, speaking softly to people. I feel awkward – as I always do in Justin's presence, thinking what a bad opinion he must have of me.

Polly has woken; she nudges me.

'Is that the vicar, Mum?'

'Yes.'

She studies him, curious. Beside us, Aggie is snoring gently on her blanket.

Justin notices us, and comes across to me, his mouth opening as though to say something – then he sees that

Eliza is sleeping, his face softening; and he doesn't speak, just smiles, not wanting to disturb her.

He accepts a drink from Mrs Dixon's Thermos, gulps it down, and leaves.

As he opens the door at the top of the stairs, there's a flash from outside like sheet lightning. I briefly glimpse a falling chandelier flare, glittering through the stained glass – ravishing, deathly. Then the door to the crypt slams shut again.

I picture him at the door of the church, then stepping out into the street. I wonder what it is like, to head directly into the devastation out there. To do the thing he asked of me – the thing I could never attempt, because I don't have his courage.

But then the thought ripples in me that perhaps I haven't understood. What if he has to force himself, to make himself take every step? I feel a shiver of fear for him. And I pray for him as well, to a God I have little faith in.

Both girls are fast asleep now. I watch them sleeping. They seem so much more at peace than in our garden shelter.

And I know I have made the right decision in coming here. This is what we will do from now on. We have neither safety nor rest, and trouble has come. We will seek what shelter we can, in front of Jemima Codrington's tomb.

29

In the morning, Eliza is better, and I decide to take her to school.

It's blustery still. The wind seems to find its way in through every crack in the house, and makes a sound like an animal in my chimney. All the branches are bare in my garden, and the margins of the lawn have a dark russet slime of dead leaves. Jackdaws are tossed around in the seethe and roil of the sky, like torn rags in a whirlpool, and in the streets, all the litter and loose things are blowing and banging about.

We pass a burnt-out building: the blackened roof timbers are silhouetted against the pale tumult of cloud. The contrast is thrilling – the stark, jagged shapes that the timbers make, with above them, the white febrile sky. I find myself wishing I had my camera with me.

After I've left the girls at school, I cycle on to the butcher's.

I've mistimed this. Theodora Dixon is just ahead of me in the queue. She looks remarkably vigorous, for an elderly woman who spent the night in the crypt. She turns to me, with an expression of rather self-righteous concern.

Please God, not my blackout again.

'So how are you finding our crypt, Mrs Ripley?' she asks me.

'It seems fine, Mrs Dixon,' I tell her.

'I wanted to have a word last night, but you were too far away. There's something I'd been meaning to tell you, Mrs Ripley. I saw Eliza in your garden. When I dropped off the parish magazine. You didn't answer your door, but I thought you might be in, so I ventured down your side alley.'

'I must have been out at the shops, Mrs Dixon,' I say.

I feel a prickle of irritation. I wish I had the nerve to tell her she had no right to do this.

'Your garden door was ajar, and Eliza was in the garden,' she says.

She leaves a pause that seems weighted with significance.

I hope that she didn't peer through my windows: I know she wouldn't approve of my rather relaxed approach to housekeeping. Theodora has a little terraced house in Rosebery Street, and it always looks immaculate – her net curtains white as drifted snow, the tiles on her front step glossy with polish, the asters in her planters trim as soldiers on parade.

I hear the click as she clears her throat.

'Mrs Ripley. I had the impression that your Eliza was *talking to herself*,' she tells me.

'I expect it was just her game, Mrs Dixon,' I say.

Theodora gives a small, definitive shake of her head.

I can sense where this is heading: I know she's going to reprimand me. But I vow to myself that this time I won't let myself get annoyed.

'She was walking round on your terrace, and talking nineteen to the dozen. Then she stopped, and she seemed to be listening. I said, *What are you doing, Eliza?* She said, *I'm listening to the people.*' Theodora pauses, for dramatic effect. 'But there was nobody else in the garden. No one except Eliza and me.'

The shop is unnervingly quiet: I'm aware that everyone else in the queue is listening in. Even Mr Bradley seems to be waiting – poised, his cleaver in the air above a lump of bloody oxtail.

I make a slight, nonchalant gesture.

'Well, you know how children are. She has a very vivid imagination,' I say.

Theodora Dixon ignores this.

'I asked her where these people were. She gave a little laugh, Mrs Ripley. She said, *They're here right now, Mrs Dixon.* I said, *There aren't any people here. Just you and me, Eliza.*' Mrs Dixon's voice is hushed and conspiratorial. Everyone else in the shop is leaning in to hear. 'And she said, *Yes, there are, Mrs Dixon. You can hear them whispering. All the dead people who got killed by the bombs . . .* To be honest, it gave me quite a turn. And I have to be careful, with my heart trouble.'

'That's Eliza all over,' I say. 'She gets lost in a world of her own.'

Theodora isn't listening.

'You shouldn't encourage her. Eliza's *five*, Mrs Ripley. She should have grown out of that kind of thing. If you indulge her, she's got you exactly where she wants you,' she says.

I feel a toxic mix of embarrassment and rage.

'I'm sorry if she upset you,' I say, through gritted teeth.

Theodora Dixon gives me a look as barbed as a fish hook.

'She didn't *upset* me, Mrs Ripley. It would take much more than that to upset me. But I did think it all rather worrying. You need to stamp down on that kind of behaviour. You don't know where it could lead.'

'Really, I don't think—'

She speaks over me. 'Mark my words. There's something not quite right there. You need to nip it in the bud, or you're setting up no end of trouble. Speaking as a mother myself, I always found the palm of my hand would make my point very well.'

I nod as politely as I can. She turns to speak to Mr Bradley.

Rage surges hotly through me, in spite of my resolve. How dare this woman insinuate that there's something wrong with Eliza? How dare she interfere with the way I bring up my child?

I find myself wishing ill on her. So many people are dying – *why not Mrs Dixon as well?*

Then I backtrack rapidly – I've shocked myself. I tell myself that of course I don't want Theodora to die. But the pictures are there in my mind, and somehow I can't erase them – all the horrible things that could happen. Lacerations, fractures, buckets of blood.

I'm startled by the ferocity and explicitness of my thought.

She goes out with her packet of sweetbreads.

'You should think about what I told you, Mrs Ripley,' she says.

30

I unpack my shopping, make coffee. My anger has all ebbed away now, and I'm left on a bleak stony shore, in an arid place without comfort. I sit at my kitchen table, my hands wrapped round the hot cup, but it doesn't seem to warm me.

There's something not quite right there.

I force myself to confront the thing I've pushed to the back of my mind: the reason why Eliza's fantasy play so disturbs me.

I think of my childhood. Of my mother. Of the black moods she had, when she seemed distant, so removed from us: times when she didn't look after us, when Sarah had to do everything. Sarah spent half her childhood in an apron – cooking, doing the laundry, cleaning the house. At these times, our mother would stay in her bedroom; she'd lie in her bed or sit by the window, staring out at the street. Sometimes silently weeping. If we went to see her, she'd seem to look past us, as though we weren't really there. To look through us.

There was a day when she was in one of her moods, when she'd taken an anemone from a vase on her dressing table. Our father had put the flowers there in a vain attempt to make her happy: he was always making these careful, solicitous gestures, though she never seemed to notice. She sat there, pulling petals from the flower and letting them fall. It upset me so much – even more than the flamboyant things: when she said she was going to kill herself, or when she saw things that weren't there. It seemed so violent to me, so casually destructive.

'Don't do that, Ma,' I told her.

She didn't respond. She looked at me, looked *through* me, with those terrible empty eyes.

Another time, she'd laid out her favourite dress on the bed: it was beautiful, the colour a deep reddish-black, like ripe mulberries. She'd taken the scissors from her sewing basket; she was cutting the dress into small neat slivers of silk. I watched, horrified.

'Ma, please don't.'

'But I have to, you see, I have to . . .'

I screamed for Sarah. But by the time she had come, the dress was reduced to a sad little heap of mulberry fragments. Our mother stood back, examined it.

'There, that's done,' she said.

Sarah mothered me. She dealt with it all by being brisk, by doing whatever needed doing. She was very capable.

'We just have to get on with it, Livie,' she'd say. 'Screw your courage to the sticking place. It's time to show some backbone.'

And if she found me crying, she'd scold me gently.

'You mustn't *brood*, Livie. You do always brood. We'll just do the best that we can. It doesn't help to dwell on things . . .'

We ate a lot of toad-in-the-hole, which was Sarah's speciality. We darned our own socks, let down our own hems, sewed our own buttons back on. Sarah tried to follow our mother's routines exactly. She'd get the fire to blaze by pegging newspaper to the fireguard. She'd wipe out the food-safe with baking soda, and bring old milk to the boil, to stop it turning overnight. On winter mornings, she'd mop the condensation from the panes, so the window frames wouldn't get mouldy. And she'd scrub the washing with laundry soap on the washboard, and put it all through the wringer before hanging it out on the line.

Looking back, I can see how the strain of the responsibility told on her. Often, she'd be frowning – just the way that Polly frowns now, the little lines chiselled between her brows. Sarah fretted about everything: thunderstorms, and vermin, and forgetting to turn off the stove; about sparks from the fireplace starting a fire on the hearthrug. Above all, she worried about intruders – about burglars stealing our things, about the murderers whose stories we read avidly in our father's *Daily Telegraph*.

'But we'll be all right,' I'd tell her, 'we've got Rufus.'

'But he's such a soppy thing, Livie. He's not exactly a *guard* dog. If a burglar broke in, he'd just wag his tail and beg for biscuits,' she'd say.

She took so many precautions. She always bolted the garden gate; she wouldn't let me sleep with my bedroom window open; and when we left for school, and our mother was ill and up in her room, she'd be absolutely scrupulous about checking the front door was locked. We might even be halfway down the road, and she'd go back, just to make sure.

'Livie. I want you to remember this.' Her sensible, bossy, grown-up voice. 'You should never leave the door on the latch. This is really important, Livie. You never know who's out there; you never know who might come in.'

She was very alert to the dangers of the city streets outside. Though really the source of all our trouble remained inside the house, up in our mother's bedroom.

Much of the time the house was dirty, all covered over with a grey pall of dust. But, somehow or other, we managed. And out in the garden together, we played as children should play – with our games of hopscotch, skipping, hide-and-seek. Though, of course, I could never manage to hide from Sarah for long. She knew me too well; she knew exactly where I'd choose to hide.

You found me.

I'll always find you.

My mother's illness grew worse, much worse, in the years after Sarah was lost. My mother felt responsible – felt that she shouldn't have let us go for that walk in the snow on our own. She never learned what really happened – that *I* was the one to blame.

Sometimes she would seem to hear things. She'd grasp my arm, her slender fingers digging into my wrists.

'They were talking about me . . .'

'What did they say?'

'Bad things . . . They were saying bad things about me . . .'

Her voice hushed and dark, as though she were sharing some terrible, secret shame.

Thinking of this now, I shudder. It's too similar to Eliza, to the way she talks about the people she imagines she hears.

The doctor had wanted to have my mother committed. But my father absolutely refused to have her put away.

'I can't do it, Livia,' he told me. 'Can't send her to one of those dreadful places with all the looney people. Just can't do it.'

He was very retiring, my father. Gentle, removed, re-served. Reluctant to take any action, to intervene in things. He was quite intelligent, well-read – he loved philosophy, ancient history – and he was fond of quoting Aeschylus: 'Like the wise man said, Livia: *Things are as they are, and will end as they must . . .*' I suppose he found this fatalism a comfort. But I was exasperated. It seemed a justification for letting things slide, a reason not to do anything.

I remember going into her room when she'd taken a

knife from the kitchen, a knife we used to slice onions, that had a very sharp blade. She was standing at the window, her left arm stretched out in front of her, the blade held in her right hand: something odd about the angle of her body, as though her left arm wasn't part of her. Yet she seemed poised, decisive.

'*Ma*.'

She didn't turn, didn't react.

She sliced delicately into her arm. I saw the shudder run through her, as the knife bit into her flesh. Blood drops beaded red as poppies along the line of the cut. One cut, then another and another.

I was paralysed for a moment – then I ran to her, grabbed the knife from her. She looked, more than anything, *frustrated*. As though this wasn't meant to happen. As though I was an unwelcome interruption to her plan.

I bandaged up her arm. I hid the sharpest knives.

I begged my father, pleaded with him.

'We have to call the doctor, she has to go to hospital, she *has* to.'

'No, Livia, no. We'll get through somehow.'

And then at last the mood passed, as it always did in the end; she began to come out of her room, looking around with an air of mingled surprise and recognition, as though revisiting a place familiar from an age ago. And she'd take up her duties, become a housewife and mother again.

As she grew older, she seemed to get a little better – the remissions lasting longer, the dark moods less intense. And after her change of life, the dark moods didn't recur. My father died, and she lived on her own in the house, seeming much like any elderly woman who keeps herself to herself: not especially strange, just rather private and solitary. Ronnie and I would visit for Sunday lunch, and she'd cook an elaborate meal – roast beef with all the trimmings – and she'd be very solicitous to us, especially once Polly arrived. As though trying to compensate for the past – all her failings, all the nurturing that she hadn't been able to give.

Is this the explanation for Eliza's strange, obsessive behaviour – a curse passed down from my mother? A malignant inheritance?

Then I think, *But what about* me? *Is this flaw in me as well?*

I think about that haunted moment in my darkroom. About the way things from the long-ago past have started to seem far too real.

These thoughts frighten me.

31

There's an incident in the crypt.

We've arranged our pillows and blankets in front of Jemima Codrington's tomb. Polly sits a little apart from us, intent on her drawing.

The man in the shabby sports jacket is sitting a few feet away. Tonight he's much the worse for wear; he's mumbling to himself, blind drunk. I'm very aware how he stares at us, stares especially at Polly: this makes me uneasy. Then he lurches across the floor towards her, dragging his chair, sits down next to her.

This is exactly the kind of awkwardness I'd always feared in coming here, in spending the night with strangers. I wish we were back in our Anderson shelter.

'Well, aren't you a pretty one?' he says to her. 'What a sight for sore eyes . . .' His voice is thick and mumbling.

He reaches towards Polly, as though to stroke her arm. His eyes are bloodshot, his gestures clumsy and vague. He's dribbling slightly, and you can smell the hot whisky fumes on his breath. Polly edges away, shrinks back against me.

I don't know how to handle this. I feel furious, helpless, repelled; but I don't want to make him angry, when we're all sheltering here together.

'Would you mind leaving my daughter alone, sir? She's shy. She's only a child. Perhaps we should all try to settle down and get a few winks of sleep . . .'

He doesn't pay any attention. He sits there, staring at Polly with bleary, lascivious eyes.

Aggie intervenes briskly.

'Oi, you. Just cut it out, will you? Let the poor child be.'

She sounds ferocious. I've never seen this side of Aggie before. I'm so grateful.

But he doesn't pay any attention. He pulls his chair a few inches nearer; the chair legs grate on the floor.

'Leave her alone,' I say, more sharply.

We hear the crypt door banging back. Briefly, through the open door, you can see all the lights of the raid, the frenzied drench of colour through the stained glass. Justin comes down the stairs, a vast shadow falling in front of him. For once, I'm so relieved to see him.

Aggie beckons to him. He comes rapidly over to us, takes in at once what is happening.

'Stop that,' he says to the drunk man. 'Leave the child alone. If you're going to stay in my shelter, you have to treat people with proper respect. If that's beyond you, I'm kicking you out on the street.'

'You wouldn't kick me out,' says the man. There's a whimper in his voice: he's suddenly obsequious. 'You *couldn't* do that to me. They're bombing us out there.'

'Oh, but I could,' says Justin. 'Just watch me. Now, move.'

The man drags his chair a few feet away from us, sits there, staring at Polly.

'Further,' says Justin sharply.

To my intense relief, the drunk man does as he's told.

Justin goes to talk to Mrs Dixon.

The bombing is distant tonight, and the crypt is quiet, except for sounds of snoring, and the soporific voice of someone reading to a child.

Polly grabs my arm. I jolt into wakefulness: I must have dozed for a moment. Beside me, Eliza wakes as well. Polly hisses at me.

'Mum, he's doing it again . . .'

It's as though the man has entirely forgotten Justin's warning. He's standing close to us, wreathed in alcohol fumes.

'Such a pretty little thing you are. Won't you give an old man a kiss . . .?' He flails around in Polly's direction.

Justin seems to appear from nowhere. I hadn't realised that he was still in the crypt. I notice how tall he is – that he can look quite menacing. He steps between the man and Polly.

The man gestures wildly, seized with a passive, ineffectual rage, trying to lurch past Justin. I wonder what Justin will say, how he will try to reason with him and pour oil on troubled waters. A clergyman should be expert at calming things down . . .

A sudden crack of fist on flesh, as Justin hits him, a fluent right hook to the jaw. The violent sound of it is startling.

There's a shocked intake of breath around me. Everyone is awake now; everyone is staring. The man crumples up on the floor, cursing, pressing his hand to his face. Then he holds out his palm in front of him. There's blood from his face on his hand, dripping black in the light of the lamps. He stares at the blood, incredulous.

'Look what you did.' His voice is whining, petulant. 'You can't do that to me, you're a man of the cloth.'

'I can and I did,' says Justin.

Justin's hands are still clenched into fists; you can see the tendons, like wires, and sense the rage coming off him, like something you could touch or smell. I feel that he's almost out of control – that it's all he can do not to beat the man up, to hit him again and again.

'I'm going to tell on you,' says the man.

'Oh yes?' says Justin. 'And who exactly are you going to tell?'

The man staggers off into a corner, mumbling and swearing. Justin follows him, stands over him.

'I'm letting you stay for the rest of the night. But you don't come here again, not ever. From now on, you find some other place to shelter,' he says.

Polly is trembling. I hold her, stroke her hair. Eliza gapes at Justin, fascinated.

Polly whispers to me. 'Was it all my fault, Mum?'

'Sweetheart, it wasn't your fault at all.'

'Mummy, he *hit* him. You shouldn't hit people, should you?' says Eliza, rather self-righteously. But there's a thread of admiration woven into her voice.

I wrap the blanket round Eliza, try to settle her again.

When I look up, Justin has left, and gone back out into the night.

I think how practised the blow seemed, how effortless, and I wonder about Justin Connelly. Where does he come from, what is his history – that he could fell another man with such unthinking ease?

The drunk man is safely asleep, and snoring raucously. But for the rest of the night in the shelter, I scarcely sleep at all.

32

The streets are littered with surprises, with fragments of people's homes and lives: clothes, toys, bits of crockery. Sometimes you see undamaged things that still might have some use in them, just scattered on the pavement, going to waste. It's hard to know what the rules are. Looting's still a crime, of course: you could get thrown in prison for it, and quite rightly. Some criminals view the Blitz as a God-given business opportunity: there are rumours that burglars have volunteered as wardens, in order to rob the houses that they're called to during the raids.

But does it still count as looting if the people who lived here are gone, if nobody has claimed these things? Is it acceptable to help yourself, if the things are just lying around?

In Elm Road, by a burnt-out house, I notice a toy Noah's Ark – battered, but perfectly usable. It's detailed, lovingly carved, with a curly red roof, a row of port-holes, a neat detachable ramp. There are no animals, but Eliza has plenty, just the right size for the ark. It would fit perfectly with her London Town. I know that she'd adore it.

I decide to leave the toy for a day or two, and see whether anyone claims it.

On Saturday, when I come back from the shops, the Noah's Ark is still there. I pick it up, guiltily, stealing a glance behind me, wondering if someone will stop me. But also imagining how Eliza's eyes will shine when she sees it.

I wedge it into my bicycle basket. Trying to look nonchalant; as though it's entirely normal to cycle round London equipped with a toy Noah's Ark.

Brisk footsteps behind me. I turn. A policeman is striding towards me. My heart pounds.

He comes straight up to me, stops abruptly. His eyes flick from me to the ark, and back again. He's young and bony and freckled, with a mournful look in his face – as though I have let him down, as though my disgraceful behaviour has disappointed him. *Damn.* Why was I so stupid? I see the entire appalling scenario spooling out in my mind: a formerly respectable mother-of-two caught looting, caught red-handed. I see myself disgraced – ashen-faced in front of the magistrates. People will gossip about me in shocked, delighted tones. Mrs Dixon will feel vindicated in her low opinion of me. And what will happen to my daughters when I get sent to jail? Oh God, my poor children . . .

I compose my face into my most penitent expression.

'I'm so sorry, Officer. I know I shouldn't have taken it, but it's been lying there all this time. I suppose you'll need me to go with you to the police station?'

His face relaxes into a small, rueful smile.

'Don't you worry, ma'am. I wouldn't dream of putting you under arrest.'

'Oh. You *wouldn't?*'

He shakes his head, rather sadly.

'The truth is, ma'am, I had my own eye on the toy. I was going to come back once I'm off duty and take it home to my lad.'

I feel a huge surge of relief that almost makes me laugh out loud.

'Take it,' I tell him. 'You can have it. Really.'

I pick it up, hold it out to him.

'No, ma'am. Fair's fair. You got it first,' he says.

There's something comical about this brief ungainly battle over which of us will take the thing, each of us being very polite.

'Really, you should have it,' I say again.

The policeman shakes his head conclusively.

'Finders keepers. I hope your little ones enjoy it,' he says.

He strides off, whistling breezily.

'Look what I found,' I tell Eliza.

She studies the ark with a look of intense concentration.

'Where did you get it?' she asks me.

'Outside a burnt-out house.'

'But that's *stealing*, Mummy.'

'Well, it would be if anyone lived in the house any more. But nobody seemed to want it. It was just sitting there in the street. It would be sad for it to go to waste.'

'It doesn't belong to us,' she says severely.

'But the people who lived there have gone. I really don't think it's stealing – if it's something that nobody wants.'

I've managed to persuade myself. But Eliza is being more moral and more scrupulous than me. She won't be moved.

'It's still theirs, Mummy.'

'Well, it *was* – but they just left it there for days and days,' I say.

She considers this.

'If I left Rabbit out in the street, would he still be mine?' she asks me.

'Yes, of course,' I tell her.

'Even if I left him there for *days and days*?' she says.

'Yes. Yes, he'd still be yours . . .'

The lines in her brow are precise, as though drawn in with blue laundry-pencil.

'What if I left him there for *weeks*? Would you let someone take him?' she asks.

'I won't let anyone take Rabbit . . .' I put my arms around her. 'Sweetheart, trust me, you mustn't worry about the Noah's Ark. There was a policeman, and he told me I could have it,' I say. Appealing to a higher authority.

Her face lights up at the mention of the policeman.

'Did he really?'

Her smile is dazzling. At last, she's reassured.

I wipe all the dust and dirt from the ark. I was planning to paint it, but Eliza wants to start playing at once. She carries it into the parlour, where I've already lit the fire.

Later, I join her, with my *Daily Herald* and a coffee. It's so pleasant, so peaceful, in here, with Hector asleep on the hearthrug, curled up like a question mark, his body stirring softly with the rhythm of his breath, and the glowing coals crackling and spitting. I've pegged washed woollens to dry on the fireguard in front of the fire, and they have a friendly, wholesome smell.

She's put the ark in pride of place in the centre of her arrangement. Her little painted animals have been moved from their usual places, and are gathered at the foot of the ramp of the ark: the spindly, blotched giraffes, the squat grey elephants, the leopards, lithe and gold-painted, with tiny indigo spots. She's singing.

> *The animals went in two by two*
> *Hurrah! Hurrah!*

I think about the story of Noah. There's something so comforting about it, this tale of cataclysm averted: the whole world threatened by the Flood – and yet so much was saved.

Eliza's play engrosses her. She has such a content look. She sings her song and arranges her animals, going up into the ark in a straggling, ragtag procession.

I suddenly feel so happy, sitting here: it's a happiness, a euphoria almost, that seems to come out of nowhere. I think how on Thursday I'm seeing Hugo, and it comes to me, with a surge of emotion, of extravagant gratitude, that he is my ark, my escape, my safe place.

Eliza walks her animals in through the door of the cabin.

'They'll be all right now, Mummy. Nothing will hurt them,' she says.

33

He shuts the bedroom door behind us and takes me at once in his arms. Not wasting a moment. He pushes my dress down over my shoulders. I help him, undoing the buttons at the side of the bodice, wanting to discard my clothes as soon as possible; wanting to feel the sweetness of his mouth, his hands, on me.

We fall on the bed, so hungry. He kisses me, his searching hands going everywhere over my body. He eases one hand up my thigh, moves his finger rapidly on me. I feel the thrill, I hear my voice crying out. He enters me: I feel my body opening up to him. He comes quickly.

We lie sprawled on the wide walnut bed, and smoke and talk for a while. He tells me about his country house in Wiltshire – the downs where he walks, the meadows where rare fritillaries grow. I talk about some of the gardens that I've visited to take photographs: about a pond that flickered with apricot carp and jade dragonflies; about the extravagant loveliness of white catalpa flowers. I like this conversation. It's so calming to talk about places that aren't London – tranquil gardens and meadows where you can see a long way, the hills heaped up in the distance, purple as damsons. Faraway, peaceful places that don't smell of brick dust and grief.

I check my watch: it's quarter past five. I think languidly how, in this strange new world we inhabit, the late afternoon is our dream time, the time for kissing and cocktails and sex. The night is for other things now. I think of all the other Londoners who are acting just as we are, grasping recklessly at life, seeking solace in the beds of people they shouldn't be with. I think of the air in a thousand London bedrooms at this moment, blurry and fragrant as parting lovers smoke a last cigarette.

I drain the martini from my glass.

'Hugo, I'm really sorry, but I ought to be heading back home.'

'D'you have to, darling?'

'Yes. Really. I really have to.' Trying to persuade myself.

But for the moment I don't move. It feels so good, in this bed. Making love has relaxed and soothed every muscle in my body: all the tension has gone from me, and now I can tell how profoundly exhausted I am. I think of the dark, harsh world out there, beyond these velvet-draped windows: it's such an effort to leave here, to step out into that world, to decide that our time together is over. My body lying beside him feels loosened and easy and warm.

'Stay, darling,' he says. As though he can tell exactly what I'm thinking. 'Stay for a little while longer. I really don't want you to go yet.' He turns to me and wraps his arm around me. He runs one finger delicately down my spine. 'To be honest, it was all over a bit too quickly for me the first time. I must have been rather too excited at seeing you again.'

He pulls me towards him: he's hard against me. He moves on top of me; I feel his warm slide into me.

To start with, it feels as wonderful as ever. But it seems to go on for such a long time, and after a while my body stops responding, and all the thrill I felt at first begins to seep away.

There's a scurry of fear in my mind, small and quick as a mouse in a corner. I open my eyes, tilt my head a little. Over his heaving shoulder, I can just see the clock on the wall. *Oh God*. Five fifty-five.

Hurry up, I think. *Please. Get a move on*. But I can't say anything, of course. I feel helpless, desperate; I can't speak, can't urge him to finish – anything I might say would only distract him and slow him down. His forehead is glossy with sweat, and I keep thinking that he's nearly there: his breathing grows noisy and rapid, and then subsides again. I'm frantic. I can hear the *tick tick* of the clock, the rhythmic creak of the bed. Measuring out my impatience.

At last, he comes, with a rushed volley of expletives; rolls off me. *Thank God*. I long to leap from the bed, but

I don't want to seem rejecting. I wonder how soon I can get dressed and go, without seeming too impolite.

He has such a satiated, replete look.

'That was amazing. You are amazing,' he says.

He reaches for his cigarettes, starts to light one for me, his movements slow and languorous.

'No, Hugo, no – I have to leave.'

He frowns a little.

'Right now, Livia?'

'Yes. Right now.'

I get up and gather my clothes, which are scattered over the room.

He looks at me lazily, so contented.

'You have beautiful breasts,' he says.

'Hugo . . .'

'Look – those daughters of yours will be fine,' he says, as I struggle into my slip. 'I know how you mothers can fret when you're not there to keep an eye on things. But I'm sure your girls can manage without you for just a little while. There's no need to get so worked up, darling . . .'

Irritation snags at me. *Of course I will worry. He ought to understand that. He's my lover, he ought to care, he ought to be thinking of me.*

My fingers fumble as I dress; I'm trying too hard to hurry. Yet everything is slowed and seems to take too long, as though I am wading through deep water.

Seeing I meant what I said, Hugo gets up as well.

'I'll call you a taxi,' he tells me.

'No, you don't have to, really. I can do it.'

But he pulls on his clothes, though rather more slowly than me.

We go downstairs, and out to the street. He flags down a taxi. We kiss quickly.

'Thank you so much. That was really lovely,' I tell him.

'For me too . . . Look, my darling, relax. Your children will be fine. I'm sure there's no need to worry,' he says again.

I think, rather uncharitably, *Well, he would say that, they aren't his children* . . .

'Can you do Friday week?' he asks me.

'Yes, I'd love that,' I tell him.

The taxi heads off, and I turn to wave to him through the window. He raises his hand; his smile is sweetly complicit. Yet, seeing him there on the pavement in all his upper-class elegance, swiftly receding from me as the taxi moves away, I have the oddest feeling. As though he's just someone who's caught my eye as I pass – a rather attract-ive stranger. As though I've been making love in the Balfour Hotel with a man who I really don't know. The thought unsettles me. It's tiredness, I suppose: it can make you feel so weird – fragmented, like you're trying to make a picture from bits of different jigsaws. As though the separate parts of your life don't fit together at all.

We travel through London. Above us, the indigo sky is cloudless; the moon hangs down like a fruit. *A bomber's moon.* The moonlit streets are full of urgency and purpose – everyone struggling to reach their homes before the bombers come over, people just visible in the shards of light from dipped headlights and shaded torches; intent, heads jutting forward; sometimes breaking into a run.

I think of all the women in the houses we pass. Preparing to take shelter, gathering everything together – their bedding, their knitting, their sandwiches and their flasks of sugary tea. Their *children*. I should be in my own home now: I should be doing those things. I keep assuring myself that the girls will be safe with Aggie. If I'm not back when the sirens start, she'll take them straight to the crypt. I think of the moment when I left this afternoon, how she sought to reassure me. *I'll look after them, don't you worry, Livia.* I recite this, like a magic spell, to try to soothe my fears: think it, *will* it. I chew my fingers, shift around in my seat. My entire body is fizzing and seething with impatience, the sweetness of my time with Hugo completely wiped from my mind.

I think of him remarking how mothers always worry. He's right, of course; and I know I worry still more than most mothers do. But how could I not? I understand how life can so easily slide from you, how cracks can open before you, everything suddenly fractured; how rapidly and fluently you can slip down under the ice . . .

I keep expecting the sirens, but the night is still silent. I dare to hope that I might be in luck: that even now, I could reach my home before the bombing begins.

The cabbie seems to be taking a rather long way round. I lean forward, tap on the glass.

'Excuse me – but shouldn't you be going down Trinity Road?' I ask him.

'Trinity Road is blocked, ma'am. An unexploded,' he says.

We're almost back at Conduit Street when the sirens start to howl. The noise makes me shudder, as it always does.

I'll look after them, don't you worry, Livia.

He stops at the bottom of Conduit Street, in the middle of the carriageway – there's debris in the gutters that could puncture his tyres.

'Sorry, ma'am, but I'll have to drop you here. I'm off to the Fountain Place shelter.'

'Of course. That's fine,' I tell him.

I pay him, and give him a handful of change for the tip – not counting it out, just thrusting it at him.

I step from the taxi into the moonlight and shadowy dark of the street. I decide to make my way straight to the crypt. I imagine running down the steps and seeing the three of them there, huddled on the blankets in front of Jemima Codrington's tomb – Aggie, Polly, Eliza.

The sirens are wailing and wailing, ripping open the seam of the night.

34

I walk rapidly along Conduit Street. I'd run – except if you run in the dark, in heels, you're likely to trip. I have to get all the way up the street, then round the córner to St Michael's. I pass my house as I go, and cast my eye quickly over it, but it all looks safely shut up, at least as far as I can tell. They'll be sheltering already. Aggie will look after them; they'll be safe and sound in the crypt . . .

But then, as I peer ahead through the dark, I make out three figures up at the junction with Stapleforth Street; a shaded torch that waves around, an air of agitation. *Please God, no.* It's Aggie and the girls: they're in a pool of white moonlight, and I can see them quite clearly. Aggie is tugging at Eliza, who is standing stock still in the road. I can tell that Polly is desperate – pleading, her pale hands fluttering. That Eliza is immovable.

I race towards them, stumbling over debris on the pavement. As I approach, I can hear them: Eliza's outraged sobbing, Polly's high-pitched entreaties. Aggie is shouting.

'*No*, Eliza. Just get a move on, will you. I promised your mother,' she says.

She smacks Eliza's arm. Eliza is startled and briefly stops sobbing, but still she doesn't move. Aggie grabs her and tries to drag her.

I rush up.

'Aggie. What on earth?'

They all turn to me, with an air of relief – certain that I will solve this for them.

'Mum – thank goodness,' says Polly.

Eliza is crying again, but now with less conviction. You can see the marks of tears on her face, luminous snail-trails that glint in the light of the moon.

'For God's sake,' I say to Aggie. 'They'll be coming over any moment. You should be in the crypt by now.'

Fear makes my voice sharp. I've never spoken so sternly to Aggie before.

'Oh, Livia. Thank the Lord you're here.' Aggie sounds distraught. 'She's so stubborn, Livia. She's refusing to move. She's forgotten that blasted rabbit – 'scuse my language,' she says.

I glance upwards. The night sky is still empty, but the planes could be here any time.

'I'll get him, Eliza, I'll get him, all right? You go now, all of you. *Now*.'

Eliza's tears are switched off. Her expression is all innocence.

'He's on the dining-room table, Mummy,' she says.

She's perfectly, maddeningly, calm now. She turns to go with Aggie and Polly.

It's all my fault that this happened. If only I hadn't been late; if only I'd been back home by the time the sirens started to sound: Rabbit wouldn't have been forgotten then. Guilt washes through me.

They walk briskly round the corner, heading for St Michael's.

And then, the sinister growl of a bomber, low overhead. My heart gallops off. But I tell myself they'll be safely there in a moment. Perhaps I should follow them, go straight round to the shelter. But I remember Eliza's expression and the shiny tracks of her tears: she's trusting me to get Rabbit. I turn swiftly back towards the house. It will only take a moment. And I've messed up today, by returning so late, and I have some inchoate sense that this is my chance to make amends. To absolve myself.

A bomb falls, off to my left: the shriek, then the vast explosion. It's close, too close: the ground trembles under my feet, as if the very foundations of London were cracking and splintering. The blast pummels me, sucks at me. My ears throb, and every hair on the back of my neck stands up: it's that strange electrical feeling, as though you're wired to the mains. I can hear the clamour of our guns responding.

I rush back to my house, pull out my key. Run in, leave the door open. Cram my key back in my bag. Switch on the lamp in the hall – then realise that the light will fall out into the street. Go back, slam the door shut.

Another huge blast. The house seems to judder and shift, and I hear glass breaking behind me, its glittery menacing percussion. I spin round. The stained-glass bluebird above the front door has shattered: just a few shards of sparkly blue glass still cling to the criss-cross tape. Plaster dust sifts from the ceiling, white as flour and suffocating. The hall light swings on its cord and flickers, throwing strange shadows over the walls.

He isn't on the dining-room table, where she said she'd left him. *Damn.* Probably I should go now; I should just give up and leave. Instead, I run through to the kitchen. He's sitting in the vegetable basket. I curse his innocent face. *Damn rabbit.*

I grab him, rush back to the door. I fumble around in my bag for my key, but can't find it – my hands aren't working properly, my fingers are thick and clumsy, useless as gloved fingers. So I bang the door shut behind me, but leave it unlocked. I head off rapidly up the street, into the full force of the raid – the cacophony, the stench of burning, everything falling apart.

You should never leave the door on the latch.

Sarah's voice in my mind. Sensible, concerned; perhaps a little peremptory.

This is really important, Livie. You never know who might come in.

I stop, swivel round to face my house.

You're right, I shouldn't have done that, I think. *I shouldn't have left it unlocked. There could be looters or burglars.*

Another bomb falls, close behind me: I can feel the shock waves moving through the pavement under my feet. There isn't time to go back to the house and still get round to the crypt.

Yet I stand there, torn, for a strange, suspended moment. In the blackout, my house looks abandoned, as though nobody lives there at all, and the moonlight is reflecting in the glass of the panes with an otherworldly radiance, like the milky glimmer of mistletoe berries. I don't know what to do now. I could leave the door as it is, and take the risk that we might be burgled. Or I could go back, lock the door behind me, shelter in our Andy – but I know how my daughters would panic if I didn't turn up at the crypt . . .

All these thoughts racing through me, pulling me one way and then the other. My body paralysed.

The raid is intensifying around me. I'm half aware that a bomber is right overhead. And there's a fire on the rooftop off to my right where an incendiary must have come down – vicious orange flames leaping, spreading. You can hear the rushing sound of burning. *Someone should put that out*, I think, with a small, detached part of my mind. *Why doesn't someone put that out?* Whatever I do, I shouldn't stay here.

Some instinct makes me look up suddenly. I have a quick vast vision of all the lights in the sky – something flashing like lightning, flares falling, the searchlights that slice through the dark. So much light, crazily pulsing. There's a sound so huge it blots out my hearing, and everything seems to slow. A wall on the opposite side of the street swells out like a windblown curtain, and all the lights are extinguished. I'm blind, in a heavy dark world that is collapsing, fragmenting, around me – and then all those buildings and broken things are falling and falling on me.

35

I open my eyes, but see only blackness. Have I lost my sight? It's so dark here.

I decide that something has happened to blind me. I consider this thought for a while, in a detached sort of way.

I move my head slightly, cautiously. Dust falls all over me, filling my nose and my eyes and my mouth. I can't breathe, the dust is choking me.

It comes to me that I must have been buried alive, and a shrill red panic seizes me. I find myself shouting out.

'Help! Help me!'

Only a small hoarse sound comes from my mouth, but it makes more dust come down, seeping into me, scratching and clogging my throat. *Dust to dust.*

I try to move my consciousness to the boundaries of my body, to work out whether all my limbs are still here – but it's too difficult, I can't do it. Nothing hurts very much; I have a strange, abstracted feeling. It's as though I have no sense of my body at all.

There's a little flutter of a thought, like a glittery fish shooting up towards the surface of my mind: *My children. Where are my children?*

And then I find myself moving down into blackness: a soft, thick black, like velour, so welcome, muffling my eyes and my mind. I sink down gratefully.

Voices come into my darkness, voices from far far away. I can't make any sense of these voices. All I can think is, *I wish they'd stop talking, I want to sleep, I want quiet.* But the voices are calling and calling; they seem to have their hooks in me, won't let me drift away. If only they'd hush, I could go back to sleep, and I long for this so very much, thirsting, yearning for it – to float away on a tide of nothingness, of dark. To stop struggling.

Something makes me open my eyes. I find I can see after all. There's light above me, off to my left, a light that is dazzlingly bright, that hurts me with its brilliance, sears me. I keep looking at it briefly, then quickly shutting my eyes. I can't work out what makes this light; then, as I manage to focus on it, the shape begins to make sense. *It's a torch. Someone's holding a torch.* Behind the light, a man's face, a tin helmet. The face is a very long way up, a very long way away, the eyes in it peering down at me. Glinting strangely in the light. I try to speak, but more dust fills my mouth, and blots and muffles my words. Then darkness blinds me.

I move off into some dreamlike state, punctured by sounds I don't understand, that trouble my sleep.

When next I force my heavy lids open, the face, the helmet, are close. There's light all around me. The mouth in the face is moving.

'Just hang on, love,' says the mouth. 'We'll have you out in a jiffy.'

But I'm suddenly aware of all the pain in my body – the pain that claws at my back, my legs; my eyes stinging, inflamed with the dust; the twisted, contorted way my body is arranged. This is intolerable to me, the way my body is placed. It's as though everything else could be borne, if I could only straighten my leg; nothing else matters.

The mouth in the helmet is still talking.

'So what's your name, love? Tell me your name.'

I have to think for a moment.

'Livia Ripley.'

But I wish he wouldn't make me talk. When I speak, I gag on a mouthful of dirt. I feel my eyes closing again, and the sensation is warm and soothing, as though soft dark velvet swathes of fabric were wrapping me closely around. Cradling me.

'Stay with me, Livia.' There's a thread of urgency in his voice. 'Just you hold on for a minute, love. We're ever so nearly there now. All we've got to do is to get your arm out,' he says.

This is surprising. I force my eyes open.

Close to me, there's a woman's arm that's pinned beneath a beam – palm upward, with cupped fingers; as though this hand had been holding a thing that has now been taken away. I wonder who the arm belongs to, and a shudder goes through me, a sense of horror. Is someone else buried beside me? A *dead* person?

'That's not my arm,' I tell him.

'Yes it is, love, it's got the same coat you're wearing,' he says.

He tugs at the beam that traps the arm, swearing under his breath. There's a sound of breaking and splintering.

'There we go. Easy does it,' he says.

He reaches down to me, puts his hands under my armpits, starts to pull. Daggers of pain slice through me. I can hear a voice crying out: it might be me, I don't know. I plunge back into darkness.

When I surface, I'm in the ambulance, and there's light around me. My face feels wet, and I'm aware that this wetness must have woken me. I touch my face: my fingers come away scarlet. Is this *my* blood? Then I realise that there's someone on the bunk above me, and this person must be horribly injured: their blood is dripping down, in vivid gouts. This seems obscene, this red blood splashing. I try to turn away from the blood, but my head is too heavy, won't move. The blood falls on my face, on my lips; I have its taste in my mouth, its salt and copper. I don't know whose blood this is, and the thought troubles me terribly – if it's the blood of a stranger, if it's the blood of a child. Of one of my children. *My children.*

I try to call out.

'My children. Are my children all right?'

But my voice is small and choked with dust and only a croak comes out.

I see that there are two orderlies in the ambulance. They're bending low over another casualty: they have their backs to me. They're talking softly, urgently.

'He's fading,' says one of them. 'Suffering Jesus. No pulse. No heartbeat. He's gone.'

They pay me no attention.

In the speechless margins of sleep, I'm still aware of the drip of the blood, falling obscenely all over me as I sink down into the dark.

36

I wake to the dazzling lights of a hospital, the starched smell of hospital linen, pain everywhere in my body. There's a nurse with a stern expression standing next to my bed. She's fiddling with something on a trolley.

'Where are my children?' It's hard to speak. My mouth and throat are like sandpaper. 'I've got two daughters . . .' A terrible anxiety surges through me. But when I try to think about them – where they are, what's happened – it's all confusion in my mind: there's something I can't get hold of. 'I have to know if my girls are all right.'

'Hush now,' she says. She holds a syringe up to the light, checks the level of liquid in it. 'I'm going to give you something to help with the pain.'

I know this will be morphine – that it will send me to

sleep. But I mustn't let this happen: there's something that has to be done, something that can't be postponed, something urgent concerning my children. I just have to work out exactly what this *something* could be.

'The pain isn't too bad, really. I don't think I need it,' I say.

But she knows I'm not telling the truth. She sticks her needle in my arm.

'There. You can go to sleep now.'

'No, I can't, I mustn't.'

But I do. Entering a fevered maze of dreams, unable to find my way out.

When at last I wake, gluey yellow afternoon sun is coming through the windows, and I feel so much more normal, so much more like myself. I glance around the ward, able at last to move beyond my awareness of my body, to take in the scene around me. The beds are full of injured people. Beside me, a woman with her leg in plaster; her skin is white as paper, her face creased up with pain. Across from me, a girl with a bandage over her eye; the cloth looks bloody, the wound must still be seeping. I can hear somebody crying, and the sound is strangely rhythmic – three ragged sobs, a pause for breath; and then it starts again.

Everything that happened comes rushing into my mind. Hurrying down the street with Rabbit, then thinking I ought to go back. Turning, hesitating. The clamour of the raid, the flames and searchlights above me; then, all around me, the houses starting to fall. Waking, with dirt in my mouth. Being dug out of the ruin.

I wonder how long I have been here. My left arm on the sheet beside me is wrapped in a stiff bandage. I wonder vaguely how badly it's hurt; I can't really tell, because of the morphine, though I know if it was fractured they would have put it in a cast. But I'm not really all that interested in the damage to my body. Because I know I don't want to live any more if my children aren't alive. I know this with a perfect clarity.

The nurse comes briskly down the ward and stops at the foot of my bed.

'Well, you're looking a lot better, Mrs Ripley.' Approvingly, as though this is a moral achievement.

I wonder briefly how she knows who I am.

'Please. How can I find out about my children? I have to know if they're safe . . .'

'Now, don't you go getting yourself in a state, Mrs Ripley,' she tells me, her voice emollient as Vaseline. 'You need to take things easy. You should try and get a nice bit of shut-eye,' she says.

Why isn't she answering my question? Does she know something, and won't tell me? Is she refusing to say what she knows, because the news is so bad?

I force myself to stay awake. I find myself pleading with God, a quick, snatched prayer before the morphine drags me down into the dark. Making a promise, a bargain.

If You give me my children back, I'll do whatever You ask. I'll be good, so very good, I'll speak to Hugo and end our affair, I'll live a different kind of life, the life You want me to live. Just do this one thing for me. Just give me my children again. Just let me hold them . . .

In spite of all my fear, I fall asleep, and dream.

I'm walking the streets of a city in a far-off, foreign land, a place where I am a stranger. This city is crowded, its colours livid, sulphurous, gorgeous, and yet the place is utterly quiet, as silent as a tomb. People walk past me, the many people who have arrived here before me. They look at me without recognition, saying nothing at all, and I have a sense of dislocation, of wrongness, in the dream – the awareness growing in me that I don't belong on these streets: that this silent city isn't my place, that this isn't where I should be . . .

A small voice enters my dream.

'Mum?'

At the sound, though I'm still dreaming, a sudden happiness opens like a sunlit flower in me. Even before I'm properly awake; even as I float up to the surface of my dream, my eyelids stuck down and heavy.

'Mum. Are you all right?'

I open my eyes.

Aggie and Polly and Eliza are standing next to my bed. The girls look fraught and pale and scruffy and rather bedraggled. Eliza's cardigan is mis-buttoned, and Polly's hair ribbon is coming undone. Eliza is hanging back a little, as though she's suddenly afraid of me. Aggie looks exhausted, but has a big, beaming smile, so pleased with herself that she's found me.

And I know one thing, with an absolute certainty. That there is nothing that has ever happened to me – nothing that *could* ever happen, nothing before or after this moment

– that could possibly compare with the joy that I feel. Nothing at all. Not ever ever.

I put out my good hand to the girls. Polly reaches down to kiss me, then sits beside me on the mattress. Eliza comes round to the other side of the bed. She's bolder now – seeing that I can talk and seem to be much the same as usual, in spite of the bandage. She climbs on the bed and presses against me. Her shoes will dirty the blankets, but I'm far too tired to care.

'Mummy, why are you crying?' She touches my bandage delicately. 'Does your arm hurt?'

'No, it isn't that, sweetheart.'

I wipe my tears on my sleeve.

'Goodness, Livia. It's been the devil of a job tracking you down,' Aggie tells me. 'I kept the girls off school, and we've been all over the shop.'

'Oh. Oh, I'm so sorry to have caused all this trouble . . .'

'It was a very nasty raid,' she says. 'They were all full up at St Peter's.'

'So where am I?'

'You're in St Jude's,' she tells me. 'The good news is – they managed to dig out your handbag.'

She pulls it out of the bedside locker. Rabbit, extremely filthy, is sticking out of the top. They must have found the handbag beside me and sent it here with me, so I will still have my crucial documents – my building society pass book and my ration book. *Bless them*, I think. *Bless them all.*

Aggie has brought in a basket of clothes for me. She dumps the basket on the floor and pulls a chair up to the bed.

'Like I say, we've been on a bit of a wild-goose chase to find you,' she tells me. 'We really caught it, last night. It was one of the worst times ever. A house just up from yours has vanished, and there's a whopping great hole in the road.'

'And you three – you got to the crypt?'

'In the nick of time,' she tells me.

'We only just made it, Mum,' says Polly eagerly. Relishing the drama of her story. 'We got to the top of the steps, and Aggie slammed the door shut. And then there was a great big bang and Eliza fell down the stairs.'

'I did *not*,' says Eliza. 'I was just rushing, is all. Polly's telling tales again, Mummy.'

'But, Livia . . .' Aggie is serious now. 'You'd have been done for, Livia, if you'd gone just a step or two further . . .'

'Oh.'

'We must thank the Lord and all His angels that you're still in the land of the living. That you hadn't got further up the street. Or it would have been curtains,' she says.

I remember how I turned back – and then the whole street seemed to fall on me.

'Our house?' I ask her. Though it isn't that important, really.

'Still standing, but not quite the same. It's rather battered, Livia.'

I can't help smiling.

'A bit like me,' I say.

'All the clocks have stopped, Mum,' says Polly. 'It's ever so weird.'

Aggie watches me and my daughters, smiling benignly.

'They said you could come home today,' she says. 'If I promise to keep an eye on you. They're desperate to free up some beds – God knows what will happen tonight.'

'Well, that suits me,' I tell her.

I think of the sampler on my wall that says, *There's no place like home*. I can't wait to get back there.

Part 3

37

Conduit Street is unrecognisable. As Aggie said, a house a few doors up from mine is now a mound of rubble. The poplar trees are shattered stumps. The road is pockmarked with holes, and littered with bricks and bits of masonry, and in the Tarmac near our house, there's a crater as wide as a room. I peer in. There's water at the bottom of it, giving back the gleam of the sky. There are smells of fire, sour earth, sewage.

I unlock the door; we go in. Aggie has swept up the broken glass in the hall, and patched the window above the door with plywood.

She seats me in an armchair, and makes a pot of tea.

'I'll stay and do your meal, Livia.'

'I can manage, Aggie, really. You've been an absolute angel. You've done more than enough.'

'What about that poor arm of yours?'

'It hurts, but I can still use it. And Polly can help me,' I say. I hug Aggie with my good arm. 'Thank you so much. Thank you for everything.'

When she's gone, I inspect the damage. More broken windows. A lot of tiles gone from the roof. Some unnerving new cracks in the walls, and doors that won't close any more. And all the clocks, as Polly said, are stopped at seven fifteen. But we can still live here.

Whenever I pass my daughters, I grab them and hold them to me, till it's all too much for Eliza.

'Mummy, we know you're happy we didn't die,' she says with elaborate patience. 'But I want to get on with my London Town.'

By some quirk of the blast, her construction has survived entirely intact. Even her cotton-reel towers are still standing.

At night, we go to the crypt, and I spread out our blankets in front of Jemima Codrington's tomb. I fall asleep quickly, still a bit drugged from the morphine. Distant bombing wakes me briefly, then I fall asleep again, my eyelids weighted, a welcome stupor overcoming me.

My dreams are happier tonight.

I dream of a beautiful wild garden, sloping down to a stream: lovelier even than the gardens I imagined in my childhood. I'm looking out at this garden from a window in a tower. There are tall trees, widely spaced, the sunlight falling between them, and many wonderful bushes – roses, camellias, azaleas: all blossoming together, as though spring and summer meld here into one long flowering season. A small breeze stirs like the softest breath, and petals fall from the flowers, white, blush pink, a tender yellow. As I stare at this place, I understand, with the faintest sense of surprise, that it belongs to me entirely, this garden is all mine. This is my place, my own. Yet I have never walked here.

When I wake, for a minute or two the sweet mood of the dream is still with me.

In the morning, after more sleep back at the house, I feel quite different. My mind is clearer: I feel restored to myself. But all the strange exhilaration of last night has left me – like when shimmering flood-water seeps away, leaving mud and mess in its wake. I feel depressed and weary, and every bone in my body hurts, and I'm acutely conscious of each scrape and graze on my skin.

It's Saturday, and the girls are home: Polly playing a Bach Prelude on the piano in the parlour, Eliza busy with her arrangement. I make a cup of coffee, and sit at my kitchen table. It's a blowy, showery day, with clouds like dirty cotton wool. Rain runs blearily down my window panes, and patters on the terrace with a sound like many people hurrying past my room.

I think about what happened on Thursday, and a wave of guilt breaks over me. I think how I risked losing my children, how close I came to losing them – and all because I was concerned with my own stupid gratification, all because I'd wanted to be in my lover's arms.

There's a chorus of accusation inside me – the voices horribly familiar, but today more strident than ever.

All you do is misguided. Loving is beyond you. You put those you care for in danger. You damage the people you love.

I put my hand to my face, and find that I am weeping.

Every decision you make is wrong. That's the kind of woman you are. Someone who damages people.

But that's only to be expected, when you killed the one you loved most . . .

I sit there, lost. I have my head in my hands. I'm only vaguely aware of the little voices of the house: they seem so far removed from me. The creakings and settlings of the timbers; Hector purring on the window sill; Polly practising the piano. She's finding this piece rather difficult; she stumbles over the phrases. Making the same mistake over and over again.

I cry for a long, long time. I feel I will never stop crying.

Then the sun comes out through the rain clouds, splitting the seam of the sky, dazzling, startling. I feel its warmth; I look up. Sunlight is falling all over the table and over my hands, which have a hundred cuts and bruises. Everything is illumined; even the tears in my eyes sparkle, making rainbows on my eyelashes. I blink the tears away. The room comes crisply into focus – the edges of things in sharp relief, everything crystalline, clear.

I feel a little stronger now.

And the thought comes to me, the sudden realisation – fully formed and distinct, almost as though from outside: that all this time I've been trying to find a way to escape from the war. That this was what Hugo meant to me. He was my ark, my sense of safety, my beautiful illusion: he gave me a place I could retreat to, a secret world where I could hide.

I see now how wrong this was, how dangerous, how deceptive. What trouble this has led me into. When the only right course is something entirely different: to face up to the things that are happening – all the horror, the bombing, the war. To find a way to live differently, just as I promised in the hospital. To work out how to make the best use of the days that are given to me.

It all seems so simple suddenly.

38

It's raining again, and the asphalt is greasy and treacherous. I thread my way carefully between the craters in the pavements. I haven't brought my umbrella, and, when I get there, my hair and the sleeves of my mac are soaked through.

Justin Connelly opens the door to my knock.

'Livia.' A frown – concerned. 'Aggie told me what happened – how you got hurt in the raid.' His eyes on me, studying me.

I feel I should shrug, and say, *It was nothing* . . . But that isn't really true; and he'd know that I was lying.

'Yes. It was all rather horrible . . .'

Behind him, I can see the shadowy hall of the vicarage. It doesn't look at all churchy – more like a cluttered, overstocked shop. A bicycle, heaps of blankets, piled-up crates of supplies – baked beans, dried milk, cocoa powder, cans of Fray Bentos corned beef. Over his shoulder, I can see into one of the rooms, where there are mattresses on the floor and bundles of clothing: perhaps some bombed-out people are sleeping here. There's just one little religious touch – a dog-eared piece of paper pinned to the wall, with a handwritten line from Scripture. *O send out Thy light and Thy truth, that they may lead me.*

I take all this in very quickly.

'It was good to see you back at the crypt last night. I'd have had a word, but I didn't want to disturb your sleep,' he says.

'I slept remarkably well. It was the morphine, probably. It was very soothing,' I tell him. Keeping my voice light. Trying to smile.

But I'm touched he was looking out for me, and there's a lump in my throat. I came here so determined, but I'm fragile as a paper doll. If this man is too solicitous, I'll probably burst into tears.

I push back my hair, which is drenched and dripping over my face, and wince slightly.

He gestures towards my arm. 'How much damage?'

'Nothing broken. I can still use it . . . I wanted to speak to you, Reverend – I mean, Justin.'

'Of course.' There's the glint of a question in his eye. 'Why don't you come in?'

I take off my coat and he hangs it up on a peg – his movements abrupt, a little clumsy, with the brittle, nervy energy of someone who never gets enough sleep.

He ushers me through to his study.

There are books all around – on shelves, on the desk, on the floor. Lots of theology, lots of political books; I notice Orwell's *Down and Out in Paris and London*, Strachey's *The Theory and Practice of Socialism*. The books are heaped in ragged columns, and all furred over with dust: you can tell he hasn't opened these volumes for months. There's a rickety table that serves as a desk – this must be where he writes his sermons. I feel a flicker of curiosity: it's an age since I heard a sermon. I remember the previous vicar from the days when I still went to church, and his homilies full of platitudes – how he'd claim to see the Hand of God in the most awful things. I try to imagine Justin's preaching. I bet he makes everyone feel uncomfortable – that they can't live up to his standards, that they're lacking in some way.

He clears some books from a chair, and I sit. He props himself up on his desk. His face is like iron in the rainy light that falls through the taped-over window.

'So, Livia, how can I help you?' His eyes on me – restless and dark, like stormy seas.

I clear my throat, which is suddenly thick.

'I've changed my mind,' I tell him. 'I'll be a warden. If you still want me.'

That smile he has, like a light switched on.

'Wonderful, Livia. Thank you so much. We'll be so glad of your help.'

I have a sense again – that this man sees something in me that I didn't know was there. That may not even *be* there. I'm sure to be a terrible disappointment to him.

He takes out his Woodbines, offers me one, leans in close to light it. His jaw is shaded with stubble, and I can see the little saffron flame reflecting in his eyes.

'So – do you know how it all works?' he asks me.

'Not really.'

'There are different kinds of warden. You can be a paid warden and get two pounds for the week. You'd be on duty every night, and during the day as well. Or you can be unpaid, and patrol for three or four nights. So, you'd be coming on duty on, say, Saturday, Monday and Wednesday. That's the kind of thing that women with families tend to opt for,' he says.

'Yes, that's what would suit me best.'

'When can you start?'

'Whenever you want.'

'Tonight?' he asks me.

I swallow hard. Somehow I hadn't imagined that it would be so soon. Perhaps I'd expected him to say, *Are you certain, Livia? Wouldn't you like to think about this for a while?* So I'd have had some time to prepare myself: time maybe to back out.

The cigarette is strong. I draw smoke into my lungs, and splutter.

'Yes, I could, if you'd like me to,' I tell him. 'I'll have to check that Aggie can look after my girls. I'll go to see her when I leave here . . .'

'Of course . . . I'll show you where we meet,' he tells me.

He doesn't hang about, I think.

He takes me down to the basement of the vicarage. It's

253

been kitted out as a wardens' post. A table and chairs; four camp beds. A darts board, draughts and playing cards. A radio, a telephone. An electric kettle, tins of coffee and tea and dried milk. On the wall, the poster you see everywhere: *Your Courage Your Cheerfulness Your Resolution Will Bring Us Victory.* The place has a thick, stale, underground smell, of cigarettes, coffee and sweat.

'This is how it happens. Just so you have a rough idea,' he tells me. 'We get the yellow alert here – that's the alert the public don't hear. It means bombs in twenty-two minutes.'

'Oh.' I realise how little I've thought about what happens during a raid.

'That's when we start to patrol,' he says. 'The red alert comes when the planes are just twelve minutes away – that's when the public hear the sirens. We tend to patrol in pairs. We help people to get to the shelters; check on the old people, and so on, hurry them up. Carry things for them. Check that the people who want to stay in their houses are all right . . .'

I feel chilly suddenly. I wrap my cardigan close.

'And what if there's an incident?' I use the neutral, official language, but there's a shake in my voice.

'We help coordinate the response. That usually means one of you coming back here and ringing through – ringing Central Control, calling the fire service if there's a fire. If the phone lines are down, you have to send a despatch rider. Usually Bobby Ainsley, who's part of our team. Then you head back to the scene and do whatever you can.

Work out who's dead and who's still hanging on. Put out any small fires. Have you ever used a stirrup pump?'

'No.'

'I'll show you . . . And we do what we can to help the injured. It's all about tourniquets, really. Trying to control any bleeding until the stretchers arrive . . .'

I think of the blood that dripped on me in the ambulance. I remember the taste of the blood of a stranger, falling all over my mouth, the copper and salt of it. I don't say anything.

He sees something in my face, perhaps. When he speaks again, his voice is gentle.

'Don't worry, you'll soon get the hang of it,' he tells me. 'You can patrol with me to start with. Your first night, I'll take you round, show you all the shelters on our patch.'

'Yes. Thank you.'

In a way, it's reassuring that I'll be patrolling with him. But in another way, it makes me more anxious than before: anxious that he might judge me – that he might learn too much about me. Discover what I'm really like. That I don't have any *courage* or *resolution* at all.

He takes me back up the stairs. My mouth is like blotting paper. I'd hoped that once I'd volunteered I'd feel a little bit braver. But nothing's changed: I'm the same self-doubting, frightened person that I was before.

In the hall, he turns to face me. My fingers on the banister are trembling, and he sees. He puts his hand on my shoulder, and I can feel the warmth of him through the fabric of my clothes.

'You can do this, you know,' he says.

'Can I?'

His sudden, startling smile.

'We're all scared shitless,' he says, and the coarse language is oddly comforting. 'But being a warden helps with the fear, in a way.'

Does it? How can it?

He pauses, seeking out the right words. Seeing the doubt in me.

'Sometimes we can feel afraid because we're trying to keep ourselves safe. But you can't do that, when you're a warden. You can't think about your own safety. You have to go where you're needed; you don't go where you feel safe. In a funny way, that helps,' he says.

'I hope so.' My voice a little shred.

'Livia. No one is born brave. No one. But it's something you can learn to be,' he tells me.

There's an intensity to him, as though he really wants me to know this. And, just for a moment – there, in the cluttered hallway, by the tattered prayer for guidance and all the cans of corned beef – I believe him. Believe I could be a different person: believe that I too could be brave.

He takes my coat from the peg and holds it out for me.

'Thank you,' I say. Though I'm not sure exactly what I'm thanking him for.

There's something in his face – a hesitancy, a question.

'Livia – I was wondering . . . Why did you change your mind?'

I don't know how to answer.

'I made a promise,' I tell him.

It sounds too heavy, too weird. But to my relief, he seems to accept this, doesn't ask me to explain.

'Tonight, then. If Aggie can help you out, come round at five,' he says.

Outside, the rain has stopped now. The world has an unexpected loveliness, each twig lifting a drop of clear water, each crater holding a bright piece of sky. The dust has been washed from the atmosphere and the air has a leaf-green freshness. I draw it deeply into my lungs as I make my way to Aggie's house.

39

Later in the morning, Phoebe comes round.

'Oh my God, Livia. Oh my God. Thank the Lord you're all right.' She hugs me delicately, as though she could easily break me. 'I heard what happened. I must say, it's a treat to see you up and about.'

She's brought me a bunch of chrysanthemums, and one of her celebrated fruit cakes.

'Oh, that's so lovely of you, Phoebe.'

She comes in for a coffee.

I find a vase for the chrysanthemums. They fill the kitchen with their subtle, powdery fragrance, and their festive colours sing out in the watery light.

'No Freddie this morning?' I say.

She shakes her head.

'He wanted to carry on playing with Bill. They were being Spitfires and Messerschmitts. Having a massive dog fight in the dining room. With sound effects, and everything.' She gives an extravagant sigh. 'It was rather wearing, to be honest. It's good to get out of the house . . .'

But I know this isn't the real reason that she left Freddie behind. I know she wouldn't want him to play with Eliza – that she won't yet have forgiven me for Eliza's behaviour, when she rejected Freddie in that cool, self-righteous way.

I fill the kettle.

'Liv, let me do that. You sit yourself down . . .'

She bustles around with practised efficiency, straightening things as she goes. Sometimes you're reminded that she was once a needlework teacher.

'So tell me,' she says. 'Tell me everything . . .'

I take a deep breath.

'Well. I'd gone to see Mr Ballantyne, to talk about my book . . .'

I see a slight shadow pass over her face. Perhaps she's wondering why I was at his office so late in the day. I wonder if she can read me, if she can tell about our affair: if she might judge me. Briefly, this disconcerts me. But then I decide it doesn't matter: it's all in the past now, anyway. My affair with Hugo is over, and I'm going to tell him this soon. Though even as I think it, I feel sadness washing through me.

'I was late getting home,' I say, 'much later than I'd intended . . .'

I tell her about Eliza and Rabbit, and how I came back to the house.

She listens intently, her eyes never leaving my face.

'I was rushing back to the shelter,' I say, 'when I turned round for some reason. After that I don't really remember . . .'

I hesitate. The green, polleny scent of the chrysanthemums licks at me.

'Yes? What is it, Liv?' An urgent note in Phoebe's voice: as though something about me unnerves her.

I think about what happened, in that moment when the clocks stopped. I don't know whether to tell her. *I seemed to hear somebody speaking. My sister, who died long ago. And I turned, and then the bomb came down* . . . I don't know what Phoebe would make of it. The world is simple to her: she doesn't believe in the shadows in the margins, the things half-glimpsed out of the corner of your eye, or heard at the very edge of hearing. I tell myself it was just my senses tricking me – that it happened because the air can feel so uncanny during a raid, all churned up by the bombing . . .

But my pulse still skitters at the memory.

I try to shrug, as people do when they're being all stiff upper-lip, making light of their misfortune.

'I felt the blast, I got knocked over. After that, I passed out. I only came round properly in the hospital,' I say.

'Oh, Liv. You poor, poor thing. How awful.'

She hands me my coffee. I drink gratefully.

'You must still be very shaken up,' she says. 'You looked almost spooked when you were describing it . . .'

The way she says *spooked* makes me uneasy. I change the subject quickly.

'I've got some other news,' I say. 'I've decided to be a warden. We're based in the vicarage at St Michael's. I'll be starting there tonight.'

I notice how I say 'we' of this group of people I haven't yet met. As though I already belong there.

Phoebe's eyes widen.

'*You*, Liv? *Really*?' She sounds incredulous.

Doubt floods me. Can I really do this – if the very idea of it so startles my best friend?

'But who will look after your girls?' she says.

'Aggie will take them to the crypt with her.'

'And what about your arm?'

'It's not too bad – I'll manage. It isn't broken or anything – it just got rather bashed.'

'I'll say. When half of Conduit Street fell on it.'

'Really, Phoebe, it's fine.'

'But you'll have to be out on the streets in the raids.' A thread of alarm in her voice.

'Yes, of course . . . The thing is . . .' I'm struggling to find the right words. 'Something seems to happen when you have such a very close shave – it changes you. I just felt I had to – I don't know – live differently. Make a contribution. Try and give something back . . . Oh Lord, that sounds so *pious* . . .'

She folds her hands precisely on the table. She looks like a schoolmistress suddenly – about to upbraid a recalcitrant pupil who has sewn a crooked seam.

'I probably shouldn't try and dissuade you,' she says. 'I suppose it's terribly unpatriotic of me. All hands to the pump, and so on. But you'll see some horrible sights, Liv. I'm really not sure you're the right kind of person for this.'

'I know it won't be exactly enjoyable . . .'

I take small sips of my coffee, which is suddenly hard to swallow.

She frowns, leans in towards me. There's a new urgency in her.

'There was this thing I heard about – an incident over in Camberwell. Connie Hughes in the fish queue told me. One of her friends was called to it – he's a warden himself. There'd been a direct hit on an Anderson shelter.' I see her throat move as she swallows. 'He told Connie the body parts were like treacle, smeared on the wall of the house. They threw buckets of water against the wall to try to wash down the remains. Then they had to clear it all up with a stiff yard broom and a spade. I mean, it's beyond imagining . . .'

I put my cup down cautiously, but it makes a rattling sound, because my hand is shaking. I don't say anything.

'Liv, you're such a sensitive person. Are you ready for that?'

I shake my head.

'You couldn't ever be ready, could you? Not really. But I've decided.'

A slight hesitation, as Phoebe studies my face. I'd like to feel it's with a new respect, because of my resolve. But I suspect it's something less flattering.

'You're sure it's not just the morphine talking? Morphine, and shock?' she asks me.

I shake my head emphatically. Though to be honest, I'm not sure at all.

'Well, that's very heroic. Good for you, Liv,' she tells me. But her voice is guarded.

I tell the girls at lunchtime.

Eliza is entirely unsurprised by my announcement.

'Is it because that man wanted you to? The man who comes to the crypt? The man who punches people?'

'Yes.'

'I like the man,' she tells me.

'I'll be on duty three nights a week. Aggie will take you to the crypt. I'll make sure that the basket of things is ready and, Polly, you can carry it. And, Eliza, you'll have to be quite sure that you don't leave Rabbit behind . . .'

Advice tumbling out of me – though I know they won't hear a word of it.

'Mum, you'll be careful, won't you?' says Polly, a speck of misgiving in her eye.

'I'll do my best,' I say lightly.

I spend the afternoon reading Polly's St John Ambulance manuals. I realise I know nothing – except how to put an arm in a sling, and that for shock you need to sip a cup of hot sweet tea. Not all that much help for the kind of thing I saw in Carpenter Street. I concentrate on tourniquets.

Aggie comes round at five o'clock.

'Best of luck, then, Livia. You show them.'

As I leave, I catch sight of myself in the mirror in the hall. All Phoebe's doubts assail me. I peer at my reflection – at this pale and frightened woman, who's never used a stirrup pump, who hardly knows any First Aid. Whose arm is damaged. Whose only obvious talent is to take pretty pictures of flowers. A fat lot of use *she's* going to be.

40

There are four of them, all in boiler suits. An elderly man with a book: he's rather spare and austere, and sits a little removed from the others. Two people playing draughts – a woman, much younger than me, with a cheerful pink complexion and her hair in bouncy curls; and a man who's probably in his forties. This man is bald, and muscle-bound, and hasn't recently shaved; he has a scar on his cheek and tattoos along his arms. And there's an older woman, making tea, who looks to be fifty or so. She has brunette hair, expensively dyed, the colour of dark chocolate. She turns, takes her cigarette out of her mouth; she has a generous smile.

Oh God, I think, *the first hurdle: all these new people to meet.* I feel so shy – intimidated already.

'This is Livia,' Justin announces to the room. 'Let me introduce you . . . We use Christian names here, Livia. I hope that's all right with you . . . This is Sebastian . . .'

The older man closes his book, gets up and shakes my hand.

'Delighted to meet you,' he says.

He has an immaculate public-school accent: he doesn't seem to belong in this room. You can picture him in a walnut-panelled study, with through the window a view of great blue cedars and wide lawns. I think that he seems utterly out of place here – then reflect that people might say much the same about me.

I glance at the book he's reading. It's about the explorer Richard Burton. Sebastian would get on well with Hugo Ballantyne.

And, thinking of Hugo, I feel a stab of longing, quickly suppressed. *That part of my life is over,* I tell myself severely.

'And this is Céline,' Justin tells me, indicating the brunette woman.

'Well done for coming, darling. It's good to have you with us,' she says.

Her voice is seductive and deep; a silken carnation scent hangs about her. Her nails are painted scarlet, and I admire her for this – still painting her nails in spite of the war: this little act of defiance. I wonder where on earth she got the varnish from.

The fresh-faced young woman is Esme: she gives an ebullient wave. The man with tattoos is Lennie. He glances up at me, studies my face for a moment, doesn't smile.

'So, lovely Livia. Welcome to the belly of the beast.'

I can see the doubt in his eyes. I'm convinced he's taken a dislike to me – that he'll feel I'm rather flimsy and feeble, totally wrong for this work.

Céline takes my arm and ushers me off to one side. As she pours a cup of tea for me, she tells me about the others, a potted biography for each. Esme works part time at Bourne & Hollingsworth, on the haberdashery counter; she's the queen of Make Do and Mend – she could make a smart suit of clothes from some pins and a roll of lining paper. Lennie's an electrician – he's a full-time, paid-up warden; he can't fight because he has asthma. Sebastian studied at Cambridge, and once walked to Istanbul.

'Sebastian fought in the trenches. In the Great War. The war to end all wars. Remember that?' she says. Her lips are puckered, as though she has a bitter taste in her mouth.

'And what about you?' I ask her.

She blows out smoke, and I see a sliver of sadness in her eyes.

'I'm a singer by trade, Liv. I used to hang out at the Monseigneur, in Jermyn Street,' she tells me. 'Before everything went haywire.'

'Oh, how lovely.'

I'm impressed, but not surprised. I remember a club in the West End that Ronnie once took me to, for a treat when we were courting. Violet-shaded table lamps casting pools of dusky light, a jazz band playing the blues, the fizz of champagne on my tongue. Just being there made me feel glamorous. I can picture her somewhere like that, swathed in tulle, a spotlight on her, singing in a dark bruised voice. *Stepping out with my baby.*

'Tell me all about you, Liv.'

'Oh – I'm just a housewife and mother. And I take photographs sometimes.'

'That doesn't surprise me one bit,' she says. 'You look the arty type.'

Though I don't know how she can possibly tell from looking at me – with my sensible slacks, my darned jumper, my hair severely tied back. Not a scrap of make-up.

'Well, good on you, Liv, for volunteering.' She takes a long drag on her cigarette. 'So where did our Justin find you?' She lowers her voice, but only a little.

'I knocked him over,' I say.

She gives me a rather salacious grin.

'And I bet he wasn't the first.'

'I mean, *literally* . . . I was on my bike,' I tell her.

I'm embarrassed by her wilful misunderstanding. Especially with Justin just a few yards away.

'And how do you get on with him?' she asks me.

What can I say? That I'm not even sure if I *like* him? That I'm bound to let him down?

'I really don't know him that well,' I tell her carefully.

'You soon will,' she tells me. 'Our Justin is one of a kind . . .'

'Yes, I can imagine . . .'

My tea is trembling in the teacup as I hold it. Céline sees.

'Feeling wobbly, darling?'

'A little.'

'Trust me – you'll get used to it. Amazingly quickly,' she says.

'But I'm worried I can't do anything helpful . . .'

She looks me up and down in a rather appraising way.

'Nonsense. You could come in jolly useful, a slim little thing like you.'

I don't know what she means by this.

'Really, I don't know anything. Not even any First Aid.'

She flicks the ash from her cigarette with one expressive finger.

'You'll find that no one knows anything, darling. We make it up as we go.'

Justin comes across to us, and the conversation ends. He gives me my equipment. A boiler suit. A webbing belt with a message pad. A gas mask, bigger than the civilian one. A whistle. Rather perplexingly, a packet of luggage labels. And a shaded torch to hang on a strap round my neck. I put on the boiler suit.

'You'll patrol with me tonight, Livia,' he tells me.

The yellow alert is sounding. A line from Eliza's story-book comes sliding into my mind.

And they set out into the forest at one point and another, there where they saw it to be thickest.

We go up the stairs and out into the moonlit dark of the street.

41

The others head off in different directions. Now, it's just him and me.

We walk down Hamilton Street towards the shelter there. The red alert sounds, the wailing siren. Doors are flung open; the street is full of people, rushing to the shelter. Justin looks out for stragglers and for anyone who needs help. I carry bags, take children's hands. For a while, it's all panicky, urgent.

And suddenly, the streets are empty.

'I'll show you the other shelters,' he tells me.

'Yes. Thank you.'

And then he's quiet, and I don't know how to fill in the silence between us.

It comes to me that London is like a foreign country in

the blackout – lit only by chilly blue moonlight. We have our shaded torches, but we still stumble a lot as we walk – there are so many random bits of rubble lying around. Above us, the ebony black of the sky, and a lavish scatter of stars, and the weaving searchlights, silver pencils that draw all over the dark. The man next to me is the only other living thing in the street.

There's a far-off droning, rapidly drawing nearer. My heart pounds. The planes are coming over. *Where are you? Where are you?* We hear guns in the distance opening up, shooting up at the planes. And missing, always missing. There's the whistle and thud of a bomb, way off to our right, not on our patch. A little scream forms in my throat, but I manage to swallow it down.

He shows me some of the other shelters – Elm Road, Howlett Street, Fountain Place.

We walk up Hurtwood Road. A heavy building looms – a deeper black against the night. I recognise the building: this is Hurtwood School, one of several local schools that were closed at the start of the Blitz.

'Hurtwood's a rest centre,' Justin tells me. 'It's just outside our sector.'

I know that the rest centres take in people with nowhere else to go, whose homes are uninhabitable.

'Right. I'll remember,' I tell him.

'The trouble is – some people are using the place as a shelter,' he says.

'That worries you?'

He nods. 'There are folk who seem to believe they'll be

safe there during the raids. The building's old, of course, and it has those big, solid walls. I've heard people say that it's stood all this time, it'll stand for a few more years yet.'

'You can understand them thinking that, I suppose—'

'But it doesn't work like that. It offers no protection at all.'

His voice is abrupt, and I chew my lip: I know I've said the wrong thing.

'It's an obvious landmark,' he goes on. 'And it's right next door to the goods yard. If they got that in their sights, the whole damn street could go up.'

I tell him what I've noticed – how people always have such faith in their chosen places of shelter.

'I suppose you have to believe you're safe somewhere, or how could you bear it?' I say.

He doesn't respond. And I find myself thinking, with a shudder: *Is that also true of me? Do I have a misplaced faith in our shelter?*

'What about St Michael's?' I ask him.

'It's safe enough . . . The truth is, there aren't all that many places that could withstand a direct hit. Well – apart from those deep shelters the government somehow neglected to build . . .' There's a shred of bitterness in his voice. 'But Hurtwood School is something else – it's a sitting target,' he tells me.

We walk for a while without talking then, and I feel so stupidly shy.

It's quiet here. The bombers have all passed over: they're bombing the docks, as so often. You can hear the distant clamour, the thunder of bombs, the crack of guns, and in the east, there's a scarlet haze of burning in the sky. There's a small night wind, like a long indrawn breath.

I clear my throat.

'I never thanked you,' I tell him. 'For what you did in the crypt. For what you did for Polly. She was so grateful. We all were.'

He turns slightly towards me. But it's dark, and I can't read his expression.

'I shouldn't have done what I did,' he says.

This surprises me.

'Well, the man didn't bother us again . . .'

He shakes his head.

'I shouldn't have hit him – though God knows I wanted to. I could have stopped him without doing that. I shouldn't have lost it like that. You shouldn't have had to see that, and nor should your children,' he says.

I'm surprised how open he is. I realise he's embarrassed by his behaviour: that he worries I'll think worse of him because he lashed out at the man.

'I don't think any major damage was done,' I say lightly.

Another silence, dense with thought; as though he's wondering whether to tell me something.

But I don't find out what he's thinking. Because as we walk down Bedford Street, past a row of small terraced houses, we notice a wash of pale-yellow light that's leaking under a door.

'D'you know who lives there?' Justin asks me.

I think of an old woman I've seen standing in her

window, or shuffling along the pavement, making her way to the shops.

'I know her by sight. She's elderly, but not housebound. I don't know her name . . .'

Justin knocks.

There's a scuffling sound: the old woman comes to the door. Her face is seamed with age, and she has a thin fuzz of pale hair. She raises a hand to her face, in a small gesture of confusion: the bones in her hands are delicate as harp strings. Loneliness hangs about her, like something you could touch or smell, distinctive as a mothball scent. Behind her, the frenetic tweeting of a canary in a cage.

'Are you going to the shelter, ma'am?' says Justin.

She stares at him blankly. She doesn't reply.

'Can you tell me if it's Tuesday or Wednesday?' she says then.

'It's Saturday night,' he tells her.

'Oh, I thought it was Tuesday,' she says.

Her rheumy eyes blink rapidly.

I can see through the hallway into her parlour. This is the poorest room I've ever seen. There are only a few sticks of furniture – a table, two rickety chairs; a naked light bulb hanging from the ceiling. The canary is in a birdcage on the table, but you can see the white glimmer of bird shit, where she's let him fly round the room.

'I think you should go to the shelter, ma'am,' says Justin. 'Mrs Ripley here can take you.'

I take a step towards her, with my most encouraging

smile, pleased to do something helpful. But maybe I've alarmed her. She shrinks a little away.

'Can I take my bird?' she asks him.

He shakes his head.

'Sorry, ma'am, you can't do that. I'm sure he'll be safe here when you get back.'

'Why do I need to go then? If he'll be safe here?' There's a sudden brief vigour to her, like the quick sulphur flare of a match. 'If the bird will be safe here, tell me, why wouldn't I be?'

There's the ghost of a smile on Justin's face.

'So we can't persuade you?' he says.

She shakes her head.

'I don't like to leave the bird. Not with all these bloody bombs going off. He could get frightened here, all on his lonesome,' she says.

'All right, then,' says Justin. 'Good night and good luck. Oh – and would you be good enough to check the blackout round your front door . . .'

We walk away.

I feel shaken. The elderly woman has shocked me: her poverty, the bleakness of her empty, desolate rooms. She's doubtless had a long life of mindless, back-breaking work, yet this is all she has to show for it: a table, a canary, a couple of chairs. I hadn't known that people lived like this.

'What is it, Livia?' Seeing something in my face, perhaps – though it's hard to read anyone's expression in the moonlight.

'Oh – nothing really . . .'

He might be shocked in his turn, if he knew how sheltered my own life has been.

We arrive back at St Michael's and Justin leads me past the vicarage, through the graveyard.

'Where are we going?' I ask him.

'To check that your daughters are fine.' His voice more gentle now.

In the church, all the lights of the distant raid are shining through the stained glass, and colouring things strangely – there's a cold blue laid on the altar, a stone angel washed red as blood.

The crypt is hushed, except for the sounds of snoring and the clack of knitting needles. Aggie is awake and doing her crochet: she waves. Polly and Eliza are curled up under their blankets, asleep.

I turn to Justin, grateful.

'Thank you . . .'

He takes me back to the post at the vicarage.

'Get some rest, Livia,' he tells me.

I lie on one of the camp beds, and doze. He wakes me with a cup of tea, and I meet the dispatch rider, Bobby Ainsley. He's about seventeen, and nervy and eager, with eyes as brown as cobnuts.

'Pleased to meet you, ma'am,' he says. He shakes my hand, very polite.

Then we patrol again.

It's colder now, and my fingers are frozen in spite of my gloves. The air is clear as gin, and frost glitters on the tarmac where the moonlight catches it. In the silence and the moonlight, it's as though no one lives here at all – as though London has been abandoned, and only wind walks on the broken pavements. How far away are we from that time? A week, a month, a year? How long before London becomes a ruin where no one can live any more?

I'm lost in my chilling vision. When he speaks again, it makes me jump.

'That thing we were talking about before,' he tells me.

He hesitates. He's silent for a long, tense moment. I wait.

'I don't have much patience with drunks. My father was one,' he says then. It's as though the words are wrung out of him.

I feel an adolescent nervousness. I don't know how to respond.

'That must have been so hard for you . . .'

My voice fades. In the silence of the street, our breathing, our footsteps, seem suddenly loud.

'It was. It was very hard,' he tells me. 'I despised him really. You know, Livia – it isn't good to have a father who you despise.'

His openness startles me. I have another glimpse of the thing I saw when he landed the blow: a sense of that different, violent world he comes from. I remember what Aggie says – how everyone has their bag of stones. Something they have to drag behind them. Something to weigh them down.

'I can see it would be hard,' I say helplessly.

I don't know how to continue this conversation, and he says nothing more.

*

At the All Clear, we head back to the vicarage.

For tonight, at least, the old woman and her bird should be perfectly safe. It's been a quiet night in our borough.

In our basement room, people are gathering their things together.

'Thank you, all of you,' says Justin.

Céline is peeling off her boiler suit to reveal a lilac twinset and a single strand of pearls.

'So how was it, Liv?' she asks me.

'Fine – though it seemed to last for months. And what about you?'

'All lovely and calm,' she tells me. 'Though I did help a woman to get to the Elm Road shelter. She had about twenty-nine children – they just seemed to keep on coming. I got to carry the baby, and very nice he was too.' She smiles, she has a dreamy look. 'I briefly considered abduction. It's that smell of Johnson's Baby Powder – it has the strangest effects . . .'

Will I ever be like Céline, I wonder – so easy with it all?

She loops a silk scarf round her throat.

'Cheerio then, darling. Sleep tight, don't let the bed bugs bite.'

My body is drenched with tiredness. I think, *At least it's over now.* But everything is slowed in me, and it takes me a moment to realise that I'm utterly mistaken – that, far from being over, it has only just begun.

42

'What was it like, Mum?' asks Polly at breakfast.

I tell them about the old woman and the canary.

'And was everything all right with Auntie Aggie?' I ask.

'It was fine,' says Polly.

Eliza nods agreement. 'Auntie Aggie and me did cat's cradles. And we had figgy biscuits to eat.'

. After breakfast, I go back to bed. In spite of my exhaustion, for a while I can't sleep. Images – feelings – from the night are passing through my mind. The old woman and her loneliness. Justin's half-glimpsed face in the dark, and the shame he seemed to feel, when we talked about the man he hit in the crypt. Céline's voice, her flower scent, her scarlet fingernails.

At last, sleep blots out everything.

*

Over the next few days, I start to adapt to my new life.

I know I will have to run my household differently. I shall do a lot less housework, and concentrate on putting food on the table, and being as alert as I can for the nights when I work. My arm is much better now, though I keep it bandaged.

I learn a lot of new things. How to put out incendiaries with a stirrup pump, or even with my tin helmet. How to do basic First Aid – the recovery position, stopping bleeding, dealing with shock. I help people to the shelters – carrying bundles, giving a hand to the old. Sometimes you have to blow your whistle and urge people to get a move on, which makes me feel rather like the hockey mistress at school. I think Céline enjoys this part – hurrying people along in her seductive, resonant voice, which belongs in a glamorous nightclub, not on these fractured, frantic streets.

Mostly I patrol with Justin. I suspect he thinks I need someone to keep an eye on me, that he doesn't yet trust me to be competent.

On Monday night, in Cross Street, I have to handle my first dead body.

There's something on the pavement that looks like a pile of old clothes. Justin moves his torch across it. Behind us, the crumbling façade of a house that was recently bombed.

I hear my sharp intake of breath.

'Oh God, Justin . . .'

The beam of light falls on an open eye – unblinking, glazed with black blood. This heap of rags is an old man, lying entirely still, his head at the wrong angle, his face

280

lacerated. There's broken masonry beside him: he must have been hit when bricks from the bombed house dislodged themselves and fell as he was on his way to the shelter.

Justin kneels, I kneel beside him. As our torchlight falls on the body, I see a deep gash in the old man's head. Something half-solid, a bit like minced beef, is seeping out of the cut, greyish-red in the torchlight: something I don't want to look at.

'Right, Livia. Show me what you'd do,' says Justin.

I feel slightly sick. I take the man's wrist, which is smooth like fabric, and chilly. I feel for a pulse. There's nothing.

'No pulse, I think. But can you make sure?' I ask him.

What if I made a mistake? What if this were to happen when Justin wasn't here beside me, and I sent a person still living to the mortuary? The thought appals me.

Justin shows me how to mark the man's forehead, to show that he has died, and he writes a tag to tie to his wrist that says where he was found. The luggage labels we carry, it seems, are used to label the dead. Everything has a new function in this disordered world we live in.

'Stay with him,' Justin tells me.

He goes to try to flag down a mortuary van.

He's in luck. Moments later, a van pulls up, and two young women pile out and take the body.

'Poor old geezer. That's awfully sad,' says one of the women. She has a wholesome Girl Guide voice and a concerned expression. She wipes the layer of brick dust from the windscreen with her sleeve. 'Well, there you go, Reverend. Good night, you two. Stay safe now.'

As the van drives off, Justin shines his torch on the ground in front of the wheels, to be sure they don't get punctured on the debris in the street.

For an hour or two, the thought of the old man – his cold, still hand, his lonely, meaningless death – these things trouble me. But after that, I don't really think about him any more. It's astonishing what you can get accustomed to.

On Tuesday, I write to Hugo. Several days have passed now since the night when I was bombed. I can't postpone this any more.

I think carefully about this letter – though the beginning is straightforward.

Dear Hugo,

I wanted to let you know I got caught in the bombing last Thursday. I was on the way to the shelter. I was incredibly lucky – just some very minor injuries – though I do still feel a bit shaken up! My daughters were fine, thank goodness . . .

Then I sit for a moment, wondering how to phrase the next bit. Wanting to warn him in some way, afraid of hurting him too much: wanting him to be a little prepared. And the thought sneaks into my mind: *Will I be able to do this? Or will I manage to do it – then find I can't bear what I've done?*

In the end, I settle for something vague and evasive.

I can still come a week on Friday, but I may not able to stay very long.

    With love,

    Livia

It's over a week; and a week is a very long time. Will he and I still be alive then?

I mark the envelope *Personal*.

I take the letter to the post box, though goodness knows if it will reach him. I picture it travelling towards him through the ruined city and carried by the postman along Paternoster Row, past the premises of all the other publishing houses, and landing on the doormat at Ballantyne & Drummond. Miss Cartwright taking it into his office and putting it down on his desk. His hands opening up my envelope – and I feel a thrill in my stomach, thinking of his hands. And then a presentiment of sadness wells up in me like tears.

I get to know the other wardens. There's Sebastian, who's polite and gracious, but keeps himself to himself. He has nerves of steel, Céline tells me: he once stitched up a gash in his own leg, when off on one of his treks. And there's Esme, who's very resourceful. On Wednesday night, she corners me when the men are out of the room. Her voice is hushed, conspiratorial. She's made some camiknickers, she says, from some scraps of parachute silk from an unexploded landmine; they worked out nicely, there's fabric left over, and would I like some as well? *You bet* . . . And then there's Lennie, who I don't warm to.

He always calls me Lovely Livia, in a rather sardonic way, which I find annoying. I'm convinced that he despises me, just from the way he looks at me, his shadowed, sceptical gaze.

Céline speaks a little about her own colourful life. She'd been married to a nightclub owner, who'd been unremittingly unfaithful.

'He'd have fucked anything with a pulse,' she tells me. ''Scuse my language, darling . . . Though, to be frank, the pulse was optional once he'd been at the Rémy Martin . . .'

Despite this dispiriting experience, her love of men seems undimmed. We're leaving the vicarage together when a couple of firemen come sauntering past, and she looks them up and down, a lascivious glint in her eye.

'Ooh, aren't they gorgeous? There's something about a fireman.' Her face lost in a sweet reverie. 'I'd love to have a fireman of my very own,' she says.

Sometimes she astonishes me.

'There was a woman in labour in Trinity Road,' she tells me on the next Sunday at the All Clear.

'Oh, goodness me. What happened?'

'She couldn't make it to the shelter – the contractions were coming too close. I sent Bobby on his bicycle to call the midwife, Miss Tate.'

Céline takes out her compact and studies herself in the mirror. I wait, fascinated.

'I'm afraid that Cordelia Tate is a little bit nervous, poor lamb. There was quite a big bang, rather close, and she made a grab for the gas-and-air. She just slumped there, grinning inanely. I could see there was nothing for it, and I delivered the baby myself.'

'Céline – you are *amazing* . . . And did it go all right?'

She pulls out a silver Coty lipstick, slicks colour onto her mouth; shrugs slightly.

'So-so,' she tells me. 'Mother and baby are doing fine – the midwife, not so good.'

I walk with Justin down a street of poor terraced houses. A bomb fell here a while ago – perhaps in the raid that nearly killed me: the front of one of the houses has been entirely sliced away. This is startling, it feels all wrong – the intimacy of it – that anyone can see straight in to other people's lives. And there's hardly anything in these rooms. Just a few sticks of furniture. A broken rocking-chair. A picture of our king that hangs askew on the wall. A mangle in the kitchen. A scrap of curtain that flaps in the wind, like a poor trapped broken-backed bird. There's something so naked about the sight.

We stand and stare for a moment. I remember the old woman with the canary. I wonder how many rooms across London look as bleak as this. There's a whole world I'm ignorant of – all these people who have almost nothing, who live such limited lives.

And also, if I'm honest, at the very edge of my mind, there's a little bat's-wing of a thought – quick, secret, illicit. *If only I had my camera.*

I glance at Justin. He's frowning.

'From those who have not,' he says.

He's speaking quietly, under his breath – but I'm struck by the anger that roughens his voice.

I remember a line from one of the Gospels, something Jesus once said. A harsh thing. *To those who have, more shall be given, and from those who have not, even what they have shall be taken away* . . . I think of Hugo Ballantyne, his Savile Row suit, gold cufflinks; the house in the country, the cocktails, the room at the Balfour Hotel. And I think of the sparse life these people lived here; how now even that is gone.

Justin turns to me. His face is ardent in the moonlight.

'We can't carry on like this,' he says; and I know he doesn't just mean the bombing, the war. 'These terrible divisions. A country run by the rich for the rich. So many of our citizens living such impoverished lives. After the war, it all has to change. It *has* to.'

His eyes blaze with impossible dreams. At least, to me they seem impossible.

A hymn we used to sing at school comes sliding into my mind. For all I know, my children still sing it.

> *The rich man in his castle,*
> *The poor man at his gate,*
> *God made them, high or lowly,*
> *And ordered their estate . . .*

'But – what can we do about it?' I ask him. 'Isn't it just how things are? I mean, there will always be poverty, won't there? Doesn't it say so in the Bible? *The poor you have with you always . . .*'

Then I feel stupid and presumptuous, for quoting the Bible at *him*.

He turns towards me. In the moonlight, I can see all the bones of his face, illumined, or starkly shadowed. He looks determined and stern – even a little angry. It's as though I've disappointed him – as though he hoped for more from me.

'Of course it can change.' His voice is urgent, as though his desire could make it so. 'If there's the will, of course it can change. We can change everything after the war. We have to believe that.'

But I can't think as far ahead as *after the war* – can't even think beyond the end of the night. Living for the All Clear – for that moment when the bombers wheel round and head towards the Channel, black-feathered birds of ill omen that flee from the light of the dawn.

Another night over.

The Blitz consumes us. We're not very aware of what's happening anywhere else in the world. Though we do hear about the battles in Africa, where Phoebe suspects that Howard, her husband, is serving. And we know that the Atlantic convoys that bring us food and munitions are under attack from deadly U-boats – silent and invisible, circling shark-like under the sea.

On Tuesday afternoon, I join Phoebe at the school gate.

She looks older, and so weary, with smudges like bruises under her eyes. This life is leaving its scars on us.

She seems distracted, watching the children surging out of the school – though Freddie and Bill are with her already.

'You're meeting someone, Phoebe?'

She nods. 'The little Munroes.'

'Oh.' I feel a wariness.

'Did you hear about Gladys Munroe?' she asks me.

There's something fractured in her voice. I feel that familiar tilt of the heart, the presaging of pain.

'Gladys? No – what about her?'

She's someone I pass the time of day with sometimes – a kindly, quiet woman with a soft, pale fall of hair.

'Frank's been reported missing. Frank, her eldest. Lost at sea,' says Phoebe. 'His ship went down. A U-boat.'

'Oh God. How awful,' I say.

My words seem so empty. I feel my eyes filling up.

'They're heroes, those lads,' says Phoebe. She sounds angry, but I don't know who she's angry with. 'Absolute bloody heroes. When you think what they have to go through to keep us fed and supplied.'

'Yes. Yes, they are,' I say.

It's such a grim death – to be lost out there, in the pitiless wastes of the sea.

'And Gladys? How is she?' I ask.

Phoebe shakes her head miserably.

'She just sits in his bedroom and cries her heart out. She keeps on saying, *If only I could bury him, and know he was resting in peace. If only I could have him back, and lay him to rest in the ground* . . . That's all she can think of.'

I have a letter from Hugo.

He says that he's so very sorry that I was caught in the bombing: it must have been absolutely terrifying. He hopes I'm making an excellent recovery. Is there anything he can do to help, just anything at all? I must let him know. And he's very much looking forward to our meeting on Friday at four, when he hopes he'll be able to find a way to offer me some comfort . . .

He finishes: *All my love, Hugo.*

I run my finger over that exuberant signature of his, which somehow looks so very male, so very assured. This gives me a bittersweet feeling. Rather more bitter than sweet, because of what I am going to tell him.

43

He touches my bandaged arm with one delicate finger.

'So, Livia, what's this?'

'It's nothing to worry about – it isn't broken.'

'You poor poor darling. Poor Livia. How completely vile,' he says. 'And your daughters? Are they all right?'

'Yes, thank God. Though I didn't find out for a while, and that was awful. I came round in the hospital. I didn't know then if the girls had survived.'

'Jesus Christ,' he says. 'Jesus Christ, Livia.'

He takes out two cigarettes, lights them.

He's so warmly sympathetic. Yet there's something different between us – just a little thing, a weed growing up through a crack. He doesn't seem quite the same to me – he looks somehow smaller, older. It's as though I'd forgotten exactly what he looked like, or as though his appearance has altered in the time since we last met. This disconcerts me.

But perhaps it's not Hugo who's different: perhaps *I* am the one who has changed.

'So how have your daughters coped with all the upset?' he asks me. 'Especially your little one, who you were so worried about?'

I can tell he's forgotten her name.

'They're fine. Though naturally it was all a bit alarming for them. And what about your family? How are Daphne and Giles?'

'Not so bad,' he tells me. 'Well, Giles is absolutely thriving. He'll be off to Harrow in September, of course. He's shooting up so fast, I barely recognise him . . . But poor Daphne's fed up in the country. She's bored quite out of her mind. She misses her life in London.' He smiles indulgently. 'You know, popping into Selfridges. Her favourite Sole Bonne Femme in the River Room at the Savoy . . .'

I nod and smile, as though I *do* know. Though I've never been to either of these places.

The waiter brings our martinis.

'To you, darling. And to survival,' says Hugo.

We drink.

'Good news on the book,' he tells me. 'It's all coming along very nicely.'

He opens his briefcase, shows me the cover. It's a picture I'm very proud of – a perfect English rose, the petals smooth as vellum, the flower shaped like a chalice; on one of the petals, a luminous raindrop. Across the image: *Summer Gardens of England* and my name.

'It's beautiful,' I tell him.

'We aim to please,' he says, smiling a little suggestively.

I study the image for a moment. I think of Polesden Lacey, of that summer afternoon.

'When I look at that picture,' I say, 'I can't quite believe that I took it. It's like something from another life – something from so long ago . . .' I suck in smoke, not quite able to put the thought into words. 'All those things seem so remote from me – you know, flowers and summer gardens. I can't quite remember how roses smell, can't imagine the scent any more.' I try to smile, but my mouth feels stiff. 'I think too much horrible brick dust must have got into my throat.'

Something crosses his face, when I say I can't remember the scent of roses. A wariness. I realise that he senses that something has changed between us. Maybe he even guesses what I have come here to say.

'I'm glad you're happy with the cover,' he says carefully.

'Yes, it's really lovely, thank you . . .'

We are quiet for a moment.

The bar is almost empty. There are the usual hovering waiters, and a couple talking quietly in the corner – the man in RAF uniform, the girl with Hiltoned hair and a frock of clingy apricot silk. The pianist is playing softly: *Dream a little dream of me.*

I clear my throat. Trying to edge towards the thing I've vowed to say.

292

'I made a decision, when I was in the hospital,' I tell him. 'To do a bit more for the war effort. I'm a part-time warden now.'

He's putting the cover away in his briefcase. Now he looks up at me, startled.

'*You*, Livia?'

It's just that he's concerned for me. He cares for me, wants to protect me. But I can't help thinking, *Why does everyone say that? Why is everyone shocked? Why do they all think I'm so bloody fragile?*

'Yes. Me.'

His eyes on me. A small frown.

'Livia – are you sure that's a good decision? You must feel shaken, of course. You shouldn't do anything precipitate.'

'Yes, I'm sure,' I tell him.

He puts his hand on my arm.

'You don't have to do it, Livia, darling.' His voice rather urgent. 'You don't have to put yourself at risk like that. To put yourself in the line of fire, as it were.'

'No, I know I don't. But it wasn't a snap decision. Someone had asked me to do it and I told him no at first.'

'*Someone?*'

I can see him wondering about this man who'd approached me: whether he's the reason I seem so different tonight. This is so entirely mistaken that it might make me laugh out loud – if only I wasn't feeling so unhappy.

'He's just the vicar at the local church,' I say.

Hugo nods, as though relieved.

'Being bombed was so awful, it made me think about things,' I tell him. 'I felt I wanted to live differently – to contribute in some way . . .'

He nods but doesn't say anything. I see the speck of doubt that floats in his eye.

I sip my cocktail, feel the heat of the fire on my skin. I'm intensely aware of his closeness – the curve of his hand on the cocktail glass, his vetiver scent, his warm, heavy body. I remember the sweetness of those brief hours in the bed with the blue satin quilt. Do I have to do this? Am I just punishing myself, when really there's no need? When we could just carry on with our discreet affair, snatching some happiness while we can in this frantic, burning city?

He puts his hand on my arm.

'Darling – shall we go upstairs?' His voice a little tentative.

Yes, I think, maybe we should: it might be easier to talk there . . . Yet I know if I go to his room, I'll slide straight into his arms. Nothing could stop me.

I clear my throat.

'No, Hugo. No . . . I wanted to say . . .' The words like pebbles on my tongue. 'I feel I can't . . . any more. I can't do this . . . You know, see you like this . . .'

He studies me, trying to read me. Then he gives a small shake of the head.

'Well, that's very sad, Livia. I can't persuade you? You're sure?'

'Yes, I'm sure. I'm sorry, so sorry. It was . . . lovely. You made me feel so different. It was . . . so good,' I say.

'For me too,' he says.

He looks wistful. But his voice is surprisingly easy.

And it suddenly comes to me that he might be rather relieved. Sad – yet relieved at the same time. That he wasn't entirely sure where our affair was going: if it might lead to complexities that he would prefer to avoid.

We sip our cocktails in a tense, rather miserable silence. I have a pain in my throat, as though saying these things has hurt me.

Then he shifts, leans back in his chair, a little away from me. It's a kind of punctuation – as though we are entering a new phase, a different kind of friendship.

'So. Livia the warden.' He smiles.

I'm grateful to him. This is easier ground.

I tell him about the woman and the canary. He listens attentively, amused.

'I admire you for doing this, Livia. Even though I'd still rather you didn't . . .'

But I sense he's not so bothered now that I'm putting myself at risk: that he feels less involved with me already.

'I'm going to find it difficult. I'm not practical at all . . .' I think of Céline. 'The others – they're all so good at First Aid and delivering babies and so on . . .'

He looks at me thoughtfully.

'Livia – have you thought of photographing some of the things you see?'

'Yes, I have. Often.' I find myself thinking of the house with all its front peeled away – the sticks of furniture, the scrap of curtain flapping. How I yearned to capture the startling emptiness of the rooms that spoke of the harsh lives that were lived there. 'But are you allowed to? Aren't there rules about that?'

'Well, yes, there are – but I don't think anyone bothers too much about them, to be honest. Think about it, Livia. These times need witnesses. The world needs to see what's happening here. *America* needs to see . . . *Picture Post* is buying a lot of pictures from London,' he says.

I know that *Picture Post* is a legendary American journal. I'm startled by what he's implying – excited, in spite of myself.

'Oh, are they? But they wouldn't take *my* pictures, would they?'

His smile says, *Here she goes again.*

'It's like I'm always telling you – all you need is confidence. You need to be more ambitious. You have such a talent, Livia. You could make good use of it now.'

I drain the last drop from my glass.

'Can I get you another?' he asks me.

'No, thank you.' I pick up my bag. 'I'm sorry, I really ought to get back . . .'

He doesn't press me. Though something illicit in me is rather wishing that he would: wishing he'd be insistent, that he wouldn't accept what I've said, that he wouldn't let me leave like this.

'I'll be in touch about the book. And, Livia – take those photographs.'

On the pavement, he hails a taxi.

As the taxi pulls in to the kerb, he kisses me lightly on the mouth. Desire surges through me.

I turn to climb into the taxi, then go back and kiss him again. He pulls me close against him. When I finally break from him, I'm breathless.

Once I'm in the taxi, I turn to wave, but he is walking away.

The cabbie sets off, driving cautiously, with dipped and shaded headlights. We pass through the ravaged city. Some streets are still untouched, unmarked; elsewhere, there are ruins, heaps of rubble, rafters sticking up like bones, the spires of churches toppled; and everything glazed with blue moonlight. I find that I am crying.

Why am I doing this? Why do I feel I have to do this?

I remind myself it's because I promised. Because I made a promise to a God I'm not sure I believe in, that I would give up Hugo if He gave me my children back. Does that make any sense at all?

The cabbie glances in his rear-view mirror.

'Now, don't you go sobbing your heart out, ma'am. I bet he isn't worth it. I bet he doesn't deserve you. There's plenty more fish in the sea.'

He must have seen our parting on the pavement, and drawn his own conclusions.

'Sorry. Please don't worry.' I blow my nose, embarrassed. 'Really – I'll be as right as rain in a moment.'

But the ruined city through the window is blurred and smudged by my tears.

I don't know if the cabbie is right – don't know what to think about Hugo and me. Was this a wrongful affair with a man forbidden to me – something illicit and sinful, that only happened because of the war? Something that *shouldn't* have happened? Or was it a startling, random gift that helped me to endure all this, that brought me back to life again?

Which was it? I don't know. Or was it both these things?

I'm home well before the sirens sound.

That night, in the crypt, I dream about him. We're in that dazzling dreamscape – the unnatural, sulphurous countryside, the livid, purple clouds, immense skies weighing on us. He's ahead of me, walking a narrow white road that winds off into the distance. I'm yearning for him, desperate to reach him. But I try to call, and no sound comes; I walk, but my limbs are heavy; and with every step I take on the road he seems to be further away.

44

On Saturday night, I attend my first major incident as a warden.

I'm patrolling with Justin when there's a flash that lights up the whole sky, then a shuddering explosion. As we pick ourselves up and head towards the area where the bomb fell, we see the flare of a fire above the rooftops. We run towards it, stumbling over debris.

We round the corner into Byron Square.

'Jesus.' Instinctively, I put up my hands to shield my face.

There's a great fan of flame, maybe thirty feet high. Its brightness is astonishing, lighting up the buildings on either side of the street, so you can see every brick, every facing, as you would on a clear spring morning. There's a sickly sweet smell of coal gas, which thickens as we draw near.

'They've hit the gas main,' says Justin. 'Right, Livia. Go to the post and report it. If you see Bobby on the way, you can leave the message with him. Then come and meet me back here. Can you do that?'

'Yes.'

I run to start with, then walk: the street is treacherous with broken bricks. I get there quickly, make the call, head back to Byron Square.

At the scene, the fire crew are there already, and are laying out their hoses. I wonder if my call was really necessary – you must be able to see this fire for miles. I think with a sense of horror that the flames will attract more bombers.

A chandelier flare is floating down from the sky, with a beautiful, deathly radiance. There's an almighty crash as every gun opens up on the flare. The noise slams into you, pummels you.

I find Justin, nod, to show I did what he asked. He puts his hand on my shoulder.

Well done, he mouths at me.

Red tracer bullets are being lobbed up in a long arc from the ground, so the gunners can see where they're firing. Every pump starts up at once, the roar of their engines enveloping everything. The ground shakes. And then the guns again, firing this time at the bombs. Missing and missing and missing.

A bomb falls close, the blast sucking at you, as though it would turn you inside out. The windows in the buildings on the right side of the street all shatter; the splinters of glass fall out over the street and lacerate the hoses, so water spurts out uselessly where the rubber is gashed. The firemen are shouting, cursing, though I can't hear what they're saying. Above us, a pigeon is flying, its pale wings rimmed with bright fire; it circles, dazed and helpless, then falls down into the flame.

There's a great wind, pushing us, tugging at us. I hadn't known this – that fire could make such a wind. It blows enormous swirling flames that come scything over the road, then are suddenly blotted out by smoke – each flame shutting off suddenly, then sweeping out red again. The heat is searing. The smoke rolls over us in hot waves that make our eyes stream with water. For a moment, we stand there, helpless before the greedy extravagance of the fire. The air is full of soot and dust, and the firemen are coughing, their faces black and scarlet in the firelight. With every breath, you drag briars into your throat.

'Justin. Look . . .'

An old woman is picking her way along the pavement towards us, a delicate black-paper cut-out against the red of the fire. She must have been driven out of her home by the conflagration. She's hunched over, taking the tiniest steps. She has a walking stick that she *tap tap taps* on the pavement, and she presses a scrap of handkerchief across her nose and her mouth.

'Go with her, Livia,' Justin shouts at me. 'Get her to the shelter. Then come back here. I want to check along the street, make sure that everyone's gone.'

I rush up to the woman, take her arm.

'I'll come with you,' I tell her. 'We'll go to the Elm Road shelter.'

She peers at me. I repeat myself, mouthing the words, but she plainly can't hear me at all. But she's grateful, she leans into me. I feel the slight pressure of her thin hand on my arm.

It suddenly comes to me – that it's just as Justin once told me: I'm not trying to keep myself safe, and I don't feel afraid.

As I open the door of the shelter, a hot breath of stale air comes out. I help the old woman down the steps. The whole structure seems to shake with the percussion of gunfire above. There's a single light bulb, flickering. The shelter is packed with people, and the air is rank with the smells of sweat and urine and fear.

I find a corner for the old woman, and settle her.

'Bless you, duck,' she says to me.

Leaving, I notice a girl and a soldier in uniform, who are standing in the stairwell. The girl is leaning back against the wall of the shelter: the man's legs are either side of hers, and he has his hands on her hips. You can tell that they've been kissing; her lipsticked mouth is blotched with red. Her hair is ebony-dark and undone, and falls over her face and her closed eyes, and shakes and seems to tremble with the trembling of the wall. The two of them are oblivious, lost in one another – drugged, as though none of this were happening round them, as though they were alone.

In that moment, I have such a yearning for Hugo.

When I get back to the site of the fire, it's raged further on down the street. The ambulance has arrived, and two men with a stretcher rush past me, a twisted, burned man or woman between them, coughing up gouts of dark blood. The other wardens have come now, and I join them knocking on doors to try to clear the area. The firemen are fighting bravely, but the fire comes hungrily on.

45

It's so sweet, sitting here in my kitchen: the horrors of last night recede, seem like a nightmarish dream. I relish the peace of this moment. Outside, my garden, rinsed with light; the breathy murmur of pigeons; on the terrace, house-sparrows pecking, flimsy, the colour of shadow or earth. In here, Hector's somnolent purring, and the smell of hot buttered toast. And my children, eating breakfast, the sunlight shining on their hair. I could just sit and sit and gaze at them and never move again.

After breakfast, the girls go off to the parlour – Polly to practise, Eliza to play with her London Town.

Later, I'm in the dining room, ironing bed linen on blankets I've spread on the dining-room table, when Polly seeks me out. Her eyes blaze.

'Mum, I've had enough of it. All that junk of Eliza's. When I go to practise, I have to wade through all her rubbish,' she says.

I feel contrite.

'But, Polly – she gets so upset if I tell her to tidy it up, and it isn't worth the trouble. Not with all the bombing and so on . . .'

'You always let her get away with *everything*,' says Polly. 'And now you're blaming *Hitler*.'

'That really isn't true . . .'

But maybe it is.

She has a perplexed expression. It's the way she looks when she's baffled by the waywardness of what happens: when life frustrates her, because it refuses to conform to her rules.

'Anyway, it's embarrassing, Mum. What if somebody visited? What if that precious vicar of yours came round, and all her rubbish was out?'

'He's not *my* vicar, Polly. I scarcely know him.'

She looks sceptical.

There's a sudden stench of scorching. The iron's been left in one place for too long: there's a scorch mark on the pillowslip. *Damn*. Scorching always upsets me – the ugly brown stain, the smell of damage. I fold the pillowslip carefully and put it to one side.

'Sweetheart.' I try to make her understand. 'I'm so busy, being a warden.'

'Yes, well, I had noticed. That's why I didn't ask you to hear my spellings,' she says.

'What spellings were these, sweetheart?'

'I wanted to ask you to hear them, but I didn't feel that I could. And we had a test on Friday, and I only got four out of ten.'

'Oh, Polly, you should have asked me.'

'How could I – when you're so busy?' A miserable mottled flush spreads over her face and her neck. 'Sometimes I think you care about all that warden stuff more than you care about us.' Her voice is small and ragged.

'Polly, I don't, of course I don't . . .'

But I feel guilty. I resolve to talk to Eliza.

She's sitting on the hearthrug in the parlour, playing with her arrangement. In pride of place, there's the ark I found in the street, with some of her painted animals in a sunburst pattern around it. In her hand, she has a little brown bear, shaggy, the colour of cocoa; she's wondering where to place him.

It's dim in here: the windows are patched with plywood. I turn on the lamp on the piano; light spills like flower petals there, a tender marigold glow, but the rest of the room is shadowy – more like evening than morning.

I sit beside her.

'Eliza. I want to talk to you – about all this,' I say.

I gesture towards her creation.

'Oh good. It looks lovely, doesn't it, Mummy?'

She has a fat, happy smile.

And maybe she's right, I think, as I look at it. There's something so beguiling about this frail construction of hers.

The animals placed with such care, the intricate matchbox houses.

'That's Old Father Thames, and that's London Bridge,' she tells me. 'And here's the zoo, with the tigers and all the men with the guns.' There's a scrap of paper she's crayoned green, with her lions and tigers grouped there. 'And this is the crypt. We're in here . . .' She points to a building-block church, with a cross made from lollipop sticks, Sellotaped together.

I notice her hands are grimy from playing here: the hearthrug needs sweeping again. There's dirt everywhere from last night's raid – a gritty soot from the chimney that's been loosened by the blast – and there are new fissures in the chimney breast. Our house is collapsing around us, and things are seeping in through the cracks – rain, cold, grit, brick dust. All manner of things coming in from outside that don't belong in a house.

I clear my throat.

'Eliza. I've let you play here for weeks now, but it's time to tidy it up.'

Her smile fades, a light extinguished. She turns to face me, outraged. Her pale eyes glitter with tears.

'*No*, Mummy.'

'Yes, sweetheart.'

'Polly's been on at you, hasn't she? But Polly's got her *whole bedroom* to be tidy in,' she says.

I think of Phoebe – thin-lipped, when she saw Eliza's creation. *Well, she's certainly gone a bit overboard on your parlour floor* . . . Of Aggie: *She'll run rings around you* . . . But I feel a great weariness. Does it really matter so much? I find I haven't the heart to insist, when it's all been built so lovingly.

'Well, listen carefully then. If you use up any more space, we won't be able to get in the parlour at all. So you must absolutely promise not to make it bigger, all right?'

'Yes, Mummy.'

I get up, feeling defeated.

I'm turning to leave the room, when something catches my eye. Something half-hidden in the shadow at the edge of the ribbon river: something she must have just added. Cold slides into my veins.

It's a music box, made of walnut, and standing on little clawed feet, with *Jewels* traced out in extravagant silvery letters on top. Sarah's jewel box.

I crouch down beside Eliza. My legs are weak as cotton wool.

'Eliza. Where did you get that?'

She sees where I am staring. She picks up the box and holds it close, as though scared I might snatch it away.

'I found it,' she tells me. 'It was packed away under my bed. I was very very tidy. I put all the other things back.'

I don't say anything.

She's looking at me anxiously, trying to gauge my reaction. Then she leans in close to me.

'Can I tell you a secret? A big big secret?' she says.

I nod.

She whispers in my ear. I feel her moth breath on my face.

'I think it belonged to a little girl, Mummy.'

I can't speak.

She's so close, I can see the fragments of marigold light in her eyes.

She turns back to the jewel box.

'It's like magic. When you lift the lid. Look, I'll show you,' she says.

She puts the box down on the floor. She's worked out how to undo the clasp. She raises the lid a little.

The music sings out – *Roses from the South*. Startling, stopping the heart. At once very familiar, and impossibly distant. The sound is rusty, rather irregular, and you can hear the whirring of the moving parts inside.

Eliza watches my face.

'It's lovely, isn't it, Mummy? Look, you can see all the little girl's things.'

She opens the lid wider.

Inside, it's lined with red velvet.

There's an elaborate glass necklace, the beads like little flowers and leaves. A frog encrusted with diamanté. A tiny pottery mouse – a present from me one Christmas. A dragonfly brooch with pink gems in the tips of its wings. A strand of seed pearls, given by an elderly great-aunt. A Christmas card trimmed with lace that shows an angel with lavender wings. All Sarah's treasures. The things are remarkably untarnished, as though they'd just been placed there.

Eliza touches the dragonfly with one scrupulous finger. As though she feels she shouldn't be doing this, but simply couldn't resist. Then she looks across at me, and frowns.

'Are you going to cry, Mummy? Your face looks funny,' she says.

'No, it's nothing, sweetheart.'

She seems to accept this, turns back to the box. The music is slowing down now, and she winds it up again.

'D'you think the little girl will mind if I play with the jewels?' she says. Rather reverently. 'If I'm very very careful?'

There's a hard knot of tears in my throat. I swallow.

'No, I don't think so. I think it was a little girl who lived a long time ago.'

I'm trying to sound casual, but there's a shake in my voice.

'Will she want them back?' she asks me.

'No. No, I don't think she will. You can have the box, sweetheart. And all the things inside. If you want to play with them.'

Should I have told her about Sarah? Should I tell her now? Is this my opening?

I'll tell her one day, tell both of them. This can't be unspoken for ever – they need to know their family story. But just now I *can't*, it's beyond me, my mouth couldn't shape the words.

She picks up the pearls, fastidiously, and drapes them over the leopard. The pearls have a subtle gleam in the marigold light of the lamp.

I leave her, go back to the kitchen, sit at the table. I feel the past brush against me, like a cool hand touching my face.

I think of a blue summer evening, in the parlour where Eliza is now. Remembering, I can smell lilac – there must have been lilacs in the room, releasing their heavy, powdery perfume. Perhaps Sarah had brought them in from the garden and put them into a vase. Outside, veils of dusk in the street, the sky a luminous cornflower colour, the ripple of a nightingale in one of the pollarded trees.

I was doing a jigsaw, Sarah was reading. But she held the jewel box on her lap, and now and then she traced her finger across the silvery word. The jewel box had been a gift from our grandmother for Sarah's eleventh birthday. Our grandmother was generous but erratic with her gifts, and this time, Sarah had done so very much better than me – receiving this wonderful, precious thing. While I, on my last birthday, had only been given a boring book of an improving kind, with a moral for every story. I was consumed with jealousy.

I sat there, my face shuttered, not speaking. I pretended to do my jigsaw, but really I was sulking.

Sarah looked up at me.

'You've been stuck on that bit for ages. D'you want some help?' she said.

I didn't reply.

'Livie, I *said* – do you want me to help you look for the piece?'

'No, I don't,' I told her curtly.

'Why are you being so horrid?'

I didn't reply.

'It's the jewel box, isn't it?' she said.

I was silent, but she knew my thought.

'Honestly, Livie. It doesn't have to be just *mine*,' she said. Her tone so sensible, rational. 'We can share it. Why ever not? There's no need to get so upset. It's stupid to sulk about it.'

She put the box on the floor between us and opened the lid. *Roses from the South* sang out.

'It's a waltz, from Vienna,' she told me. 'I can do the waltz, I know how.' She jumped up. 'Clemmie taught me at school . . . I'll show you.'

I shrugged. I tried to look as though I didn't care.

But Sarah pounced on me, pulled me up.

'This is how grown-ups do it. It's what they do, when they're falling in love. Look, I'll be the man, I'll lead you . . .'

She put her hand on my waist, and I could feel the heat of her skin. She took my other hand in hers. She whirled me round and round the room, and our braids swung out, and the skirts of our sprigged summer frocks, and all my bad temper left me and flew away like a bird. I remember the warmth of her hand against me, the musk of her hair, the scent of her breath; the music playing and playing, her eyes laughing. The smell of lilac, the nightingale. Through the window, the last bright gleam of the day.

But I was clumsy, I couldn't keep up, and trying to steer me, she lost the rhythm. We spun randomly, faster and faster, till we toppled and fell in a heap, giggling, a tangle of limbs and braided hair. We were laughing so much it hurt my stomach. While the music wound down, sounding strange, and making us laugh even more.

Eventually, we quietened. I could feel my heartbeat slow. Sarah sighed, a replete sigh, a sigh of pleasure.

'That's how you do it. That's how you dance,' she told me. 'Well, the first bit anyway. We were doing all right when we started. Before you fell over your feet.'

'It's difficult,' I told her. I rubbed at the stitch in my side.

'We need to practise, of course,' she told me. 'So we can get good at it, Livie. And one day we'll have those special dresses with really long swishy skirts that ladies have for dancing in. Imagine. It'll be heaven . . .'

She grinned at me, flushed, breathless. Thrilled by the thought of the future spooling out before her, bright and deliciously patterned as a bale of silk flung out.

'We'll go to such beautiful dances when we grow up, Livie,' she said.

Remembering this, I find that I am crying.

46

Elm Road is empty: all the people who wanted to go to the shelter must be there by now. Above us, the dentist's-drill stutter of planes – but they seem to be passing over.

Someone calls out from a doorway.

'Evening, Reverend. Evening, ma'am.' There's a hot smell of alcohol on the man's breath, a bleary note to his voice.

'You need to get to the shelter, sir. It's a bomber's moon,' says Justin.

We walk for a while in silence through the dense dark of the shadowy street: it's narrow, the moonlight doesn't penetrate here. Suddenly, shockingly, Justin slams his arm into my front. *He's hit me.* I'm too stunned to react for a moment.

'That could have been nasty,' he says, and slants the beam of his torch to the ground.

I look down. My feet are on the edge of a crater. It's deep, perilous – you can't see to the bottom – and there's a stink of sewage, where a drainage pipe must have cracked. I'd have fallen in, if he hadn't stopped me.

My heart is pounding. For the moment, I'm paralysed. He grabs my arm and pulls me back from the brink.

'Oh goodness. I didn't see it. Thank you.'

We move on carefully down the street, and my heart begins to quieten. I can feel the imprint of his fingers, from where he pulled at my arm.

There's a bit of a wind tonight, which rustles the litter and dust on the pavement. Above us, a tatter of cloud blows across the white face of the moon. You can hear the lurch of the gun barrage as it opens up in the distance.

Something has shifted between us, because he grabbed me like that. As though some barrier has been broken down, because we touched each other. I feel a little easier with him, and perhaps he feels this as well – because suddenly, out of nowhere, he starts to ask about me.

'So, Livia. Tell me about your family. Tell me about your children.'

There's no decision that I'm aware of – the words just come spiralling out. I must be disinhibited, after the shock of nearly falling in the crater.

'They worry me – both of them, really. Polly's still grieving for her father, and one of her school friends died in the bombing. She doesn't talk about it, but I think she's taken it hard. There's something despairing about her . . .'

'Poor kid,' says Justin.

'But it's my little one, Eliza, who disturbs me the most,' I tell him. 'She has such a vivid fantasy life. It's like the world she conjures up is more real to her than this one. And sometimes I hear her talking to people who aren't there. I feel that can't be healthy . . .'

He's silent for a moment. This isn't how people usually react – I think of Phoebe, leaping in with her explanations and theories. But Justin just thinks for a while, as we thread our way on down the street.

'I suppose people try to reassure you,' he says then. 'They tell you it's a way of coping, in these terrible times.'

'Yes.'

'There's something in that, of course. We all have our own ways of getting through – some stranger than others,' he tells me.

Immediately, I find myself wondering about *his* ways of coping. Prayer and reading the Bible, presumably. Sometimes, letting fly with his fists.

'Perhaps it's my fault,' I tell him. I think of Mrs Dixon. *It's important not to be too indulgent, Mrs Ripley.* 'I probably ought to be stricter. I shouldn't let Eliza get away with so much – I mean, she's taking up half the parlour floor with this town she keeps on building . . .'

He turns to me, and the colours of the lit-up sky glint briefly in his eyes – topaz, copper, crimson.

'You have so many ways to blame yourself, Livia.' I can't

see his face properly; I have to work out what he's feeling from the tone of his voice. But I can hear a kind of warmth in him – even a touch of amusement. 'Why do you always blame yourself for everything?'

Because I am to blame.

I don't answer.

There's a vast eruption in the distance – a long way off, towards the docks. I wait for the reverberations to die.

'But in a way, I can understand her,' I tell him. 'I'm probably rather the same.'

I think of that feeling I have of the past bleeding into the present. Of that strange, haunted moment in my darkroom. Of Eliza opening the jewel box, and my sense of the past leaking through. How my memories seem too vivid to me. Almost as though those things were still happening . . .

'I guess I have too much imagination as well,' I tell him. 'Things from my childhood seem too real to me . . . Especially living in that house . . .'

'I remember you told me it was where you lived as a child. I can see that might feel strange,' he says.

'It used to be fine, it wasn't a problem,' I tell him. 'Before Ronnie died. Before the bombing began . . .'

And I think, but don't add: *Before I opened up Sarah's old room.*

There's a wide white ribbon of moonlight down one side of the street, and we walk in it, close together, so we can see where we're going. I'm aware of the smell of him – a smell of work and sweat. Warm, masculine, somehow comforting.

317

He doesn't say anything. He often seems so restless – turbulent, losing his temper. But tonight there's a stillness to him.

I draw in a long, shaky breath.

'It's almost as though . . . I don't know how to put it . . . Justin – do you believe in *hauntings*? In – you know – the unquiet dead?' The phrase sounds literary and pretentious. And utterly unreal.

He considers this.

'Well, maybe. I believe in the world of spirit. That we're surrounded by the unseen. That there's so much more to life than what we see or hear,' he says.

We pass a block of Victorian mansion flats. Moonlight falls on the building, so it seems to be carved from ivory, a great cold lunar palace. You can hear the distant cacophony of bombs and explosions and guns, and far off over Stepney, the sky is red with burning. The street is utterly deserted, except for Justin and me. *Is this the end of the world? Is this what the end of things looks like – these broken buildings and moonlight and scattered corpses and raging fires, this city of ghosts and flame and ruin?*

I think of that moment when the clocks stopped.

'The night I got bombed, something happened.' My voice is a little thin thread. 'I heard a voice, or thought I heard it, telling me to go back. It was in my mind, but it wasn't *my* voice. I stopped and turned round, because of the voice, then the street seemed to fall on my head.' I clear my throat, which is suddenly thick. 'Later, I found out the bomb came down just a little further along. At exactly the place I'd have got to if only I hadn't turned back . . .'

It's the crucible of the night – the fear, the dark, the damage; and it's something about Justin and the way he waits for me. You end up saying so much more than you'd intended to say. I can feel pulses skittering off all over my body.

He doesn't speak for a while, and I know that he's musing on what I've told him. Turning it over in his mind and wondering how to respond.

'So – did this voice mean anything to you?' he says then. 'I mean, to you, personally?'

He's speaking quietly, lightly, as though playing around with the thought. As though his words are marbles that he slips from his pocket and holds out up to the light, to see the patterning in them.

I don't, *can't*, say anything.

He asks me again.

'Livia – who did you think was speaking these words?'

I don't reply. My heart is beating everywhere, down to the tips of my fingers.

The question hangs there between us in the moonlit dark of the street.

47

Tuesday afternoon. It's time I did some housework. Though it's hopeless, really – the house is coming apart at the seams, like a suit of worn old clothes. There are cracks that shouldn't be there; clocks I can't get going; doors that are wedged open and that won't be closed again. The front door is worst affected: the door frame must have shifted, and you have to slam it to shut it. Rain has dripped into the loft space where tiles are gone from the roof, and mould is blooming whitely across the ceilings below. The ominous fissure in the wall of the girls' old bedroom is widening, and the ceiling in there is sagging. There are draughts in the house that never used to be there: they eddy around our feet when we're sitting in the parlour, or finger the fringes of the lampshades. One of the windows has broken in the room that is now Eliza's, and this room always seems to feel especially cold, so I've heaped more blankets on her bed. The piano is horribly out of tune because it's been jarred by the blast, though Polly still practises conscientiously. And the glass on *The Light of the World* is starting to splinter, and Jesus's face is blurred with cobwebby cracks.

I've never been very house-proud – Ronnie complained about this often. And sometimes Phoebe has commented, teasingly: 'Well, of course, Liv, your idea of housework is to sweep the room with a glance . . .' But it's all got beyond the pale now.

So I busy myself with my mop and scrubbing brush and dusters. In the parlour, I hoover carefully around Eliza's arrangement. I've started to find it touching: that in these nightmare days, with our great city laid waste around us, she works so assiduously at this – her dream of how London should be. I understand her obsession now – that she wants to create a city that's perfect, that isn't at war: a city where wonderful things can still happen. And, mysteriously, through all the bombing, her frail creation survives.

I wipe down the paintwork, and scrub the kitchen floor, and polish the dining table. I clean the window panes with ammonia. I sweep all the dust from the corners – the gritty grey dirt that lurks everywhere, and seems so hard to get rid of. But my work is wasted really: the house still looks a mess when I'm done.

I've made myself late. I hurry through the streets that seem so different during the day – full of colour and vibrant, all the shops with their wares on the pavement, all the women in headscarves rushing, like me, to pick up their children from school. There are lots of reminders of the shortages. A grocer has painted in whitening on his window: *No Eggs, No Leeks, No Paper Bags*. But there's a kind of cheerfulness, in spite of everything. A horse-drawn coal-cart clatters past; the coal-merchant is whistling exuberantly. There's a jokey notice in someone's shop, where half the roof has gone: *More Open Than Usual*. The chill ruin where we walked last night is utterly transformed. I think of walking here with Justin – of all the things I told him: things I could never tell anyone, ever, by the light of day. I'm astonished I was so open.

Phoebe is at the school gate before me. There's something brittle in her face. I weave my way urgently towards her through the crowd of waiting mothers.

'Phoebe – what is it, what's happened?'

'I'm a bit shaken up, Liv.' Her summer-blue eyes are clouded. 'I thought last night that we might have caught it. One came down incredibly close.'

'Oh, Phoebe.' I grasp her arm. 'But you were in the shelter, surely?'

Her mouth works.

'Let's face it,' she says, 'if there was a direct hit on the Milton Street shelter, you probably wouldn't survive.'

I murmur something. Remembering what Justin said – how the government should have built deep shelters.

'The whole place shook. And you know that weird feeling you get – when it's like the blast squeezes you in. And all the lights went out,' she says. 'I was crouching there, clutching Bill and Freddie. Thinking, *So this is how it happens. This is how we die . . .*'

She smiles, though the smile doesn't reach her eyes.

'Oh, you poor thing. How awful.'

'I didn't feel how you'd think you'd feel,' she tells me. She has a puzzled look: there are lines between her brows, fine as though cut by a scalpel. 'I felt a kind of acceptance, really. Kind of: *Let it be.* Just this one silly thing that upset me. I've got a nice tin of peaches in my larder, and I was going to open them yesterday and have them with custard for tea, but then I'd decided to save them. And I just felt so regretful. That we hadn't eaten those wretched peaches while we still had the chance . . . It's strange the way your mind works.'

I put my arm around her. She rests her head on my shoulder for a moment.

I'm cooking bacon and potato cakes.

As I fry the bacon, I glance into the dining room, where Polly has dumped her satchel and her gas mask on the table. Her hair is frizzing with damp and arranged in rather haphazard waves, because she's started to borrow my hair-curlers: it frames her face, a soft dark halo. She undoes the straps of the satchel and takes out all her things: her exercise books, her pencil case, her book of comprehensions.

And a little winter posy: mistletoe, and Christmas roses, white-petalled, now browning at the edges – all thoughtfully put together and neatly tied with string.

She turns, sees me looking at the flowers. A blush as deeply red as strawberries spreads all over her face.

I'm startled – touched, too. She's growing up. My solemn little girl with the colour-coded hair ribbons is turning into a woman. I shouldn't be so surprised. Children don't stop growing up just because it's wartime.

'Colin Parker gave them to me,' she says. Offhandedly.

'They're so pretty. We'll put them in water . . .' Keeping my voice carefully neutral, so as not to embarrass her further.

But Eliza, coming into the room with Rabbit under her arm, has heard everything. She dances a jig around her sister.

'He *loves* you, he *loves* you,' she chants gleefully.

Polly grabs at Eliza, but Eliza is too quick for her. I find a vase for the posy.

After tea, while we wait for the sirens, I go to the parlour to damp down the fire. Polly is at the piano, playing a Mozart minuet. She's playing beautifully – it's music that seems to suit her, as trim and decorous as she is. But, seeing me, she takes her hands from the keyboard. She has an expression of limpid sadness that brings a lump to my throat.

'Sweetheart, what is it?'

'I want to grow up, Mum. I want to grow up and marry someone and have lots of babies,' she says. Her voice is full of misery.

'Oh, sweetheart. You'll be able to, of course you will,' I tell her.

'And before I get married, I really want to be a nurse,' she says. She's speaking quickly, as though the words are rising in her like steam.

'You will be, and I know you'll make such a wonderful nurse. You've got so much to look forward to, Polly.'

Her face darkens.

'But I'm frightened of looking forward to things. If I do, I just jinx them,' she says.

'No, you don't – you *can't*, Polly. Really.'

She brushes a tear from her cheek.

'But it isn't safe to look forward, Mum. I was looking forward to Dad coming home, and look what happened,' she says. 'If I let myself look forward to things, then everything always goes wrong.'

'Polly, that isn't true. Trust me. You can't stop things from happening by hoping for them,' I say.

I put my arm around her, breathe in her rose geranium scent and the faint citrus tang of her sweat.

'Sweetheart, you'll be a nurse, and get married, and do all those lovely things,' I tell her. 'Of course you will. One day.'

She swallows down her tears. She moves a little away from me.

'I bet that Nancy Baxter's mother said just the same,' she says.

48

In the crypt, I take out the book of King Arthur stories. Eliza nestles against me. Polly is drawing a picture, but I know she's listening as well.

I read about Nimue, the dazzling young enchantress: how she brought about Merlin's downfall. How she led him into the wilderness, and he went quite willingly with her – though, with his gift of sight, he knew exactly how things would play out.

I hesitate. I realise that the story is rather upsetting.

'Mummy, don't stop,' says Eliza. 'I want to find out what happens.'

So I read on. The story tells how Nimue wrapped her enchantments around Merlin, and imprisoned him for all eternity in the bole of an oak.

'Poor old Merlin,' says Eliza. 'Why did he let her do it?'

'I don't know, sweetheart. But Merlin could see into the future. Perhaps he felt it had to happen . . .'

So many magical tales have this kind of inevitability. A turn of events can seem ineluctable. There are rules that must be obeyed, that you can't oppose yourself to. Is this how the people who first told the stories believed the world to be? That it is all laid out before us, that everything goes its own way, that nothing can be changed or altered? I remember my father: *Things are as they are and will end as they must* . . .

Eliza frowns, as though she finds my answer less than satisfactory. She examines the illustration, which shows the tangled, sinister woodland – brambles and creeping ivy and woven shadows and ferns; twigs crooked as arthritic fingers; secrets hidden in ditches; menacing lilies like wide-open mouths, and hairy, intricate orchids, flecked with red like spattered blood. You can just make out Merlin's anguished face in the striated bark of the oak, as though he's become one with the oak tree.

'He doesn't look very happy,' she says. 'He got away one day, didn't he? He did a spell and escaped?'

'Yes, I expect so. Yes, I'm sure he did . . .'

It's what mothers always do – pretending to our children that the world isn't cruel; even softening the edges of the stories we tell.

'I liked the other one better,' she says. 'When the knights rode off into the forest.'

So I read that story again, about the knights who rode out so bravely and searched the wide world for the Grail, and I still haven't reached the ending when she falls asleep in my arms.

49

Wednesday: a very bad night.

Bobby screeches to a halt beside us, and almost falls from his bike.

'Mrs Ripley! Reverend! There's a fire in Mandeville Street.' His voice is shrill with drama. 'Lennie's there already.'

In Mandeville Street, a timber yard is burning. Incendiaries have fallen and there are a lot of different fires, all rapidly joining together into a vast conflagration. The flames shoot up into the night, a searing, dazzling red-gold. There's an unnatural rosy light, long shadows, a great sound of roaring. The fire crew are struggling: the water from their hoses hisses and steams in the heat, and seems to leave the fire untouched. The puddles on the asphalt are hot, and rainbow-coloured with oil.

A man is sprawled on the Tarmac, writhing, screaming for help. Justin goes to him. The man is bleeding profusely from a shrapnel wound in his leg. Justin presses his palm on the wound, but blood spurts from under his hand.

There's a sound of rushing through the air, a flash that lights the whole sky; a shuddering explosion. I find myself ducking instinctively. Some of the fire crew fling themselves down on the road.

And then I see Lennie, in the timber yard.

'Oh God, Justin. Look.'

Lennie is standing on top of a pile of timber. He's throwing planks off the pile, trying to reach down to the seat of one of the fires, where an incendiary has fallen in a gap between the planks. The light from the incendiary is a dazzling flashlight-white, the wood around it a brilliant yellow. Lennie has lost his tin hat, and his body is black against the brightness. His strength is astonishing as he flings plank after plank off the pile: it's as though he has been gifted with some superhuman power. The other fires edge in around him.

Justin calls to him.

'Lennie – get out of there!'

But Lennie doesn't hear, or chooses not to hear.

Justin turns to me.

'Livia. Press on the wound,' he tells me.

I kneel by the man and do as Justin told me, but it doesn't seem to help, the blood still seeps round my hand. It's as brightly red as by daylight in the light of the great fire, and feels warm and slippery against me. There's a shrill scream of panic inside me: this man is bleeding too much. His cries and curses are fainter now, his voice shivery, fading away.

Justin runs towards Lennie, shouting, trying to get his attention.

'Lennie, leave it, come down!'

Lennie holds up one finger, indicating *one moment*.

Justin keeps shouting at him, but Lennie doesn't respond. Justin shakes his head, then rushes back. He's swearing under his breath.

'Right, Livia. Go round the corner to Hawksville Road. Get people out of their homes. This fire could spread very quickly. Any stretchers you see, you should send them round here at once.'

He pulls a length of cord from his pocket, ties a tourniquet round the man's thigh.

In Hawksville Road, there are people out in the street, dazed, wounded – people who'd unwisely not gone to the shelter tonight. They're in torn pyjamas and night-dresses, and there are cuts on their faces and hands, from shrapnel and bits of broken glass. They're wandering around, bemused, their hair and skin all grey with dust, their faces shocked, blank, dazzled: I think of the pigeons you sometimes see walking in circles near the flames.

I urge people to get to the shelter. I give my arm to a shaky old man.

'A bit of a close shave tonight,' he says. 'I thought that last one had my name on.'

He clings to my arm. He's gangly as a crane fly, and he

has a smell of tobacco, onions, old clothes. He won't stop talking.

'I wouldn't say I'm a religious man . . . Well, I am and I'm not. I reckon no man is an island . . . But tonight I did find myself having a word with the Lord.'

I pat his hand reassuringly.

A chandelier flare is falling. The flares are like strange bright blossoms, I think, like great yellow peony flowers, malign and beautiful.

'Are you a believer yourself, ma'am?' the old man asks me.

'Well – yes and no. A bit like you,' I tell him.

I take him to the Elm Road shelter, which tonight is packed full. Then I go back to Hawksville Road, and on down Hamilton Street. I knock on doors, get people to leave, try to help the injured. I send an ambulance to pick up the man on Mandeville Street – hoping he's still in need of an ambulance.

Something happens then that disturbs me. I'm about to return to the fire, to join up with Justin and Lennie, when a bomb falls, very near to me. I throw myself to the ground. The bomber moves off, and I get up and rush to the scene. A house has been entirely destroyed, but Sebastian's arrived here before me, and he's taking charge, and sending Bobby for help. There's nothing I can do here. I decide to check out Selborne Street, just round the corner from the blast.

At number 11, the door is ajar, and I see the glow of a hearth fire that's been lit in an upstairs bedroom. I climb the stairs, go quietly into the fire-lit room. There's a woman

332

cradling a baby; she has her back to the door. It's such a tranquil scene to come on, amid the chaos of the raid. I stand there, stilled for a moment: the mother and child seem so peaceful, sitting there by the fire. But when I step round in front of them, I see that they are both dead – outwardly untouched, but their organs destroyed by the blast. The memory of this stays with me. I wish I could erase the image from my mind.

When at last I get back to our basement, I find Céline there already, sitting at the table with a cigarette in her hand. I expect her usual smile, but she stares, as though not seeing me properly, seems to look straight through me. Her cigarette is all burned down to a sagging column of ash. The column trembles, ash falls on the table, she doesn't brush it away.

I go to her.

'Céline, what is it? What's happened?'

'Lennie didn't make it,' she tells me.

Her face is desolate. With one hand, she tries to push the tears from her face, as though she is angry with them.

I think of this man – who I didn't like very much, and never got to know: I think of his astonishing courage. The way he laid down his life. Nothing is simple.

'I saw him fighting the fire. He was being so brave,' I tell her.

'That man was a fucking hero. He was the best of us,' she says.

50

Saturday 23rd November

Justin is quiet as we walk the streets. I can imagine what he's thinking: how tomorrow he'll bury Lennie. How he has to offer people hope, when his own heart is torn. I think how hard that must be for him.

It's another clear night, very cold. I'm wearing two pairs of gloves, but my fingers are still frozen. Where the moonlight slants across us, our breath makes pale, ragged clouds.

'Justin – I was wondering . . . Why did you . . .?' I feel awkward. This question is rather impertinent. 'Why did you become a clergyman?'

He doesn't say anything for a moment. Though he must have a ready answer: this surely must be a question he's often been asked.

'I guess you could say I had a calling,' he tells me.

It's not an unfamiliar phrase. Yet it suddenly strikes me what a strange expression it is.

'I was a labourer, for years,' he goes on.

'Yes.'

This makes sense to me. I think of his callused hands, of the strength of his grip when he grabbed me on the edge of the crater. You only get muscles like that from years of very physical work.

'There was an accident on the building site,' he tells me.

'Your leg?' I say.

He nods.

'I fell from the scaffolding. They said I was lucky to be alive, but, trust me, I didn't *feel* lucky . . . I was in hospital for months. I thought I'd never walk again. I felt I had no future . . .' His words sound brittle, dry. 'I was working out how to kill myself. It was a bit of a problem. Believe me, it's not so easy to end it all, when you're stuck in bed and your leg's in traction,' he says.

There's a slight, cracked smile in his voice.

I murmur something sympathetic. But this is all too big for me.

'I was lying there in despair one night, and suddenly everything changed. I became aware of something. Or, rather, something made itself felt – from beyond or behind or beneath it all . . .' His voice is spare, tentative. 'The trouble is – it's so hard to put into words . . . It was rather like finding there was something in the thin air to lean on. Something that would hold you up. So long as you tipped

yourself madly forward and asked it to take your weight . . .'
He's walking very slowly, and I match my pace to his. 'Or
some*one*, maybe. A presence. I felt like I feel when there's
someone beside me . . .'

He speaks so haltingly. I sense how he's struggling to
express this, how the precise words elude him. And it comes
to me, and surprises me, that he isn't used to telling this;
that maybe it isn't something that he's ever tried to describe.

He pulls out two cigarettes, hands me one, lights them. He
takes a long drag.

'I started getting better.' His voice more ordinary now.
'There's nothing mystical in that. I stopped being quite so
bolshie. I probably tried a bit harder, gave the poor physio
a chance. I'd been a terrible patient.' He thinks for a while.
'I wanted to understand what had happened. When I finally
got out of hospital, I started going to church. A lot of it
didn't make sense, or even made me see red. In spite of
that, I found I still wanted to understand more. I studied
– I went to classes at the Workers' Educational Association.
I went to theological college. Here I am . . .'

He turns towards me. In the blue bolts of the moonlight,
I can see his small, crooked smile.

'Yes, here you are,' I say, smiling back.

We pass a row of terraced houses, several of them gutted:
ceilings lie on floors, and there's a smell of decay. There's
a bright spray of stars high above us.

He's silent for a long time. I'm used to this now – how we
drop, then pick up again, the threads of our conversations.

'It wasn't all easy, of course,' he says then. A hesitation,

336

as though he's not sure if he should say this. 'I'd been engaged to be married, when the accident happened. But afterwards she left me. She said I wasn't the man she'd fallen for any more.'

It disconcerts me that he's telling me this. That he's being so open.

He thinks for a moment, and I resist my urge to fill in the silence between us. I'm learning to wait for him, as he will sometimes wait for me.

'You can understand it, of course. I'd become a cripple. The poor woman had found herself hitched to a cripple who kept harping on about God. It wasn't what she'd signed up for . . .'

His voice is striped with scars. I can tell how much this still hurts him.

'That must have been so sad for you,' I say.

Swallowing down all my questions. *Who was she? How did you meet her? What did she look like?* Feeling an intense and inappropriate curiosity about this woman who was engaged to him. Wondering what kind of woman he might be drawn to, might *love*.

'Yes, you can say that again,' he tells me.

We hear the roar and thud of distant bombs, and the obscure throb of the barrage.

'It's . . . extraordinary – what you described,' I tell him. 'It makes me feel – I don't know – *envious*, really.'

He's quiet, thinking. For a little while, the guns are still. I can hear our footsteps, our breath.

'There's never been another moment like that moment,'

he says then. 'I've had times since when I've needed something desperately – some kind of affirmation. Times when I've needed God's presence. And I haven't felt it. I've never again felt the thing I felt then.'

There's a gun-flash off to the east, and you can see a chandelier flare falling, over towards Bermondsey, the flares floating down with languid menace like fiery pearls on a string. He hesitates for a long moment.

'On a bad day, I can believe that I dreamed it all,' he tells me. 'Or that it was just my traumatised brain misfiring in some way. Some weird brain chemistry, perhaps.'

His voice is more fragile now. I can't see his face, but I can imagine his expression – a kind of perplexity. Sadness, even.

'You know – when you're confronted by the utter randomness of things. The randomness of suffering. Lennie dying, that brave man . . .'

There's a knot of tears in his throat: I can hear this.

'Some days, I can think that that moment meant nothing,' he goes on. 'But I have to hold on to it – what I felt that night in the hospital. Because if I don't have that, then what do I have?' he asks me, and his voice is bleak when he says this.

We walk on through the blackness, stumbling over the wreckage of things.

51

Sunday night. I send the girls on ahead of me and stand at the door of the church, enjoying what's left of my cigarette. I don't like to smoke in the crypt.

Theodora, passing, gives me a look full of disapproval. She has her knitting basket, and she's wearing a furry stole that has the tail and head of a fox. Her mouth is thin as the slash of a razor.

'You need to put that out, Mrs Ripley. Remember what I told you, when there was that problem with your blackout. Even a little thing can look very bright from up there.'

She gestures skywards.

Even now I'm a warden, she's still trying to give me advice.

I swallow down my impulse to say something horribly rude. I relish my cigarette down to the very last puff.

When I join the girls in front of Jemima Codrington's tomb, I see that the refugees from Frankfurt are sitting there, with Aggie. They have a plaid blanket spread out, a Thermos, a basket of books. Aggie introduces us.

'This is Dr and Frau Rosen . . . This is Mrs Ripley and her girls . . .'

He's stooped and long-necked, like a heron; she's a small, plump, faded woman, and her eyes are dark as sloes.

'What beautiful daughters you have,' says Mrs Rosen, with a smile that drives the shadows from her face and her eyes.

They tell me they've moved out of Orchid Villa and have started renting some rooms on Kimberley Road.

Polly peers at their basket. On top of the books, there's the musical instrument case that I've noticed before.

'Is that a flute, Dr Rosen?' Polly asks him.

He smiles at her.

'Yes. I keep it safe with me. Would you like to see it?' he asks.

He takes the flute out to show her, and the silvery metal shoots arrows of brightness across the walls of the crypt.

'Would you play it for us now?' asks Polly, her passion for music emboldening her.

He's hesitant.

'But people might be trying to get to sleep,' he says.

Polly glances around.

'Nobody's sleeping quite yet. *Please*. It would be so lovely.'

'Yes, play for us, Gregor,' Aggie urges him. 'It would

340

really cheer everyone up. There's nothing like a bit of music to lift the heart,' she says.

He gives a slight nod, and raises the flute to his lips.

A hush falls. Even Theodora's knitting needles are silent.

As the music shimmers round the room, there's a small, shared sigh of pleasure. We're caught in luminous webs of melody, lulled by long-held ravishing notes. I know the piece. It's Debussy, *Syrinx*: it tells of the god Pan waking in a wooded glade, full of desire for the nymph Syrinx, who will run from him and turn herself into a reed. The music speaks of summer, of sunlight – of the blues and greens of trees and sky, a small breeze blowing, the scents of the forest, the dancing light on the leaves.

We are enchanted, there in the crypt, down beneath burning London. The music takes us to a different place. We believe in another world again – a place where war doesn't come, where all good things are possible. I think that I have never heard so beautiful a thing.

Something wet falls on my hand; I find that I am weeping.

A bomb comes down very near, with a sound like a freight train speeding towards us. The blast moves through the earth beneath the crypt: you can feel the foundations shudder. But Dr Rosen scarcely falters. When the sound and fury have all died away, the music is still singing out, telling of other countries, other worlds.

52

Early December

It's colder. When we come back home in the morning, our windows are scribbled over with frost. And the evenings are drawing in now, the daylight dying around us as I walk the girls home from school, long sepia shadows falling.

One afternoon, Polly follows me into the kitchen, where I'm about to make tea.

'So, was it a good day?' I ask her.

She shrugs slightly.

'It was semolina for pudding *again*. And our history class was so boring that I started to eat my own hair. It's always the wretched Tudors . . .'

But there's a troubled look in her face, and I know she wants to talk to me – to tell me something she couldn't say out in the street. I always dread hearing of the death of another of her classmates.

I put my arm around her. She rests her head briefly on my shoulder.

'Polly – there's something else, isn't there?'

She moves away, and I see her throat move as she swallows.

'There's a new boy in our class. Isaak Baumann,' she tells me. 'He says he comes from Germany. He used to live in Berlin.'

Eliza is wandering through, with Rabbit under her arm.

'We don't like the Germans,' she says.

'He's not a Nazi, though, he's Jewish.' Polly has a small, puzzled frown. 'He tells these stories, Mum. About people being arrested. He says the people get sent to Poland, and they never come back.'

I feel a chill. But I have such an urge to reassure her.

'There are always rumours, in a war,' I tell her briskly – remembering the stories that people all believed, during the Great War: that the Germans would use their bayonets to cut off children's arms; that they crucified people. But those things never happened. 'The thing is, Polly, you don't know quite what to believe in wartime.'

She moves her hand over her face in a small, uncertain gesture.

'I suppose not,' she tells me. 'Anyway, boys are always telling stories and trying to impress you. But he wasn't making it up, Mum. He had such an unhappy look, when he talked about it,' she says.

343

I'm desperate to comfort her.

'It must have been difficult for him – leaving Berlin and all his friends there. Like Dr and Mrs Rosen. They had to do that as well, they left their whole life behind. It must be terribly hard for people . . .'

Polly's forehead is creased with thought.

'He says the people get taken away on trains, and his parents say we could stop it by bombing the railway lines,' she tells me. 'Because if the railway lines were destroyed, the Nazis couldn't do it. They've tried to tell people about it – you know, the people who run the country. But nobody believes them. Nobody listens,' she says.

I tell myself they must know what they're doing – Mr Churchill and the war cabinet. They must have masses of information to base their decisions on – intelligence reports from their spies all across the Continent. We know about the ill-treatment of the Jews in Germany – how they have to wear a yellow star, how on Kristallnacht so many of their businesses got fire-bombed. But I've never heard about people disappearing like this. If these stories were true, Mr Churchill would try to stop it from happening, wouldn't he? These stories must be just rumours – which people are ready to believe because they feel so afraid.

Polly's eyes are shadowed.

'Imagine, Mum. To have something like that to tell – and for no one to listen,' she says.

53

There's an incident in Curzon Street – a house entirely destroyed, leaving a huge mound of rubble. Four men are already digging in the ruin when we get there.

One of them lowers his shovel as we approach. He's gap-toothed and has a checked cap; he doffs the cap, seeing us. I recognise him – Dickie Wheeler, a local odd-job man and builder. He made some shelves for my kitchen, back before the war began.

'Morning, Reverend. Morning, Mrs Ripley,' he says.

I'm startled that he says *morning*. But the faded stencil of the moon is sinking down in the sky. The night must be nearly over: soon the All Clear will sound.

'How's it going?' asks Justin.

Dickie Wheeler scrapes a filthy handkerchief over his face.

'The neighbours told us they used their basement – the poor blighters who lived here,' he says. 'But we haven't heard a peep from them. We're making a bit of a tunnel in the side of the mound. So we can see if anyone's down there.'

He shows us. In the side of the heap of rubble, there's a ragged hole, leading inward and down into darkness.

'It's a bloody small tunnel, mind,' says Dickie Wheeler. 'But if someone could get to the end of the tunnel, we reckon you'd able to see into the basement from there. It would take someone on the small side, though.'

Justin looks at the tunnel sceptically, shakes his head.

'I'll say.'

I'm aware of the way Dickie Wheeler is eyeing me up and down, as though he's sizing up my body. I remember something Céline once said, something I couldn't make sense of: *You could come in jolly useful, a slim little thing like you.*

'Mrs Ripley could get through there. If she was willing,' he says.

'Yes. Of course. I'll do it,' I say.

I'm scared – but also excited, that at last I can do something helpful.

But Justin turns sharply towards me.

'Livia, no. You don't have to.'

His voice has a rough edge, and I'm perplexed. Why is he angry with me – when I'm volunteering to help?

'But that's what we're here for,' I say.

'*No.* Let's face it – it's pretty unlikely that anyone's still alive down there. We should wait until they've opened up a bit more of a gap. One of the men could go through then.'

346

His look startles me. His eyes in the torchlight are widely dilated; and I suddenly see he's afraid. Afraid for *me*. As I would be afraid for someone I cared for – someone I *loved*. *Oh*, I think. *Oh*. The world tilts, everything rearranging itself around me.

But I push the thought away from me. For now, I have something to do.

'I'm the obvious person. I'll be all right. Really,' I say.

Justin puts his hand on my shoulder, grips me briefly.

'Then for God's sake, be careful, Livia.'

I can hear the catch in his voice.

I edge into the hole, wriggling forward on my stomach.

It's instantly very dark around me. But by the thin beam of my torch, which is wedged in my belt, I can make out the sides of the tunnel – everything that was in the house, all of it shattered and smashed together. Most of it ground to a pulp, but you can still make out some of the things, the crushed remains of people's lives. Scraps of floorboard, curtains, crockery. A picture frame, the spout of a kettle, a children's teddy bear.

I start to bitterly regret that I put myself forward like that. The space is claustrophobic, oppressive. Panic stalks me, ready to pounce, to seize me. *Don't think, don't think,* I tell myself. I try to keep my mind carefully blank, start to recite my seven times table, but the numbers skitter around, elude me. The panic edges nearer: soon it will have its claws in me. The air is thick and sour with dust; it's growing hard to breathe.

Then, out of nowhere – or perhaps because of the kettle

spout – one of Eliza's nursery rhymes comes sliding into my mind. I seize on it gratefully, chant it under my breath.

> *Polly put the kettle on*
> *Polly put the kettle on*

The rhyme is the rope that I cling to, creeping on into the blackness. Reciting the words in my head, keeping all my attention on them, timing them exactly with my movements, my breath.

> *Polly put the kettle on*
> *We'll all have tea*
> *Sukie take it off again . . .*

I reach out a hand, and feel emptiness, just hollow air in front of me; here, the sides of the tunnel have fallen away. I sense space opening out below me: if I go any further, I'll fall. There's the foulest smell in the world, filling my nose and my throat – like rotten meat, like a sewer, but ranker than either.

I rest on my elbows. I pull my torch from my belt and move the beam around.

I'm looking down into the basement of the building. Amid the dust and wreckage, I can make out the forms of people – sprawled out awkwardly, covered in dust, making shapes that are wrong. So still, so silent. *Dear God.* I see that this is a family – mother, father, grandmother, two children. Timbers and joists from higher up have crashed right through into the basement: the old woman's chest is pinned down and crushed beneath a fallen beam. Some light from my left, where the debris is thinner, leaks in – a searchlight, perhaps, or the flash of another bomb falling: the light briefly illumines the paleness of those ravaged, broken bodies, their faces swimming in the darkness like the faces of the drowned. The old woman's hand sticks up, like a drowning hand, reaching out: it's so close that I could touch it. I stretch out cautiously, brush her fingers. Her skin is utterly cold, the coldest thing I've ever touched.

'Mrs Ripley – can you see anyone?'

It's Dickie Wheeler's voice, from the other end of the tunnel. I'm startled how near the man sounds – when I have passed through some grisly portal and entered a different world: an underworld, a sepulchre.

I don't call back. It all feels so fragile around me: I'm scared of making any vibration that I don't have to make. My only thought is to retreat; this is all I want in the world, to be anywhere else but in this terrible place. This desire consumes me.

It isn't easy. If I could only turn round, if I could only see where I was going . . . I push with my hands, slide backwards, my body catching and snagging on the broken corners of things. My throat is thick and scratchy with brick dust and wood dust and plaster. I try to stifle my cough, frightened I could disturb the wreckage around me, fearing the slightest puff of breath could make it shift and fall.

Sukie take it off again
Sukie take it off again
They've all gone away

Flurries of dust and mortar sift down on either side of me. Some solid things – fragments of masonry – are falling onto my head, bouncing on my tin helmet with an ominous clattering sound. With a sudden new urgency, I push very hard with my hands.

As I slither out of the tunnel and feel ground beneath my feet, the roof of the tunnel collapses in the place where I have just been.

I wrench off my helmet – wanting to feel the air on me, wanting to shake the smell of death out of my clothes, my hair.

Justin has his hand on my shoulder, his fingers digging into me. He's holding me so fiercely it hurts, but I welcome his touch. I want him to keep me close – to hold me here in the land of the living, to pull me away from that grim place of burial under the mound.

'Livia. Thank God. Are you all right?' he asks me.

I nod. Though I'm not *all right* at all. Every part of my body is trembling: my teeth are clashing together.

'They're dead. Five people,' I say to the men with the shovels. Stupidly, I hold up the fingers of one hand, to show them. As though I'm a traveller from some far-off land, and they won't understand my language. 'I'm pretty sure there's no one left alive. You'll need to check, though.'

'Poor sods,' says Dickie Wheeler.

'Thank God you got out,' says Justin.

There's a shake in his voice.

I can still feel the coldness of the old woman's hand on my hand; it goes right through me. I have a startling impulse to throw myself on Justin, to lose myself in his arms, his strength, his *aliveness* – to do whatever it takes to forget the touch of that hand.

I start to cough; then my whole chest heaves. I turn away and vomit. Justin holds back my hair. The heaving goes on and on, until there's nothing left inside me.

At last, I straighten up.

'Sorry,' I say. 'God, how awful.'

I wipe my mouth, feel ashamed.

'You were so brave, Livia,' says Justin.

I wasn't brave at all, I think: *I was terrified*. But I hug the compliment to me.

He takes out a Woodbine for me, but I'm shaking too much to hold it. So he pushes it between my lips, and leans in to light it, his face very close. I can smell the warm smell of his body. I feel a jolt of desire, which utterly disconcerts me.

I turn from him, smoke the cigarette, take a deep grateful drag.

The long long shadows of dawn are all around us, and there are rags of pink glimmery light in the sky. We can make out each other's faces now. At last, the All Clear sounds; a thin cheer goes up from the men.

A vehicle trundles up – the WRVS canteen. The men fling down their shovels and gather in line, but gesture for

351

me to go first, with a chivalry that touches me. The drinks are served by a robust woman with pillar-box-red lipstick and her hair in a Victory roll.

'That'll set you up nicely, dear,' she says, as she hands me my cocoa. Her voice is extravagantly upper class – I think of a Georgian house in Chelsea, and G and Ts at the Café Royal.

'Yes. Thank you. I'm sure it will.'

I cradle the cup between my hands. Its warmth is very welcome. I realise that I'm frozen: I've been sweating, and now my sweat is turning to ice on my skin. I drink, and the cocoa rinses the bile from my mouth. But the stench of the basement still lingers about me.

54

I can't sleep, can't bear to close my eyes. The faces are waiting for me in front of my closed eyelids, floating in the dark of my mind, dead things in a black pool.

In the end, I get up, and pull on my warmest clothes. I leave a note for Polly, in case she worries, finding me gone. I hang my camera round my neck and step out into the morning.

The ruins and barrage balloons are all tinged rose pink with the dawn, and there's a slight wind rising, lifting my hair from my neck. Dead leaves rattle like tin on the asphalt. In our street, there's no one about.

I feel unreal, and the world feels unreal around me – as though this whole vast city were something I'd hallucinated or dreamed, some great palace of illusion. These streets, once so familiar, are now disfigured, changed. You could get lost here. You could walk and walk and still not know where you were, not recognise anything. I think of the wildwood in Malory's stories, the great wasteland; of the knights who rode out with such faith, wherever the woods were thickest; who searched and searched, yet never found what they were looking for.

It's so cold. I shiver, pull my threadbare coat close about me.

I walk on, photographing as I go. I suspect I shouldn't be doing this: Hugo told me there were rules. But there's no one here to stop me. I'm clumsy in my gloves, but without them my fingers would freeze.

Fragments of people's lives are crunching under my feet. It's mostly little things that catch my eye, domestic details, misplaced but precisely preserved, their sadness tugging at you. A woman's necklace, the coloured glass beads scattered across the Tarmac. A shattered mirror, in which I can see small random shards of myself. The floral wallpaper in someone's parlour, now opened up to the street; the roses are pallid in the shadows, their colour all leached away. On the pavement, a partly burned book: the dawn wind is rifling through it. The pages are scorched at the margins, but you can still read some of the words.

Two boys are sitting on the kerb, poking with broken table-legs in a puddle. The oil in the puddle makes rainbow patterns as the water is stirred, fluid swirls of rose and indigo. The boys' faces and clothes are filthy. One of them looks up as I pass. Eager, a little furtive: a mercenary gleam in his eye.

'Read your palm, miss?'

He's wearing a dirty dressing gown over his clothes, and a fireman's hat he's found somewhere that tips down over his eyes.

'No, thank you.'

'Go on, miss. Just for a copper?'

'*No*. Really.'

But I give them some pennies anyway.

At the fishmonger's in Fountain Place, the boxes outside are still neatly stacked, undisturbed by the bombing, and there's a drenching smell of kipper. A ragged cat skulks off into the shadows, its footfall as soft as though it were made of shadow itself. I hear someone coming out of a house and banging a door behind him, whistling. *When the red red robin comes bob bob bobbin' along* . . . I welcome the sound, its ordinariness, puncturing my strange mood. It's a cheerful song: I imagine the whistling person thinking something encouraging, hopeful – the sort of thing that Aggie says. *Time to rise and shine* . . . *Keep your sunny side up* . . . Then the person turns a corner and the sound is abruptly shut off.

I come to a row of terraced houses that were caught in the bombing last week, the front of one of them peeled away, as though it were a doll's house. The people who lived here would have been poor: there's so little in these rooms. I think of Justin raging at people's poverty, of the dazzling dream of the future that blazed in his eyes.

We can't carry on like this. After the war, it all has to change. It has *to* . . . I can hear his words again, as clear almost as if he were walking beside me. When you're together in the dark and you can't see the person you're talking to, their words can seem to stay with you, to resonate in your mind.

What would it be like – to have the faith that he has, the faith that things could be different? I can't imagine it.

I think of that moment when I sensed how much he cared about me. And I remember the unnerving jolt of attraction I felt, but I tell myself it meant nothing: it was just a random thing that happened because I was so glad to still be alive. Really, I scarcely know him. We can walk so close in the darkness, hearing one another's breath – yet we remain strangers to one another.

There's a low rumble behind me, the dull, hollow, sinister sound of masonry shifting, falling; then the echoes fade and die away, and all is quiet again.

I find myself in Curzon Street. I didn't intend to come here, yet something has drawn me. The place where I crawled through the tunnel has been opened up to the sky, and they have the bodies out now. The bodies are laid on the ground, covered in grubby bits of sheeting in a desperate striving after decency. Two men are waiting with the bodies, sitting hunched on the rubble. Everything about them speaks of their utter weariness. One is staring at his cigarette, with a blank, unseeing look; the other has his elbows on his knees, his head in his hands. They don't see me: they're beyond noticing anything. I know they will be waiting for the mortuary van.

I put my eye to the lens. But I stand for a moment, torn, uncertain. Would it be intrusive to photograph this scene? Or even in some way immoral? But this is *my* scene: I tell myself I have a right to be here, to lay claim to this sight, because I crawled through that terrible tunnel. I press the shutter.

I walk on. Now I have started, I have such a need to take photographs, a feeling so strong it's a compulsion – an instinct that would be hard to put into words. A hunger to capture something – an image that will catch the eye, make people stop and turn. *Yes, I recognise that – the ruin, the bleakness, the dawn light, everything. Yes, I was there, and that is exactly what it was like.*

When I've used all the film in my camera, I make my way back home.

55

Monday. Justin isn't at the post. After what happened with Lennie, I feel fear rushing through me.

But Céline smiles at me sagely when I enquire about him.

'Don't you worry your pretty head, darling. Our Justin's a cat with nine lives.'

I sense that she knows quite well where he is, but for some reason won't say.

I patrol with Céline. She's subdued tonight, grieving for Lennie: she doesn't talk much at all.

We come to Hurtwood Road, at the edge of our sector. Hurtwood School looms before us, and I remember how Justin once told me that people were using it as a shelter: how he feared for their safety. But it all looks shut up and quiet; perhaps they've stopped sheltering there. I don't ask Céline about this: she doesn't feel quite present. She seems to be moving more slowly than usual, as though she is mired in wet sand.

It's an uneventful night for us. Though over towards Battersea, there's an ominous brightness in the sky. After we've checked all our streets and shelters, we go back to our basement and play dominoes, smoke, drink tea. Esme is knitting a pullover from mismatched scraps of wool; Sebastian is reading a book on John Hanning Speke, a Victorian explorer who tried to discover the source of the Nile. When there isn't much to do, you're more aware how tired you are. We're intensely conscious of Lennie's absence.

All the next day, I worry about Justin, grim scenarios spooling out in my mind. But I try to reassure myself: if he'd been bombed and killed or injured, surely Céline would know something? I tell myself all will be well – that I'll see him tonight at the crypt, when he drops in to check on us.

But when night comes, I sleep deeply in front of Jemima Codrington's tomb.

As I walk home with the girls through the chill morning streets, I ask Polly if she saw him.

'Not tonight. But I could have been fast asleep when he came . . . Why are you asking anyway?' She gives me a narrow look from under her eyelashes. 'Mum, you're as bad as Aggie. What is it with the pair of you? Please, please don't say *you've* got a crush on him as well.'

This startles me. But I try to sound nonchalant.

'Goodness, Polly, of course not. I just wondered if he was around . . .'

Wednesday evening: my next night on duty. I go down the stairs to the wardens' post, and hear his voice before I enter the room. A ridiculous, disproportionate happiness floods me.

He turns.

'Livia.'

He smiles, as though he's pleased to see me as well. But he hasn't shaved, he looks exhausted, the lines etched too deep in his face.

We set out together. He's walking faster than usual: I've learned that this can happen when he's tired and his leg is hurting – as though he's taking the weight off his painful leg as quickly as he can.

'You weren't around on Monday. I was worried about you,' I tell him.

He glances towards me but I can't see his expression. I sense a hesitation in him.

I shouldn't have said I was worried about him, shouldn't have been so open. I wonder, as so often, exactly what he sees when he studies me with his dark, fierce eyes. I remember what I felt when I first met him: that he'd think me a sheltered, standoffish woman – over-protected, knowing so little of life.

I was so happy to see him; yet now I feel awkward again. As usual.

'I was visiting my brother.' There's something withheld in his voice. 'I got stuck and couldn't get back. There were an awful lot of street closures. I helped out at an incident, then I had to spend the rest of the night in the shelter at Tooting Bec tube . . .'

'I didn't know you had a brother,' I say.

A small pause – just a heartbeat.

'Yes, I have a brother. He's in Wandsworth Prison,' he says. His voice rather level and careful.

'Oh.'

What do you say? Would it be too forward to ask, *What did he do, your brother? What was his crime?* I'm so curious – I ask it anyway.

The street is hushed for a moment. I can hear the tiniest things – the creak of his shoes as he walks, a kicked pebble rolling away.

'He killed someone,' says Justin. 'Or – he *may* have killed someone.'

'Oh my God.'

And yet I'm not as surprised as I might be. I think of the little I know of Justin. How his father was an alcoholic. How he worked as a labourer on a building site for years. How he hit out at the drunk man – the effortless, practised blow. The rage I sometimes sense in him.

'I don't exactly come from what you'd call a good background,' he says.

'Well, none of us . . . I mean—'

'Our mother died, when I was eight and my brother was ten,' he tells me. 'Our father couldn't cope. He drank, like I told you before. My brother got the worst of it . . .'

I feel a disconcerting tenderness, picturing Justin as a child – wanting to reach back through the years and put my arms around him, protect him.

'Your brother . . . what's he called?'

'Danny. His name is Danny. He got into fights at school. We used to get picked on. Well, you can understand it – we didn't wash very much, we had nits in our hair. Danny was very ready with his fists – he stood up for both of us really . . . One time, I was being bullied, and he knocked the boy to the floor. The boy hit his head and was badly injured. Danny got sent to Feltham.'

'Oh, how awful.'

Feltham is a borstal. I've heard of these institutions, where they lock up boys too young for prison. They're said to be rough, brutal places.

'That place was a school for criminals,' Justin tells me. 'When Danny came out, he knew a lot that he hadn't known when he'd gone in. None of it good stuff. And he got to know people he might have done much better not to have known . . . He started robbing banks. He was clever, he didn't get caught. Well, not for a long time . . .'

'Did you know – I mean, what he was doing?'

A hesitation, that feels like assent.

'I couldn't stop him. But I didn't turn him in,' says Justin. 'Looking back – of course, I can see that what I did was wrong. Or rather, what I failed to do . . .'

'It must have been so hard.' My words sound flimsy, empty.

'The time they caught him, the robbery had all gone horribly wrong. The men panicked, they started shooting, they shot a bank clerk. By the time the ambulance arrived, the man had bled to death. Danny said he hadn't fired the shot that killed him. But there were two other men in the gang, and they both swore that he had. There was enough uncertainty that he just escaped hanging,' he says.

I hear the catch in his voice, as though these words snag at his throat.

'Now Danny's doing life. The other two men just got a few years.'

'Oh.'

'One of those men is now a warden, not so far from here,' he tells me. 'You sometimes see him around. Tom Coster. He has a scrap metal business. That's life, I suppose – you can't get away from these people. He's a bastard, and dangerous with it.' There's a harshness in Justin's voice now. 'He has a way with him, Tom Coster. He can reel people in, he can make them do what he wants.'

I glance at Justin. A shaft of white moonlight is lighting his face and his eyes: I can see a spark of anger in him. Then, sensing my gaze, he gestures, as though to push all these things away.

'So there you have it, Livia.' His slight crooked smile. 'Not what you'd call a good family . . .'

'Well, nobody has a perfect background, I suppose . . .'

We walk for a while in silence, breathe in the dust of

London's buildings; above us, far above, a gorgeous panoply of stars, and a moon as yellow as a wolf's eye.

'Do you have brothers or sisters, Livia?' he asks me then.

For most people, such an ordinary question. But it isn't to me.

'I have . . . I *had* a sister.' My voice seems to come from far away and sounds like someone else's voice.

He hears the past tense: perhaps he also hears how my voice sounds all wrong. He waits.

'I lost her,' I tell him.

In the stillness between us, I can hear the thud of my heart.

When I don't say more, he turns a little towards me.

'That sounds sad, Livia.'

Above us and off to our right, an enemy plane is drumming, drawing up bursts of gunfire, dragging around in the pool of the night. The barrage bangs, coughs, retches, and then is silent again.

'There's something I've felt about you – that you've been hurt,' he says. A question in his voice.

'Well, that isn't quite right. *I* did the hurting,' I say.

A bomb swings whistling down, the detonation dulling off into the roar of a building split open. A direct hit, somewhere else: this time, not on our patch. The reverberations fade away; the silence waits for me.

'She died when I was ten, and she was twelve,' I say. 'She drowned in an icy river. It was an accident – or that's what everyone said. But it wasn't really . . . I don't talk about her much. Well, I don't talk about her at all.'

'But you *think* about her.' Slowly, gently.

'Every day. I think about her every day.' It's as though I've forgotten how to breathe: I exhale too loud and raggedly. 'I've always felt responsible – felt it was all my fault. Well, it *was* my fault . . .'

I shudder.

I expect him to ask me: *Is this why you're always blaming yourself for things?* But he doesn't.

I feel my throat close like a fist. I can't say anything more.

High above us, the solitary bomber is moving away. It's so quiet. The asphalt is a shining river in the moonlight, with sapphire shadows exactly laid all down one side of the street.

I can hear his breath, before he starts to speak.

'They can possess us. Take us over. Can't they? The untold things. The things we can't bear to tell.'

'Yes,' I say.

'An untold thing can shape a life,' he tells me.

'Yes. Yes, it can.'

But now I feel afraid – afraid about what I've revealed. As though he could see straight into me, and hate me.

And this suddenly seems strange to me – that I face death every night in these streets, yet I'm frightened, so very frightened, because of something I've *said*. In the silence and the darkness, my words seem solid as stones. They can't be taken back again.

56

It's nearly Christmas.

Every morning, my letter box rattles and Christmas cards land on my mat. I'd thought that people wouldn't bother with sending cards this Christmas – with the bombs, the paper shortage, the risk that the post might not get through. But there are so many of them.

There's one from Hugo. He's written a line of bland good wishes: he sends his love and the Season's Greetings, and hopes that I am well. I run my finger over that swooping male signature, feeling a pang. But our affair feels very remote now – as though it happened to somebody else, or in some far-off place or time.

I'm cutting mistletoe in my garden when a snowflake lands on my sleeve. I look upwards, feeling a thrill: I always love the first snowfall, its purity and freshness. The sky is bulging like the breast of an overfed goose, grey and heavy. More flakes come spiralling down, at first just a few, then a flurry, furring the wool of my cardigan, spreading immaculate white all over the mud and dead leaves on my lawn. It's very early for snow. This winter could be a harsh one.

I pin the mistletoe up in the doorways, and hang the cards on red ribbons.

Phoebe remarks on all the cards when she comes round with our present – one of her marvellous fruit cakes. Her face is ruddy with cold, and snow is melting in her hair.

'Well, your house *is* looking lovely, Liv. We've had masses of cards as well, even more than usual. People wanting to stay in touch. Saying, *We won't let the bastards grind us down.* It's just so cheering, isn't it? Your heart seems to lift a little, with every card that comes.'

Her eyes glitter briefly with emotion. Then she shrugs, with a slight rueful smile, as though worried this sounds sentimental.

She sits at my table; we drink coffee. Phoebe wraps her cold fingers gratefully round the warm cup. Outside, feathers of snow are still falling.

'There are rumours that the raids will stop for Christmas,' she says. 'That there will be some kind of truce. Peace on Earth, and all that.'

'Yes, I've heard that as well.' People were speculating about this in the queue at Mr Bradley's. 'But I'll believe it when it happens. There are always rumours,' I say.

'But – think about the Great War. You know, the

Christmas Day truce. There's a precedent,' she reminds me.

I remember the pictures of enemy soldiers, showing each other photographs of their children or their sweethearts, kicking a football around together in no man's land.

'Well, here's hoping . . .'

But it seems too much to wish for – a whole blissful night without bombs: sleeping all night in our own beds.

'So how's it going – the warden thing?' Phoebe asks me.

I hesitate. Pictures swim into my mind. The dead family in the basement. Lennie on the woodpile, just before he died.

'I think I'm getting the hang of it,' I tell her.

Phoebe hugs me when she says goodbye, wrapping me in her beneficence and her sandalwood scent.

'Liv, you have yourself a wonderful Christmas,' she says.

I buy a Christmas tree from Mr O'Callaghan's shop. It lies trussed-up in our hallway and fills our house with a wonderful resinous fragrance. The girls are excited.

'Eliza, listen.' I kneel beside her, and cup her face in my hands. 'Sweetheart, I'm going to put up the tree in the parlour. And we'll have to move your London Town, to make a space for the tree. We'll put it all carefully in boxes. It'll be perfectly safe there . . .'

But she slides away from my grasp, slippery as a minnow.

'No, I don't want to, Mummy.'

I have a sudden inspiration.

'Well, how about if I take a photograph? So you can see where everything goes.'

She considers this for a moment.

'Could I keep the photograph?' she asks.

'Yes, of course you can, sweetheart. And you can build your London Town again when we take the Christmas tree down.'

To my relief, she accepts this. I take several photographs for her, and then we tidy the room.

Polly is ecstatic.

'At *last*, Mum. Thank goodness. I thought you'd never do it,' she says.

I hunt out the Christmas decorations: some rather battered paper chains we made before the war; glass baubles; an angel in a white crêpe-paper dress to go on top of the tree.

The girls work together surprisingly well, decorating the tree. Then they stand back to admire their handiwork, and Polly sighs with pleasure.

'It's pretty, isn't it, Mum? I *love* Christmas. It's so nice to still have Christmas, even though there's a war.'

Eliza has a smug expression.

'I bet the Germans wish that they could have Christmas, like us.'

'They do, though, sweetheart,' I tell her. 'The Germans have Christmas as well.'

'But they don't have Christmas trees. They don't have cards and presents and things.' Eliza is intransigent.

'Yes, they have all those things. Just like we do.'

She refuses to believe this.

I dress up for Christmas Day – my smoky-blue shantung

silk frock, a splash of Après l'Ondée. Aggie comes to join us, and I've invited Dr and Mrs Rosen as well. The Rosens bring a gift for us, a book of German *märchen* – fairy tales – wrapped in a scrap of red silk.

Mrs Rosen is apologetic.

'It isn't much, when you're being so kind. But it was the best we could do . . .'

I'm touched: the book will be precious to them; they must have brought it with them from Frankfurt. The language looks simple to translate – I'll be able to read the tales to the girls. The pictures are taken from engravings, and bordered with woven garlands of flowers and tendrils and leaves: they're enchanting. I flick through. The princess disguised as a goose girl. Hansel and Gretel being so clever and cunning, defeating the witch. Huntsmen and fearless kitchen maids and the gentle sons of poor millers. Poisoned fruit and cloaks of feathers and magic dancing shoes. Rewards for kindness; happy endings.

'It's so beautiful. Thank you.'

I roast a chicken for dinner; there isn't all that much meat on it, but I bulk it out with sausages cooked with potatoes in a tin, and sage and onion stuffing. Aggie has made a Christmas pudding, and I set it alight with a spoonful of brandy: I have a bottle from years ago that I've stored at the back of the larder. The girls always find this thrilling – the implausible spurt of blue flame. Eliza's eyes are shining.

After the meal, we move to the parlour, where I've made a good fire, and we listen to the King's Message on the wireless.

The future will be hard, but our feet are planted on the path of victory, and with the help of God, we will make our way to justice and peace . . .

I hear these words rather doubtfully. I suppose he had to say those things – to try to keep up morale. But the news from the war doesn't really suggest we're on the *path of victory*. I think of the way that Hitler has cut a swathe through Europe. Of the losses and reverses in the Western Desert. Of our airmen, beyond exhaustion, flying perilous sorties night after night after night. Of the sailors out in the Atlantic where poor Gladys Munroe's son died, under constant threat from U-boats. There have been no victories for us, just defeats and retreats.

I keep these thoughts to myself.

I serve slices of Phoebe's fruit cake, and we listen to Children's Hour, which has a dramatisation of Dickens' *A Christmas Carol*. The girls listen raptly. Sipping tea, gazing at the benign red blaze of the fire, I think about Dickens' story, about what happened to Scrooge. How in order to be reborn, to become a better person, he had to repair his relationship with the lost, the forgotten, the dead. But how can you do that, outside a story? Is such a thing possible?

I'd like to talk about this with Justin. I'd like to know what he thought.

After tea, Polly sits at the piano and Dr Rosen takes out his flute, and we gather round to sing carols. *Hark the Herald Angels Sing. Silent Night, Holy Night.*

We listen for the siren, but it doesn't come. At eight, it still hasn't sounded.

371

'Well, girls, I suppose you might as well go up to bed,' I say.

'In our *own rooms*?' says Eliza.

This seems so novel to them.

'Mum,' says Polly, with a small, happy sigh, 'it's been a really nice day. The best day ever. Since Dad . . . you know . . .'

I kiss her.

Then it's just the four of us, drinking brandy in the firelight. I feel a deep contentment. As Polly said, it's been a happy day. I feel that nothing tonight could upset me.

Silence falls between us. You can hear the little shift and stir of the glowing coals on the fire. I turn to Dr and Mrs Rosen.

'Tell us what happened. Tell us how you came to London . . .'

So they do.

They tell us about their life in Frankfurt, under Hitler's Third Reich. How the patients had all stopped coming to Dr Rosen's surgery. How old friends would cut them dead when they met, or spit if they passed in the street. About Jewish businesses defaced. About Jews beaten up in broad daylight, and people gathered to watch. About uncles and aunts taken off in the night, and never seen again.

Cold spreads through me. Our vision is so narrow, here in ravaged London. All we can think of is the Blitz, and where the next bomb will fall. I remember Polly telling me about the new boy in her class, whose parents said we should bomb the railway lines. Again, I try to assure myself that Mr Churchill knows everything, that we're doing all we can to stop these terrible things from happening. That must be true, mustn't it?

We say goodbye at the open front door, letting lamplight spill into the street. For once, the blackout doesn't matter. The night is silent, like in the carol; the sky is dark and clear and empty, like a bolt of black velvet flung out.

This is the very best gift of Christmas.

57

There's no bombing on Boxing Day, either. But on the night of the 27th, it all begins again.

With Lennie gone, I offer to do some extra nights on duty. So I'm at work on Sunday 29th December.

It's a very bad night in our sector. A parachute mine falls on Fountain Place, and seven people are killed. A fire in Pembroke Road rages for hours: the fire crew struggle manfully, but there's a fierce wind that whips up the flames and they're impossible to extinguish. I have to tend to some nasty injuries. There's an elderly woman whose leg is broken in two places, a jagged piece of bloody bone sticking right out through her skin. I fix her injured leg to her sound one as a kind of makeshift splint, tying her knees and ankles together. My hands are cold, and I fear I'm clumsy. She's crying with pain as I do this, a high-pitched keening like a wounded dog, and the ambulance seems to take an age to arrive. And there's a young man collapsed on the pavement: his body seems undamaged, but he wipes his mouth and you can see a bright stripe of blood on his hand. He looks rather like Bobby Ainsley, and this upsets me. His breathing grows more constrained, each breath a desperate gargling heave, as though he's lifting some terrible weight that is far too heavy for him. The ambulance men look grave, and I know it's just a matter of time.

And then, at midnight – very early – we're astonished to hear the All Clear, the bombers all wheeling around and heading back towards the Channel. But away to the north and west, in the very heart of London, the night is as dazzling as sunset, the scarlets and ochres of vast conflagrations lighting up the dark sky.

The next morning, the BBC news is evasive: *Enemy aircraft attacked towns in the south of England during the night, causing some damage. Fires were started and casualties have been reported . . .*

But I hear more in the butcher's queue: I hear that in the night the City of London burned.

'The damage was terrible. My Eddie said it was Hell, a scene from Hell, in the City. A wall of flame all around. Embers falling like rain. The tyres on the fire engines melted . . .'

'I heard that all the fire stations were down to bare poles . . .'

I know this means that all the engines, men and equipment

were out, leaving just the poles the firemen slide down when answering a call.

'Those poor brave men. They were fighting the fires with just a dribble of water. The bloody tide had gone right out in the Thames. They couldn't get to the water, they couldn't drag their suction pipes through the mud and into mid-stream . . .'

'My Mary was at the Barbican, in the operations room. She reckoned she was done for. It got that hot, she said, the paint was blistering on the walls. They managed to make it out, thank the Lord, but just by the skin of their teeth . . .'

'And then, to cap it all, there was that vicious westerly wind . . .'

During the next few days, I learn more about the damage. The City of London – Moorgate, Aldersgate, Cannon Street, Old Street – all burned. Bombs fell on St Paul's, but the wardens there managed to put out the fires, and the cathedral at least is still standing. But so many other wonderful churches have been completely destroyed: St Andrew by the Wardrobe; St Mary-le-Bow; St Augustine-with-St-Faith; St Mary, Aldermanbury; St Anne and St Agnes; St Vedast alias Foster; St Lawrence Jewry . . . Their names like poems.

Eliza sings to herself as she plays: it's one of her favourite rhymes, the one that tells of London's churches.

> *Oranges and lemons*
> *Say the bells of St Clements*
> *I owe you five farthings*
> *Say the bells of St Martin's . . .*

I think of all the churches that are now gone for ever. All built so cleverly, so lovingly, with so much labour and craft. I think of the gracious, soaring pillars, of the carving like lace on the altar screens: of the jewelled coloured glass, the saints, the angels, the tombs. So much loveliness destroyed, in one night of fire and terror.

On Thursday, a letter comes, from Hugo.

Dear Livia,

I write to you with a heavy heart. I expect you will have learned of the events of the 29th of December, and the terrible devastation in the City of London. Very sadly, Paternoster Row was caught in the bombing, and all the offices and warehouses of the publishing firms are now gone, including Ballantyne & Drummond. It seems likely that upwards of twenty million books have been destroyed.

I was in Wiltshire with Daphne and Giles. I came back to find everything ruined. It was beyond belief – the whole place a debris-filled wasteland. Where once our offices had stood, you could pick your way from brick to brick along a smoking causeway, sulphurous flames from buried fires seeping up under your feet, on either side great glowing caverns, once basements full of stock, now the crematoriums of London's book world.

I have to confess, Livia, that I wept.

I'm going to try to rebuild from Marlborough. Though just at the moment I don't really have the heart for it, I'm afraid. But when we get into production again, of course I'll be in touch.

Until then, take care, Livia. And I'd like to wish you and your dear ones a happy and fortunate New Year, if such a thing is still possible.

With love,

Hugo

When I've read his letter, I weep myself, as well – for *Summer Gardens of England*, and all the hope I had. A book seems such a small thing, amid so much destruction and death. But it was *my* book.

58

Is there any point in photography, when the whole world is on fire? When my book has burned, with all the other books? But nothing can stop me.

Early one morning, I'm in Laurel Road with my camera. The place is quiet, and thick with smoke and shadows: a couple of streets away, a fire is burning itself out.

At first, I think the street is empty – then something catches my eye, just a slight movement ahead of me.

There's a little girl in the road. She's not much older than Eliza. The dawn wind lifts her mousey hair and pushes it back from her face. She's filthy – a grubby frock, soiled cardigan. She's wearing tap shoes that are too big for her, and her cold bare legs are mottled with purple and red. Beneath the dirt, her face is white as wax, as though she lives a subterranean life, as though she never sees sunlight. She's thin, her wrists like little twigs. Her expression is watchful, wary, and she has an uncared-for look: I wonder if she's an orphan. She's pushing a small toy pram with its hood up that must have a doll inside. Behind her, a bombed house, a ruin.

There's something about this child – motherless, old before her time, holding tight to her pram, with her white skin, colourless blown hair; her shifting, cautious eyes. Something that calls out to me.

She's seen me. She knows I want something – but doesn't know what to make of me.

'Can I take your picture?' I ask her.

She nods. There's the slightest upward movement of the corners of her mouth. As though this makes her feel special, or pleases her in some way.

I kneel on the dirty pavement, in the dust of broken homes. The child's face is turned towards me, her pale hair stirred by the wind. There's a look in her eyes that I want to capture – rather withdrawn and remote. As though she's witnessed things no little child should ever have to see.

I feel a thrill, taking the picture: I know this will be a good shot. It's the way the light falls on the child, the look in her eyes, the ruin behind her.

I try to move nearer to her, but she takes a step away, maintaining the distance between us.

I want to get a shot of her cradling the doll in her arms.

'Have you got a baby doll with you? I'd love to look at your doll . . .'

She gives one shake of her head, her eyes never leaving my face. Then she turns and slips away from me, pushing the toy pram deftly through the rubble on the pavement, moving softly as a shadow in her clumsy, too-big shoes. I'm so cross with myself that I've frightened her off, when I've only taken one shot.

As she goes, I glimpse inside the pram. She doesn't have a doll at all. The pram is stuffed with scraps of things she's scavenged from bombed houses – tins of baked beans, a battered saucepan, a silvery tray she might sell; firewood. She's been looting. Surviving.

I understand her wariness then. She's worried I'll get her into trouble. I'd like to follow her – to comfort her, to take another shot, but I know I'll never find her. The world is more vivid around me now, the outlines of things coming clear and filling up with colour, but the little girl has vanished, as though she'd never been there. As though I'd dreamed her.

59

Our guns never hit their targets – everybody knows that. We like to hear them firing, attempting to defend us; but their only real achievement is to keep up morale.

Except for one January night.

I'm patrolling with Justin, when something makes me glance upwards. There are searchlights, tracer bullets, a bright cold crackle of stars.

Then a sudden flare as I watch, the night sky ripping apart like torn cloth.

'Oh God, Justin. Look.'

I stare up at the fire in the sky: it must be a German bomber. The thing circles like one of the birds you sometimes see flying into the flames, spiralling round, doomed, helpless.

'Looks like a Heinkel,' says Justin.

I stand there, not breathing. I feel my heart beat in my throat. It comes to me that I've never thought at all about the men up there – the young men doing this to us – beyond cursing them and directing an impersonal rage and hatred towards them. I find that I'm suddenly willing the crew to escape from the fire, for their parachutes to open. But you can't work out what is happening, high up in the terror and blaze of the sky.

The plane is entirely engulfed now. We stand there watching, transfixed. Young men are burning to death, up there, before our eyes. I can hear Justin praying.

The plane loops, spins, spirals, suddenly falls like a stone. We hear a vast explosion. A great flare goes up from the ground.

It's a long way away – not on our patch. We have incendiaries to put out, and in Kimberley Road a woman has tumbled into a crater. But all the night I wonder about the German plane.

In the morning, in the greengrocer's, everyone is talking about it.

'That Jerry plane landed in Camberwell. There was nobody killed on the ground,' Mr O'Callaghan tells us. 'It was a miracle really.'

'There were three Jerries in it,' says Mrs Yates. 'I heard two of them bailed and survived.'

'More's the pity,' says an old woman at the head of the queue. Her voice is grating, hard as metal.

'They've been taken off to POW camp . . .'

'They'd have died if there was any justice . . .'

'They're bloody lucky they didn't get lynched . . .'

'I hope the dead one burns in Hell,' the steely old woman tells us.

'Too right,' says someone behind me.

But he already did, I think.

I'm putting away my shopping, when there's a knock at my door.

'Justin. Oh.'

His face seems weirdly unfamiliar to me. It's as though I can't remember what he looks like. I'm so used to sharing the darkness with him – rarely looking at him, just hearing his voice.

I stand aside to let him in. But he hesitates on my doorstep. He rubs his hand over his face, as though to wipe away the sticky webs of sleep that cling there. His eyes are fogged with tiredness.

'Thanks, but I won't come in. I just wanted to ask you something.'

He shifts from one foot to the other, as though his body hasn't been put together properly. Sometimes he seems so awkward, and then I feel awkward as well.

'It's about the German, the airman who died,' he tells me. 'I'm burying him at St Michael's – tomorrow at half past two.'

I'm surprised. I've never considered what happens to an enemy who dies here. But I suppose everyone has to be buried.

'But why you?' I'm puzzled. 'The crash was a long way away. Why not someone from Camberwell?'

'I offered to,' he tells me.

The words are restrained – but he sounds angry. I'm reminded of the moment when he punched the drunk man in the crypt; of the harshness in his voice when he talked about his brother, and Tom Coster who his brother was nearly hanged for. Of the way he is when he's raging at people's complacency or weakness. I know there's something he's not telling me, and I wonder what has happened. Maybe other clergymen refused to bury this man.

'Livia, I wanted to ask if you could come?' he goes on. 'It'll only take a few minutes.'

This startles me. But there's no reason not to do this.

'Yes, I could, if you'd like me to.'

'Thank you so much.' He seems disproportionately grateful.

I watch him for a moment as he walks off down the street, with that rapid, stumbling step, as though someone has pushed him.

The next day, it's dark and dismal, with a persistent, gritty rain. The dust and ash are washed from the air, but the smells of the bombing linger – sewage, smoke, and ruin. It's so still as I walk to the graveyard, not many people about, just the splash of horses' hooves, the lisp of water in the drains, the swish of tyres in the puddles. London can seem very quiet now, when we're not being bombed.

In the graveyard, the ground is sodden, the gravestones

shiny with wet. I see things that I don't notice when I come rushing through here with the girls, with the dark and the bombers closing in. Random objects have landed in the graveyard – guttering, masonry, broken glass – but there's little bomb damage. The gravestones still tilt at odd angles; the Victorian angels are hunched and pensive, hands pressed together, cold wings folded, crusted with lichens and moulds. It all looks much as it always did. Except that where I'm heading, along the wall of the churchyard, the earth is raw, turned-over, and there's a long line of new graves.

I don't know why Justin asked me to come. Perhaps because he thought that no one else would be here – though there are already several people gathered with him at the graveside: one or two familiar faces, though no one I know well. Or perhaps he expected trouble, that someone might try to stop the burial, might even desecrate the body. But the people who've gathered are silent, their heads bowed, their faces composed. The men have removed their hats, as a mark of respect. But they shuffle a little, uncertain. Perhaps they, like me, don't really know why they're here.

Justin opens his prayer book, starts to read out the words.

'*Man that is born of a woman hath but a short time to live, and is full of misery. He cometh up, and is cast down, like a flower; he fleeth as it were a shadow, and never continueth in one stay.*

'*In the midst of life we are in death; of whom may we seek for succour but of Thee, O Lord?*'

The sexton prepares to lower the coffin into the ground.

A woman steps forward. I've seen her around but I

386

don't know her name. She looks as so many of us look – middle-aged, tired, haggard, her face rather wrinkled, her brown hair fading to grey. Her clothes are at once stylish and shabby – the coat well-cut, but threadbare; a hat with a little black veil. She has a bunch of flowers in her hand – snowdrops, the very first flowers of the year, white as skimmed milk and graceful, their delicacy all out of place in the gloom of this chill, rainy day. She looks across at Justin as though for permission; as though she'd had an impulse to do this, but now is doubting herself. He nods. She places the snowdrops on the coffin, then stands back, shy and flustered, blushing a little. There's a piece of paper tied with string to the stalks of the flowers. She's written on it in careful letters: *For Some Mother's Son.*

The others gathered at the graveside are reading what she has written. Will they be angry with her, try to snatch away the flowers?

Nobody speaks, nobody moves. But something passes around the group – a shared, elusive thing, a slight exhalation of breath: a softening, an undoing. My face is wet, and it isn't just from the rain, but I don't know who I'm weeping for: there are too many people to cry for. It's for all of us, maybe. For the people who are bombing us, and the people who we have bombed. For all of us enduring this, and for those who have gone before: Nancy Baxter, Lennie, the family in the basement; this young German pilot who burned to death as I watched. *For all of us.*

We stand there in silence. The rain begins to wash the words away.

Then the sexton lowers the coffin into the grave. He throws a spadeful of earth on the coffin: the earth becomes mud at once, from the wet.

The other people are leaving, and I'm about to go too.

'Livia,' says Justin.

I turn.

He just stands there, looking at me. As though there's something he wants to say to me, but it's too difficult.

'It was important to me that you were here,' he tells me then.

But I feel he still hasn't said what he was trying to say.

His face in the daylight has an astonishing clarity. I can see the new lines coming, and all the colours in his eyes. I think how he has to be so strong, to offer consolation – when in the midst of life we are in death, when all this is beyond anyone. How can we bear it? How can we? And yet it has to be borne.

'I'm glad that I came,' I tell him. 'Well, maybe *glad* isn't quite the right word. But — you know . . .'

'Yes,' he says.

The rain is falling and falling on us, the sky the colour of ash.

'The thing that woman did . . .' I don't know how to go on.

'Yes,' he says.

We are silent for a moment. I think of the woman's

gesture, and more tears spill from my eyes. I'm embarrassed. I scrabble around in my handbag for a handkerchief.

'Really, it's so silly – the smallest thing can make me cry . . .'

'It's not a small thing,' he tells me.

He reaches out one finger, and wipes the tear from my skin. He leaves his finger there for a moment, then trails his hand down the side of my face. I feel his touch go all through me, a thin tongue of flame running over my skin. The intensity of the feeling shocks me. I want to reach out, to hold him, I long for the comfort of that, but I don't move, can't move.

The silence spills over between us, threatens to drown us. I feel so frightened suddenly. I murmur something vague and bland, and turn and walk away.

60

The temperature has dropped again, and on Friday, the crypt is freezing: the little paraffin heater scarcely takes the edge off the chill. I glance around the room, at all the familiar faces; tonight, everyone's wrapped in blankets and quilts and several layers of clothes.

It's then that I notice that Theodora Dixon is missing. She always sits in the exact same place, on the opposite side of the crypt from us, her knitting needles clacking briskly, her glance taking everything in – looking, as I always feel, for someone to disapprove of.

'No sign of Mrs Dixon,' I remark to Aggie.

'I bumped into her in the butcher's,' Aggie tells me. 'She had a touch of tonsillitis, did Mrs Dixon. She was thinking of staying at home in the warm and taking her chances, she said.'

A shadow crosses Aggie's face.

The bombing sounds rather too close for comfort, for most of the night.

It's a relief to see that there's no new damage in Conduit Street.

I tuck the girls up in their beds. But, myself, I can't sleep at all. I feel at once drained and restless, as so often after a heavy night of bombing.

In the end, I get up. I pull on two jumpers and my boiler suit, and tie a woollen scarf round my head, with my warden's tin hat on top. I leave a note for Polly, so she won't worry if she finds me gone. I have my camera with me.

It's so strange, after all the cacophony of the bombing, to walk out into the bleak morning stillness of the aftermath. A little snow is falling, and the air is bitterly cold.

I head east, towards the place where the bombs were coming down during the night. There's a lot of damage here. I pass a house where the front has been entirely torn away, as though by a giant tin opener. By some quirk of the blast, one of the rooms is undamaged, and you can see the table set for tea, the forks and plates laid out there, for a meal that will never now be eaten. There's so much rubble that I'm confused; it all looks unfamiliar. I lose my bearings, I can't make sense of these streets.

I reach a scene of massive destruction – a street where three adjacent houses have been completely destroyed, leaving a crater in the middle with heaps of rubble on either side. Five men are working on the rubble, and a van that must be an ambulance is waiting in the road.

Suddenly, I know where I am. This is Rosebery Street; and one of the houses that stood here would have been Theodora Dixon's. Theodora – who during the raid was *taking her chances* at home. There's a weight of dread in my stomach.

I look round for Justin, but can't see him. I guess he's busy elsewhere: this won't be the only incident on our patch, after all the bombing last night. But I recognise one of the men in the gang: wiry, a narrow, clever face, a shock of greasy dark hair, a cigarette hanging from his lips. He's Johnnie Dee, from the ironmonger's.

He sees the camera round my neck before he's aware of my face.

'Sorry, ma'am, that isn't allowed . . . Oh, it's you, Mrs Ripley.'

He courteously raises his hand to his helmet, then carries on with his work.

Mostly, the men aren't using their shovels, but working just with their hands, filling buckets which they then empty down at the edge of the mound. Now and then, they breathe on their hands to try to warm them. It's snowing more heavily now, and there's a hush that seems to fall from the sky with the snow, so that the little nearby sounds – the shifting of rubble, a swear word from one of the men – seem lost within a much larger silence. It's so desolate.

Some people are watching the work, not talking, not moving. A scrawny woman in a headscarf. A man and a woman standing close, their faces blank as papier mâché masks. On the Tarmac, the usual sad little pile of possessions – a woman's handbag, two ration books, a flowery china bowl: small remnants of the life that was lived here. I wonder if any of these things belonged to Theodora Dixon, whose house would have been where the right-hand mound of rubble is now. I think of the asters in her window boxes, standing up like sentries; of her front step so clean and sparkling it put all other housewives to shame. Of the careful, proud, fastidious life she lived here.

I think how once I wished her dead, and a cold horror creeps through me.

Some of the men are using their shovels now. They're attempting to dig a small shaft vertically down through the mound on the right. From here, I can see a little way down it. The walls of the shaft are composed of all the everyday things, all mashed together – shattered floorboards and beams, pieces of broken furniture, carpets, bits of crockery; everything compacted into everything else: the shapes, the distinctions, of things all taken away. All pulverised into some tight-pressed, clayey substance.

One of the men tries to let himself through the opening. But you can see at once this won't work: the opening needs to be wider to take the width of a man. The others watch him, frowning.

'Damn,' says Johnnie Dee, with an edge of desperation. I step forward.

'What is it, Mr Dee? D'you need someone to go down there?'

He nods.

'We thought we heard a voice calling earlier, Mrs Ripley. There must be some poor bastard buried under all that crap. Someone needs to get down there and see if they can hear anything.'

'Was it a man or a woman?' I ask him.

'You can't tell, not really,' says Johnnie. 'Not when they're buried like that. They all seem to sound much the same.' He chews his lip. 'A bit like an animal, to be frank with you.'

'It could be Mrs Dixon,' I tell him. 'She lives – lived – here. I know her.'

He absorbs this silently.

I think again of the fate I wished on her.

'Let me try. I'm quite thin,' I say.

Johnnie looks at me doubtfully.

'Are you sure, Mrs Ripley? This is really man's work,' he says.

'I've done it before,' I tell him.

I assure myself that this isn't as frightening as the other hole I crawled through: at least with this one, you can see where it ends. But a flicker of fear still moves through me. I try to steel myself – remembering what people always said when I was a child: *Screw your courage to the sticking place.*

Johnnie frowns: he doesn't like this. But he's too

394

exhausted, too desperate, to protest any more. He moves the beam of his torch across the sides of the hole. They've dug down into a kind of hollow in the rubble. The drop looks to be about ten feet.

'There's a crack down there, at the bottom.' He focuses the beam of light on the place. 'Somebody needs to get down the shaft and have a shout through the crack . . . If you're really willing?'

I nod. I put down my camera. He hands me his torch, and I tuck it into my belt.

I kneel with my back to the hole, then let myself slither down. The ragged ends of floorboards and wooden beams catch at my body. It quickly becomes oppressive, and I regret my moment of heroism. If the sides of the shaft cave in, I know I'll be buried alive.

I slide down as far as I can, then let myself fall. I land awkwardly on the rubble at the bottom of the shaft. There are flurries of brick dust around me. A single snowflake feathers down and settles on my sleeve.

I call up the shaft to Johnnie, who is peering over the rim.

'All right. I've made it! I'm here!'

I look round the bottom of the shaft. I can see the crack he showed me, where some of the rubble is propped up by a broad piece of wood – a door, or the top of a table. Beyond, there's darkness.

Johnnie Dee calls for quiet. All movement stops above me. It's utterly silent, muffled, with all the weight of things pressing in: no sound but the rustle and sigh of my clothes as I move, and the *thud thud thud* of my heart.

I move the torch around. There's a sickly-sweet stench of coal gas; the gas that's escaped from the shattered pipes must be seeping out through the mound as the men dig deeper. I try not to think about this. I listen. But there's nothing, except for the tiny siftings and tricklings of dust; and around and through it all, a desolate empty stillness.

I crouch, put my mouth to the space.

'Hello? Anyone there? Can you hear me?'

Nothing. There's a heavy feeling like grief in me. I try again, without hope.

'Mrs Dixon? Could you call out if you're there?'

And then – startling me – the faintest wail, leaking through the gap in the rubble. A small, broken sound, not quite human. I feel my heart skip a beat.

'Mrs Dixon? We're going to get you out of there.'

I shine the torch through the space – I can see a blood-stained leg, a bit of grubby candlewick fabric.

I call up the shaft.

'I've found her.'

'Is the old biddy alive?' shouts someone.

'She is. I can hear her,' I say.

I start to pull at the rubble, delicately, as Johnnie Dee's men were doing. Pulling at it piece by piece, trying to widen the gap. It's like one of those children's games when you build a house with playing cards: when a single wrong move – or a fraction of a move, a hair's breadth – will bring the whole thing catastrophically tumbling down.

'Mrs Dixon? Can you slide forward? Can you push yourself this way at all?'

I sense something shifting beyond the crack. She's scrabbling her way towards the light of my torch, dragging her body inch by inch, a wounded slithering animal. She manages to push her head, her shoulders, through the gap. I slide my hands under her arms and pull at her. I have a weird fear that if I tug too hard, some part of her might come off, but there's no other way to get her out. She's covered in heavy white dust and smears of dried, blackened blood. As she edges through the gap, a jagged nail snags at her arm, and the fresh blood drips, red as tulips, the colour startlingly bright against the grey of rubble and dust. She doesn't seem to notice.

'You're doing so well, Mrs Dixon . . .' I keep my voice gentle and cheerful, as you might talk to a child. 'Just an inch or two more. That's wonderful. We're nearly there. That's the way . . .'

She's entirely through the crack now; she collapses onto my feet. She's still wearing the soiled and tattered remnants of her dressing gown. I crouch down, hold her, touching her very tentatively, in case anything is broken. Her body is thin and light and fragile as a bird's. She clings to me.

'Well, Mrs Ripley . . .' Her voice is hoarse, crackling with brick dust and pain. She coughs, a spluttering, choking cough, spits out a thick grey sputum. 'Mrs Ripley, I have to say, you certainly took your time.'

I feel a delirious light happiness.

Johnnie calls down: 'Where are you hurt, ma'am?'

'My legs don't feel too good,' she says.

'We'll hoist you up,' he tells her.

I pull her to her feet. We're pressed together: there isn't room for the two of us.

Johnnie lowers a loop of rope, and I help her to sit in it.

'I'm going to pull you up now, ma'am. If you could try and keep her steady, Mrs Ripley,' he says.

I push; the men haul on the rope. Somehow they get her out of there. As they drag her out of the top of the shaft, the men all clap and cheer. And then it's my turn. They lower the rope, I scrabble up, and there's applause for me, too. I can feel the adrenalin coursing through me, and a wild exhilaration – as though there are trumpets, as though I'm drunk on champagne.

'Thank you, Mrs Ripley,' says Johnnie.

'It was my pleasure,' I tell him.

Two men from the ambulance come over. Theodora looks with distaste at the stretcher they carry between them.

'If you think I'm going to lie on that thing, you've got another think coming.' She clutches the rags of her dressing gown close, with an air of defiance. 'I can walk, thank you very much.'

But she can't walk, really: she staggers, drunkenly sways. They wrap a blanket over her shoulders, and one of them pulls her arm round his neck. They hobble like that to the ambulance.

Johnnie Dee turns to me, with a wry grin.

'She's a tough old bird, that Mrs Dixon. You've got to respect that,' he says.

'Yes. Yes, she is. She always has been . . . I needed to

tell you, Mr Dee – I could smell gas down there in the shaft.'

He nods laconically.

I expect him to put out his cigarette, but he doesn't. Isn't he worried there might be an explosion? Should I insist?

'You'll have to be careful,' I tell him.

He smiles a slow, tired smile, takes a luxurious pull on the cigarette.

'Trust me, Mrs Ripley, we're always careful,' he says.

Polly is out of bed when I get home, making a pot of tea in the kitchen, her hair a soft unbrushed cloud, her face flushed and blurry with sleep. She smells of rose geranium and warm bedclothes.

'Mum, you look filthy.' She studies me quizzically. 'And what's that disgusting brown stuff on your front?'

'It's just a bit of blood. Don't worry, it's not mine, it's somebody else's . . .'

'Yuk,' says Polly. She frowns. 'Anyway, why are you grinning like that?'

'I rescued someone,' I tell her. 'I rescued Mrs Dixon.'

I collapse into a chair. Dust and dirt fall on the floor around me. Exhaustion washes through me, but I know I'll be able to sleep now: I feel a profound sense of peace. There's a perfection, a completeness, to this moment: the apple-scented warmth of my kitchen; outside, snow stitching its pattern; and Polly in her pyjamas, making tea, her face like a flower.

Just for this moment, I am entirely happy. Just for this moment, there's no guilt in me at all.

Polly hands me my teacup. Perplexity floats in her eye.

'Mrs Dixon? But I thought you didn't like her. I thought she was always on at you about your blackout,' she says.

I don't know how to explain. I don't really understand it myself.

'It's true, I never used to like her.' I sip the hot tea gratefully, feeling it sliding into my veins, warming every part of me. 'But today it's different. Today I love her to bits.'

61

Saturday night. The snow has mostly melted, but the air is still very raw, with a mist obscuring everything. Moisture beads on our clothes and our hair. For the moment, the skies are quiet.

'Theodora told me what happened,' says Justin, as we walk the streets. 'I went to see her at St Peter's.'

'Did you? How is she?'

'A little the worse for wear, but picking up quite nicely. She couldn't stop talking about you, and what a marvellous person you are. *That Mrs Ripley, she's the bee's knees.*'

'Oh.' I can't help laughing. 'She's certainly changed her tune. That isn't *precisely* what she used to think . . .'

'What you did was wonderful, Livia.' I can hear all the warmth in his voice. I could wrap it round me like a blanket.

'I was lucky. I was in the right place at just the right time. It all worked out rather well . . .'

'I'll say.'

'It was a special moment for me, too. It made me feel so happy. It made me feel that I could do something good for a change . . .'

He turns to me, but I can't see his expression. But I can imagine, it, sense it. That familiar look: the look he had when we first met, when I'd just knocked him down. The look that says: *Do you always do that – think that things are your fault?*

I'm more nervous with him, since the airman's funeral. I often think how he touched my face, and I don't know what to make of it. Maybe it meant nothing, beyond the emotion of the moment. But I remember the sensation so exactly – the warmth, the precise texture, of his fingertip on my skin. The tenderness of it. And, in a secret part of myself, I want him to touch me again.

We walk down Kimberley Road. The murk has trapped all the smells of broken London, and the air has a strong, unwholesome taste – metallic, as though you've been sucking a handful of change. With so much cloud, there's no moonlight, and we stumble a lot as we walk, tripping on sandbags, bits of masonry, potholes. You can scarcely see your hand in front of your face.

'Livia,' he says then. 'I was thinking about you.'

'Oh. Were you?'

'I was thinking about what you told me, and the thing you never say. About what happened with your sister.'

My heart canters off. I don't respond. The street around us seems claustrophobic suddenly – I can feel all the buildings, the mist, the thick, raw air, pressing in.

'Do you want to tell me?' he asks me.

'I've never told anyone. Never ever.' My throat is narrow as a needle's eye.

'Yes, I'm aware of that. But perhaps you could tell me now.'

Could I? Could I tell him?

And it comes to me – that here, on this raw, blind evening, as I walk the disfigured streets with this weary, difficult man, when death at any moment could fall from the sky above us: this is the only place, the only time, that I have felt that I could.

'Yes. I'll tell you.'

Rufus was my dog. Well, Sarah and I shared him, but he was especially mine: it was *my* bed he slept on, a warm, heavy lump at my feet. He'd been given to me as a puppy, on my seventh birthday, after years of yearning and pleading. He was a cocker spaniel – long soft ears, golden-brown eyes, that spaniel air of being so eager to please. You could bury your face in his coat and feel such comfort. I loved him so much; I'd never loved anything more. Or so I thought.

That morning on the river path, Rufus was frisky, playful – running circles around us, then skittishly darting ahead. Beside us, the frozen river, opalescent in the sunlight. Our grandmother had told us that it hardly ever froze here: the water-course was deep, the water fast-flowing in spring. The ice fascinated us – we sent pebbles skimming across it. Mostly, the ice was white, opaque, though there were streaks here and there that had a bluish translucency, and the colour deepened to violet in the shade of the holly trees on the bank. There didn't seem to be any warmth in the sunshine, but the icicles that fringed the banks were just beginning to drip.

Suddenly, Rufus scampered out onto the ice. Turned, stood there, looking at us – tail wagging, pleased with himself. His eyes huge, mellow, trusting.

I called him to heel. He paid no attention, ran off along the iced river, excited and impetuous.

As he ran, I heard a thing that I thought was the sound of his claws on the ice; but it wasn't. At first, it was just a small thing, a tiny rattle or creak. It grew louder: a sound of cracking.

'Oh God, Sarah. *Oh God.*'

The ice was starting to splinter around him. You could see it shifting like a live thing, jagged fissures opening, a glimpse of black water below. I could picture how it would happen, the scene all spooling out in my mind, filling me with blind terror. The ice pulling apart and breaking up; how he'd fall, be trapped by the ice floes; how he'd drown in the bitter black water under the ice.

I stumbled, slithered, down the bank, my breath in painful, choking gasps, my body seized by trembling. I was about to step out on the ice, which was still solid near to the bank.

But Sarah was close behind. She grabbed me.

'Don't, Livie, don't, it's not safe.' Her voice high and ragged from running.

'I have to, I have to. The ice is breaking. Look at him . . .'

'No, Livie, *no*. For God's sake, you can't even *swim*.' Shrill, insistent, her fingers pinching the flesh of my arm.

Rufus was in the middle of the river, the white surface cracking all round him, his front paws slipping and scratching and skidding on the edge of the ice. His tail was rigid between his legs, his ears were flattened with fear. He was whimpering pitifully.

The tears were scalding my cold face.

'But he's drowning, he's going to drown.' I was sobbing, gasping for breath.

'No. I won't let you. I'm meant to be looking after you. I won't let you do it. It's far too risky.' Her fingernails dug into me, her voice was rasping and harsh.

So I screamed at her.

'Then *you* have to get him, Sarah. *You* have to.'

I can still see it, hear it – all of it – in the dark of my mind: every detail, every word I said.

'You have to save him, Sarah. You can't let him die.' Shrieking at her.

She stood there.

'Livie . . .'

I wrenched her fingers away from my arm. I pushed her towards the frozen water.

'*Now*, Sarah. *Please*. He's going to die, he's going to

drown. *Please*, Sarah. If you love me, do it for me. Go and rescue him. *Now*.'

She hesitated. I remember the exact look in her face, all the terrible doubt in her eyes: how hard this was for her. She was torn. She knew this wasn't wise. She didn't want to do it.

'Sarah, you *have* to. If you love me, you can't let him drown. *If you really love me.*'

She hesitated a moment longer, then stepped out onto the ice. Because she loved me. Because she didn't want me to be unhappy.

We walk on down the quiet street. Every sound is shockingly loud to me, in the silence between us: our footsteps, the creak of our boots as we walk, the sigh of our breath. A single plane passes over; incendiaries fall, to our right – probably not on our patch.

Just for a moment or two, I have a sense of lightening. Almost as though the telling of this has healed me in some way. As though the very act of doing this – of plucking the words from deep inside me and putting them out in the world – has freed me.

But the feeling doesn't last.

He's quiet for a long time, and I try to imagine what he will say – how he will seek to comfort me. *You were only a child, you weren't responsible for what happened* . . . And I won't accept that, because it's not how it feels. *You didn't want to hurt her, that was the very last thing you intended* . . . But it still happened, and I killed her. *You have to forgive yourself. That's*

406

what she would have wanted . . . And I'll have to explain that I can't forgive *myself*, of course I can't, it's not possible. Only *Sarah* could forgive me. And she can't do that, being dead . . .

But he doesn't say any of these things. The silence seems to last for ever – and I start to be afraid. Afraid that he's appalled by me. That my terrible story has silenced him, and there are no words to say. And that by telling this, by revealing myself as I am, I have wrecked whatever there was between us – the new and delicate thing, the wild flower growing up between stones. All the friendship – *love*, even. Because in this moment, I realise it is love. *Was* love. And by telling my story, by revealing myself as I am, I have trampled all over this new, fragile thing, and destroyed it.

There's a slight wind getting up; the fog begins to thin and tatter. And Justin stirs and clears his throat, and gives a little sigh.

'Oh, Livia.'

My breath is stopped, waiting for what he will say.

A commotion in the street behind us. Shouting, a sound of someone rushing, a frenzied bicycle bell. A shape emerges from the shadows, coming rapidly nearer.

'Reverend! Mrs Ripley!' Bobby Ainsley screeches to a halt beside us. 'Thank God I've found you. There's a fire in Cranleigh Gardens. They've seen a shape at the window, they think some poor sod must be trapped. You have to get round there *now*, Reverend . . .'

I have a sense of something broken, the moment ripped away.

For the rest of the night, as we help the firemen get the man down, comfort people, tend to burns, I'm never alone with Justin. There's no chance to talk, no chance to hear the thing he wanted to say. It's as though something has been torn from me.

62

I'm up well before the girls. I lay the table, make breakfast. Outside, the mist has cleared, and sunlight seeps between sooty grey clouds. The world looks dirty to me.

I think back over those moments in Kimberley Road with Justin. Why on earth did I tell him? What came over me? I wish I hadn't confided in him – I can't begin to imagine what he must think of me now. I remember something Phoebe once said: *We're like snails who've had their shells ripped off* . . . That's how I feel: so vulnerable, raw, my safety all taken away.

The girls come down in their pyjamas, as it's Sunday. Eliza has an imperious look. She grabs me, tugs at my sleeve.

'Well, Mummy, have you found him? Have you found

Hector?' As though she's continuing a conversation we've had.

'I haven't seen him,' I say vaguely. 'I guess he's somewhere around.' Not really paying attention.

'No, he isn't *somewhere around*. If you haven't found him, he's *gone*.'

'She's right,' says Polly, for once agreeing with her sister. 'He disappeared yesterday evening. He wasn't here when the siren went off, and Auntie Aggie wouldn't let us look. She said you'd probably kill her if we didn't go straight to the crypt.'

I glance in Hector's bowl, which I filled last night before I went out. It would normally be licked clean by now, but the food is entirely untouched.

'Where is he?' asks Eliza.

'I'm not sure, sweetheart. It's probably nothing to worry about. Animals hate the bombing. I expect he found a secret place to hide away for a while.'

'He's never done it before,' says Polly.

'I'm sure he'll be back,' I tell them.

Eliza sips her milk, then puts her mug down on the table – precisely, with a small, crisp sound, like the snap of the bone of a bird. She studies me, with a thoughtful expression.

'If you really think that, Mummy, then why do you look so upset?'

'Oh, do I?' I try to paste a cheerful smile on my face. 'It's probably just that I'm tired. It was a busy night,' I tell her.

We eat our breakfast in silence, each with our own preoccupations.

A slice of pale sunlight falls into the room as the cloud peels away in the sky. The light is searching and clear, and you can see the flaws in everything, all the new signs of damage – a spidery crack in the ceiling, a cupboard door hanging askew – as the whole house shifts, subsides, breaks up along its fault lines. It's cold, in spite of the sunlight. I cradle my teacup in my hands, but it doesn't warm me at all. I have a dull, sad, worn-out feeling – a sense of the pointlessness of everything.

Eliza licks her finger and traces it over her plate, to pick up the last few toast crumbs. Then she heads off to the parlour to play with her arrangement – which we've rebuilt carefully together, using the photo I took. Polly goes up to her room, to read and listen to music. I wash the breakfast dishes, and start to make the vegetable broth with sausage-meat dumplings for lunch. We'll have treacle tart for pudding.

Once I've put the broth to simmer, I decide I will go to my darkroom – hoping that this will distract me from all my thoughts and fears. That I'll find a tentative peace there.

In the parlour, Eliza is building a delicate pyramid of matchboxes.

'It's St Paul's Cathedral,' she tells me.

'That's very nice, sweetheart,' I tell her routinely. 'Now, Eliza, I wanted to warn you – I'm going to be in my dark-room. You absolutely must remember not to open the door.'

'But what about Hector, Mummy?'

'Don't worry, I'm sure he'll turn up.'

'But aren't you going to look for him?'

'Really, there's no need, sweetheart. Cats can look after themselves.'

Her face clouds over.

'No, they can't.'

There's a little frown etched in her forehead. But I'm keen to get to my darkroom.

'Now, don't forget, Eliza – if you want me, you'll have to call out.'

'Yes, we *know* that. You don't have to keep on saying it.' A little impatient with me.

I close the door behind me, and work on my latest reel of film. I slide the film into the washing-up bowl of developer; I rinse the strip of film and peg it up on the line. I look at the negatives through the magnifying glass. Ruins, the smokes of dying fires. A book on the pavement, the pages blowing. A row of terraced houses with their façades peeled away, to reveal the rooms, so poorly furnished. Curzon Street, where I crawled to the sepulchre under the mound: the two men sitting silently, with such weariness etched in their faces. Waiting for the van to come and take the bodies away.

I come to the picture of the little girl with the doll's pram. I stare at it for a moment, not breathing: the hairs stand up on my arms. The image draws the eye, and the composition is perfect. She stands there like a little bird – poised, about to take flight, the dawn wind lifting her pale hair, the ravaged building behind her. I'm thrilled that I've managed to capture something so ephemeral – this tender, eloquent moment, amidst all the chaos of war. I long to see how the picture will look when it's developed – whether it will be as good as I'd hoped.

I move on to the end of the line of negatives.

My eye falls on my wristwatch: I've been in here far too long. And it suddenly comes to me that the house is very quiet. I feel a flicker of guilt, that I've been neglecting the girls. I ought to give Eliza some attention. I'll find a task we can do together: she could help me roll out the lattice pastry for the pudding for lunch.

I close the door of my darkroom behind me and go to the parlour to find her.

She isn't there. The matchbox cathedral has fallen, and her animals are scattered, lying abandoned, disordered, as though she left quite suddenly in the middle of her game. Rabbit is flung on the hearthrug.

I stand in the hallway and listen out for her voice. You can usually hear her around the house – singing a scrap of nursery rhyme in her husky, tuneless way, or chattering to the people she imagines. But today I can't hear her. Music drifts down from Polly's room: *Begin the beguine*. Apart from that, the house is silent.

I call for Eliza. She doesn't come.

I look in her bedroom, in the bathroom: I can't find her. There's a rapid wingbeat of panic in the pit of my stomach. I go to Polly's room, assuring myself that Eliza's just hiding, that I will find her soon, that there's no need to worry; but

413

the handle of Polly's door slides from me – my palm is slick with sweat.

Polly is sprawled on her bed, with one of her *Chalet School* books.

'Polly – have you seen your sister?'

'Not since breakfast. Why?'

'I wanted to speak to her. I don't know where she's got to.'

'She was worried about Hector. Perhaps she's looking outside.'

Polly is always so sensible.

I rush out into the garden. The sodden lawn sucks at my feet, spiky branches whip at me. I hunt in all the usual hiding places – behind the jasmine trellis, between the laurel hedge and the raspberry canes. Though it would be hard to conceal yourself out here in the winter garden, everything bare, the leaves all fallen.

'Eliza. Where are you?'

My voice is shaky and shrill.

I look in the Anderson shelter. I peer up at the cherry tree that I used to climb as a child. No Eliza.

I go back into the house, search everywhere again: in my darkroom, under her bed, behind the boxes in her bedroom. It's as though some big, soft, muffling thing is pressing into my chest.

'Eliza. Come out. Stop hiding. I'm getting really cross now.'

I wait, listen out for an answer. The song is over in Polly's room, and there's nothing – just the echoey sound of my voice.

As I come back down to the hall, I see with a thrill of alarm that the front door is slightly ajar. It's so difficult to shut now: I must have failed to close it properly when I brought the girls home this morning – worn out from the night, almost sleepwalking. Preoccupied with Justin, and what he thought about me. Not thinking about what I was doing. Or maybe Eliza opened it? But she knows she isn't allowed.

I run out into the street. She shouldn't be here, she's strictly forbidden to come out here on her own. Especially since the Blitz began, and the streets became so unsafe.

The street is almost empty. No vehicles: they rarely venture down here, with all the damage to the Tarmac. No one on the pavements. No sign of Eliza.

I don't know which way to turn. I glance to my right, where the houses are all still standing. At the end of the street, I see Mrs Cavendish, scrubbing her doorstep. I run down the street towards her. It hurts to draw breath.

'Excuse me, Mrs Cavendish. Have you seen Eliza – my little one?' My voice as distant as if it were coming from the bottom of the sea.

'No, sorry, Mrs Ripley. But I'll keep an eye out,' she says.

She goes back to her scrubbing.

My heart is pounding with painful blows, as though someone were hitting my chest. I retrace my steps back up the street, and arrive at the place where the bomb came down, the night I nearly died. The ruins are much as they were when I returned home after the bombing: the skeleton of a house, charred timbers sticking up like burned bones; heaps of masonry and rubble; in the road, the water-filled crater that seems as wide as a room.

I come to the edge of the crater. Stop. Some instinct makes me look down.

What I see there doesn't make any sense to me for a moment. There's something thrown or flung there, at the bottom of the crater. A pale thing, splayed out like a starfish, and still, so utterly still. Face down in the oily water, with fair hair that's muddied and drenched.

Oh God oh God oh God.

I jump down, grab her, turn her over. She's floppy, inert as a roll of fabric, a dead weight in my arms. Her eyes are closed, her skin is white as paper. I search for a pulse but my trembling fingers can't find one. I clasp her to me, clamber up out of the hole. It's a struggle: she's awkward to move, as heavy as something soaked through with water, and I'm clumsy, my body won't seem to work properly. I haul her out of the crater and lay her down on the road.

Polly comes running out of the house.

'Mum, Mum . . .' Her voice fraying, as she sees Eliza. 'Mum, is she . . .?' She starts crying.

I shake Eliza.

'Eliza, my darling, come back to me.'

Her head lolls backwards, her eyes stay shut.

I panic, my First Aid all forgotten. I sit her up, bang on her back, like you do if somebody's choking, my movements desperate, violent.

'Sweetheart, come back. *Please please please.*'

'Mum, you'll hurt her . . .'

But I shake Eliza, hit her again on her back, on her chest.

A spasm passes through her body. Her eyes snap open, her chest heaves. She retches, her whole small body convulsing. A gush of dirty brown water comes spewing out of her mouth.

Thank you thank you thank you.

I hold her tight. We are both trembling.

'Oh my darling.'

'Hector,' she says, in a strangled voice. And vomits up more water and mud, all over me.

Mrs Cavendish dashes up.

'Oh dear, Mrs Ripley. Can I do anything? Shall I fetch the doctor?'

'No, thank you, we can manage . . .'

I stand, and pick up Eliza. She has a rank, sour smell, of mud and soil and petrol: the odour of ruined London has soaked into her hair and her skin. Polly is still crying, but more quietly. She goes ahead of us and pushes open our door.

'Is she all right, Mum?'

'She'll be fine now.'

I collapse on a chair in the parlour, with Eliza close against me. I take out my handkerchief and wipe the mud and blood from her face. There's a nasty gash on the side of her head, where she hit herself as she fell: this must have been what concussed her. She's juddering as though with a fever. Polly fetches a blanket and a towel, and I wrap Eliza up tightly, and towel the water from her hair. I press her to me for a long moment. I can feel her heart beating against me, as though we are one body.

'Eliza – what happened?' I ask her then.

'I fell in.' Her voice rasps, as though her throat is hurting her. A slick of muddy saliva is edging out of her mouth.

'But why were you out there anyway? You know I don't let you play in the street. What on earth were you doing?'

'Looking for Hector,' she tells me.

'You shouldn't have been out there, Eliza. You know perfectly well that you're not allowed to go in the street on your own,' I say again.

'But Hector was walking round the crater. I saw him out of the window . . . Well, I *think* I saw him . . .' She hesitates. I can see the doubt, the confusion, that floats in her eye, as though the memory skitters away from her, even as she tries to grasp it. 'He could have got stuck in the crater. What if he fell in and couldn't get out? I didn't want him to *starve*.' She frowns. 'Are you very cross, Mummy?' she says.

'No. Well, only a bit. But you must *never* do that again . . .'

I boil several kettles, to heat her bathwater. When she's had her bath and I've tended her cuts, I tuck her up in her bed.

I close the door softly. Polly comes to find me. Her eyes are wide, her face hollow.

'How did it happen?' she asks me.

'She must have tripped on the edge of the crater and

418

knocked herself out when she fell, and her head slid into the water.'

'Mum, I thought she was . . .' She can't say it.

'I know, sweetheart. But she's all right now. I promise.'

Polly brushes a tear from her face.

'I was scared, Mum.'

I put my arm around her.

'Oh, sweetheart. It was frightening, but it's over now,' I say.

Polly shakes her head a little.

'To think that Eliza nearly . . . you know . . . And just because of an *animal*. Just because of *Hector*.'

I think of Sarah and Rufus, and I feel a jolt of cold. I don't say anything.

I'm in the kitchen, making coffee, when Hector comes sauntering through. His fur looks entirely pristine: whatever he's been up to, I doubt he's been out in the street, skulking in muddy bomb craters. I swear at him under my breath.

I have a sudden need for fresh air: it's as though I can't breathe in the house. I fetch my coat, take my coffee cup out to the garden. I seat myself on the mossy bench beneath the cherry tree.

My garden seems so dreary. Everything still looks dead out here, the roses a tangle of crooked blood-red twigs and thorns, the trees a black snarl of branches, the flower-stalks in the borders thin and pale as finger bones. Only the laurel hedge seems alive, with its glossy evergreen foliage, the shiny leaves stirring and rustling with a sound like a sibilant voice. All else is grey, dull, dormant, the touch of the air still so cold. Will this grim winter last for ever?

Yet, as I sit there sipping my coffee, I start to notice the faintest scent on the air, something I'm still aware of, in spite of the stench of the broken city. It's the scent of the changing seasons: a green fresh wetness, a smell of rain and damp hedgerows, and something subtle and polleny, a hint of the first flowers of spring.

Grass, and dew, and violets.

Sarsaparilla drops . . .

I rub my eyes, rub my hand over my face. I'm imagining things.

Guilt weighs on me. I've been so self-centred and preoccupied. Distracted when we came home this morning and not securing the door. Not paying attention to my children. Not seeing that Hector's disappearance had troubled Eliza so much that she'd do anything to find him. Staying all that time in my darkroom, when I should have helped her to look. Obsessed with my own fears. Selfish.

It's happened again. It keeps happening. I damage the people I love.

63

I'm desperate to talk to him.

I go down the stairs to our basement room. Bobby Ainsley is there, speaking to him in an urgent undertone.

'Evening,' I say.

Justin glances up, nods briefly. His eyes like winter: no smile.

Perhaps he's appalled by what I told him. Perhaps he won't ever want to talk with me in that intimate way any more. Perhaps our friendship is over . . .

Céline must have noticed my expression. She takes my arm, pulls me aside.

'He's in a bit of a state, Liv. He's got a lot on his mind.' She lights two cigarettes, gives me one. 'It's Hurtwood School,' she tells me.

'Oh.' At once, I'm ashamed of myself – because I was so self-absorbed. Because I'd thought *I* was the reason for his wintry mood.

Hurtwood School. I think of the rest centre that he showed me, one street beyond our sector. How he'd said that people imagined that it would be safe to shelter there – believing in the protective magic of its thick, old walls.

'What's happening there?' I ask her.

'Bobby's got the latest – he's just been round there,' she says. 'It's stuffed full, Liv. With all the poor sods from miles around who got bombed out in yesterday's raid. There are an awful lot of people there, and they look stuck in for the duration . . .'

'They're planning to stay at Hurtwood School? But what if there's bombing tonight?'

Céline's lips are pursed, as though something tastes bitter to her.

'They say they've been told that coaches are coming, to take them out to the country. Justin says it's just a rumour. But you know how these things can happen, as soon as word gets round . . .' She takes a long pull on her cigarette. 'Someone says something – maybe just that something *might* happen, *ought* to happen. And then, before you know it, it's taken as gospel,' she says.

'Well, maybe it *is* true. Maybe—'

She interrupts me, bats at my words as if shooing an insect away.

'Justin made some phone calls to check. Rang the authorities in Whitehall. No one knows anything about it. No coaches are coming,' she says.

'But those people won't be safe there, not if those streets get bombed.'

'No, they sure as hell won't,' she says. 'But people will cling to anything. They can convince themselves that something will happen because they *want* it so much.'

There's a new note in her voice: she's not usually solemn like this. There's a flicker of misgiving in the margin of my mind.

'But – we can't do anything, can we? Hurtwood School's not on our patch.'

Céline gives a slight, weary shake of the head.

'He's not going to let it go, Liv. He's not the kind of man to do that. Well, you know our Justin.'

It's very clear, very cold, the night sky seeded with stars, the streets glazed with blue moonlight. The bombers are droning in, and far away to our right we hear the gun barrage opening up, sending a blinding, percussive thrill through the heart of London.

Justin's silence presses in on me: I couldn't possibly break it. All the things I long to say fill up my throat like stones.

We come to Hurtwood Road, and I realise where we're heading. The school looms in front of us up at the end of the street, the bulk of the building a denser black against the dark of the night.

He turns to me.

'Céline told you?'

'Yes.'

'I'm going in. Will you come with me?'

'Yes, of course I will. But what do you want me to say?'

'You don't have to say anything. Just be there beside me,' he says. He has a small, wry smile. 'See I don't do anything stupid.'

We arrive at the school. He opens the door and pushes the blackout curtain aside.

There's a little light in here, and a distant sound of many people – talking, laughing, babies crying, bronchitic coughing. We walk down a narrow corridor towards the source of the sound. There are toilets, with a line of people waiting. On the walls along the corridor, there are still school things displayed: pictures of Bible stories; photographs pulled from a *National Geographic* magazine, showing far-flung places, oceans and mountains and shores; sports trophies in a glazed cupboard.

We come to the door that leads to what would have been the school gymnasium. The noise spills out and washes over us as we open the door. There must be at least a hundred people here. They have their belongings with them – the scatter of things that remain to them: blankets, handbags, children's toys. Whatever they'd taken to the shelter before the bombing began, or whatever they'd managed to salvage when they went back to pick through the rubble.

The place smells appalling – of sweat, fear, filthy nappies,

424

unwashed clothes. But there are comforts here that you wouldn't find in a regular shelter. A trestle table, spread with a cloth and strung with Union Jacks, where you can get tea and biscuits. A table-tennis table, where two men are playing a game, with others gathered to watch, cheering, passing a bottle around. Some boys with dirty faces are rolling marbles in a corner – all pent-up energy, laughing, boisterous. There are child-sized chairs, and the school gym mats to lie on, and the toilets out in the corridors. You can see exactly why these people would want to stay, after everything they've been through.

Justin approaches a woman. She looks exhausted: her eyes are dull and opaque, her brown hair tangled and undone. She has a toddler on her lap. The child reaches up and kisses her face and she gives a small, weary smile. The sight is touching.

'Who's in charge here, ma'am?' he asks her.

'That would be Mr Coster,' she says.

I hear Justin mutter something under his breath. And I remember what he told me – about the man that his brother took the rap for, the robber who only got a few years, when his brother so nearly was hanged. Something plummets inside me.

The woman gestures behind her, towards the table-tennis table. We look where she is pointing.

He isn't what I'd expected. I'd envisaged a big, heavy man, a bruiser; but this man is small and dapper, with something very controlled about him. He's smartly dressed – a suit, a tie; his hair dark, oily, slicked down. Around him, a huddle of men in similar suits, with hungry, shifting eyes.

Justin strides towards him.

Tom Coster looks up, frowns. He lays his bat precisely down on the table.

'So. Here comes trouble,' he says.

He has a soft, lisping voice, but when he speaks, people listen. I notice a lavender scent that hangs about him, rather too sweet for a man.

'These people have to get underground,' says Justin.

'This isn't your patch, Connelly. I'll thank you to keep out of it. We don't need cunts like you barging in here and telling us what to do.' All said in a very reasonable tone – still not raising his voice.

'They're a sitting target,' says Justin. 'You need to get them out of here. They should go to the Fountain Place shelter.'

Tom Coster raises one eyebrow.

'And have you seen it tonight, by any chance? Fountain Place is jam-packed. Looks like a bomb hit it,' he says, with a tight, sour smile at his own joke. The men standing round him laugh loudly.

'It's safer than here,' says Justin.

'We can look after ourselves,' says Tom Coster.

'But you've no protection here at all.' I can hear the steel in Justin's voice. 'If the bombers aimed at the goods yard, there'd be carnage here,' he says. 'These people wouldn't have a prayer.'

Tom Coster shakes his head. 'There are coaches coming. Haven't you heard? To take them out to the country.'

'The coaches aren't coming,' says Justin.

Tom Coster scarcely reacts to this. He flicks some lint from his sleeve.

'That's your story, is it? Why the fuck do you think I would listen?'

'You have to, you can't let this happen. You're putting these people at terrible risk.' Justin's fists are clenched, the veins knotted like string in the backs of his hands.

I'm aware of the other men around us; forming a circle as boys will in the playground when there's a fight. My heart is beating wildly.

Tom Coster shrugs.

'So what will you do? *Land* me one? We know you can't keep your hands still. It's in the blood, I reckon. That rather nasty tendency. You Connellys are all the same. It has to be said – what a crew.'

Justin says nothing. But I know his fierce loyalty to his brother, and I can feel his rage. I'm worried he might indeed lash out.

Tom Coster senses this as well.

'Go on, then,' he says, taunting Justin. 'If you're itching to. Just do it.' He turns to the man who was playing table tennis with him. 'You can be my witness, Charlie, if the reverend assaults me,' he says.

I glance at Justin. His lips are white with anger.

This man is dangerous. He's clever, he can read people, immediately scent weakness. I remember what Justin once told me: *He has a way with him. He can reel people in, he can make them do what he wants.*

427

More people are pressing in around us. I know that the angrier Justin becomes, the less willing they'll be to believe him.

I put my hand on his arm.

'Justin . . .'

Tom Coster seems to notice me for the first time. His eyes slide over my body. He has a satirical smile.

'So you've brought your floozy with you, to try and keep you in line? Just what we'd expect of a man of the cloth. Fucking hypocrites, the lot of you.'

I see Justin's throat move as he swallows hard. When he speaks, there's a flare of rage in his voice.

'The coaches aren't coming. You have to tell these people. I made some calls, and there aren't any coaches. It's just a rumour,' he says.

Tom Coster examines his fingernails.

'What is it with you, Connelly?' Thoughtful. As though he's genuinely curious. 'Always interfering . . .' He glances up sharply. 'You should look after your own first. And you didn't do such a great job of that, it has to be said . . . Just cast your eye over these people.' He makes a wide gesture, encompassing all the families gathered there. 'Their homes have all been bombed, they're desperate to leave London. By what right do you march in here and take their hope away?'

There's a swell of murmured agreement from the men around him.

Justin starts to speak, but Tom Coster is speaking over him.

'Connelly. I've heard enough.' His voice is harsh now. For the first time, I can clearly hear the fury in him. 'You can just fuck off and die, as far as I care.'

He turns his back on Justin, picks up the table-tennis bat.

Justin spins round and leaves, and I follow. The men near Tom Coster are laughing. Their gaze is like a hot breath on the nape of my neck.

Justin is cursing under his breath, and I can feel his helpless anger, as though it is my own, and all his sense of failure. As though his thoughts are my thoughts.

'You did what you could,' I tell him. 'You can only do what you can.'

He shakes his head heavily.

'I handled it all wrong. I let him get to me,' he says.

'You couldn't have made it turn out any differently,' I tell him. 'He's convinced that the coaches are coming. There's nothing you could have said that would have made Tom Coster listen. If we'd stayed any longer, those men of his would have kicked us out of the door.'

Justin frowns, says nothing. As he walks, his limp seems more marked, as though some weight were dragging at him.

I hear a bomber chugging overhead. I look up, fearful. But the plane edges on through the black sky; we aren't its target tonight. I think of all the people who we saw at Hurtwood School – the grubby boys playing marbles, the woman tenderly holding her son. I think how utterly vulnerable they would be if there was a raid. But I tell myself: *Perhaps it will all turn out fine. Perhaps the bombs won't fall here. Perhaps the coaches will come after all and take the people away—*

My thoughts are abruptly cut off. There's someone crying out, round the corner ahead of us – a chilling, high-pitched keening that splits the darkness apart. We rush towards the sound.

Two women are standing in a pool of moonlight; the younger one is pulling at the older woman's arm. They must be heading for the Fountain Place shelter. The younger one looks desperate: I suspect it's with a superhuman effort that she's dragged the old one this far. But the old woman won't go any further – she stands there, stubborn as a child. She's moaning.

'My arm! It's broke! My arm!'

'I'll deal with it,' I tell Justin.

I go to them, put my hand on the old woman's shoulder. The moonlight falls across the white dazed mask of her face.

'Let me help you, ma'am,' I say.

I'm fortunate. Seeing my official-looking appearance, she quietens, clutches my hand.

'My arm,' she says, more tentative now.

'Your arm's right as rain, Ma. We've been through all that . . .' The young woman's voice is shredded with exhaustion.

The old woman stares at her daughter, as though these

430

words have no meaning for her; and then her face collapses, and slow tears spill from her eyes. I wonder if her mind is going.

'Why don't we try and get you both to the shelter?' I say.

'Bless you, love,' says the younger woman.

We creep along the pavement. There are more planes overhead now, and incendiaries are falling, over towards Camberwell.

The old woman suddenly stops, looks up at the sky.

'Too many lights! There are too many lights!' Her words are shaky with dread, frayed with a presaging of disaster. 'They'll see us! They'll see us!'

I pat her arm reassuringly.

'Don't worry, ma'am. You'll be safe soon.'

Her voice rises to a terrified shriek.

'Make them do it! You have to! Tell them to put out the lights!'

I manage to steer the women to the entrance of the shelter. But the old one grabs me with sudden strength, her nails like claws on my skin.

'Tell them! You have to tell them!'

The young woman peels her mother's fingers like bandages from my arm. I see them safely down the steps.

Some incendiaries have landed quite near us, back towards Hurtwood School, though the bomber that dropped them is heading off towards the east, towards the docks. There's a white flare, where a fire has started. I head towards the flare.

The fire is in Hurtwood Road, at the opposite end of the street from the school. Justin is there already; he's putting it out with a stirrup pump. The magnesium brilliance of it illumines his face and his eyes, making everything too harsh and clear: his frown, his desolate look. I join him.

Then the fire is out, and I can't see his face, and the street is just shadows again.

It's quiet. The bombers have all moved off, the guns drop down into silence. A little breath of cold night air rattles a leaf on the Tarmac. Where the moonlight pours whitely across them, the buildings seem carved from bone.

There's so much I want to say to him, so much that needs to be said. But now there's a chance to say those things, here in the dark and the silence, the words elude me; I don't know how to begin.

I try to rehearse my thoughts in my mind. *Justin – you know how I told you about the death of my sister. I need to talk about it; I need to know what you think . . .*

But he's in despair, and it seems all wrong to want to talk about *me*.

To the east, the London rooftops are black against an ochre sky. A few clouds drift, their edges washed with a bilious, coppery light. The searchlights cluster, sweep apart. Now, it feels colder than ever: our breath makes a tattered smoke that looks translucent in the moonlight.

The bitter air has found its way inside my gloves, my clothes: my fingers are stiff, frozen. I feel that I'm chilled to the marrow, that I shall never again be warm. Suddenly, I can't bear it – this chill. Can't bear any of it – the cold, the dark, the danger. Our life feels unendurable to me.

Blindly, not thinking, I find myself reaching out for his hand. Forgetting all my fears, forgetting everything. No longer struggling with the impossible things that can't be put into words. Just wanting to give him comfort; and for him to comfort me.

He wraps his hand around mine, but our fingers are gloved and clumsy. He stops abruptly, turns to me. He puts his hands on my shoulders, pulls me towards him.

The street is suddenly still around us: as though the whole city – the great old buildings, the ruins – as though all of this has dissolved, into mist, into dream. It's so silent. All I can hear is the thud of my heart, and our breathing, shockingly loud.

'Livia.' He says my name slowly, as though he doesn't want to let go of it. His face is so close to mine, I can feel the graze of his skin on my cheek, and I sense his voice rather than hearing it, like a vibration passing from his body into my body. I'm so hungry for him, for his warmth, his closeness, his touch.

There's a growling in the sky above us, the sound building rapidly, with a terrible urgency to it.

We break apart. We look up. Exactly above us, there's

433

a bomber circling, circling, that seems to have come out of nowhere. I stare at it, unable to make any sense of it for a moment – still transported to some other place where none of this is real.

'Dear God,' says Justin.

The plane seems to hang there, suspended, not moving.

And then we see the bomb fall.

All these things happening at once. The flash, lighting up the whole sky. The great blast, sucking at me, so I feel as if my lungs and my heart were being sucked from my body. The sound, unimaginably huge, like an express train hurtling towards us. Debris twisting and sweeping in a wild, hot wind. And up at the end of the street, the massive stone wall of Hurtwood School, billowing outwards as though it is sailcloth.

I throw myself to the ground. I feel the Tarmac kick and shudder beneath me.

The sound of the vast eruption dies away, in endless, overlapping echoes. I rub the filth and grit from my face. I find I can open my eyes.

I look up. The air is thick with dust, in gauzy pale layers that merge and billow like fog.

As the dust clouds swirl and drift apart, I see Justin, sprawled beside me. He's unmoving; for a moment, I think he must be badly injured. But as I watch, he struggles up. He staggers down the street towards the place that was once Hurtwood School.

I try to get to my feet, try to follow, but my legs are like cotton, won't take my weight, won't move.

The bomber is still above us, circling, preying on us. I can hear the drumming of its engines. *Where are you? Where are you?*

I look up. The night sky is full of lights, full of dazzle. *Too many lights.*

And then a black flash, and the whole world implodes, and all the lights are put out.

64

I push myself up on my knees.

He isn't there. Where I last saw him, just a few yards ahead, there's now a ragged heap of fallen masonry. Though it's hard to make anything out, with all the dust and smoke in the air. Strange lights are shining through the dust – a chandelier flare falling, and the reds of the fires that burn in the place where Hurtwood School once stood, which is now a smoking pile of rubble, filled with the dead and dying. I can hear many voices, screaming, cursing, wailing: some of them have an inhuman, animal sound. A woman lurches past me, stretching her arms before her like somebody blind, covered in dust and dripping blood, her clothes in tatters. I ought to go to her, but I don't move, *can't* move.

More bombs fall; guns shoot wildly. These sounds slam into me, pummel me. When the noise briefly thins, I hear the engines of vehicles, all of them struggling towards the site of Hurtwood School. As the dust clouds part, I make out an ambulance stopping in a side road: it can't get any further. Men clamber out and rush on into the ruin.

I rub my eyes with my sleeve, look around me. I can see more clearly now. The Tarmac is tumbled and buckled up, the shadows are skewed and falling awry, the roadway is treacherous with debris, some of it frosted with a thin ash that has a white look in the moonlight. Random objects from the school have been flung this far by the force of the blast. On the pavement beside me, a boot, a doll, some shattered shards of crockery; and a thing like a large, long-legged insect, pale, bloody, curled in on itself. I stare: there's something so wrong about this blood-spattered, spidery thing. Then I see it is a severed hand. Bile fills my mouth. I retch; my whole body heaves.

All this – and Justin is dead or dying, somewhere beneath this devastated street. And no one will come to help me, there's too much horror tonight. Every rescuer will be heading straight to Hurtwood School, to all the poor people buried there, beneath those massive old walls – that had stood for years but were broken down in an instant, as though turned to some substance flimsy as fabric, that briefly swelled outwards, then fell. There will be no one at all to help me.

I haul myself to my feet; I stumble along the ruptured Tarmac. I come to the place where I last saw him, where there's now a tangled heap of rubble and splintered timbers and bricks. If anyone's going to dig for him, I know it has to be me. But my body is weak as paper. I just stand there, then sink to my knees. He's dead, I know he is dead. It's hopeless, all beyond me. There's no point in trying, it's futile, utterly futile. *I can't do this.* Despair falls all over me like a fisherman's net, a heavy dark thing that entraps me, that can't be shrugged or shaken off. Everything is purposeless, pointless, however hard you try. In the end, this is the truth of life: this is the only truth. There is no meaning, no consolation.

I kneel there in the ravaged street, at the very end of things. *I can't do this.* Tears fall, and I don't even move my hand to wipe them away.

Time to show some backbone, Livie.

Sarah's voice. Urgent, rather bossy. As clear as if she were standing here beside me.

I cling to the thought of her. I see her in my mind's eye – her apron, her dark dishevelled braids, her flower-sprigged summer frock – and this image seems utterly real and vivid to me, more real than this whole terrible street of nightmare. As real as in that moment when she stood beneath the cherry tree. Grinning, looking up at me.

You found me.

I'll always find you.

I feel a sudden stillness amid the chaos, the devastation. And it's as though I can smell the faintest scent on the air that mingles with the smells of burning and cordite and dust. Devon Violets. Sarsaparilla drops.

I'm sorry, so sorry, I whisper.

Livie. Never mind that now. There's no need to get so upset.

As though the past and the guilt and the weight of these things have all simply melted away, melted into thin air.

Just get on with it, Livie. Her voice is quiet but commanding. *Do what you have to do. What you are here to do. Find him.*

I can't, I say. *There's no point, he's dead, I know he is dead. It's all too difficult for me. It's how it always happens, I always mess everything up. I can't do it.*

Oh yes you can. Stop thinking about the past, Livie. You do brood. You always did dwell on things. Things are as they are, and will end as they must, she tells me.

It was all my fault, I say.

Forget it, Livie, she tells me. *It was just the way things happened.*

And suddenly, I know it, truly know it. It was just the way things happened. Things are as they are and will end as they must. I hold the words close to me, press them close to my heart.

But that's enough of that. You need to get digging, Livie.

I have only my hands to work with, so I dig around with my hands, dragging out handfuls of dirt and broken bricks and debris. Scrabbling, my fingers bleeding, tears streaming down my face. Picking through rubble and joists and piping and bits of floorboard.

I hear the whine of another bomb falling. The blast sucks at me, the sound hurts my head, and all my hair stands on end. I pay it no attention.

I reach through to a place where some timbers seem to form a kind of cave. The way they've fallen, there could

439

be a space, a hollow, between them. Someone could still be alive in there.

But then I remember how I crawled through the hole to the sepulchre under the mound. The horror of what I found there. And again my heart fails me.

Don't you give up, Livie. Her voice is fainter now. *Screw your courage to the sticking place. Don't give up, whatever you do.*

I tug at the timbers, wrench out a shattered floorboard. I push my hand back into the rubble. My hand breaks through, into air.

You know what to do now.

Her voice receding from me. Her scent seems to hang in the air a moment longer, and then that fades as well.

The street feels different – furious, loud, chaotic: the stillness that I felt for those few sweet moments has gone. Everything hurts again – every muscle in my body, and my hands are lacerated and bloody. Exhaustion drags at me, weighs me down, as though stones are tied to my limbs. But I keep on scrabbling at the hole, one brick, one scrap of wood, at a time. Moving cautiously through to the space beneath the timbers.

I pull out my hand, I put my mouth to the space.

'Justin. Are you there?'

Nothing.

'It's me, it's Livia.' I call as loud as I can. 'Can you let me know if you're there?'

I listen for an age.

And then a slight sound – a rasp, a whisper. I can only just hear it above the thud of my heart.

I push my hand between the timbers.

'Justin? Can you reach me?'

I feel his hand, warm, living, his fingers clutching my fingers.

'Justin. It's me.' I say it over and over. 'It's me. It's Livia. Stay with me. Just hold on, hold on to me.'

And when at last they arrive – Céline, and Johnnie Dee and the rescue squad – I'm still lying there in the broken street, talking to him to keep him conscious; stretched out on the buckled Tarmac, holding his hand in my hand.

Epilogue

On Saturday 6th October 1945, I set out on a journey.

I straighten my hat in the over-mantel mirror; I tuck the newspaper cutting into my bag. I've not told the girls where I'm going – just that I'm visiting someone, and I should be back by teatime. I didn't want to invite their questions, when everything is unclear – when I don't know what will happen when I get there. Or even whether I will manage to find the place at all.

I glance round my dining room to check that everything is in order. The walls are newly painted, I've had decorators in. The house survived the war, even the doodlebugs of '44, and all the bomb damage is mended. The furniture has a battered look, and I long to make new curtains, but our life here in Conduit Street is more or less back to normal. The girls are in their old bedroom, and the room that once was Sarah's is just a box room again.

Polly is doing her homework at the dining-room table, in a sea of coloured pencils. I glance at her drawing over her shoulder. It has an anatomical look.

'It's the heart, Mum,' she tells me.

The diagram is detailed, immaculate, done with great concentration. Biology is Polly's favourite subject. Next year, she'll start her nurse training, and she can hardly wait, she says. She's happier, so much less solemn than in the years of the war: she's learned to dare to hope for things. She's fourteen now – almost a woman. Last week, Colin Parker took her to the Gaumont to see *Blithe Spirit*; she wore a shapely red frock, a touch of lipstick, court shoes. It was startling: she looked so grown up, not my little girl any more.

'Your drawing's beautiful,' I tell her.

'It's not meant to be *beautiful*. It's meant to be *accurate*, Mum.' She studies the drawing a moment, smiles. 'It does look nice, though, doesn't it? I thought the heart would be difficult, but I think I'm getting the hang of it.'

'I'm sure you are, sweetheart.' I drop a kiss on the top of her head.

I find Eliza in the parlour. She's curled up on the sofa with Hector, deep in a book: *The Midnight Folk*. She doesn't live shut away in a fantasy world any more, but she loves to read about other worlds and secret, hidden kingdoms: *Lost Horizons*, *King Solomon's Mines*. And she writes stories of

444

her own now – long, intricate tales of monsters and demons and ghouls, and the brave, clever girls who fight them. She has a talent, I think: her teacher is always reading out her compositions in class.

Just yesterday, after I saw the article in the newspaper, I found myself thinking about those months when London was bombed, and all the things that happened then.

'Eliza,' I asked her, 'd'you remember that arrangement you made in the parlour during the Blitz? I think you called it your London Town.' I'm smiling a little, remembering. 'Polly used to get really cross; she thought it looked so untidy. And our house cracked up all around us, but your whole fragile city survived.'

Eliza shrugged – a sophisticated, world-weary gesture she's borrowed from her sister. 'Mum, that was an awfully long time ago,' she said.

Now, she glances up at me.

'You look really nice in that dress,' she says.

It's a new dress, made of damson silk. I smooth down the full floaty skirt.

'Thank you, sweetheart.'

I put my arms around her.

She breathes in appreciatively.

'Mum – I don't believe it. You're wearing *scent*,' she says.

She gives me a quick hug; her eyes flick back to her book.

I study her for a moment as she sits there reading, a little light through the window glistening in her fair hair. I think how I used to worry about her. But she's fine now;

I know all is well with her. I'm so grateful. I have a sense with both of them – that as they grow up, they're becoming more themselves, maturing into the people they were always meant to be.

I fetch my handbag from the dining-room table.

'Remember, there's shepherd's pie for your lunch. It needs a couple of hours in the oven.'

Polly smiles indulgently, an adult at an anxious child.

'We *know*, Mum. You've told us at least a thousand times,' she tells me. 'Anyway, isn't it time you left? If you're going to catch that train?'

I sit with a cigarette, looking out of the window of the carriage. It's a day of shifting, watery light and sudden squally showers, and everything looks so shabby in the fickle sunshine. London is being rebuilt, but it's slow, there's so much damage. By May '41 and the end of the Blitz – nearly four months after all those people were killed at Hurtwood School – great swathes of our city had been destroyed. There are ruins and vacant lots everywhere, grown over with brambles and nettles, and the magenta spikes of fireweed that flare on any broken ground.

You can see into the backs of people's houses from the train. Random moments; all the drab ordinariness of peacetime. A man pulling on a string vest in an uncurtained window. Children squabbling in a garden. A woman in a thin cardigan pegging out her washing. It's blustery, and the heavy wet sheets are filling with wind like sails.

These last months haven't been easy for everyone – the

transition back to peacetime. Phoebe's husband Howard returned to his old job in insurance, and she told me how, on his very first day, he'd opened the drawer of his desk, and found there some papers from five years ago, before the outbreak of war. He'd felt such depression, in that moment: he'd felt that everything was different, and nothing. Peace brings its own dilemmas: war makes everything simple. Strange as it sounds, there are people who wish that we were still at war – missing the drama, the adrenalin, the sense of urgent common purpose. And life certainly isn't perfect – there's still rationing, and all the rebuilding: there's still a long way to go.

But there's hope as well. Especially since the election in July, the Labour landslide. All those returning servicemen voting for things to be different. *We've won the war, let's win the peace.* Voting for a better life. Voting for change.

Not everyone was happy with the result, of course. Aggie was distraught. She sat at my kitchen table; her kindly eyes glittered with tears.

'How *could* people, Livia? How *could* they?' She took out a handkerchief, dabbed at her eyes. 'Winnie did so much for us, and this is how we repay him. It's dreadful, Livia, *dreadful.* It's so *ungrateful.* How could people do such a terrible thing and live with themselves?' she said.

I thought it was better not to tell her I'd voted Labour myself. That to my mind the election result is thrilling.

I think of what we are being promised: what we have voted for. A different, fairer country. Pensions. A National Health Service. Council houses with indoor toilets and gardens where children can play. No more babies will die because their parents can't afford medicine. Those who have laboured all their lives will be cared for in old age.

I remember talking about all this with Justin. How he said: *It has to change.* How we disagreed about that, how I believed that the poor would be with us always. I thought he was a dreamer, that what he dreamed wasn't possible.

But now it is starting to happen. Now the world will be changed.

I wrote to him for several months: he'd been sent to a Birmingham hospital that had a specialist unit. But I never went to see him. I'm not exactly sure why: maybe it was just cowardice, yet another failure of nerve. But it was a difficult journey in wartime; and whenever I suggested a visit, he seemed to try to discourage me. I could tell he didn't want me there. He would have felt wrecked, ruined – his injuries were so severe. They had to amputate one of his legs below the knee; he had to learn to walk again, and it was the second time in his life that he'd had to rebuild his body like this. It must have been agonising. Perhaps he preferred for me not to see him in that ravaged state.

There was something else, too, that made me uncertain. I didn't know how that night at Hurtwood School would have marked him – when he tried so hard to save all those people, and failed. I didn't know how to talk about it – didn't know what I could say to make it more bearable for him.

448

In time, we lost touch – the demands of our lives enveloping us, unable to think beyond the immediate tasks of the day. For him, his rehabilitation; for me, caring for my children, and the struggle to make ends meet with all the shortages, and to keep putting food on the table for the rest of the war. You live from day to day, the sand trickles through the hourglass – and then you find four years have passed, and you don't know quite where they went.

And now this: his picture in the *Daily Herald*.

I take out the newspaper cutting and look at the photo again, to see what I can learn from it. He's been elected MP for a borough in South London: he's in a photograph with a group of other new London MPs. He looks older than his years now. He's rather gaunt, rather stooped: his appearance hints at what he's been through. He's at the front of the group; you can see he has two sticks to walk with. The article states: 'Mr Connelly was formerly the vicar of St Michael and All Angels, Stapleforth Street, and is still suffering from injuries sustained while serving on the Home Front . . .' As far as I can gather, he isn't married.

Seeing his picture in the paper brought so many things back. The Blitz, and those dark, intimate streets where we walked, where my fear and my guilt seemed to stalk the pavements beside me. All the fevered closeness of those nights, when we told each other things that we'd never told anyone else. And, remembering, I'd had such a sense of something that never quite happened: something I felt I had no right to, or was too frightened to reach out and grasp. That there were times when it would have only taken a word from me, or a touch, and I couldn't do it: not till it was all too late, on the night when Hurtwood School was destroyed. I can see this more clearly now – how afraid I was then. Afraid that if I were truly known, if I were seen as I truly was, I would be found damaged and damaging. And if you damage people, how can you love, or be loved?

He's not called 'the Reverend' any more, and I'm curious about that. I doubt that he's lost his faith, but he must have left the ministry. I wonder what he believes now – what he has allowed to slip away, and what he holds to, still lives by. Perhaps he and I have grown more alike in the way we understand the world, for my own beliefs have changed as well across the past four years. Exactly what I have faith in would be hard to put into words. But I've learned that more can be mended than I ever dared imagine; and I have such a sense of mystery – of things not seen, yet real.

The article gives the places and times that the MPs hold their surgeries. Justin's is on Saturday mornings, in St Edmund's church hall.

I step out onto the platform, into a gurgle of pigeons and a fresh green scent of rain. I speak to the station master and he gives me directions.

I walk up the High Street, which is full of Saturday bustle. There are shoppers everywhere, chatting, waiting in queues. There's a baker's, a fishmonger's, a dress shop with pastel Viyella blouses hanging on racks outside. A bookshop.

I glance in the bookshop window, and see, with a surge of pleasure, that my book is there. *London Witness: a photographic diary of the Blitz*, published by Ballantyne & Drummond, from their shiny new offices in the Marylebone Road. The cover image leaps out at me: it's my most famous picture, the one that was bought by *Picture Post*. The watchful child with the blown hair, holding onto the little pram that was full of things she'd scavenged, because she was doing whatever she had to do to survive. Getting through as best she could; as we all did. It's strange to think of: there was that fragile moment in the dawn light after the raid – when I asked to take her picture, and she gave the slightest smile. And now her face is everywhere, in every bookshop window.

It surprises me still: that this is what I am known for, these pictures of devastation – when all I wanted was to photograph flowers.

I think of the pictures I first sent to Hugo Ballantyne: the roses at Polesden Lacey, the camellias and fountains. All so like those elaborate gardens I'd conjured up as a child. So like the landscapes I still dream of sometimes.

I remember the loveliest of those dreams, the one I dreamed in the crypt at St Michael's, the night after I nearly died. As I walk on up the street, I recall all the detail of the dream: it's imprinted on my mind for ever. The wild and beautiful garden sloping down to a stream, a garden that I knew was mine, a little breeze stirring the branches, the trees in leaf, the bushes blossoming. And I know that one day I will walk there, beneath those trees, among those flowers, pale petals softly falling.

But there's a lot of living to do first. And I hold the image close for just a moment, then shut it away.

At the top of the street, there's a church, and beside it, a red-brick Victorian church hall. There are notices pinned to a board – Girl Guides, the Mothers' Union. One of the drawing pins has fallen out, and the paper cracks in the breeze. There are wilting geraniums, dustbins, a bicycle padlocked to a fence post.

I don't go in. I just stand there for a moment, uncertain.

The door bangs open, a man comes through. He's wearing a cap and work overalls. He unlocks the bicycle, then bends to fix his bicycle clips.

'Excuse me. I wondered – is this where Mr Connelly sees his constituents?'

There's a shake in my voice, but the man doesn't seem to notice. He straightens, doffs his cap politely.

'That's right, ma'am. You'll find him inside.'

I step into the hall foyer. There are smells of cabbage, drains, disinfectant. I glance through an open door into a little kitchen, where biscuits and bottles of orange squash are stacked on open shelves. A woman with a hairnet over her curlers is mopping the lino.

'He's through there.' She angles her head towards the opposite side of the foyer.

I'm suddenly very afraid – as afraid as when I walked

the streets in the dark of the Blitz, my mouth like sawdust. And I think how we do this over and over, like the knights in the old story. Setting out into the forest. Not knowing what we'll find there.

I come to the door the woman indicated. There's a line of tubular chairs, but nobody seems to be waiting. I don't know whether to knock. I push at the door.

It's a long, airy hall, with windows set high in the walls and an expanse of polished parquet. Outside, the clouds have blown away, and bright sunlight pours into the room. He's at the far end of the hall, sitting behind a table with papers strewn across it, and talking to another man, who could be a party official. The two chairs in front of the table are empty; it looks as though his surgery is over for today.

His appearance shocks me. He's even thinner than in the photograph; in the light that floods through the windows, the bones in his face seem too clear. The sticks he walks with are resting against the table. But his expression is as it always was – eager, determined, intense.

I absorb all this, in the blink of an eye.

My mouth is sealed: I can't speak for a moment. He hasn't seen me. The party official is talking, and Justin is listening – concentrating, focused, his eyes on the other man's face; then he glances down, writes on a notepad.

I could just turn and go. No one would be any the wiser. I could leave everything as it is, accept the good life that I have – walk out of this light-rinsed place, forget him, never come back . . .

453

But I don't do that.

'Justin . . .'

My voice has a strangled sound.

He looks up, sees me. His eyes widen. He says my name as though it is the answer to a question.

I start to make my way to him, across the sunlit room.

Here are some of the books that helped me in my research for *A Brief Affair*:

Elizabeth Bowen, *The Heat of the Day*, Vintage, London, 2008.

Mike Brown and Carol Harris, *The Wartime House: Home Life in Wartime Britain 1939–1945*, The History Press, Gloucestershire, 2011.

Joseph Campbell, *Creative Mythology*, Penguin, Harmondsworth, 1976.

Eating for Victory, reproductions of official Second World War instruction leaflets, Michael O'Mara, London, 2007.

Lara Feigel, *The Love-charm of Bombs*, Bloomsbury, London, 2013.

Juliet Gardiner, *The Blitz*, HarperPress, London, 2011.

Henry Green, *Caught*, Harvill, London, 1991.

Graham Greene, *The End of the Affair*, Vintage, London, 2004.

Stephen Grosz, *The Examined Life: how we lose and find ourselves*, Chatto & Windus, London, 2013.

Jacqueline Hollings, *Teddy Bears and Doodlebugs*, Book Guild Publishing, Brighton, 2010.

Catherine Horwood, *Keeping up Appearances: Fashion and Class between the Wars*, The History Press, Gloucestershire, 2011.

Nella Last, *Nella Last's War*, edited by Richard Broad and Suzie Fleming, Profile Books, London, 2006.

Ken Loach, *Spirit of '45*, documentary film, UK, 2013.

Alison Maloney, *The Forties*, Michael O'Mara, London, 2005.

Frances Partridge, *Diaries 1939–1945*, Phoenix, London, 1999.

Charlie Richardson, *The Last Gangster*, Century, London, 2013.

Nevil Shute, *Requiem for a Wren*, Vintage, London, 2009.

Francis Spufford, *Unapologetic*, Faber & Faber, London, 2013.

Luca Turin and Tania Sanchez, *Perfumes*, Profile Books, London, 2008.

Philip Ziegler, *London at War 1939–1945*, Pimlico, London, 2002.

Reading Group Questions

1. What purpose does Livia's love affair with Hugo serve for her? Did you feel critical of her behaviour?

2. How are these characters changed by their experience of the Blitz: Livia, Justin, Polly, Eliza?

3. Do you think Livia takes more responsibility than she should for Sarah's death?

4. Justin tells Livia that courage can be learned. Do you agree with this?

5. Consider the use the author makes of these images: Livia's photographs of gardens; Eliza's London Town; the damaged house in Conduit Street.

6. Livia's work as a warden means that she has to leave her children with Aggie during the raids. Do you feel she was right to make this choice? Have there been times in your own life when you've had to choose between your children and your duty to others?

7. How do you understand what happens to Livia during the raid on Hurtwood School? Do you see this experience as psychological or supernatural?